THE
UNQUIET
GENIUS

A CONOR THORN NOVEL

THE
UNQUIET
GENIUS

A CONOR THORN NOVEL
GLENN DYER

TMR PRESS, LLC

ALSO BY THE AUTHOR

The Torch Betrayal

The Ultra Betrayal

TMR PRESS, LLC
2057 MAHRE DRIVE
PARK CITY, UTAH 84098

The Unquiet Genius is a work of fiction. References to real people, events, incidents, organizations, or locales are intended to provide a sense of authenticity. All other characters, and all incidents and dialogue, are drawn from the author's imagination or are used fictitiously.

THE UNQUIET GENIUS A Conor Thorn Novel (Book 3)

First Edition

ISBN
978-0-9991173-7-8 (ebook)
978-0-9991173-9-2 (paperback)
978-0-9991173-8-5 (hardback)

Library of Congress Control Number: 2021949847

Printed in the United States of America

Cover and Interior Design: Jane Dixon-Smith Design
Edited by: Kimberly Hunt of Revision Division and Gretchen Stelter
Author Photo: Terry Moffitt

The OSS logo is a registered trademark of The OSS Society, Inc. and is used with its permission.

You can grab a free short story that pits Winston Churchill against the leader of the Soviet Union, Joseph Stalin, when you subscribe to my newsletter.

You'll also get the prologue and chapter 1 of *The Torch Betrayal*, the first book in the Conor Thorn Series, and notice of upcoming releases, promotions, and personal updates.

Sign up today at:

WWW.GLENNDYER.NET/SUBSCRIBE

For my parents, Thomas and Eleanor

...only the living who are clever enough can disappear without a trace — or if some trace is unavoidable, can foresee and calculate precisely how wrongly it will be interpreted by others and how clumsily followed up.
　—Leonardo Sciascia, *The Mystery of Majorana*

Despite the vision and the far-seeing wisdom of our wartime heads of state, the physicists felt a peculiarly intimate responsibility for suggesting, for supporting, and in the end, in large measure, for achieving the realization of atomic weapons...In some sort of crude sense which no vulgarity, no humour, no overstatement can quite extinguish, the physicists have known sin; and this is a knowledge which they cannot lose.
　—J. Robert Oppenheimer, head of the Los Alamos Lab

Physics is on the wrong road, we're all on the wrong road.
　—Ettore Majorana as quoted by Amaldi Edoardo

PROLOGUE

The disembarkation announcement startled his cabinmates, ruining what seemed to him a deep sleep, given the raucous snoring the two men had emitted during most of the voyage from Palermo. But for him, sleep did not come. He may have looked like sleep had overcome him, with his shut eyes, lying in his berth, coiled tightly like a child in the womb. That peaceful image clashed with the battle taking place inside his head. His overwhelming desire to end his torment sparred with his previous acceptance of the church's teachings that to do so, he would be proclaiming sovereignty over God's creation, himself. His failure to carry out the plan the night before, which he had spent so long devising—the plan to let the Tyrrhenian Sea take him—produced pangs of confusion that were heightened by not knowing what he was supposed to do next. But there had been one moment of clarity—he knew he could not return to his past life.

Before his cabinmates could toss off their blankets, he was already out of his berth and had slipped into his iron-gray overcoat. Then he snatched his suitcase from under his berth and opened the cabin door. He looked back as the door shut and glimpsed the two men looking at one another, one scratching his head, the other wiping the sleep from his eyes.

He waited midship on the port side while four deckhands

1

wrestled the gangway into place. Several other people waited with him, but no one spoke. They focused on the movements of the deckhands, all seemingly eager to find themselves on firm ground. The sun had not yet risen, but the sky, with its growing yellowish tint, hinted that soon the morning sun would arrive and another day in his tormented life would be set upon him.

Some measure of time passed after stepping off the gangway. He didn't know how long it was, but he found himself standing in the middle of a piazza. The light was much brighter now, though he remembered little of his walk from the ship. Not his surroundings, his thoughts, or if he'd passed by people along the route. His head was in a thick fog that seemed to smother any attempts to focus on the details of his environs. He closed his eyes, a minute later—maybe it was longer—swaying as if he were being buffeted by a stiff wind. He put out his hands to brace his fall, but one still held his suitcase, so his chin hit the cobblestones hard, causing his vision to short circuit. He rubbed his jaw while his vision returned, and then he rose and looked around the expansive piazza. It was devoid of people except for a moonfaced, timeworn man stooped over a broom, sweeping the trash in front of a large baroque-style building—the Church of San Ferdinando. He was standing in the Piazza Trieste e Trento. Nearby was the Royal Palace, as was the Gran Caffè Gambrinus, a place that he and his friend and superior, Professor Carrelli, frequented before the martial prefect decided to close it due to its reputation for attracting antifascists.

He looked at his watch. It was approaching seven. He picked up his suitcase and headed toward the church, kneading his aching jaw along the way. The old man, his sweeping motion slow and weak, watched him as he passed by and climbed five steps. As he grabbed the door's tarnished brass handle, he could feel the old man's eyes on him. But before he pulled it open, the old man spoke.

"No, no, no. It is too early. Two more hours. Come back then." He turned and saw the old man shaking his head and then resume his sweeping, leaving him standing there, not sure what he should do. A drenching disappointment washed over him. Not because of the closed church, but because of his weakness, his failure to carry out his suicide.

He took in the piazza. There were more people now, some on

bicycles, a few walking, some with faces raised toward the rising sun. He descended the steps and headed across the square in the direction he thought he'd come from. He moved slowly, head down, thinking about where he should go. He had determined he would never return to teaching, so making his way to the Institute of Physics in Naples was out of the question, and he couldn't go back to his hotel room at Albergo Bologna. He was just passing the opera house when someone rushed past him. A moment later, he heard his name.

"Ettore?"

He stopped and turned toward the voice. He recognized the woman. She was a nurse who had helped him with his stomach ulcers several months before. She was kind and patient. He liked her. Anna. That was her name.

"It is you," she said as she moved closer. She was dressed in her nurse's uniform, but the white outfit was dingy, wrinkled, and spotted. She was most likely headed home. "How are you feeling, young man? Have your ulcers calmed down?"

"I am...well. Thank you for asking, Anna."

She reached up to touch his chin.

The move startled him, and he backed away.

"I...I just wanted... What happened? Did you fall? Your chin is bruised. You didn't get into a fight, did you? You don't seem the type, Ettore."

Her questions surprised him. He rubbed his chin and felt a bruise. *Did I fall*, he asked himself. "No, no. Not a fight. I slipped and fell. But I am fine."

Anna looked at his suitcase. "You are traveling, I see. Where are you headed? To Rome to see your family?"

His family. The letter to his family, in which he'd written:

I have a single wish: that you do not wear black for me. If you want to bow to custom, then bear some sign of mourning, but for no more than three days. After that, remember me, if you can, in your hearts, and forgive me.

Anna tugged on the sleeve of his coat. He flinched at her touch. "Ettore? Are you all right?"

He turned and hurried away, leaving her standing in the piazza, calling out his name.

CHAPTER ONE

1430 Hours, Thursday, November 5, 1942
MI6 Headquarters, No. 54 Broadway, London

Miles Stoker, at first, was surprised, but that surprise slowly turned to anger. As Kim Philby's deputy, he had grown used to being at the man's beck and call. Some days, he lamented he was just an errand boy. It shocked him that Philby summoned him by sending a lowlife, pock-faced courier who he didn't recognize but who had no problem identifying him in his favorite hangout: the Arts and Battledress. Stoker had been keen to keep his sexual activities well out from under the microscope. He knew there were others in MI6 who felt the same as he. Homosexuality was a long way from being accepted as a way of life in the hallways and offices of the Secret Intelligence Service or Scotland Yard.

Stoker finished his gin martini and passed his phone number to the BBC presenter he had just met. The young man, whose startling good looks captured the attention of nearly all the club's patrons when he entered, was a new face at the Arts and Battledress. Stoker had wasted no time in being the first to introduce himself. Now, he bid the man farewell, grabbed his Burberry trench coat and black fedora, and exited the bar.

On the taxi ride from Orange Street back to No. 54, Stoker mentally prepared himself for his meeting with Philby. He hadn't seen Philby since Monday, and he had heard that he was in a deeply foul mood ever since his widely reported run-in with

Conor Thorn at a party at Ian Fleming's. Philby had been a no-show at No. 54 since it had taken place. Stoker hopped in the undersized elevator in the lobby, punched the button with the faded B, and headed down to the basement bar. The elevator door screeched as it opened, revealing a spacious, weakly lit room filled with cigarette, pipe, and cigar smoke. At least fifteen men gathered around several tables, hunched over in quiet conversations, sharing state secrets they couldn't breathe a word of to anyone outside the long-standing spy institution. A bar in a spy agency. *A very British touch*, thought Stoker as he walked over to a table in the far corner of the room where a lone figure sat. Philby, a cigarette dangling from his lips, held up an empty tumbler, signaling Stoker to not join him empty-handed. Miles Stoker, errand boy.

A minute later, Stoker joined the sour-looking Philby with a tumbler of cognac and a gin martini in his hands. Stoker noticed Philby's blackened eye and swollen nose. A little annoyed at having to fetch his drink, he decided to poke the slightly flushed spymaster, asking, "So, was it a tripped and fell or was it—"

"Don't push it, Miles," Philby said. "You'll find me in no mood for any probing inspired by mockery." Philby, slouched in his chair, took a whiff of his glass, then a healthy swallow of the smoky liquid. "So, was it love at first sight or just two men passing in the night?" Obviously, the pockmarked courier had reported back to his master with details.

Stoker decided to disengage from the scrum, knowing too well that the acid in Philby's tongue was top grade. "What do you need from me, Kim?"

Philby sat up and leaned in. "Conor Thorn. You remember him. From your run-in at Paddington Station?" Philby's cognac-scented breath sluiced over Stoker. Of course, he remembered. Thorn had almost bagged him at Paddington when he finished briefing Henry Longworth on how to get the stolen invasion plans for Operation Torch into the hands of his Nazi friends. But he was sure Thorn didn't get a good look at him—well, as sure as he could be.

"What of the man?"

"You may have heard that he and his accomplice, Emily Bright, have foiled another operation that Moscow had a deep interest in. That makes two."

Stoker was well aware of the first failed mission, but not the second. He also knew that Moscow Center's reaction to the initial failure had been very harsh regarding what they considered Philby's mounting shortcomings.

"Two failed operations. A number that will not grow," Philby added.

Stoker loosened his ascot, took a sip of his martini, and waited for more.

"I want him out of the way. He's been too much of a nuisance. And I need you—"

"To take care of it." Stoker took his martini, tipped his head back, and drained it. "Where is he?"

Philby sat back and picked up a pack of Woodbines from the table and shook one free. "That's the problem. He hasn't been seen since..." Philby lit the cigarette with the nearly spent one between his fingers.

Since he punched you in the face, Stoker mused.

"Since Tuesday." Philby blew a cloud of blue-gray smoke toward the maze of pipes and ducts that hung below the ceiling. "I suggest you have someone follow Bright. She's back at No. 10. Given their relationship, she's bound to rejoin her friend in due course. When that happens, you take charge. I don't care how long it takes, how you do it, or where it's done."

Stoker nodded and began thinking first of the how. He was very fond of knives. They were quiet and brought death fast, if used properly. As to where, that wouldn't be in his complete control. Unless he was to lure Thorn into some sort of trap, possibly one that used his friend, Bright, as bait.

"What about Bright? What if she was collateral damage?"

Philby smiled and picked a speck of tobacco from his tongue. "Ah, all the better, Miles. All the better." He leaned forward and in a soft voice said, "One more thing. Do not underestimate Thorn. That would be a mistake."

CHAPTER TWO

0230 Hours, Monday, November 16, 1942
Aboard Inflatable Boat on Open Water

"It's up to you, Conor. You gotta make the call to go or no-go." Those were the words Jack Taylor was saying to Conor Thorn, Office of Strategic Services operative and former US Navy officer.

Taylor, who headed up the training for the experimental OSS maritime units, and Conor got along fine. Taylor gave Conor all the rope he wanted as the mission leader. Enough to hang himself. Which didn't bother Conor, he preferred it that way. He was confident in his decisions concerning the missions he was sent on... usually. But this time, Conor was questioning his decision to go on with it, given the lousy weather coupled with the area they were being sent to having a reputation for severe ebb currents. If asked, he would deny that some of his self-doubt sprung from a previous experience as a child with tidal currents that ended in tragedy. But that would have been a lie.

The two rubber inflatables, Taylor called them *Goodyears,* were one thousand yards off the coast and headed for the beach, where they were to pick up two high-value assets, an unnamed male and female. Conor knew Taylor couldn't get them any closer because of the sandbars. The rain alternated between beating down on them in sheets and horizontally directed rain that stung their faces like red-hot buckshot. White phosphorescent caps, whipped into a frenzy by the wind, broke the inky darkness of the night. Despite the howling squall, he could hear Flanagan breathing hard behind him. One of the OSS's newest recruits, Flanagan was out of shape but seemed to be game for anything. In the second boat, Oliver Shoemaker, a Yale grad and former Olympian in swimming at the '36 Berlin games, took the lead. Will Sanders, another Ivy Leaguer, though from which school Conor couldn't recall, was behind Shoemaker.

Shoemaker and Conor had butted heads from the beginning. The same age as Conor, Shoemaker had spent his postgraduate days at Yale law school, then getting his first job out of law school at his father's firm making $100,000 a year, and he made sure everyone on the team knew about it. That and his prowess in a pool. When they first met, it had not surprised Conor that Shoemaker had brushed off Conor's question about whether he'd won any medals.

Each member of the team was carrying a rucksack and had an M1 Garand slung over their shoulder. In Conor's pack was a relatively new piece of equipment—the SCR-536, a portable transceiver with a range of one mile that gained the nickname "handy-talkie." The wind-swept seas proved a treacherous challenge for the two boats, but both boats made it ashore, Shoemaker's boat nearly capsizing in the process.

After collecting their two assets, Conor radioed Taylor and reported their status. On hearing Taylor's response, both boats immediately headed back into the raging waters, which had now been whipped into swells that hit five to six feet. Shoemaker pushed his boat off the beach, followed by Conor. Shoemaker was the first to board. Ten seconds later, Conor couldn't see Shoemaker's boat; it was swallowed by darkness and the sheets of pelting rain. Ten feet off the beach in water four feet deep, Conor felt his footing give way. The ebb current was pulling him out to open water—he was being pulled under the boat.

Conor's mind jumped back to when he was ten years old, in the clutches of his mother, Bridgett, as she struggled to pull him ashore after he had fallen prey to a vicious riptide off a New Jersey beach. Her strength being drained, she'd managed to toss him toward the beach as she was pulled under. Four days later, the sea gave up her sodden, swollen body.

In the present, he kicked hard, hitting the bottom of the boat, then pulled his M1 from his shoulder and freed himself from his rucksack, letting both sink to the bottom. He continued kicking as he grabbed the rope that ran along the top edge of the boat and pulled hard, raising him to a point where his head was even with the boat's rounded side.

"Grab my hand!" Conor screamed above the roar of the wind and angry surf. Flanagan stopped paddling, reached for Conor's right hand, and yanked. A series of waves was pushing them back to the beach as the asset in their boat, the male, grabbed his other hand. On their second attempt, Conor was pulled into the boat and fell, ass first, on something hard. He reached underneath him and found a paddle, then dug it deep into the white-capped waves. He yelled at Flanagan to push harder. The rain didn't let up, and neither did the wind. The cold temperature created a sleet-rain mix; the sleet stung his face and hands. They were making headway, finally, putting distance between them and the shoreline. They both kept paddling. Conor looked off their starboard side, trying to locate Shoemaker's boat. He yelled for him twice. On the second attempt, he heard a response. It was Shoemaker.

"Do you have everyone?" Conor shouted.

There was no answer.

The wind picked up and with it the size of the swells, now reaching heights of seven feet. He had the lives of Flanagan and the asset in his hands. He couldn't do anything for Shoemaker. He shouted at Flanagan to keep paddling toward the PT boat.

#

The two deckhands and Jack Taylor pulled them aboard the PT boat's stern, Conor coming on last.

"Where's Shoemaker?" Taylor shouted into Conor's ear. It was his turn not to answer.

Conor looked out toward the shoreline; the black, storm-incensed night revealed nothing. Then a paddle clattered on the boat's foredeck, startling Conor and Taylor.

"Over here," Shoemaker screamed above the snarling wind.

The deckhands, Taylor, and Conor rushed down the boat's starboard side and looked over into the water, the deckhands quickly going to work with a long boat hook pole to pull the inflatable in close.

In the boat were Shoemaker and the asset. No Sanders.

"Ah, shit," Taylor spat.

Conor suddenly remembered—Sanders had gone to Princeton.

Taylor turned to Conor. "Colonel Donovan won't like to hear we lost someone on a training mission."

Conor thought about the trust Taylor had put in him as far as making a go or no-go decision on the mission. A fucking training mission. "No, Jack. Not we. I lost a man. Sanders. From Princeton."

CHAPTER THREE

The panic-stricken call from the administrator of the Certosa di Trisulti monastery, or charterhouse, came early in the afternoon. Bruno Fabrizio was a fifty-year-old, broad-shouldered man who most people accused of lying when he revealed his age, given that his weather beaten, leathery, and creased face belonged on a man in his late sixties. As Collepardo's only plumber, he had been to the monastery on the occasions when he or someone in his family needed medicines or ointments that the monks produced from herbs found on the surrounding rocky slopes of Monte Rotonaria, a peak of Monti Emici. The sight of the sprawling, multilevel baroque-style monastery that came into view as he guided his dilapidated Fiat truck up the steep mountain road always impressed the man. The monastery was surrounded by imposing limestone walls at least twelve feet high. The buildings visible above the walls were taupe in color, with brownish-red terracotta roof tiles capping the buildings. But it was the sheer size of the landmark that always captured his imagination.

As he got closer to the monastery, he spotted a monk, clad in a snowy-white habit complete with a cowl that enveloped his head, waiting for him outside the gatehouse. Bruno got out and pulled his soiled canvas bag of tools from the back of his truck and approached the monk, who was standing motionless, his arms

11

folded into the wide sleeves of his vestment. The monk introduced himself as Brother Alfieri, Certosa di Trisulti's administrator, even though Bruno had met him before. He was slightly built and sported a long nose that drooped so much at the tip, it came alarmingly close to touching his upper lip. His long, flowing, white serge garment was donned with a long, wide band of similarly colored cloth. Bruno noted the vestment was spotless except for the hem, which hung barely an inch off the ground and was marred by a layer of brownish grime.

He asked if Brother Santino was still assigned to the pharmacy, which Brother Alfieri chose to ignore. Instead, the monk marched past Bruno, heading away from the gatehouse.

"Wait, where are you going? Do you have a burst pipe or not?"

Brother Alfieri stopped and turned back to Bruno. "The problem is not inside the monastery itself. It is in the hermitage. The Sanctuary of Our Lady of the Cese. I thought I mentioned that."

"No. No, you did not." Bruno's response seemed to displease Brother Alfieri, who huffed, then adjusted his habit's cowl and headed down a narrow pea gravel path.

Less than five minutes later, they stood in front of a two-floor, aging, white stucco building that sat under a towering cliff in the mouth of a cave.

"This is the Sanctuary of Our Lady of the Cese. This is where you will find your burst pipe." With that pronouncement completed, Brother Alfieri turned and retreated up the path to the Certosa.

Bruno had heard something about the sanctuary but had never visited. It was a story about a hermit that withdrew to the Grotta delle Cese to lead a life of repentance when the Virgin Mary appeared to him and left her image imprinted on a rock. Bruno was reluctant to believe such stories. His skepticism, which his wife chided him for, made him question such stories as well as people who displayed a deep faith in matters that were difficult to explain. He dropped his tool bag and walked around the building, inspecting the cave walls that surrounded it. He found nothing except for some crude words in fading paint referring to someone named Lucia.

Bruno retrieved his bag of tools and entered the building. The first thing he saw when he entered the large, sparsely furnished room just inside the door was a frozen patch of ice that covered over half of the room's plank floor, worn smooth from years of traffic. The bottom third of a wall on the right side of the room was darker than the upper two-thirds. There was water still seeping out of a one-square-foot section. He heard a muffled voice; it seemed to come from an adjacent room with a door slightly ajar. Bruno dropped his tool bag to the floor with a bang to announce his arrival, prompting the emergence of an older plump man, stooped in posture and similar in attire to Brother Alfieri.

"Ah, the plumber. I am the prior, Father Misasi. Thank you for coming. But please work as quietly as possible." The squat framed, ruddy-faced priest smiled and tapped both ears with his hands to underscore his request.

Bruno thought about just nodding but decided that being more civil would make his fervently Catholic wife, Teresa, happy when he told her of his day. "Yes, Father. I shall do the best I can. But this is...how shall I say...a big problem," Bruno said as he pointed to the damaged section of wall.

Father Misasi nodded, gazed at the scene of the plumbing disaster, and retreated into the room, leaving the door slightly ajar. Bruno knelt on one knee and yanked a claw hammer and a chisel from his tool bag as he heard Father Misasi resume his conversation.

"Ettore, listen to me. Signora Majorana has been through enough, as have your brothers and sisters."

A soft-spoken man answered, but Bruno couldn't hear the specifics.

"Why leave here now? Are you not content serving the Lord, Ettore?"

Another indecipherable reply.

Ettore...Majorana. Bruno mulled over the names as he broke up the sheet of ice that covered the floor. The clang of his hammer on the head of the chisel brought the prior back into the room, where he again tapped both ears, this time unaccompanied by any smile, to remind Bruno what he had asked of him earlier. The prior then turned back and shut the door behind him.

Bruno dug into the lower section of the wall that looked like it was the prime location of the trouble. *Ettore...Majorana.* He had heard those names spoken before. He rose from the floor, pulled a pack of Alfa cigarettes from his shirt pocket, and lit one. He threw the match onto a pile of sharp-edged ice littered over the floor's surface. The match hissed for a moment as it was extinguished. He took a deep pull from the cigarette, filling his lungs with the tarry, dark tobacco that was his favorite. Then it came to him. Anteo Tardino had spoken of an Ettore Majorana. Tardino, the cocky blowhard, was his brother-in-law, Teresa's only living relative. He was also a high-ranking official with the Italian political police—OVRA.

Tardino bragged he'd had fun banging the heads of antifascists and communists. Bruno recalled two visits from him about four years ago, when Teresa had again been ill. Tardino was in a foul mood on both occasions and complained about the pressure from his superior to find a missing scientist, some brilliant scholar of physics. He needed to find the man so the pressure his superior was feeling from Mussolini would stop. Tardino said that he wished he never heard the name *Ettore Majorana.*

The Majorana disappearance had been a major news story in 1938. The newspapers had covered it for months after the scientist disappeared while sailing from Palermo to Naples. There was a theory that he had sought refuge in a monastery of which there were hundreds in Italy. The prominent Majorana family put up a generous reward for anyone who could provide information as to their son's whereabouts. Majorana was not a common Italian name. Could it be possible that Ettore Majorana was alive and living in the Certosa di Trisulti?

Bruno tossed his cigarette onto the pile of cracked ice. The idea of visiting his overbearing brother-in-law in Rome took root in his mind.

CHAPTER FOUR

1430 Hours, Saturday, December 5, 1942
Equus Bar, The Royal Horseguards Hotel, 2 Whitehall Ct., London

The glass of Watney's Red Barrel was sweating. So was Conor Thorn. The air in the Equus Bar was sweltering. Maybe one of the two elderly ladies that occupied the settee ten feet from Conor's table had complained and had the furnace in the basement turned to maximum output. Conor took off his dark, navy blue suit coat and draped it over the back of his chair.

His emotions during his trip from Port Washington, NY, to Southampton on the Pan American Yankee Clipper had run the gamut. Losing a young OSS agent in the training exercise in the Chesapeake off the eastern Maryland coast preyed upon his thoughts for much of the long flight. Jack Taylor had tried his best to convince Conor that he had done what he could, that there was no fault to put on anyone. He said it was just the way the waves broke and that he couldn't have prevented it. He took a needless risk for a training mission. It was something he would not soon forget. Nor did he want to. Then there was the other black cloud that added to his sour disposition. News that his father Jack passed on to him. Buster Seaker was headed to trial.

Seaker, an academy classmate and football teammate, was the assistant military air attaché in Stockholm—and his late wife's rapist. A letter from Grace's maid of honor, Sue Ryan, revealed that Grace told her of being raped at a dinner while Conor was on convoy duty in the North Atlantic in early '41. It took some leg-work by Conor before he felt he could confront Seaker about his suspicions, but then, with a little prodding from his Colt 1911AI, it didn't take long for Seaker to admit his guilt, though not before he had the balls to claim that Grace welcomed it.

A few fingers of Jameson during the flight helped tame the images of the fouled-up exercise and Seaker's guilty-as-shit mug, but they couldn't completely extinguish them. Competing for his attention, and eventually winning out after a long struggle during the protracted flight, were the warm thoughts of seeing Emily again.

It had been nearly a month since he last saw her, when they'd shared a compartment on the train from Southend-on-Sea to London. They had spent a few restful days at her mother's house after their mission to bring back to England Lars Lind and Gunnar Lind's wife, Eve, after foiling their attempt to sell British Ultra code-breaking secrets to the Nazis.

The few days spent there were the happiest Conor had had since before he'd lost his wife, Grace, in 1941. The loss of Grace and their first child, a son, in childbirth had been enough to nearly choke the life out of Conor. The demons that the tragedy sum-moned had contributed to the demise of his naval career. Dealing with that loss was a burden he never thought he could withstand. While at Grace's bedside, the USS *Reuben James*, the four-stack Clemson-class destroyer he was the executive officer of, had been on convoy duty in the North Atlantic and had been torpedoed by a U-boat, sending him deeper into his emotional tailspin. He had only started to escape its grasp when his career had been officially sunk by the wife of his then-superior officer. She was drunk and neglected, and Conor was an easy target. And his superior, Captain Bivens, wouldn't believe that Conor had no interest in his drunk wife. She stated otherwise and the man, of course, believed his wife. The suggestion that Conor resign his commission was deliv-ered in the same way a punch to the gut was used to communicate an extreme dislike of someone. Conor left the US Navy. The only organization he had ever wanted to be a part of.

It was soon thereafter that Colonel William Donovan, a close friend and law school classmate of his father, Jack, came knocking, essentially throwing him a life preserver. Conor had taken it—a chance to contribute to the defeat of the Axis Powers while helping build a clandestine organization the United States had never even thought of before Pearl Harbor.

He reached back into his suit coat pocket. The prize was still there. He took a swig from the Watney's, and before he could put it down, he heard a voice behind him. Her voice.

"Aah, just what a girl needs—a swig of beer to put her right." He turned to see Emily Bright, a dark coat draped over her arm, a pair of gloves in her hand. Conor jumped to his feet like his chair seat was electrified. She was resplendent in a teal dress that hugged her five-foot-six slender frame. Her light brown hair bounced softly on her shoulders as she took the last steps toward him, her green eyes sparkled as she wrapped her arms around him and kissed him softly on his cheek. Conor felt a delightful fluttery sensation in his stomach. He took a deep breath, inhaling her lavender scent, returning the hug but refusing to let go.

"Hey, I'm a thirsty girl. Release me at once." Conor freed her, and Emily plopped down in her chair and took a drink of his Watney's. "Aah, that's better."

He sat and took in the sight of her, but his gaze shifted to an elderly, lanky-built man dressed quite inappropriately for the Equus Bar that entered just behind her. The man looked about furtively as if he knew he didn't belong in the swanky bar. He took a seat at a small table and focused his gaze on Conor and Emily, making no effort to hide his interest in the couple. Conor returned to studying Emily. She looked worn down; she wasn't smiling like he had envisioned she would when they first saw each other.

"Good to see you too," Conor said.

That smart-ass remark was greeted with a smirk. "So sorry. I may not look it, but you are the bright light of my day. I'm just a bit exhausted."

Conor took a taste of his beer and noticed that the elderly man waved off the server and then rose and beat a hasty exit. "Winston cracking the whip again?" Not long after their return from Stockholm and the wrap-up of the Lind mission, Prime Minister Churchill had reclaimed his prized assistant from MI6. The letters Emily had sent Conor while he was back in the States didn't go into details about what she was doing, but she made it clear she was working long hours with her "old boss."

"Yes. I feel like I'm stuck in the center of a whirlwind of activity with no chance of ever seeing a calm day again. I'm sorry I'm a little late," Emily said.

"A long-winded Churchill leading a war cabinet meeting?"

"Actually, no. I just had a checkup with my doctor. He was running behind."

"Everything all right?" Conor said. Wise move or not, he tried his best to steer clear of doctors given past experiences.

Emily shrugged and took another sip of his beer. "I have news. Winston notified me I'm going along with him when he meets with your president."

"Oh?" Conor said, noting the obvious evasion.

"Sometime next month, many rumors as to location. I heard North Africa mentioned. It's quite hush-hush. Much to discuss, Winston says."

Conor drained his beer and asked if she wanted to order something. She shook her head. Emily was twirling the ends of her hair around an index finger, lost somewhere in her whirlwind. Conor raised his glass in the direction of the waiter, who gave Conor a nod. "Well, maybe we'll run into one another. I'm hearing some talk that Bobby and I are headed to Algiers. Maybe by the end of the month. Something about the next phase of the war in the Med. No other de—"

"Conor...I'm pregnant."

The sensation that Conor was in an elevator in free fall washed over him. Then the elevator slowly stopped, and he felt the pressure of gravity on his legs and a sense of relief. Then joy. Pure joy. He succeeded in holding at bay any thoughts of Grace. And the hospital. And doctors. Emily was studying his reaction; her eyes locked on his face. Conor smiled, reached into his coat pocket, and pulled out the small, felt-covered box. He opened it and showed its contents to Emily. Conor's face slackened when he saw that she didn't signal any joy or surprise.

"I knew you were going to propose. It's just something that good men do. And you are a good man, Conor Thorn," she said, rapid-fire, like she had rehearsed it many times over.

Conor closed the box and set it on the table. He glimpsed the women on the settee taking in the scene.

"The thought of bringing a child into this world, at this time, makes me so terribly sad," Emily said, stretching out the last few words. She sat for several beats, her gaze fastened on her hands that lay limply on the table. "I told my doctor that you would propose in less than a minute after I told you. And I was right."

"You see, you know me too well. We were meant to be together."

Emily bit her lower lip. Her chin quivered. Tears rolled down her cheeks.

CHAPTER FIVE

1510 Hours, Saturday, December 5, 1942
Certosa di Trisulti Charterhouse, Outside of Collepardo

Bruno stood in the monastery's cloister, just past the gatehouse, and waited for Brother Alfieri to arrive so he could report his findings. He took in the view of the courtyard; it was surrounded by the cloister he now stood in and was filled with precisely trimmed boxwood shrubs. Two monks were tilling the soil beneath the shrubs silently, engrossed in their work. Bruno lit up an Alfa and started to toss the match but stopped. The sight of the cloister's glistening tiled walkway made him reconsider. He placed the spent match in his pocket. He was halfway done with the Alfa when he saw Brother Alfieri trudging his way down the cloister toward him, head bent down, his arms shoved into the wide sleeves of his garment.

"Signore Fabrizio. You have good news for me?" Alfieri asked. His cowl rested on his shoulders, revealing the mottled surface of the brother's bald head. The patchy, irregular colors reminded Bruno of an old topographical map of Italy.

Bruno took one last pull from the Alfa but did not dare stomp it out on the brother's sparkling floor. Brother Alfieri watched Bruno as he fumbled for a solution to his dilemma. Bruno snuffed out the cigarette between his index finger and thumb and placed it in the same pocket with the match that lit it. "I'm afraid not, Brother Alfieri. The pipe that burst is old, like everything else in Italy. It succumbed to rust. The whole pipe in the lower section of the wall must be pulled out and replaced."

"And how long will that take?" the stone-faced monk asked.

"I will have to go to Rome for the pipe that I need. With the travel back and forth and the repair itself, it will take…hmm, at least three days. Then the repair to the wall will take another day."

Brother Alfieri mulled over Bruno's response and nodded slowly. "I assume you will take into account that we here in the Certosa have little means. Perhaps you could take payment in the form of some herbs from our pharmacy?"

Bruno had expected the brother's response. Teresa had suggested he offer his services at no cost. He told her they couldn't afford to do that. So now he was ready with his reply. "Brother, the Fabrizio family most likely has even fewer means, as you say." He waited for Brother Alfieri to say something, but he remained silent, like his brother monks tilling the boxwoods nearby. It was pointless to push harder. His wife would make his life miserable. "Perhaps some herbs and several bottles of sambuca." Bruno liked his wine, but his wife was quite taken by the anise-flavored liqueur that was supposedly invented at the Certosa.

"I will accept those terms, Signore Fabrizio. But please work as quickly as possible. This incident has upset the spiritual routines of the Certosa."

"Of course, Brother Alfieri." With that, Brother Alfieri spun on his heels and started down the cloister. "One more thing," Bruno said.

The monk stopped and turned to Bruno.

"Is there someone here named Ettore?"

Brother Alfieri looked at Bruno quizzically, his eyebrows knotted tightly, and took two steps back toward him. He waited a long moment before answering. "Yes, there is. Why do you ask?"

"Is his full name Ettore Majorana?" Brother Alfieri gave Bruno a stern look, making sure Bruno knew he didn't like his question being answered with another question.

"No. His name is Brother Ettore Bini. He is a lay brother who lives in the sanctuary." Brother Alfieri turned to leave and end the questioning but stopped again. "But you must not bother him. Only speak to him when spoken to, and that will be seldom. Good day, Signore Fabrizio."

Bruno watched Brother Alfieri retreat down the cloister at a much faster pace than he'd arrived.

#

His walk back down the path from the monastery to the sanctuary gave Bruno a chance to process his thoughts about Brother Alfieri's demeanor and the tone of his responses. The brother's hurried exit was most telling. The hooked nose man seemed rattled.

The sun struggled to break through the low, dark clouds as he arrived at the sanctuary. It felt like snow to Bruno. He hated snow. There was blackish smoke billowing from a metal pipe that jutted out from the red-tiled roof. Before he knocked on the door, he walked to a window to the left of the door and peered inside. There was a man seated at a table about ten feet from a smoldering fireplace. He was dressed similarly to Brother Alfieri, with his cowl pulled over his head. Two lit oil lamps sat at opposite ends of the table. Nearest the window, there were two books—one was a Bible, another he could only make out one word—*fisica*. Physics—a subject that the famous Ettore Majorana was an expert in. A brother named Ettore and a book on the subject of physics. It gave some much-needed credence to his theory that he had found the famous scientist—credence that his brother-in-law would certainly require before doing anything on his behalf.

Bruno approached the door and knocked. A moment later, it opened. Bruno stared at the brother's expressionless face. His skin color was darker than other Italians, like the complexion of Sicilians. Majorana had been born somewhere in Sicily. He was of a slight build that featured a sunken chest. He stood a few inches short of six feet tall. His cheeks were hollow, but his dark eyes sparkled. With his right hand, he was holding an open book that Bruno could make out the title of: *La guerra sul mare* (*The War on the Sea*). He noticed a long, pinkish hued scar on the back of the man's hand that held the book.

The two men stared at each other.

"Brother Bini, is this a good time to resume my repair?"

Without answering, Brother Bini stepped back and swung the door open wide to let the beaming Bruno inside.

CHAPTER SIX

1515 Hours, Saturday, December 5, 1942
Equus Bar, The Royal Horseguards Hotel, 2 Whitehall Ct., London

Conor leaned across the table and handed Emily his handkerchief. She accepted it, said thank you, and took several deep breaths. He sat back, allowing Emily time to collect herself. What he thought would be a dizzyingly joyful encounter with the woman he loved was anything but. Seeing the tearful Emily completely disarmed him, as it had whenever Grace had a vulnerable, emotional moment. The waiter dropped off Conor's beer and asked Emily if she needed anything. Without looking up, she shook her head.

"So, before I boarded the Pan Am Clipper, I met up with my dad for dinner. He asked about you, which got me talking about you and our last mission, or at least what I could tell him. But mostly it was about you."

Emily sat up and rested her elbows on the table and her chin on her clasped hands.

Conor leaned into her lavender scent. "I guess I went on a bit because he interrupted me. Do you want to know what he said?"

"Of course. Go on."

"He said, 'You realize that you've been talking about Emily nonstop for the last ten minutes. You barely came up for air.'" That made Emily smile. And that made Conor do the same. "And that's when it hit me."

"It?"

"That's when I knew I was going to propose the minute I next saw you." Conor opened the ring box again, glanced at the engagement and wedding ring set; the yellow gold of both shimmered as did the row of six smaller diamonds that were set in the engagement ring's band, but both features were outdone by the one-carat diamond set in the prongs of the wedding ring that shot off sparks of bright light. He slid it toward her.

Emily picked it up and studied it. "It's lovely, Conor. It really is. But what is the point? This damn war will go on for years. It won't—"

"It won't stop us from doing what people in love do and that is to get married."

Emily closed the ring box, placed it on the table, and pushed it toward him. The three seconds it took her to reject the rings made Conor swallow hard.

"Let's not let Hitler and his Nazi psychopaths mess with our lives any more than they already have." Conor took her hand in his. "Emily. This is the right thing to do. Especially given the wonderful news."

Emily breathed in deeply and smiled. "Ten minutes...nonstop? Just what did you tell Jack?"

"That it was time to move on from Grace." He paused, feeling once again the weight of his words. "And I wanted to do that with you."

"Oh, I see," Emily said in a throaty voice. Her eyes welled up, and she looked away, dabbing at her eyes with his handkerchief.

Conor squeezed then let her hand go and sat back. "So?"

Emily mimicked his move and smiled. "Yes," she said softly. "You know, besides telling the doctor that you were going to propose the minute you heard the news, I also told him I would be the luckiest woman in the world to have you."

Conor feigned a look of annoyance. "Then why did you make me work so hard to convince you?"

"I don't know. A woman's prerogative, maybe," she said, a mischievous look on her face, which faded quickly. "But I was dead serious about bringing a child into this horrible world."

"Well, we'll both do all we can to make the best of it," Conor said.

Emily reached over and took a healthy swallow from his beer. "We have little time to plan anything."

"Agreed. How about Sunday the thirteenth? Eight days from now will give Jack time to get over here and me time to find out where Bill Donovan has Maggie holed up." Conor's sister, Maggie, was Bill Donovan's latest recruit to the ranks of the OSS. He knew she was in training somewhere in Scotland. And there was his brother Johnny. Conor was almost certain that Johnny, a captain in the US Army's military intelligence, or G-2, was currently somewhere in Morocco, working for General Patton. It would be a stretch thinking Johnny could get leave, but it was worth the effort to get word to him.

"I am sure the prime minister can spare me for the day." She grinned. "Let's ask Sean to officiate the ceremony."

Conor smiled and began nodding. "That's a great idea."

Father Sean Sullivan was a Thorn family friend going back to their time in Dublin, where Jack had been the US vice-consul. Sean had been just a little kid, of course, as was Conor. Sean's parents had managed the household, while Conor's parents busied themselves with growing the relationship between the US and the Irish government through lobbying and entertaining. Sean had been along on Conor and Emily's mission to reclaim a document from General Eisenhower's personal diary that contained key directives for Operation Torch, the Allied invasion of North Africa. He had been a critical asset as they navigated the environs of Vatican City and Rome.

I hope he's still talking to me, given that I almost got him killed.

"Okay, I think we have a plan," Conor said.

They were both about to push away from the table when the waiter came over with two flutes of champagne. "These are offerings from those two lovely ladies over there," the waiter said, nodding toward the ladies seated on the settee. "It seems they think you have something to celebrate. Cheers." Conor welcomed the gesture—even though it was initiated by two busybodies, because it put a smile on the blushing Emily's face.

CHAPTER SEVEN

0930 Hours, Monday, December 7, 1942
No. 10 Downing Street, London

Churchill looked on as David Bensusan-Butt, Frederick Lindemann's private secretary, set up three easels on the other side of the table from where Churchill sat smoking a Romeo y Julieta, one of his favorite cigars—the Cubans made the best cigars in the world, he would tell anyone who would listen.

What he most liked about his dear friend Lindemann, who was his most reliable scientific adviser, was his uncanny ability to process vast amounts of data into a concise statistical presentation. Today's session would include bar charts that Lindemann promised would shed some light on Allied bomb tonnage dropped on Germany versus German tonnage dropped on Britain and the effectiveness of each belligerent's bombing campaigns. Lindemann's uncanny ability to distill vast amounts of data allowed Churchill to render swift decisions on the prosecution of the Allied war effort.

As fond as he was of Frederick, he was tiring of defending him to those in Parliament who questioned Churchill's loyalty and reliance on someone they considered to be the most arrogant and insufferable man in government service. Churchill had once had to chastise a complaining MP for not knowing that Frederick was his oldest and greatest friend.

Lindemann, the washed-out gray color of his mustache matching the remaining sparse hair on his head, whispered something to Bensusan-Butt, who then left his superior and Churchill alone. He fiddled with the tight tie knot at his throat and turned to Churchill. He was about to speak when he, being a nonsmoker, attempted to wave away the stream of blue cigar smoke making its way toward his face, a mannerism Churchill was very familiar with. "Winston, before we begin, I must ask how the planning for Operation Gunnerside is going. Hopefully, it is progressing toward a sounder and cleverer plan than Operation Freshman, which—"

"Yes, yes, I know what you think of Freshman. It was a debacle. One best forgotten." The subject of destroying the heavy water processing facility at Norsk Hydro's Vemork plant, outside Rjukan, Norway, and its stockpile of the heavy water moderator utilized in the nuclear fission process, had become a favorite of Frederick's. "We have learned our lessons. Or so I am told by Roundell Palmer. It's his task to make sure the SOE gets the job done." The Special Operations Executive, better known as the "ministry of ungentlemanly warfare," had done a masterful job of cocking up Operation Freshman, and Churchill made sure Palmer knew it. Two crashed gliders, heavy casualties, Gestapo executions of those who survived the crashes—all of it was hard to live with.

"If Heisenberg gets a steady supply of deuterium oxide, his Uranprojekt will far outpace our program and that of the Americans." The German-born Lindemann stressed the German name for their nuclear weapons program, a program Churchill had been hearing about ad nauseam. Werner Heisenberg was their lead scientist on the project. "Heisenberg is a brilliant nuclear physicist, and we should not underestimate his abilities. He's a Nobel Prize winner in physics, Winston."

"So you have mentioned several times."

"The Americans want to send a bomb group to level the plant. Why not let them do it?"

Churchill spewed a thick stream of smoke in a show of exasperation. "Frederick, the heavy water processing facilities are in the plant's basement with several floors of concrete and steel above it. Success would not be attainable."

"Ach, we should let them try," Lindemann said, bearing clenched yellowed teeth, and then leaned on the Cabinet Room table. "And another related matter. The Americans seemed to have slowed the sharing of research from their Manhattan Project to a trickle. This worries me and should worry you. You must think about where Great Britain's position as a world power will be after the war. You trust your friend Roosevelt too deeply. We must have our own atomic weapon and not rely on the Americans to protect us from the Red Menace."

Churchill remained silent. What could he say? He agreed with everything his dear friend said. But Britain didn't have the resources and brainpower to match the Americans. Nor did it make sense to duplicate efforts. He knew if Operation Gunnerside—which was targeting February as its D-Day—was successful, it would severely harm, but not stop, the Nazi program. *If* it was successful.

"Get on with it, Frederick." As Lindemann turned to retrieve his secretary, Churchill took in a lungful of his cigar and wished he had a tumbler of brandy in his hand.

CHAPTER EIGHT

The rusted pipe liked where it was. It resisted the brute force Bruno brought to bear on it. Resting on one knee, he looked over at Brother Bini, who hadn't moved from his reading table or uttered a word since Bruno had begun extracting the pipe two hours earlier. His head was bent down, and the cowl of his habit hid much of his face.

Bruno ceased his efforts in order to reclaim some energy and lit up an Alfa. He leaned against the wall and watched Brother Bini, if that was his actual name, scribble on an envelope and then place it on a corner of the table. The monk's head rose, and he turned to look at Bruno. Not directly at him, but at the glowing, red-tipped cigarette he held in his hand. There wasn't a look of displeasure, but it was the look of a wide-eyed child who was staring at the assortment of candies in a shop's display case. Bruno didn't take him for a smoker, but he was wrong about many things—or so said his wife.

"Do you smoke?"

Brother Bini shifted his gaze from the Alfa to Bruno's face. His mouth opened, but he did not speak. Instead, he took in a deep breath and slowly let it out. "I used to. Quite a lot."

Bruno nodded.

"It is frowned on here at the Certosa."

Bruno responded with a shrug. "Would you like one?" he said, holding out the packet.

Brother Bini looked at the front door of the sanctuary, then back at Bruno. "I shouldn't."

"It's okay. I can keep a secret."

Brother Bini rose from his chair and walked over to Bruno, who passed the packet to him. The monk slipped a cigarette from the packet, like he had done it hundreds of times, and returned the packet to Bruno. He delicately held the cigarette between his index finger and thumb and carefully brought it to his lips as if it was a communion wafer. Bruno struck a match and lit it. After the first puff, Brother Bini just nodded slowly, eyes closed. He released the thick smoke solely through his nostrils and then raised his eye lids halfway. "I used to smoke the Nazionali brand," the monk said before inhaling and expelling another lungful. "My mother did not approve of my habit."

"If you want, you can have this pack," Bruno said, holding out the packet of Alfas. "There's only a few left."

"No, no. That would not be right." Brother Bini took another drag on the Alfa. "You are called Bruno?"

"Yes."

Brother Bini nodded. "Were you aware that Saint Bruno of Cologne was the man responsible for the founding of the Order of Carthusians?"

"No, I wasn't." Bruno dropped his spent cigarette on the floor. The monk looked at it. "Don't worry, Brother. I'll sweep it up before I leave." Bruno took out another cigarette.

The monk took another puff. "Saint Bruno built the first hermitage in the valley of the Chartreuse Mountains in France in 1084. Have you heard our motto?"

"I didn't know orders had mottos. You mean a motto like *Me ne frego?*" Bruno recalled his father, who was a member of the *arditi*—the "daring ones"—who fought for Italy in the Great War, would say the phrase often: *I don't care.* The volunteers did not care if they died defending their country. Bruno did not speak of his father often, as the *arditi* had become the backbone of the fascist Blackshirts. Bruno kept his antifascist political ideology a secret, even from his wife.

"I have not heard of that. It seems quite mindless. What does—"
Bruno waved him off. "It is too pointless to discuss. What is the Carthusian motto?"

"*Stat crux dum volvitur orbis.* It's Latin that translates to 'the Cross is steady while the world is turning.'"

Bruno's religious zeal had moved on from him long ago, so he had no interest in discussing it further. "Brother, when I visited you in sanctuary two days ago, you were reading a book: *The War on the Sea.* I was surprised at your interest in such a subject. And physics as well. May I ask if the study of those subjects is allowed at the Certosa? I thought the monks only studied religious works."

This change in the conversation's direction only served to shut down Brother Bini. The monk handed the stub of his still-lit cigarette to Bruno, turned, and returned to his table. Bruno shrugged, then stamped out their cigarettes and returned to the battle with the rusted-out iron pipe.

It took another thirty minutes for Bruno to wrestle the pipe from the wall. And thirty more for him to pack up his tools and sweep up the debris from the extraction. Brother Bini stirred little while he sat at his desk, busy scribbling words and diagrams in a leather-bound journal. As Bruno made for the door, the monk rose and turned to Bruno, who stopped, canvas bag of tools in hand. Brother Bini had the envelope Bruno had seen earlier in one hand and a Bible in the other.

"Bruno, are you a God-fearing man?"

The question puzzled him, as did the hopeful look on the monk's face. Standing in the sanctuary in front of a Carthusian monk, Bruno assumed an affirmative answer would be better than a direct denial of a deep belief in God. When Bruno answered yes, he heard Brother Bini release a long breath.

"Yes, I thought so. If you would be so kind, Bruno, to mail this letter when you leave here today, I would be deeply grateful. I am not allowed to travel into Collepardo, and I would like to keep my letter writing from my brothers. I fear they wouldn't understand." With ink-stained, boney fingers, he extended the envelope to Bruno, who took it. On the face of it was just an address: Vaile Regina Margherita, 2057, 00187 Roma RM. "The letter is very important to me. Would you please place your hand on my Bible and promise me and the Lord that you will not read the letter, nor tell anyone of its existence?"

Bruno shot another look at the envelope. It didn't take him long to get over the fact that Brother Bini lacked trust in him. "I...I'm not—"

"You doing me this favor will not be forgotten in my daily prayers."

Bruno knew he was going to read it and, even though he wasn't spiritual in any way, he would not help any deity in bringing down its wrath on him. "Brother Bini, the Bible is not necessary." Bruno took the letter and dropped it into his canvas tool sack. "You can trust me implicitly."

CHAPTER NINE

1000 Hours, Monday, December 7, 1942
Claridge's, Brook Street, London

The breakfast meeting with Emily at the Museum Tavern, where they made some hasty decisions regarding their wedding ceremony, left Conor in a buoyant mood. Emily was beaming and didn't take her eyes off him, nor did she let his hand go the whole time. He had to tap the table with his free hand a few times to get her to snap out of her reverie and answer his questions about the guest list. He didn't think he stopped smiling once on the taxi ride to Claridge's after their meeting.

When he arrived at the famed hotel, he took in the magical sight of the front entrance. The portico's overhang hosted a line of Christmas trees that glowed in the morning sun. The seven flags represented the countries of some of the hotel's illustrious guests, including the Union Jack, were not flying that morning. Conor thought that possibly management wanted nothing taking an observer's attention away from their lavish Christmas display.

He headed into the lobby through the revolving doors, aided by one of the footmen on duty. Standing in the black-and-white tiled foyer, he again took time to take in his surroundings. He had been through the lobby many times in the past three months. Colonel Donovan had a room in the basement assigned to Conor because he didn't want him too far away from his suite on one of the upper floors. But the past two days, since Emily had agreed to marry him, he seemed to be noticing things, little things, for the first time.

In the foyer, Conor studied two metallic leaping deer lamps perched atop crystal pedestals nestled inside wall niches. The art pieces gleamed against black backgrounds. He headed to the bank of elevators as he passed through the lobby and marveled at the display of several more Christmas trees of varying sizes that must have been adorned with several hundred white lights. If it weren't for the pile of sandbags at the front entrance of the landmark hotel, one would never guess there was a war on.

There were ten people waiting for an elevator, so he decided to head up the massive staircase to the third floor to catch the elevator there. As he did, he remembered it was just six weeks before that he'd run into—almost literally—Queen Wilhelmina of the Netherlands as she strode down the staircase dressed in orange flannel pajamas. On a prior visit to the reception desk, one of the hotel's desk staff told him the queen wasn't the only royalty waiting out the war at Claridge's. Others included the kings of Greece, Norway, Yugoslavia, and Czechoslovakia. As if to back up the story, the gentleman had taken a call just then, and all Conor had heard him say was "Certainly, sir, but which one?" When he hung up, he'd told Conor someone had wanted to speak to the king but hadn't specified of which country.

The elevator dropped Conor off in a foyer connected by hallways to other foyers on either side. This allowed the entourages of various high-ranking guests to stay in close contact with one another. One of those high-ranking guests was David Bruce, head of the OSS London office, who was never far from the colonel.

His knock on the door to Colonel Donovan's suite was met with a sharp response: "Enter." He found the gray-haired, freshly shaved colonel seated behind his large art deco desk. His khaki cotton blouse, open at the neck, was crisply ironed, showing two sharp creases down the front. His eyes were locked onto the contents of a file. It occurred to Conor that the colonel spent a lot of time with his head buried in a file. Something the man of action undoubtedly didn't revel in. On the desk was a copy of that day's *Daily Mirror*.

"Hello, Conor. Welcome back," Donovan said without looking up from the file.

"Good to be back closer to the action, Colonel," Conor said as he took a seat in front of the desk.

Donovan slid the newspaper across to him and sat back. Conor picked it up. The boldfaced headline read "One-Year Anniversary of the Attack on Pearl Harbor." The lone picture above the fold was of the USS *Arizona* engulfed in an oil-fed conflagration. Conor said nothing. Neither did Donovan. Each sat in silence, lost in their own thoughts, knowing there were few words that could properly and fully address the tremendous loss of life.

A long minute passed. "Where were you when they attacked?" Donovan asked, slumping back into his chair.

Colonel Donovan knew most of the facts about Conor's last days in the US Navy. Ever since his wife, Grace, and son, Timothy, died on October 31, 1941, the same day that the *Reuben James* was sunk, his life hadn't been the same. He had been crushed from both sides. He had needed and wanted to be by his wife's side but had also needed and wanted to be with his crewmates. As the executive officer, he had responsibilities to the crew of his ship. One hundred and fourteen of the crew died. They were sailing without an XO, given Conor's abrupt departure. He always felt he could have helped save some lives that day. Both events sent him spiraling into a deep chasm of self-pity and loathing. He had given up on himself.

He had been stationed at the Brooklyn Navy Yard while the USS *Iowa* was going through its final outfitting before being commissioned in February 1942. Being falsely accused of accosting the captain's wife at a holiday party on December 6, Conor had sought some solace in a bottle of bourbon. He was sleeping it off the next morning when he was woken in the officer's quarters with the news. He had learned a week later that his captain, Leslie Bivens, had already started the process to get him court-martialed. The US Navy was done with Conor Thorn. He made it easier on them both by resigning his commission.

"I was stationed at the Brooklyn Navy Yard, waiting for the finishing touches on the *Iowa*. It hit me hard. I lost a lot of friends... classmates that day."

Donovan nodded. "As did I. As did I," he said with a weak voice. More silence. Then he sat up, cleared his throat, and picked up the file he had been reviewing when Conor first arrived. "You remember Colonel Eddy, don't you?"

"He's a hard-to-forget kinda guy, Colonel."

Colonel William Eddy, head of the Tangier OSS station and his old boss, was a decorated US Marine veteran of World War I. He was also the one who sent him back to London for reassignment because of some complaints from Conor's fellow OSS agents that he was too reckless. A claim that he himself couldn't fully deny. It seemed Colonel Eddy agreed with Conor's associates. He hoped he could one day reunite with Eddy and prove he was effective, if a little impulsive.

"I sent him along with some of his staff from Tangier to Algiers to set up camp there."

When Conor and Emily returned from their R and R at her mother's house in Southend-on-Sea on November 9, London newspapers had been abuzz with the daring action that involved a direct landing by two destroyers of the Royal Navy and the US Army's Third Battalion, 135th Infantry, to secure the port of Algiers before the Vichy French forces could destroy the port's facilities. Operation Terminal had HMS *Malcolm* and HMS *Broke* carrying six hundred troops, with the mission to land the troops directly on the quay. HMS *Malcolm*, severely damaged by shore batteries, withdrew, but HMS *Broke* pushed through the port's boom after three attempts and landed its troops. When *Broke* withdrew, she came under heavy fire from shore batteries and sank two days later from the damage. After initial success in securing the port, the Third Battalion, 135th Infantry came under fire from Vichy troops. The battalion's commander, Lieutenant Colonel Edwin Swenson, facing French tanks with only mortars and grenades, sought to save some of his remaining men and surrendered. But for the French, it was a hollow victory. After the surrender, the Vichy commanders failed to destroy the port's facilities or scuttle any ships inside the harbor.

"Quite the show securing the port, Colonel. Those British destroyers had some balls trying to breach the port's boom. Too bad we couldn't count on the Vichy troops to back the Allies up."

"Please, don't get me started on that subject," Donovan said, making no attempt to mask his disdain. "So, tell me, how's your Italian?"

Conor had hoped that subject wouldn't come up. There were two reasons for his assignment back in the States: help Jack Taylor pull together a training program for agents assigned to future maritime units and spend as much time as the first mission would allow learning passable Italian. "Ah, well…I got as much classroom time as possible. I can't have a deep conversation on fascism, but I can order a meal—as long as it's pasta and mussels, along with a glass of wine."

Donovan stared at Conor.

Wrong approach. Humor was a dangerous thing. Time for damage control. "Colonel, I spent as much time with the tutor as possible. I wanted to make sure Commander Taylor had a well-thought-out training program. I know how much of an impact you think the maritime units will have once deployed. I can muddle through."

Donovan's look remained one of displeasure, but thankfully, he decided to press on. "All right. When you get to Algiers, Colonel Eddy will brief you more fully. But we're going to infiltrate you into Sicily, after you've had some paratroop training."

Conor hoped the large gulp he took wasn't as visible as it felt. He hated flying. He could muster the nerve necessary to do so, but there wasn't enough nerve in his body to jump out of an airplane.

Not taking notice of his silent but wide-eyed reaction, Donovan continued. "Sicily looks like the next major offensive for the Allies. We need some friends there when we land on their beaches. Hopefully, more dependable friends than the Vichy French were in North Africa."

"Who are we targeting as potential friends?"

"Believe it or not, the Mafia."

"Whoa. We're going to reach out to the Sicilian Mafia to help us invade Sicily? Their homeland?"

Donovan rose but didn't move from behind his desk. "I take it you don't think that is a good idea."

Careful, Conor. "I'm sure that someone has figured out a damn solid reason why it is a sound strategy." Conor was very tempted to ask whether the colonel thought of sending in someone of Italian descent. Maybe an actual Sicilian.

As if he'd heard his thoughts, he replied, "We thought of sending in someone with roots to Sicily, but the Mafia are very distrustful of their own kind. An American, that would be you, with a generous cash offering and…let us say, promises from Hoover's FBI to look the other way when dealing with their American cousins, was determined to be a more intelligent approach. Your thoughts?"

Conor listened first to the devil on his shoulder, then to the angel on the other, and simply said, "That makes sense, Colonel."

"All right, then. We'll team you up with someone—someone who knows Italian better than you and can help when you get on the ground. Not sure who that may be. David Bruce and I are still working on that. Colonel Eddy will know once you land in Algiers."

"What's the timeline, Colonel?"

"You leave on Christmas Eve. Sorry about the timing. It couldn't be helped."

"I understand. The timing could be worse."

"How so?" Donovan asked as he spread his arms behind his back in a long stretch.

"Emily and I are getting married on Sunday the thirteenth."

Donovan finished the stretch and sat back down. A smile crossed his face. "What took you so long?"

Conor sighed. "It was a little complicated. You know. Grace and…" Conor stammered.

"Yes. I'm sure it was," Donovan said, his tone thoughtful and reassuring. "But she would be so contented that you found a new happiness. Focus on the future. And that includes your next mission, Conor," Donovan said, his tone shifting back to business in the blink of an eye.

Conor, gratified at his mentor's heartfelt reaction, could only nod and bow his head.

"Is Kim Philby invited?" Conor scoffed and checked to make sure Donovan was joking. His answer came in the form of a sly smile and a wink of the eye.

#

It was almost two months ago that Conor and Emily last found themselves in the sitting room of the Westminster Cathedral Clergy House. Nothing had changed in that time—the same couch sat along a wall adorned with photos of the cathedral at various times of the year, and two other walls also displayed cathedral photos. Across from the couch they were seated on was a large, faded reproduction of the Sacred Heart of Jesus. Just as in their last visit, on a small table below the painting was a vase of lilies flanked by two flickering devotional candles. It seemed as if time had stopped in the clergy house.

"Here they be, Father Sean. Your old friends have come to visit," Edith, the diminutive housekeeper and cook who was dressed in the same washed-out floral-print smock as the last time, said as she entered the room. Father Sean Sullivan was right behind her. On their last visit, the barrel-chested priest had bellowed his greeting and promptly gave Conor a bear hug that made his back crack. This time, Conor did the bellowing, and Emily was the one who gave Sean a hug like she had never given Conor.

Sean nodded at Edith, who took her leave. He smiled briefly and weakly, shook Conor's hand, returned Emily's embrace fleetingly, and pushed away. Some things did change—Father Sean Sullivan looked as if he was in mourning.

"It's great to see you again, Sean," Emily said as she and Conor took their seats on the couch. Sean sat in a well-worn club chair across from them. Conor noticed that the slouching priest's thick mop of black hair was turning gray near his temples, and his emerald green eyes appeared to have lost some of their sheen.

"Ah, you are both a sight for sore eyes, believe me when I say that."

Knowing Sean wasn't one for exaggeration, Conor had no problem believing it.

"Sean, you look a bit cut up about something. Everything all right?" Emily asked.

Sean leaned forward and put his elbows on his knees, his head lowered as he gazed at his meaty hands. "Well, truth be told, I have been a bit off my game."

"What does that mean?" Conor said.

Sean sat back. "Let's call it for what it is. It's a crisis of faith. My crisis of faith."

Conor and Emily exchanged a quick worried glance.

"Ever since I returned from our foray in Rome, I have struggled. My faith in the Lord did not shatter, but it has cracked. The fissures…they creep and grow slowly each day."

"I'm sure that happens to many people who have pledged their lives in the service of God," Emily said as she reached out and touched Sean's knee lightly.

"What triggered this crisis? Was it what happened in Rome? Or Lisbon?" Conor asked.

The firefight with Russian agents at Portella Airport outside of Lisbon had been a shock to Sean, who was transporting the diplomatic pouch between Westminster Cathedral, the seat of the Catholic Church in Great Britain, and the Vatican. It had surprised Conor that Sean was carrying a small pistol and said he was prepared to use it to protect the cathedral's pouch. But Conor knew that the loss of life on the tarmac that day had been a deep shock to his cloistered religious sensibilities.

"I say mass every day. I hear confessions once a week. I visit hospitals to soothe the sick. Yet the scourge that is fascism continues to grow. It seems what I do with my life does not have the impact that I desire."

Conor was so taken aback that he didn't know what to say. Thank God Emily was not, so she told Sean, "You're a strong-willed man. You will see your way through this crisis."

Sean smiled faintly. "You're so kind, Emily. I plan to do just that. I'm headed up to a monastery in Scotland to sort things out. I'll pray. Take walks. Pray some more. And search for some answers."

"When do you leave?" Conor asked.

"This Saturday. The twelfth."

Conor looked at Emily. She nodded, so he spoke. "Sean, we came here today to ask you to officiate a wedding ceremony. Ours. On the thirteenth." He reached for Emily's hand.

Sean leaned forward. His eyes lit up. "Oh, my Lord. You won't believe this, but in a conversation I recently had with your Colonel Donovan, I told him this was in the cards. I couldn't be happier." Sean sprang out of his chair and raced over to the door of the sitting room. "Edith," he shouted. "Edith, come quick. And bring my special bottle and three glasses. No, make that four."

He turned back to Conor and Emily, who had both stood. Sean's emotional transformation amazed Conor, but he was even more surprised the priest had been talking with Colonel Donovan. "Sean?" Conor said.

"I just want to toast you both. This is wonderful news. And of course, I would be thrilled and honored to be your celebrant. Wouldn't miss it for the world."

"But Scotland," Emily said.

"Scotland and my crisis can wait for one more day." Edith entered the sitting room with a tray holding four glasses and a bottle of Kilbeggan Irish Whiskey. "Edith, my friends here are going to get married. Do you believe that?"

Edith raised her right hand to cover her gaping mouth. "Oh my. The first time I saw them, Father, I just knew they were meant for each other."

Conor remembered when they had shown up at the clergy house's door back in October looking for Sean, Edith had called Conor and Emily "two lovebirds" and asked if they were looking for banns of marriage.

Sean poured, and they toasted. Edith corralled Emily, who showed off her ring. Conor and Sean just watched them, Emily beaming and Edith oohing and aahing.

Sean poured them both another round, then pulled Conor aside. "Conor, do you have a few minutes to talk one-on-one? It's a family matter."

Conor looked at his watch and grimaced. "Can it wait? Emily and I are already running late for a reception at the US Embassy. Colonel Donovan invited us and told me not to be late."

Sean hesitated and then said, "I'm sure it can." He put his glass down on the table below the faded painting of the Sacred Heart of Jesus and gave Conor a bear hug that made his back crack.

CHAPTER TEN

1800 Hours, Monday, December 7, 1942
Farmhouse of Bruno Fabrizio, Collepardo, Italy

Bruno told his wife their meal could wait as he pushed plates of antipasto and cacio e pepe to the center of the table. His wife, Teresa, her ashen face, and sunken cheeks looking worse than he remembered from the morning, followed his lead obediently.

Bruno took a table knife and carefully pried the envelope open. Before he could slide the letter from it, Teresa placed her hand, its skin blotchy and translucent, on his arm.

"What if it is a harmless letter? With no information that he is who you think he is?"

"Then I will post the letter like the brother asked me to."

Teresa pulled her hand away and nodded.

Bruno took a sip of red wine, then opened the letter and read.

"Bruno, aloud, please."

Bruno took another sip of wine and began.

7 December 1942-XX

Mother, brother, and sisters,

I am alive. And I am deeply apologetic for having put all of you through so much pain and agony. I cannot tell you where I am. But I can tell you I am safe and healthy. The gloom that I lived with for several years before I took leave from my life with you has been lifted with help from the Lord my God and those who surround me.

42

When I wrote my last letter to you in those dark days, I asked that you remember me and, in your hearts, to forgive me. It is my hope that you have found the forgiveness that I beseeched you for. If not, it is my fear that you will not grant my wish to return home, to be amongst you once again. If you can see that a reunion could take place, I will be forever grateful. You can communicate your willingness to allow my return by placing an advertisement in the II Messaggero *on 15 December. All the advertisement need say is: "You are forgiven. We await your return to us with joyful expectations."*

Should you reject my plea and not respond, I will never complicate your lives with any further correspondence.

Your humble and repentant son and brother,
Ettore

"It's him." Bruno tossed the letter on the table. "The disappeared scientist. He has been in the Certosa for God knows how long." He took another sip of wine, then a greedier swallow.

"What will you do now?" Teresa bit her lower lip, a familiar sign that she was curious.

Bruno picked up the letter and gingerly placed it back in the envelope. "More wine."

Teresa rose and retrieved a bottle from the kitchen counter, then filled his glass. "I have a suggestion."

"I know what your suggestion is: let your brother in on our little secret. I have already thought of that."

Teresa nodded and took her seat. "It makes sense, Bruno. This man's disappearance consumed Anteo. And his stature within OVRA has grown. He could be of great help to us."

"He hates me. He thinks you married below your station."

"You're right. He hates you." She shot him a wily smile, and he shook his head slightly at her brazen admission. Truthfully, he'd always known it, but she'd never voiced it before. "But he loves me, and he will help if we ask him to."

Bruno gave her a slight, incredulous smile and drained his glass before pulling the plates toward him and his wife. He nibbled on a small wedge of cheese wrapped in a slice of prosciutto. He could sense Teresa was staring at him, but he went on eating. Finally, she cleared her throat.

"Yes, yes," Bruno said, a speck of cheese caught in the corner of his mouth. "Tomorrow, I will go to Rome. I will buy some pipe for the Certosa. Then I will call upon Anteo. If there is still a reward for information about Majorana, he will know. I am sure a promotion will come his way if this man is the scientist that has come back from the dead." Teresa nodded and poured Bruno more wine.

"Drink and eat. Then meet me in the bedroom. We can celebrate our good fortune in a more meaningful way."

CHAPTER ELEVEN

0900 Hours, Tuesday, December 8, 1942
OVRA Headquarters, Forte Braschi, Rome

The trip to Rome took two and a half buttocks-numbing hours. The condition had not been helped by having to sit in a wooden chair in front of Anteo Tardino's desk for the last twenty minutes. Bruno couldn't help but think that his brother-in-law was purposely making him wait, thinking it would prove he was superior.

Above the dark wood credenza behind the cluttered desk hung two framed photos; the larger of the two was of Benito Mussolini. He was wearing a black uniform, shirt, and tie, and a soft black hat. Mussolini's head was turned to his right, his chin elevated and pointing proudly outward, his hands resting on his hips. The smaller photo was of a man Bruno didn't recognize. He was wearing glasses, dressed in a double-breasted suit and a wide-brimmed fedora with a dark band. He was in a crowd of people who were all gazing at the man somewhat reverentially.

There were footsteps behind him—the heavy footsteps of a fat man. "I'm busy. What do you want, Bruno?"

Tardino was wearing a wrinkled dark suit, the jacket unbuttoned, giving up the sight of a midsection well out of proportion with Tardino's short frame. He had a sheaf of haphazardly arranged papers tucked under his arm. Bruno noticed the man's hair was thinning and that, despite the cold office, he was perspiring. When he dropped into his desk chair, it creaked loudly under its load. He dabbed at his brow with a handkerchief and dropped it on the desk.

"My sister is all right, no? I have not heard from her for several weeks."

"She is fine. Now. A few weeks ago, she was not well. But she recovered. She sends her love."

"Please tell her to come and visit me. I will send a car for her. My new position here allows me that privilege. Tell her that."

"What is this new position you speak of?" Bruno said, registering mild surprise.

Tardino wiped his brow once more, then turned and pointed, with the hand still holding the handkerchief, at the photo of the man Bruno didn't recognize. "Guido Leto, head of OVRA. A great man. I am his new deputy. He has others, but it is me he trusts the most." Tardino didn't turn back to Bruno for several seconds. He just eyed the photo of Leto and wiped the perspiration from his forehead. When he turned back to face Bruno, he was smiling, but it disappeared almost instantly when he looked at his sister's husband. "Why are you here? I have much work to do."

Bruno decided he would get to the point—no need to prolong this. "About four years ago, on a couple of your visits, you talked of an investigation that you had been assigned to."

"What investigation? I don't remember discussing any investigation with you. That would have been inappropriate of me."

"Maybe so, but you did it anyway." Bruno gave a thought to mentioning that it was after the first bottle of wine he consumed, but he abandoned the idea as quickly as it came to him.

Tardino stiffened, eyebrows furrowed. "Get to the point."

"It was the Ettore Majorana disappearance. You were searching for a body. He left a suicide note for his family. You told us he asked for forgiveness from them, and to not mourn more than three days. Teresa has a better memory of it than I."

"What of it?"

Bruno pushed the letter across the surface of the desk. "Read the letter, Anteo."

Tardino kept his eyes on Bruno as he pulled the letter from the envelope and spread the folded paper on his desk. Finally, he looked down and read it. Bruno watched as his brother-in-law's eyes bulged. He darted a look at Bruno, then back at the letter. Bruno eyed his lips moving as he read it the second time.

"This is a hoax," he said roughly. "Where did you get this letter? Did you write it?"

Bruno snorted. "What would be the point of that?"

"I don't know. To impress my sister? To trick me into helping you in some scheme?"

Bruno wanted to slap Tardino, but he needed information. "Do you have a photograph of Majorana?"

Tardino pressed his lips together and hesitated before finally replying, "First, describe the man you think is Majorana."

"Medium height, a slim build, dark hair turning gray. He has dark eyes and a darker complexion, like that of a Sicilian."

Tardino shrugged. "The person you just described numbers in the millions in Italy."

"He has a scar on the back of his right hand."

Tardino jerked his head back, then pushed away from his desk. "You are sure it was the right hand?" Tardino said, his tone much less imperious.

"Yes. The right hand."

Tardino rose from his chair, stepped over to a file cabinet, and opened the bottom drawer, retrieving a brown accordion file from the furthermost confines of the drawer. Dust rained down to the floor as he undid the elastic cord that secured the file's flap. He stepped back to his desk and thumbed through the contents, which Bruno could not see. Tardino eventually found what he was looking for and studied the photo for a moment, then handed it to Bruno. "Is this your man?"

Bruno immediately saw the resemblance between the young man in the picture and his Ettore Bini. The photo he held in his hand was that of a man in his early twenties, dressed in a light-colored suit, a white ironed shirt with a striped tie, and a buttoned vest. His short, dark hair was parted sharply on the side. Majorana was looking straight into the camera. His furrowed eyebrows nearly touched above the bridge of his nose. He looked as if he was thinking of an answer to a complex problem. "It is." He handed the photo back. "That is the face of the man who now calls himself Ettore Bini."

Tardino placed the photo back in the accordion file and retook his seat. "Where is he? Collepardo?"

Bruno had expected this question and had decided that morning he was going to withhold that piece of information. He didn't trust his brother-in-law. "He is nearby."

Tardino leaned forward and crossed his arms. "Don't play games with me, Bruno. It could get you in quite a bit of trouble."

"I will tell you where he is if you can find out if there is still a reward for information that leads to his discovery."

Tardino didn't move or respond. Nor did Bruno. A few moments passed before Tardino unfolded his arms and searched for something under the scattered papers on his desk. He pulled a pack of MS cigarettes from under the papers, slipped a cigarette out of the pack, and lit up with his lighter, all while he stared at Bruno.

"You believe me now, Anteo?" Bruno asked, hoping his gloating tone wasn't noticeable.

Tardino blew a stream of smoke in Bruno's direction. "Maybe. Maybe you have seen pictures of him and read about the scar. His disappearance received much attention in the press."

Bruno nodded. "I am interested in the reward. Please find out if there is one still being offered. Then I will tell you where he is."

Tardino plucked a speck of tobacco from his tongue and flicked it to his right. "If there is a reward, maybe you can finally treat my sister to some finer things."

Bruno's jaw muscles tightened. His breathing quickened. But he remained silent.

"Wait outside," Tardino finally said. "I need to make a call."

CHAPTER TWELVE

0930 Hours, Tuesday, December 8, 1942
Kaiser Wilhelm Institute for Physics, Berlin

Werner Heisenberg hated politics with the same intensity as he loved science. It hadn't always been that way. But ever since June of that year, when he was named managing director of the institute, the politically charged interference from high-ranking military staff and Nazi Party members had become an enormous distraction. Which, in his mind, characterized the nature of the meeting that he was just summoned to attend.

His superior, General Emil Leeb, listened sympathetically when he complained. For the most part, Leeb was careful not to bother him with trivial matters, so he knew that today's hastily called meeting must be over a significant matter. Leeb had taken on his role as the chief of the Waffenamt, the Army Ordnance Weapons Depot within the War Ministry, in April 1940. Leeb had confided in Heisenberg that it was a posting he had not aspired to, and he would have rather remained in the field, commanding his old unit, the XI Corps. He prided himself on the XI Corps' effectiveness during the invasion of Poland and wished to be reassigned to a field unit—even if that meant a unit on the Eastern Front, he'd revealed to Heisenberg. Leeb was told it was because of his successes in the field that they had appointed him to head the Waffenamt, which was in desperate need of new leadership. His predecessor, Karl Becker, had taken his own life after receiving criticism from Hitler for shortfalls in munitions production.

When he entered Leeb's office, the midmorning sun pouring in the three windows opposite the office door made it difficult to see who was seated in the overstuffed leather chair facing Leeb's massive desk. As he drew closer, he saw who it was and was not pleased—Kurt Diebner. Heisenberg knew that his coworkers called Diebner his *wettbewerb*, his competition. Diebner, a bespectacled experimental physicist, who wouldn't miss a chance to poke a metaphorical finger in Heisenberg's chest over some scientific failing or disappointment, was an adversary. The German nuclear weapons project, Uranprojekt, was broken up into two forms of attack: the research and development generated by theoretical physicists headed by Heisenberg and the research and development generated by experimental physicists headed by Diebner. Leeb's key task was to keep Heisenberg and Diebner at each other's scientific throats—a task he was quite adept at.

"Ah, Herr Heisenberg, please take a seat. And I apologize for the interruption. We won't be long, I assure you," Leeb said. The general was resplendent in his sharply tailored, greenish-gray Wehrmacht uniform, his hair slicked back, his back straight. The fingers of his right hand drummed the gleaming surface of his desk.

"No apologies needed, General. I am sure you have something important to report." Heisenberg took his seat and nodded toward Diebner. "Kurt, it is good to see you. Are you well?"

"Better as each day passes. Success in the laboratory makes that possible, Werner," Diebner said without looking directly at him. Leeb ceased drumming his fingers.

Heisenberg scoffed, and Diebner turned and squinted at him before responding. "Werner, you look completely spent. I can see it in your eyes. Late nights calculating critical mass is my guess."

Heisenberg knew he had a mole within his team, someone who was leaking information to Diebner. Someone who knew that he and his protégé, Carl von Weizsäcker, were struggling with the critical mass calculation. Determining the amount of fissionable materials, namely uranium-235, was a problem that had persistently hounded Heisenberg and von Weizsäcker. Heisenberg worried that their troubles determining how to effectively induce criticality might have also been betrayed. He was about to respond to the taunt when Leeb noisily cleared his throat.

"Tell me what progress you've made." Heisenberg had nothing remotely positive to report and knew he had to alter the direction the meeting was about to take.

"Progress is…slow but meaningful. Construction on the nuclear pile is moving along at the proper rate."

"Proper? What does that mean exactly?" Diebner sneered.

"It means that I have to oversee every phase, inspect every piece that is added to the pile. There is no room for mistakes. I am sure you would agree with that, Kurt."

"Of course, Werner," Leeb interrupted. "But you must know there is pressure…pressure from outside the institute to show genuine progress in producing a weapon." Heisenberg noted the anxious tenor in Leeb's reedy voice. "The Allies grow stronger every day, with the American factories turning out war matériel at unprecedented rates."

"I assure you, General, I and my team are acutely aware of our current situation."

"Well, you haven't convinced me," Diebner said. "And others I will not name."

Heisenberg ignored Diebner's jab. "General, I was reminded to ask about the next shipment of the deuterium oxide. It is overdue." The heavy water, which was to be used as a moderator in his nuclear pile, seemed to perpetually be in short supply.

"It should be here in the next three days. The Allies' recent bombing of the rail yards in Eindhoven has delayed the arrival."

Heisenberg jolted forward. "Has the shipment been damaged?"

"I…I am unsure of that. But—"

"General, if the supply of heavy water from Norway is going to continue to be unreliable, then we must consider using another moderator."

"No, no, no. We've had this discussion and agreed that the deuterium oxide was the best route. Gathering enough graphite to act as a moderator to keep the program going could not be guaranteed. I do not want to revisit the subject," Leeb said as he slapped his palm on the desk.

"I agree with General Leeb. To switch moderators would set the program back months," Diebner said, twisting in his chair to face Heisenberg. "I think that is what you want. You are dragging your feet and that—"

"Stop," Heisenberg shouted, slamming his fist down on the arm of his chair. "Do not question my loyalty to my country. I pledged to do all in my power to see to a successful nuclear weapons program. We will be successful. I will stake my life on that."

There were thirty seconds of silence before General Leeb dismissed Heisenberg and Diebner. Outside Leeb's office, Heisenberg and Diebner turned to each other.

"I don't like you," Diebner said. "You are arrogant. But I love my country more than you know. Do you need my help?"

Heisenberg did need help. But not from Diebner.

#

When Heisenberg strode into the lab, all ten members of his team stopped what they were doing and gawked at him.

"Gentlemen, please get back to work. We have much to do." He walked up to von Weizsäcker, who was leaning against a worktable. Heisenberg waited for the question.

"Was the meeting productive?" von Weizsäcker asked. "Do we still have the general's backing?"

"Yes, Carl. But because of external pressures, his support is weakening. We must push harder."

Von Weizsäcker nodded. Heisenberg watched him pick up a pencil and make a note on a clipboard full of papers. "I brought up the subject of changing moderators. He was not pleased."

"That's not shocking news. What about the deuterium oxide shipment?"

He delivered the news about the shipment, which elicited a nonresponse from his friend. Heisenberg leaned over the workbench to study a blueprint of the pile.

von Weizsäcker bent down next to him and whispered, "This policy of rounding up Jews has done nothing but damage our ability to outthink the Allies. Virtually every brilliant Jewish physicist worth a damn has left the country. If they had been given some sort of special treatment, this program would be much further along than it is now. I mean no disrespect to you, Werner, but you know that."

Heisenberg's head sagged. He did know that. He stood upright and turned to von Weizsäcker. "Carl—"

"What if we worked more closely with Diebner? That could help."

"That won't happen. He will get in the way."

"Then what about help from our Italian friends?"

Heisenberg knew that Enrico Fermi had established a group of physicists at the Via Panisperna Institute in Rome in the 1930s. But Fermi had fled to America, like Einstein had in 1933. The Via Panisperna Boys—so called because they were so young—that Fermi surrounded himself with had all moved on except for Gian-Carlo Wick. Heisenberg's attempts to convince him to come to Germany went unheeded. Giovanni Gentile Jr. had died in March of that year. "Too many promising theoretical physicists have long ago escaped or..." Heisenberg's words drifted off.

"Or what, Werner?"

"Or died. Like my dear friend, Ettore Majorana."

"Aah, Ettore. He was not an easy figure to forget. I remember your efforts to make him and Gian-Carlo at ease when they attended the seminars in Leipzig and Göttingen. The evenings in your apartment, the spirited discussions, the music—"

"And the Ping-Pong. Don't forget that, Carl," Heisenberg said, smiling at the memories von Weizsäcker's words conjured up.

"His suicide was such a loss for science. He was brilliant. Answers to complex questions just came to him when others had to struggle, fail, and struggle more before they finally realized they were completely lost."

Heisenberg's smile faded slowly. "He was a good friend. Deeply troubled, but brilliant."

"They never did find his body, is that correct?"

Heisenberg grabbed his white lab coat from the top of the worktable and put it on. "No, no body was found, so suicide could not be confirmed." He picked up a clipboard after he finished buttoning the lab coat and headed over to the pile with von Weizsäcker at his side. "Yes, nor could suicide be ruled out." Von Weizsäcker paused. "But the lack of a body does give rise to another conclusion, does it not, Werner?"

CHAPTER THIRTEEN

1030 Hours, Tuesday, December 8, 1942
OVRA Headquarters, Forte Braschi, Rome

Both Guido Leto, the head of OVRA, and Baron Carl-Ludwig Diego von Bergen, the German ambassador to the Holy See, were smoking cigars and sipping amber-colored drinks when Tardino, clutching a brown folder, interrupted their meeting. The late-morning sunlight streamed through the office's windows, dust particles intermingling with the hazy cigar smoke. Through the pungent miasma, Tardino saw an opened bottle of Campari on the olive wood table behind Leto's desk. The bottle sat next to several framed photos, among them ones of Leto's wife and mother. Another was a large, framed photo of a cape-wearing Arturo Bocchini, the former head of the State Police and OVRA. Tardino was aware Leto considered him his mentor. But the most prominent of the displayed photos was of a black-suited Il Duce, Benito Mussolini, his arms folded across his torso, lips pursed, and a shiny bald crown. The equally bald von Bergen, dressed in a dated, tuxedo-style suit and a red armband with a black swastika, asked Tardino if he would partake of one of his Toscano cigars; Tardino looked at Leto, seeking permission.

Leto met his gaze with a slight nod. He thanked von Bergen and took the offered cigar and placed it in his breast pocket, explaining that he wanted to save Italy's finest cigar as an after-dinner indulgence.

"What is it, Anteo?" Leto asked as he flicked ash into a gold-colored Cinzano ashtray.

"Excuse the interruption, but I thought I should inform you about a...sensitive and most unusual matter." Tardino glanced quickly at von Bergen.

"I'll step out for a moment, Guido," von Bergen said as he rose from his chair.

"Nonsense, Carl. You are a trusted ally. Stay." Leto dunked the tip of his cigar into the shot glass of Campari. "Now, what is this sensitive matter that can't seem to wait?" he asked, a pinched expression on his face.

Tardino took the letter his brother-in-law had brought him from his folder and handed it to Leto, waiting while Leto read it. The man's expression changed into one of puzzlement. Without looking, he reached to place his Toscano in the ashtray, but it rolled out onto the desk. Tardino retrieved it, careful not to touch the Campari-soaked tip.

"What is the meaning of this, Anteo? Who is this Ettore, and what makes this...sensitive?"

"You remember the case of the missing scientist Ettore Majorana? It goes back to 1938. We reported that—"

"Oh, yes. Of course. The brilliant physicist." Leto paused, his head tilted to one side. "He's alive?" Leto looked again at the letter. "This was written yesterday?"

"Yes."

"Where did you get this?" Leto asked, tossing the letter on the desk.

Tardino disclosed the details of his meeting with his brother-in-law and the probable location of Majorana.

"What monastery?" Leto said.

"The Certosa Trisulti." When he told Bruno there was still a reward offered by the Majorana family, he had excitedly given him the location of the scientist. "It's located very close to Collepardo, in the Province of Frosinone." Tardino glimpsed von Bergen sit up and move to the edge of his seat, placing his glass of Campari on Leto's desk.

"I know of this man. Quite a mystery, if I remember correctly," von Bergen said. Leto picked up his cigar and took a long drag, nodding at von Bergen as he did so. "His Holiness, Pius XI, and his secretary of state at the time, the current pope, received repeated petitions from the Majorana family and his colleagues for any assistance they might offer. The family was convinced that he had fled—"

"Yes, yes, to a monastery. The entire case was a major headache for Bocchini. He told me that Il Duce screamed at him that he wanted the man found." Leto shook his head, then drained his glass. "I told you about that, right, Anteo?"

Tardino nodded.

"Guido, if this Majorana is alive, he could be of great assistance to the German weapons program. They are starved for scientists, especially physicists. So many have been sent away or have abandoned the Fatherland," von Bergen said.

"Listen, my friend. If he has fled to a monastery, he is most likely a pacifist. And they make horrible creators of weapons." Leto, amused at his own witticism, let out a laugh. He handed the letter to Tardino and sat back.

"It would be a significant achievement for you and OVRA if he could be enlisted in our collective endeavors to win this war." Von Bergen rose and placed his nearly spent cigar in the ashtray. "I must take my leave," he said as he looked at his watch. "I do not want to be late for my meeting with Secretary of State Maglione. He is not very tolerant of tardiness," von Bergen said. A partial bow preceded the sharp sound of clicking heels.

Leto leaned forward and placed his elbows on his desk, silently puffing on his Toscano. Tardino waited for instructions. A minute passed; with two inches of his cigar remaining, Leto added it to the ashtray. "Anteo, I fully believe that this is nothing but a hoax." Leto paused, then rose from his chair. "But I would be negligent if I didn't report this development to Il Duce. You are dismissed, but I want no one other than us to know of this…letter. Am I understood?"

Tardino's posture stiffened. "Completely, sir."

CHAPTER FOURTEEN

1630 Hours, Tuesday, December 8, 1942
No. 10 Downing Street, London

Conor stood in the entrance hall of the prime minister's residence, waiting for Emily. His stomach growled loudly, announcing to those in proximity that he hadn't eaten all day. The Cambridge professor that Colonel Donovan had enlisted to do a deep briefing on the current makeup of Sicily's Mafia had cracked the whip and wouldn't let him leave the musty library at No. 70 Grosvenor Street, the headquarters of the OSS in London. For the last hour of the briefing, he couldn't stop thinking of his plan to take Emily to her favorite restaurant, Wilton's on King Street—a good meal followed by some dancing to celebrate their upcoming marriage was just what they both deserved.

Then he heard the first shout. It was followed by a second higher-pitched shriek, then a commotion at the end of the narrow corridor that led directly from the entrance hall toward the rear of the residence, which also served as the office of the prime minister. Conor spotted Elizabeth Nel, Churchill's personal secretary, pushing her way through a gaggle of women gathered near a doorway, straining to see what was going on inside the room. "Make way, ladies. Make way, please," Nel said, her voice calm like she had routinely experienced shriek-producing scenes many times before.

Conor started to make his way down the corridor when a gray-haired man carrying a black medical bag pushed past him and approached the group at the doorway.

"Excuse me, please. Let the doctor pass," the gray-haired man said as he slid past the women.

Thinking he might also be of some help, Conor made his way through the group of women and stood next to Nel. When she noticed him, her jaw dropped. "Conor, thank God you're here. It's Emily."

Conor drew in a quick breath at the mention of her name. He knelt beside the doctor, who was about to apply his stethoscope to Emily's chest. Her eyes were closed, her face pallid. Tears stained both cheeks.

"No, no, give her some space, young man."

Ignoring him, Conor took Emily's hand; she opened her eyes and squeezed it.

"It's all right, Dr. McMoran," Nel said. "He's Emily's fiancé."

"Oh, I see." He turned to Emily and listened to her heart.

"Doctor…" Emily's voice was faint, and raspy. "I think I might have suffered a miscarriage. I can feel some—"

"Call for an ambulance straightaway, Elizabeth," he said without turning to Nel.

Conor heard Nel sprint down the corridor, his own heartbeat racing at the sight of Emily lying there.

"Em, everything's going to be okay, right, Doc?"

"Indeed. She'll be fine, but a thorough exam at the hospital is certainly called for." The answer calmed Conor. For a moment. The doctor took a deep breath and lowered his voice. "But I'm…I'm…"

Conor's posture stiffened. *Did the doctor have a stutter*, he wondered. "You're what?"

"I'm…I'm not sure about the baby. I'll know when we do a more thorough examination at St. Thomas Hospital."

Conor heard a gasp and someone say "Dear God" but his ears felt like they were being muffled and his head swam.

This can't be happening. Not again.

He looked down at Emily. Fresh tears rolled down her face. Conor reached out, lightly brushed the hair off her face, then leaned over to kiss her on her forehead.

"We'll get through this. You and me. We'll get through this together." And he desperately wanted to believe it.

CHAPTER FIFTEEN

1015 Hours, Wednesday, December 9, 1942
Apartment of Monsignor Puchini, Via di Porta Fabbrica, Rome

"I thank you, my loyal friend. You can expect your usual gift in the mail soon. I shall initiate it today." Monsignor Puchini gently placed the handset back in its cradle, careful not to startle Zitto. The spotted tabby was lying in his lap; its rhythmic purring never failed to calm Puchini, and Zitto's antics, as the cat roamed about his lavishly appointed apartment, constantly delighted him. He turned his attention to the wall above his desk where a framed photo hung of a mosaic that was determined to have originated in Pompeii. In the photo, the tabby, wild-eyed with the toes of its front paws spread wide, was mauling a delicate, vibrantly colored bird of some type. Blood had not yet been spilled. Puchini grinned. He was lucky to have found such a creature to brighten his days. He was also lucky to have such friends as Anteo Tardino.

"That was an excellent conversation, Zitto," Puchini said as he stroked the back of the cat who raised its head from his lap and stared at him with its amber eyes. "Unexpected but very welcome. Tardino's news will certainly greatly interest the secretary of state. He will not vacillate over my request to meet this time when I hint as to the value of my news."

Puchini's role as the head of the Vatican's press office provided numerous opportunities to roam the hallways and salons of the Vatican, gathering snippets of information—some, never him, called it gossip—which he routinely turned into financial gain by selling it to various embassies. And OVRA. Guido Leto, OVRA's chief, was unaware that the flow of information traveled in two directions. His source, Tardino, was always reliable and cheap. He could have charged Puchini more for his high-grade intelligence, but Tardino never pushed hard for increased compensation.

Zitto rolled over on his side and licked his paws. Puchini rubbed the cat's left ear between his thumb and index finger while he stared at the photo of the mosaic. Puchini was drawn to thoughts of his last meeting with Cardinal Maglione. It had not gone well. It seemed that the secretary of state was uninterested and went so far as to reprimand Puchini for revealing information regarding another episode of Milan's Cardinal Idlefonso Schuster's profascist behavior. Puchini thought his reaction was fueled more by the Vatican's embarrassment over the Mussolini-fawning Schuster than anything else.

"Cardinal Maglione may not want to hear my news, Zitto, but he must be made aware of it, nonetheless. The famous Ettore Majorana has been discovered in a monastery. And that news has already reached multiple sources, including the Germans, according to that last call." Zitto stopped licking his paws, turned to Puchini, and purred. "But maybe they knew where he was all the time. Perhaps they were involved in arranging Majorana's placement at the Certosa di Trisulti. It certainly wouldn't be beyond the secretary and His Holiness to be involved in a little intrigue, now would it."

Puchini remembered hearing reports from inside the Vatican years ago about the annoyance Pope Pius XI and his secretary of state, Pacelli, the current Holy See, felt over receiving repeated petitions from the Majorana family at the time of his disappearance. The thought that making the cardinal secretary of state aware of Majorana's discovery might help improve Puchini's standing with the cardinal and the Curia, the papal court at the Vatican, prompted a smile from the priest.

"Regardless of Cardinal Maglione's reaction, Zitto, I am sure that the Americans and the British will be very interested in hearing that their adversary, Nazi Germany, received the Majorana news with great interest." He picked up his cat, brought him close to his face, and smiled once more.

Multiple streams of income always warmed Puchini's heart.

CHAPTER SIXTEEN

1030 Hours, Wednesday, December 9, 1942
St. Thomas Hospital, Lambeth, London

Three of the hospital's buildings still standing were positioned at the south end of the property, at right angles to the river Thames, directly across from the Houses of Parliament. Conor slowed his pace when he approached what remained of the three northern buildings—he was eager to get inside to see Emily, but the destruction of the northern buildings shocked him. When he'd told Duncan Lee, Colonel Donovan's assistant, that he was going to St. Thomas Hospital to see Emily, Lee had mentioned that the hospital had been one of the Luftwaffe's targets on the first two nights of the Blitz over two years ago. Conor had seen overwhelming evidence of the German attempts to destroy the morale of the citizens of London all over the city and didn't think he would be emotionally impacted, but the sight of the hospital's destruction and the thought of the hundreds of patients and staff who died stunned him into numbness. The rubble, mangled steel, and broken glass on the site had been organized behind temporary barriers into orderly piles of wartime debris.

Something bumped into the side of his left leg, rousing him from his stupor. A woman in a black-and-white checkered wool coat carrying a small suitcase was walking past him, part of a steady stream of Londoners walking past in both directions, chatting away, seemingly anesthetized to the sight of the ruins.

Emily, he thought, hustling to the building he'd been told she was in. He needed to get her out of the hospital as soon as he could.

"How is she?" Conor asked of the doctor he found standing outside her room, looking over a clipboard. His discolored plastic name tag said Mulgrew.

The man kept his eyes glued to his clipboard as he scratched out a note. "The she you're referring to would be…?"

"Bright. Emily Bright," Conor said with a tinge of annoyance over the lack of eye contact, which received the desired reaction when the doctor lowered the clipboard and looked at Conor.

"You must be that Thorn fellow," the doctor, a bespectacled fortyish man of average height with graying coarse hair, said, his tenor a bit accusatory to Conor's ear. "She's resting. Or that's what she should be doing. She's, in my opinion, overly keen to get out of here for someone who's been through a miscarriage."

Smart girl, that Emily.

"Thank you," Conor said as he moved past the peeved doctor.

"Don't get her riled up, Mr. Thorn. She's been through quite an ordeal."

Conor stopped and turned to the doctor. "No plans for riling up anyone. At least not today," he said, eliciting a look of disdain from the man.

Conor entered the room and walked past a young woman lying in a bed with her lower right leg in a cast, suspended above her bed by a pulley system. She was snoring, her mouth agape, a strand of her blond hair falling across her forehead, down past her nose.

Emily's bed was only about eight feet from her roommate's bed, and she was under a gray wool blanket, her upper body propped up by two pillows. Her head was turned away from the door, facing the window. She appeared to be sleeping, despite the orchestra of snores emanating from the woman next to her. From the foot of her bed, Conor could now see her face. She was not sleeping. She was weeping.

He went to her and took her hand in his. "Em, it will be all right. I promise. We'll move on. We'll try again. It—"

"Stop. Please." Her cold words felt like slaps to his face.

He sat on the edge of her bed as she turned to him and wiped her cheeks with her free hand. "I'm not crying about the baby. Losing the baby is terribly upsetting. But it's…" She turned her head to the window again and took back her hand.

"It's what?" Only silence answered, but he waited.

"It's the war. It's us." She looked back at him. "It's you," she said, her voice thick with emotion.

It was Conor's turn to look for an answer out the window. She'd been through a lot, going back to their first mission. That had to be it. He didn't want to entertain any other explanation. *Give her time. Give her space. Give—*

"I want to put off the wedding until after the war, Conor. It's the right thing to do now that the baby isn't…"

He didn't hear the rest of what she said. There was a ringing in his ears. He felt flushed. He turned back to her.

She was staring at him, still talking, and then she grabbed his hand and kissed it.

It was his turn to take back his hand.

CHAPTER SEVENTEEN

0030 Hours, Thursday, December 10, 1942
St. Thomas Hospital, Lambeth, London

Conor couldn't feel his ass from sitting in the chair alongside Emily's bed for the past twelve plus hours. They had spoken little. Which seemed as fine for Emily as it was for him. She had spoken her piece, and he left it there—for now, at least.

There was a point, sometime around when they brought the evening meal, that he got up and gathered his coat, and she asked him to stay. It surprised him slightly, after she'd shut him down earlier. She'd said she didn't want to be alone. Her snoring roommate had been discharged earlier that afternoon, and the hospital had not reassigned the bed to anyone. Conor had nowhere he had to be, so he complied. He sat and took her hand. *Anyway,* he thought, *shut down or not, there's no one I'd rather be with than Emily.*

As they sat in silence, Conor's thoughts turned to the last time he was in a hospital. It was Boston's Mass General. The bed that Conor sat beside then was his wife's. Grace had ignored her doctor's strongly worded advice not to have children. The bout of rheumatic fever that hit her in her teen years had weakened her heart severely. But she was stubborn and expressed often that Conor Thorn deserved to have a child because he would be the best father. Early labor had taken them to Mass General. The doctors were in and out of the room at least fifty times, and each time, they spent a long minute listening to her heart, after which each would mark her chart and leave without saying a word. There was one occasion when Grace was asleep that her primary doctor asked Conor to follow him into the corridor. He wasted few words: her heart was failing, and childbirth would, except for a miracle, not end well.

All he could do was nod at the prognosis, as it was not a surprise. He almost wished it were. Her doctor had a right to gloat, but he didn't. Conor was upset that he'd failed to convince Grace to forgo having children. Upon returning to the room, he'd found Grace awake. He'd sat and taken her hand, and she'd begun to sing, her voice low and raspy. It was her favorite song, "Mad About the Boy." She'd squeezed his hand when she got to her favorite lyrics.

Conor felt his hand being squeezed and opened his eyes. Emily was looking at him.

"You…you're crying. Whatever for?" She let his hand go and sat up. "If it's about me, please don't. I'll be fine." She paused. "Conor, we'll be fine," she said.

Conor picked up on the genuine concern in her voice, which wasn't enough to lessen his deep disappointment when he saw she had removed her ring.

He hesitated. Removing it made sense. The wedding was called off. She'd called it off. "Yes, I know. I'm sure of it," he said, unsure he believed it himself.

Midnight approached, and Emily insisted he leave and get some sleep. Conor, exhausted, both physically and emotionally, gave in. He told her he would return in the morning, when she was supposed to be released. In the doorway, he stopped and looked back at her. She was staring back at him with a dreamy smile, and she gave him a wink. That helped. Maybe they would be fine.

#

Just outside the entrance to St. Thomas Hospital, Conor stood on the steps and buttoned, then cinched, the belt to his trench coat. He took a deep breath and slowly released it. The long day at the hospital was over. No one had died this time.

He headed down Thames Path toward Westminster Bridge.

He decided he didn't want to call Miss Hollis, the driver Colonel Donovan had assigned to him when he first arrived in London. It was late, and he needed to sort some things out—the walk back to Claridge's would give him time to clear his head and do some sorting.

Once up on the bridge, the moon shed a gauzy light on the barrage balloons that hovered above the Houses of Parliament and the clock tower, which housed the famous four-sided clock and bells. Miss Hollis, who also acted as a tour guide early on, had once mentioned that the bells fell silent after a Luftwaffe bombing in May 1941, the first month of the London Blitz. Vehicle traffic on the bridge was scant, and pedestrians were not to be found. He was alone.

Midway across the river, Conor stopped. He stepped over a pipeline that ran along the balustrade and railing. There were about twelve inches between the pipeline and the railing, just enough space to stand. He leaned on the railing as his thoughts turned back to Grace. He hadn't cried over her in quite some time—it brought no relief, didn't lessen the loss. Down river, thanks to the moonlight, he could make out the Hungerford Railway Bridge and he noted barge traffic that plodded along on the river's swift current. One was just emerging from under the Westminster Bridge. The stink that wafted up from it announced what it was hauling—garbage, and quite a lot of it— convinced Conor he needed to be on his way.

#

Stoker followed the slow-moving Thorn across the bridge from a safe distance, then stopped when Thorn pulled up to the railing. The illusive Conor Thorn. It had been over a month since Philby had charged him with tracking down and eliminating the American agent. His lack of progress had served to cool their relationship quite thoroughly. The old Russian from the Soviet Embassy that he had assigned to keep an eye on Bright had finally yielded results. Stoker stationed himself outside the hospital and waited patiently for the American to exit. He contemplated taking them both inside the hospital but thought better of it. There would be less risky circumstances that would present themselves as long as his patience held out. He watched Thorn as he gazed down river. He surmised Thorn was an inch or two over six feet, had a medium build. He also assumed the man would have a weapon.

Don't underestimate Thorn, Philby had said. Stoker had no plans to do that. He would need to move fast as soon as he saw an opening. He felt for his Puukko knife in his right coat pocket, then touched his left breast to confirm that his Tokarev semi-automatic was there.

He moved closer. He was thirty feet away when Thorn turned and headed toward the clock tower.

#

As Conor turned away from the railing and stepped over the pipeline, he heard someone speak.

"Hey there, friend, might you have a light? It seems I've lost my lighter."

Conor noted the British accent. It was on the cultured side, he thought. The man wore a dark trench coat that was tightly belted around his waist, his long arms out of proportion for his frame, which looked to Conor to be about three inches short of six feet. A wide-brimmed fedora that matched his trench coat obscured most of his face.

"Sorry, I don't smoke. Wish I could help you," Conor said, then turned around to resume his trek to Claridge's and his bed.

"Ah, one more question." Conor stopped and turned to see the man take a step closer. Conor noted the ascot he was wearing. It complemented his cultured accent. "I'm not from around here, and you look like you'd be comfortable around the ladies. Any idea where I might find a...hospitable female companion for the night?"

The jump from bumming a light to the location of the nearest prostitute shocked then amused Conor. "I can't help you there either, I'm afraid."

The man slumped, but in an exaggerated way. "No lighter

because you don't smoke. And no tips on where to go to have some innocent fun. What good are you, Yank?" he said, drawing out the last word like a slur.

This guy was overstaying what little welcome there was to begin with.

"Whoa, there. That's out of line. Why don't you just crawl back in the hole you came out of?" Conor spun on his heels and left the ass standing there. He had taken five paces when he heard heavy footsteps. He started to turn back, and then an arm wrapped around his neck and clamped down hard around his throat. He expected a gun to his head or a knife at his throat. Then he felt something sharp—the tip of a knife in his lower back, too close to his kidneys. Conor's right arm dangled at his side; he dug the fingers of his left hand into the asshole's forearm. He could have ended this quickly if he'd had his Colt. But the hospital didn't allow weapons inside, so he'd left his 1911A1 in his room at Claridge's. He was going to have to get creative.

"You don't recognize me, do you?"

So, he wants to talk. Fine. I need a few seconds to figure out my next moves.

"Let me see your face again, maybe it'll come to me," Conor said, his voice strained.

"A comedian. It was Paddington Station…just a few weeks ago. You were interested in talking to me, but I was in a rush."

Holy shit. I know this bastard.

The guy in the overcoat and fedora that had a long conversation with Henry Longworth the day Eleanor Roosevelt arrived to visit the king and queen. Conor had wanted to do more than talk to him. He'd come close to getting sliced up by this guy's knife as he slipped behind a moving locomotive on his escape from the station. Maybe it was the same knife that had just sliced through Conor's trench coat and shirt. He felt the sting of the knife's tip puncture his skin. A warm, damp sensation followed.

His attacker tightened his hold around his neck and began shoving him with his left hip toward the bridge's railing, the knife continuing to gouge his lower back. A good portion of his attacker's body was exposed to Conor's right, leaving Paddington man's groin not far from his dangling right arm.

But first things first.

Conor rotated sharply to his right and into the attacker, raised his right arm, then rammed the elbow backward like a piston into his solar plexus. A blast of air rushed past Conor's right ear. With his hand balled into a fist, he now sent it in search of Paddington man's groin. Finding it, he buried it deep.

The hold around his neck loosened, and Conor turned his back toward the struggling man, raised both arms to his right, reached around his assailant's neck, interlocked his fingers, and bent forward, yanking the man off the ground and pulling him up and over Conor's head. Paddington man's lower body smashed onto the top of the railing, and his fedora fell to the ground. His upper body leaned against Conor, who was looking directly at the man's now unobscured face. The man's eyes were open wide, his breathing labored. The knife was still gripped in his right hand, but the body flip had loosened his ascot.

"Do you have a name, asshole?"

The man reached up and swiped across where Conor's neck had been a second before. A barge passed below, making the smell of garbage more potent. Conor pushed forward, looking to dump the man onto the barge, but that also meant he would get away. He stopped, and the man lashed out again, cutting through his coat sleeve, the warm flow of blood running down his right arm unmistakable. Conor backed off, and his attacker fell to the ground but got to his feet quickly.

A vehicle was approaching, its engine loud. It sped past, blowing its horn, but it didn't stop. Both men crouched and circled each other. Paddington man held out the knife, its sharp edge facing up. Conor's close-in combat training he'd received at the OSS's Area F taught him that a knife in that position was going to enter one's body and be yanked upward, leaving multiple organs damaged.

His attacker cut the air with his knife in a tight circle.

"No gun, no knife—that doesn't sound like a proper OSS agent. Donovan will not be pleased to hear that one of his agents was so ill-prepared." He lunged like a fencer.

Conor grabbed his forearm with his left hand, halting the lunge, the knife's tip two inches from slicing through his rib cage. He spun on his heels, so his back was to his attacker. He forced the knife hand's wrist backward until he heard the joint crack and the knife clatter to the ground. Conor powered backward shoving the man into the sturdy railing with all the leg muscle he could muster. His attacker hit the railing hard, producing a loud grunt. Conor disengaged from him by stepping forward, then wheeled around to the man, sweeping the legs from under him with his right leg, collapsing his attacker to the ground. He kicked the knife into the roadway behind him, then thought better of it; he spun around, then took a step to retrieve it, which gave Paddington man a moment to get to his feet.

"Not good enough, OSS man," his attacker said.

Conor stopped and turned, watching as Paddington man reached inside his trench coat. He knew a gun was about to make an appearance.

This is gonna get noisy.

The attacker struggled to pull his gun, and Conor took a step toward him just as it emerged from inside his coat. Before his attacker could aim, Conor flung his left leg in a sweeping arc, contacting with the pistol and launching it over the railing into the Thames.

"No knife. No gun. What's next? You got a cricket bat inside that coat?"

His assailant glanced over the railing. When Conor's sense of smell was assaulted by another garbage barge passing under the bridge, he knew what was going to happen next. Paddington man hoisted himself up on the railing. Conor lunged, hoping to tackle him, but when he reached out, all he grabbed was his ascot. He leaned over and watched his attacker land on his back on top of a sprawling mound of stinking trash.

Conor picked up the fedora and flung it and the ascot into the Thames. The man was gone for now, but he knew: when someone wants you dead and they fail, they will strike again.

CHAPTER EIGHTEEN

1100 Hours, Thursday, December 10, 1942
MI6 Headquarters, No. 54 Broadway, London

In Stewart Menzies's left hand was a decrypt that had arrived that morning from Bletchley Park. In his right hand was a cup of tea; it hovered two inches above a saucer that held some of the cup's spilled contents. He looked up from the decrypt and dropped it on the desk, gently placed the cup in its saucer, and sat back. He commenced tapping the desk with the tip of his index finger while staring into space. He rose and started pacing.

As head of Britain's Secret Intelligence Service, also known as MI6, he often received information that, at first, he couldn't ascertain the importance or true value of. He would employ a series of what-ifs in his head to guide him in determining what action he needed to take. This morning, the what-if that dominated his thinking was "What if Ettore Majorana fell into the hands of the Nazis?" He knew the Nazi atomic weapons program was starved for high-value, intellectual talent. And when one is starving, you will do anything to acquire what you need to stay alive.

Menzies strode over to his office door and opened it. His assistant, Miss Pettigrew, sat at her desk, her back to the door, her fingers rapidly pecking at the typewriter's keys like a pianist playing a snappy jazz tune.

"Miss Pettigrew, ring up Frederick Lindemann, please. Tell him it's urgent."

"Right away, sir. Can I tell him what it is about?"

"I'm afraid not," Menzies said, turning back into his office and shutting the door. Two minutes later, the intercom on his desk buzzed, and he reached for the handset.

"Sir, I have Mr. Lindemann for you on line one. But he's very—"

"Annoyed, yes, I'm not surprised. Thank you, Miss Pettigrew."

Menzies admittedly disliked dealing with the quarrelsome Lindemann. His brilliance in scientific matters was outweighed by his arrogance. But his standing with Churchill made it imperative that he and Lindemann were on the same page when it came to matters concerning any threats to Allied weapons research and development.

"Frederick, I hope this call finds you well."

"Stewart," Lindemann barked. "Get on with it, please. You've pulled me away from a critical briefing." For Lindemann, everything he was involved in was critical, mused Menzies.

"Right. Won't be but a minute." Menzies explained that he received information from D'Arcy Osborne, the British ambassador to the Holy See. Osborne claimed it was from a somewhat unreliable source inside the Vatican. "It was regarding—"

"This sounds like a colossal waste of time," Lindemann said.

"I don't believe it is. His information was regarding an Italian physicist who was thought to have committed suicide." There was silence on the other end of the line. Encouraged, Menzies continued. "But just this morning, I received news from Bletchley that confirmed much of what Osborne related to me. It comes from decrypts of traffic between the German ambassador to the Vatican and Berlin."

"Go on."

"Is the name Ettore Majorana familiar to you?"

There was a heavy sigh on the other end of the line. "Stewart, he's dead. Committed suicide over four years ago."

"No body was found, Frederick. I'm sure you know that," Menzies said. He realized there was an admonishing tone to his last statement, so he added, "At least to my knowledge."

"I am well aware of that."

Menzies needed to get to the point before Lindemann hung up on him.

"Our intelligence points to him being alive, that he's been hiding in a monastery in Italy."

"What?" A pause. "Alive, you say?" Lindemann asked in a lowered, less irritated voice.

"Yes…alive."

"That…that is startling news to say the least."

"What are his scientific credentials, if I may ask?"

"Well, before he succumbed to what many said was a deep depression, he was a brilliant theoretical physicist. He published little, but what he did was head and shoulders above what others in the field were theorizing."

"What—"

"Let me finish," Lindemann blurted. "Fermi thought the world of him. Referred to him as one of the greatest scientific minds, along with Newton and Galileo. He was the first to hypothesize that the fermion is its own antiparticle. Those are named after him. The Majorana fermion is in contrast to the Dirac fermion that are not their own antiparticles. Then there is his and Heisenberg's introduction of exchange forces. Not to be overlooked is he was the first to correctly interpret Joliot and Curie's discovery of the neutron." A pause. "Oh my God. If the Germans…" Lindemann mumbled something Menzies couldn't make out. Then the line went dead.

#

Sitting in Cardinal Maglione's antechamber, Puchini brushed some of Zitto's hair off his lap. He should have done it before he left, but he had been in a rush. The cardinal, who Puchini knew was in his midsixties, seemed to be allergic to cats, given the sneezing fits Puchini had witnessed during previous visits. It contributed to his strong perception that the cardinal secretary of state and his office were not very responsive to his requests for meetings—but this time, their response had been swift. No doubt the mention of the name Majorana struck a nerve.

The white-haired cardinal was placing a phone handset back in its cradle when Puchini strode into his office, ushered in by his assistant, who gathered some folios from an outbox on the corner of the desk before scurrying out. The cardinal, his arms resting on the desk's surface, a handkerchief in his right hand, had a cape draped over his shoulders. The Palace of the Governorate, like many buildings on the Vatican grounds, did not have a heating system. The room's temperature reminded Puchini of the well-known joke among Italians that followed the Vatican closely: The Italian word for sweater was *maglione*. It was said, given the cardinal's very close relationship with the Pontiff, whenever His Holiness went out without his *maglione*, he caught cold.

The chilly air seemed to match the look on the cardinal's face when Puchini took his seat. He greeted the cardinal with all the reverence a monsignor would be wise to use when addressing someone in such standing, but the cardinal waved him off.

"The news of Majorana, where did you get it from?"

"Your Eminence, my sources are many. This particular source is one I trust unreservedly."

"You didn't answer my question." Maglione's steely gaze told Puchini he had to give up more information.

"I have a source inside OVRA. He trusts me to do what is right with this information. That is why I did not delay in reporting it to you."

Maglione sat back in his chair. Puchini was unsure if it was a sign that his answer satisfied him or not. "What else does this—" Maglione sneezed, then sneezed again. A third time proved to be the last for the moment. The cardinal, with three loud honks, blew his nose. "What else does your OVRA source tell you?"

Puchini cleared his throat. He knew that what he was about to report would represent the worst news as far as the secretary of state would be concerned, given his well-known fears about a German victory. It would not only further threaten the Catholic church in Germany, where the Vatican was already walking a tightrope, but it would threaten the church in all countries conquered by Hitler. "He believes the Germans are interested in enlisting Majorana's services in their struggling weapons development programs." After a long moment of silence, the cardinal sat up and tucked his handkerchief inside his left sleeve.

"Thank you, Monsignor. That will be all," Maglione said as he placed his left hand on his phone's handset and waited for Puchini to exit before picking it up. Back in the antechamber, Puchini heard the cardinal's assistant say into his own handset, "His Holiness, yes, Your Eminence. Right away."

CHAPTER NINETEEN

1150 Hours, Thursday, December 10, 1942
Kaiser Wilhelm Institute for Physics, Berlin

"Ah, Werner. Thank you for coming so quickly. I know you are very busy," General Leeb said, his delivery hushed as if he struggled for the breath to form the words. Werner Heisenberg hadn't seen the general in two days. He knew that he had been called away for meetings with Albert Speer in Hamburg. The general, who looked agitated, was standing behind his desk with a document in his hand.

"General, welcome back. I hope your travels were productive. Do you have any news that I need to be aware of?"

Leeb tossed the document onto his desk and took his seat. "Just that Speer is growing more and more impatient with us. With your Uranprojekt." Heisenberg expected such news. He struggled to keep a look of apprehension from washing over his face. "Do you have news of progress to report?"

"I can say the construction of the pile moves along. I am very pleased with the brisk pace of the construction."

"Not too brisk, I hope. We can't afford any setbacks due to hasty efforts of your scientists."

"Of course, General, I completely agree."

"Speaking of scientists," Leeb said, steepling his hands below his chin. "I just read a message from Foreign Minister von Ribbentrop. Actually, it arrived while I was traveling to Hamburg.

He notified me that his office has received word from his Vatican ambassador that an Italian scientist, a theoretical physicist, once believed to have committed suicide, has been discovered hiding in a monastery in Italy. Are you aware of a—"

"Ettore Majorana," Heisenberg nearly shouted.

Leeb jerked his head back at Heisenberg's outburst.

"Tell me, is it Ettore you speak of?" Heisenberg said.

Leeb picked up the paper and slid it toward Heisenberg. "Yes. You apparently know of him."

Heisenberg read von Ribbentrop's message. It was brief. It ended with a request: *Please advise immediately as to what value this man would be to your weapons program. If he could provide some value, we must act quickly.* Heisenberg looked at the date the message was sent—Tuesday, the eighth. He looked up. "General, the response to the foreign minister's request is the value is virtually incalculable."

Leeb appeared somewhat stunned at first, and then his expression morphed into disbelief. He began shaking his head. "Incalculable? Who is he, and what is your experience with this man?"

Heisenberg's heart raced as he paced back and forth in front of Leeb's desk, explaining his friend's visits to Leipzig and Berlin in the early thirties, his display of brilliance, his ability to grasp convoluted concepts with ease and seize on complicated solutions to confounding nuclear physics problems. He talked of Majorana's accomplishments. His speech pattern quickened with each glowing reference to the towering intellect of Ettore Majorana.

"Please sit, Werner. You exhaust me just watching you." Heisenberg realized he was perspiring. He wiped his forehead with his pocket square and took his seat. "I take it you were close?"

"Yes. Very close. There was, of course, the challenge of language at the beginning of our friendship, but I had begun to instruct Ettore in the German language. He, no surprise, was a quick learner and, in return, he taught me some Italian. He was shy, but when we were together, he was noticeably more at ease." Heisenberg told a story where Majorana, one night during a deep discussion of a theoretical problem, scribbled out the solution to the problem on the backside of a cigarette packet and presented it to him. The solution was so obvious in its simplicity as to have escaped anyone Heisenberg had ever discussed the problem with. Majorana had sheepishly taken the packet back, crumpled it up, and tossed it into the trash. His solution had so dumbfounded and impressed Heisenberg that he couldn't speak for several minutes. He still possessed the packet he retrieved from the trash. "I am so overwhelmed to hear that he is alive, General."

Leeb sat quietly. Heisenberg wasn't sure if the man had moved since he began telling the story of the cigarette packet solution. "A cigarette packet. That's quite a story," Leeb said. "You seem to claim a special friendship with this man. Do you think you could convince him to join his German friends? His scientific brethren? His friend Werner Heisenberg?"

Heisenberg realized that the thought hadn't even entered his mind. He was so overjoyed to hear that he was alive and not at the bottom of the Tyrrhenian Sea that he hadn't envisioned the possibility that he could be rejoined with his friend. "I…I'm not sure."

"Well, Werner, you've convinced me he couldn't hurt the program." Leeb stood and leaned on his desk. Heisenberg also stood. "Make plans to travel to Italy. Upon your return, you can introduce me to this marvel of a man."

CHAPTER TWENTY

0800 Hours, Friday, December 11, 1942
Metallurgical Laboratory, Stagg Field, University of Chicago

Enrico Fermi stood on the mezzanine, shoulder to shoulder with his fellow physicist, Herbert Anderson. Both were staring at CP-1. Chicago Pile-1 was their prized creation—the first nuclear reactor that produced a controlled nuclear chain reaction. Fermi was the lead physicist on the project and Anderson handled the day-side twelve-hour shift that built the pile. The structure, to an outsider—not that an outsider would ever gain access to the cavernous space beneath the north and west stands of Stagg Field—would come across as a hideous edifice. Standing twenty feet high and some twenty-five feet across, it was made up of over five tons of uranium metal, forty-five tons of uranium oxide, and 360 tons of graphite. To Fermi and Anderson, it was their shared crowning achievement, their Pietà.

"How do you feel right now?" Anderson asked him.

"How do you think?" Fermi smiled. "Look at my feet. Tell me. Are they really on the ground, or am I floating in midair?"

Anderson laughed. "Yes. Quite an accomplishment it was. I haven't slept in days."

"That's two of us," Fermi said. Eleven days prior was the breakthrough with the first controlled chain reaction followed by CP-1 achieving a power output of two hundred watts the day before. Granted, it was only enough to power a light bulb, but it was another first.

"The radiation?" Anderson asked.

"Yes. Without shielding, we have created a radiation hazard for all in the area. For further testing, let's pull the power output back to point five watts." Fermi turned to his mustachioed friend. "Do you agree?"

"Yes. Of course. I will see to it," Anderson said. He turned away quickly and left Fermi standing there, wishing he could share the news of their accomplishments with his old friends back in Rome—Segré, Amaldi, and Rasetti. With thoughts of his days at the Via Panisperna Institute darting around in his head, he didn't hear the footsteps coming up behind him.

"Enrico. Congratulations are in order, I hear."

Fermi turned and was surprised to see the barrel-chested US Army officer standing before him dressed in a neatly pressed, olive green uniform, his service cap tucked under his left arm. Lieutenant Colonel Leslie Groves, who headed the Manhattan Project, was at least a foot taller than Fermi. His looming presence always made Fermi ill at ease. Groves had a reputation for being rude and arrogant, as well as holding a meaningful level of contempt for the rules. But he got things done. Which, for Fermi, meant that he got whatever he wanted from Groves, such as sixty tons of graphite.

"Ah, thank you, sir. I understand I should congratulate you as well." Groves's already broad chest swelled with pride. "Your promotion to lieutenant colonel is very much deserved and overdue, I must say."

"Thanks for the kind words, Enrico. But I don't have time to shoot the bull with you. I'm here on a sensitive matter."

"Aren't all the matters we deal with sensitive?" Fermi noticed Groves's jaw muscles clench. A clear signal of annoyance.

"Tell me about Ettore Majorana."

Fermi's head tilted to one side, and his brow furrowed. He hadn't heard the name spoken in quite some time. Internally, Fermi invoked it often, especially when a theoretical physics problem flummoxed him. "Colonel, why bring up the late Ettore Majorana?"

"Just tell me what you know of him."

"As you wish. Let me say this of Ettore Majorana. There are

geniuses like Galileo and Newton. Well, my friend Ettore was one of these. He had what no one else in the world had."

"Is he smarter than Oppenheimer? Than you?"

Fermi took note of Groves's use of the present tense but thought it was a simple grammatical mistake. "He was smarter than me. And I am sure if he were to have matched wits with Robert, Ettore would not have embarrassed himself. But, Colonel, why do you ask? Ettore is no longer with us."

Groves grabbed Fermi by his elbow and led him to a dark corner of the mezzanine. "This is classified." Groves looked over his shoulder, then back at Fermi. "Word has reached us from our British friends that Majorana is alive and in hiding at a monastery in Italy."

Fermi reached out and placed a hand on the cold concrete wall to steady himself. "*Mio caro dio…mio caro dio,*" he said breathlessly as he made the sign of the cross.

"Steady, man. Get ahold of yourself."

Fermi pulled a handkerchief from his pants pocket and wiped his forehead. "Colonel, I will tell you what I wrote to Mussolini when Ettore disappeared. Of all the Italian and foreign scholars whom I had the opportunity to meet, Ettore was the one who, for the depth of his genius, had impressed me the most."

"Could he help us?"

"Simply put, there is no doubt."

"Was he friends with any American scientists?"

Fermi rubbed his chin and scratched along his jawline as he thought. "Joseph Feinmann. He studied alongside Ettore in Leipzig and Rome. They became very close, even though they didn't speak each other's language. I believe he is working in the MIT Radiation Laboratory, the Rad Lab, on their radar project."

Groves took out a small pocket notebook and jotted something down. After putting it back in his breast pocket, he looked over his shoulder again. "One last question. Would Majorana work for the Nazis?"

Fermi had been expecting the question. It surprised him Groves hadn't asked it sooner. "I do not know. He was mildly profascist. I can tell you this: he was close friends with Werner Heisenberg. They both admired each other's intellect greatly."

Groves put his service cap back on. "That's all I need to know."

CHAPTER TWENTY-ONE

1200 Hours, Sunday, December 13, 1942
OSS Headquarters, No. 70 Grosvenor Street, London

Conor's mood was foul. It was Emily; it was the resurfaced memories of Grace's death and that of his son; it was his run-in with Paddington man and his escape, riding a garbage scow down river. The bitter wind on his walk from Claridge's to the OSS London office did nothing to improve his outlook. As for the meeting with Colonel Donovan, it was doubtful that it would adjust his disposition for the better.

He knocked on the door of suite 323 and, not waiting for a response, opened the door. The last time he was in the suite, it had looked more like a hotel room, with its art deco furniture. In the time since, its inhabitants had transformed it to look more like an office with several gray metal pedestal desks along the walls. There was a large wooden desk in the center of the room, occupied by the silver-haired Bill Donovan. Seated at a small desk nearest the colonel was Duncan Lee, his personal assistant.

"Hello, Conor. Thanks for coming over so quickly," Donovan said, motioning to one of the Bentwood armchairs in front of his desk. "All patched up?"

"Fine, Colonel. The house doctor at Claridge's took care of it. A few stitches in the arm and back. Almost good as new," Conor said, his report drawing a nod from Donovan. "Has MI5 passed any information to you about the wacko who wants me dead?"

"Afraid not. I don't have a relationship with its director, David Petrie. I've asked Stewart to get involved on my behalf. If they learn anything, he'll pass it along to me."

Conor nodded slowly. Donovan didn't continue, but his gaze remained locked on Conor, who broke it by looking out the window.

"You know, you've been through a lot, what with Emily's miscarriage and now this attack out of nowhere. I would understand if you wanted to stand down for a week or so."

Stand down and do what? Roam the streets of London looking for an ascot-wearing Brit that smelled of rotten garbage?

He turned back to Donovan. "Colonel, I appreciate your concern. But actually, what I need right now is an assignment. I'm ready to leave for Sicily as soon as you give the word."

Conor needed some time away from Emily, which is what he thought Emily wanted also. That notion did nothing but sour his mood further.

"You're sure you're up to another assignment?"

"As I can be, Colonel," Conor said, making sure there was no hesitation in his voice.

Donovan nodded thoughtfully, then looked over at Duncan Lee. He cleared his throat and said, "Duncan."

Lee got the message, picked up a notepad, and left the two men alone.

"All right. That plan to get you into Sicily pre-invasion is off the table. For now. Something's come up. And it could be more important than the Sicily mission. Or so I'm told."

Conor knew the best-laid plans in wartime always went up in smoke when the first shot was fired. He just wasn't sure who had fired the first shot this time—the good guys or the bad guys. "Where am I headed, Colonel?"

"It's still Italy. But this time, it's the mainland."

Donovan spent the next five minutes telling the story of the disappearance of Italian nuclear physicist Ettore Majorana. It sounded more like an Agatha Christie novel than a breakdown of an OSS mission. Donovan handed Conor a black-and-white photo of Majorana. It showed a young Majorana, somewhere around early to midtwenties. He was looking slightly off to his right, dark eyes avoiding the camera, and he was dressed in a dark, double-breasted suit, white shirt, and black tie. Conor thought the man looked anxious, like he needed to be somewhere else, not waiting for the photographer to take his photo.

"What makes this physicist so special, Colonel?"

"Well, for one, he's brilliant. He's a major leaguer while everyone else is playing minor league ball. But more concerning at this point is that he has friends in Germany. Friends that are working on top secret projects." Conor passed the photo back to Donovan.

"It's been, what, over four years? If he was interested in helping the Germans, wouldn't he have already made that move?"

"Listen, Conor, I can't tell you much, but I can tell you that the Allies and Germany are actively working on atomic weapons. It's a race, one we can't afford to lose. It's not him volunteering to go; it's him being dragged to Germany, kicking and screaming, that we're worried about."

"Right. Fanatical Nazis who won't take no for an answer."

"Something like that."

"So why has this boy wonder surfaced now, after hiding for over four years?"

"That's not clear to me. What has been made clear is that we have to get our hands on him before the Nazis do."

Donovan handed Conor a brown file stamped in red ink *Eyes Only*. He opened it and saw, on the first page, in all caps, the mission objectives:

KEEP SUBJECT FROM FALLING
INTO GERMAN HANDS

CONVINCE SUBJECT TO JOIN ALLIED
TOP SECRET WEAPONS PROJECT

FAILING SECOND OBJECTIVE,
USE AS MUCH FORCE AS NECESSARY TO
PLACE SUBJECT IN ALLIED HANDS

Conor continued to scan the file's contents, including a family photo of an older, matronly woman dressed in holiday finery flanked by five children. A note below the photo labeled them Dorina Majorana, her sons, Ettore, Salvatore, and Luciano, as well as her daughters, Maria and Rosina. Donovan ran down the mission's details. When Conor heard the mention of a PBY-5, he looked up. Flying. He hated it. And flying hated him.

"You leave for Gibraltar in three hours, then on to Algiers from there. The PBY will get you close to the shore, near the town of Anzio. You'll be traveling with a person who knows their way around Italy, someone who will help keep you out of the hands of the OVRA."

"Who might that be? The pope?"

"No, but close. Your friend Sean Sullivan. He's taking a bit of a break from his official duties to help us out. You'll catch up to him at Tempsford."

Well, that's a surprise.

Given the body count at Portella Airport outside of Lisbon and the gunplay on the bridge over Rome's Tiber River just a few weeks before, it shocked Conor to hear that Sean would agree to go on another mission.

"Take care of him. He may become one of us officially if I can twist his arm a bit more."

"It sounds like you've twisted his arm plenty," Conor said, hoping he wasn't out of bounds. He was relieved when his comment triggered a smile from Donovan, which disappeared as quickly as it materialized.

"Conor, Emily's going with you."

His jaw dropped slowly. Emily had mentioned nothing about a new assignment when he'd picked her up at the hospital on Friday. She had been quiet, distant, which he'd chalked up to the ordeal of losing their baby. But it seemed there had been more on her mind than that.

Conor leaned forward. "Colonel, that can't happen, it—"

"I knew you wouldn't like it, but I inquired about her…condition. Churchill says Elizabeth Nel told him that any concerns about her condition are nonsense. She says that Emily is stronger than half the men she answers to."

"Yes. But she's just lost a baby."

Our baby.

Donovan stood. "It's done, Conor."

He slumped back in his chair. It seemed he had no say as to who would comprise his team. He knew he would have no sway with Emily either. She was as stubborn as he. Maybe more so.

Conor and Emily had spent Saturday with her mother, Bertie, in Southend-on-Sea. Bertie waited on them hand and foot, and he had been able to see that Emily had recovered physically, but he could also see she was still struggling emotionally. Her bouts of silent contemplation had been frequent. They had slept in separate rooms, which Bertie took note of but said nothing about.

"You should know that there is some level of distrust between the US and the Churchill government. They don't think we're sharing everything with them from our weapons development program. I'm sure we're selective about what we share, and we believe they're just as selective, though they would deny that. They want a dog in the fight."

Conor stood as Donovan came around his desk. "Pack what you need and collect Emily at No. 10, then head out to Tempsford. Colonel Eddy will have a more detailed briefing when you land in Algiers. This mission came out of nowhere, so we're still pulling some details together. Meantime, I need you to work out a plan to get inside the monastery. Lay it out when you see Eddy. Let him tweak it if he thinks it needs it," Donovan said as he walked Conor to the door. "Eddy will also have all the gear you'll need."

Donovan stopped short of the door and turned to Conor. "And Conor…"

"I know, Colonel." Conor thought of Donovan's last words after giving him the assignment to track down the missing directives for Operation Torch. "I won't fuck this up."

CHAPTER TWENTY-TWO

1210 Hours, Sunday, December 13, 1942
Country Road, Banbury, England

His code name was *Otto*. His handler's was *Sonya*. It was only his sixth meeting with her. But when they would walk arm in arm like besotted lovers down various country roads near Banbury, never too far from the train station, they never used any names. Always anxious and tense before their meetings, her soothing and calming demeanor always disarmed all his thoughts of doom.

Klaus Fuchs, a German-born theoretical physicist, hoped that his mentor and friend, Rudolf Peierls, hadn't been too put off with his vague reply about where he was going that morning. Peierls, also a German-born physicist, had hired Fuchs as his assistant the year before, and since housing choices were extremely limited, he had offered Fuchs the option of staying with him and his family in Birmingham, where they both worked at the University of Birmingham on the British atomic bomb project, code-named Tube Alloys.

Today's meeting was different for two reasons. It was the first of their meetings during unpleasant weather; the light sleet-snow mix made for slippery walking conditions. But the most important distinction was what he was going to pass along to her. Besides the packet of documents that were now stuck in his waistband at the small of his back, it was the information that Rudolf had excitedly passed along to him while they enjoyed a cigarette and a glass of schnapps after dinner the night before.

Fuchs, standing near the tree that was their designated meeting location, lit up a cigarette and tossed the match into a puddle. He looked down the road toward the Banbury train station and saw no one. In the distance, he could see trains arriving and leaving the station. The wind shifted and it was then that he caught the scent of decay. Death was nearby.

He looked in the other direction and took in the sight of a young woman walking a cocker spaniel. The dog was pulling her down the street. She was slipping and nearly tumbled as the dog continued to pull. Fuchs surmised that the dog had picked up the same scent of death. It scrambled into the low brush along the roadside and promptly exited with what looked like a dead rabbit firmly clenched in its mouth. The young girl screamed and dropped the leash. The spaniel laid down in the road and commenced making the dead animal his lunch. The girl continued to scream.

Fuchs flicked his cigarette onto the road and raced to the dog and its owner, who was now yelling at her dog to cease. Fuchs picked up the leash and handed it to her.

"Please make him stop. It's disgusting, what he's doing."

"What's his name?"

"Sir George. His name is Sir George. Make him stop."

Fuchs bent down and grabbed the spaniel's collar. The dog growled, which didn't surprise Fuchs. When he slapped the dog on its rear, that did surprise Sir George. Fuchs, with his left hand, yanked the rabbit carcass from the dog's open jaws. He tossed the carcass farther into the low-lying field that ran along the road. "Hold tight to the leash, young lady. Sir George may still be hungry."

After the woman, with tears in her eyes, thanked him, she headed back in the direction she'd come from. Fuchs could hear her reprimanding Sir George using words that Fuchs thought were entirely inappropriate for a young woman.

He made his way back to the tree, wiping his left hand on the outside of his overcoat, wishing he hadn't forgotten his hand-kerchief. As he was wiping away, he saw Sonya walking up from the station. She was dressed in an orangish-brown pinstripe skirt and jacket; her hands were encased in black gloves. A floppy hat was pulled down low on her forehead, covering most of her short, styled hair. Tucked underneath the wide-lapelled jacket was a white-and-red tie. Her walk was purposeful, her smile welcoming. She stopped about ten feet away from Fuchs, which confused him. "There is a stink on you. What in God's name is it?"

Fuchs chuckled. He no longer noticed the smell. After explaining the incident with the dog, he handed over his packet of documents. She accepted them and slipped them inside her jacket.

"Shall we walk?" she asked. Fuchs nodded, and she slid her arm through his as they started down the road in the direction away from the station. The sleet and snowy conditions had lightened. "Is there anything I need to know about your package?"

Fuchs thought for a moment. "Nothing out of the ordinary. Just more reports from the Tube Alloys project. Quite a few documents. You'll have to take photographs. There's too much material to put in a coded message."

Fuchs never considered himself a spy. When he brought his position on the subject up to Sonya, she scoffed, which perturbed him. He explained to her he couldn't grasp the reasoning behind why the British and the Americans chose not to share their research and development of atomic weapons with the Soviet Union. They were fighting the same enemy. If all the major players on the world stage possessed the knowledge to create the enormous, devastating power of a nuclear bomb, it would prevent its exploitation by a single world power.

Sonya didn't respond to his comment about the number of documents, so Fuchs continued. "There is something else. It's not in the packet. It's something I heard last night."

"And what might that be?" Sonya asked, picking up the pace of their stroll as the weather began to clear.

"Rudolf brought back news from a Tube Alloys Technical Committee meeting that he attended Friday. Apparently, the members were buzzing about news of an Italian physicist, an Ettore Majorana, who has been discovered living in a monastery in Italy."

Sonya stopped abruptly and turned to face Fuchs. "What makes that startling news?"

"Well…Majorana was reported missing back in 1938. Some thought he committed suicide," Fuchs said.

"Interesting. That would make an attention-grabbing novel." They resumed their walk while Fuchs recited a brief list of Majorana's papers, described his reputation, and gave her a pointed description of how brilliant a nuclear physicist he was. "Or *is*, if this report is accurate."

"I'm assuming that you think he could be of some help to our program?"

"You assume correctly. What's most important is that Majorana had strong ties to Werner Heisenberg. You recall, I'm sure, that we talked about Heisenberg a few months ago. They grew very close on Majorana's visits to Germany in the early and midthirties."

Sonya stopped, then quickly turned around and led them back to the train station.

"Tell me everything Rudolf told you. Leave nothing out."

CHAPTER TWENTY-THREE

1500 Hours, Sunday, December 13, 1942
No. 10 Downing Street, London

Conor navigated the army green Buick Roadmaster off Whitehall on to Downing Street and pulled up to the curb in front of No. 10. The two strapping, armed British Army sentries that flanked the glossy black door to Churchill's residence both cut piercing looks inside the Buick at Conor, then broke off their icy stares when they recognized him. He shut the Buick down and remained in the sedan for several minutes, dealing with his apprehension over confronting Emily about why she hadn't told him of her assignment to the Majorana mission. He worried doing so would make things worse between them. He worked hard to convince himself that she must have had a good reason and that he was becoming too thin-skinned.

In the time it took Conor to exit the sedan and open the trunk, Emily and Elizabeth Nel appeared. Emily was dressed in an olive-drab, waist-length wool jacket and matching trousers, along with thick rubber-soled boots. Her light brown shoulder-length hair, pulled back and gathered at the back of her neck, shined. He noticed a hint of rouge on her cheeks.

Conor greeted both ladies and grabbed Emily's duffel bag, then shoved it into the trunk. After slamming the trunk lid shut, he turned to see Nel and Emily in an embrace. Nel was gently patting Emily's back. Conor looked on, thinking the two strong women could have been sisters. Emily whispered something to Nel, and she responded by giving Emily another hug. When they broke off, Conor saw Nel wipe away tears. Emily opened the passenger door and took her seat.

Conor went up to Nel and extended his hand. Nel surprised him by ignoring it and wrapping her arms around him.

"I don't know where you two are going. But I know it can't be…a picnic in the country. Do stay safe and please make sure you both come back." Conor was about to say that he had intentions to do just that when Nel continued. "What I mean, Conor, is please don't do anything foolish. Bring her home. And yourself. We need you both." Nel released and looked at him intently, waiting for the answer she needed to hear.

"Please, don't worry. Emily and I have a long future ahead of us."

Nel beamed. "I know you do. She told me so in almost the same words." She moved to reenter No. 10.

"Elizabeth, one question." Nel turned around. "Has anything turned up on my"—Conor looked to make sure Emily was out of earshot—"my friend from the bridge?"

"They're still searching for him. No one has turned up as of yet. MI5 and Scotland Yard are working closely on it." Conor nodded. "Come back…soon, Conor. But don't forget your mission objectives." Nel's tone shifted so effortlessly from sincere concern to *there's a war on, sonny* that Conor's jaw dropped slightly. She responded by tilting her head and smirking. Conor loved that woman.

"What did she say?" was the question Emily asked as he took his seat behind the wheel of the Roadmaster. "You two talked for a while."

Conor's mood upon arriving at No. 10 had shifted from apprehensive to pleased given Nel's comments. "She said you loved me and to—"

"And to what?"

"To come home soon."

Home. Conor realized he was becoming very comfortable in war-torn England. It wasn't the weather, for sure. But the people, their resilience in the face of the German Blitz and the defeats in the early stages of the war, their unchallenged ability to just get on with life in the face of such devastating setbacks.

"That woman is a saint," Emily said, emotion caught in her throat.

Without hesitation, Conor said, "She is your biggest fan...next to me."

Emily smiled. Conor thought he saw her face flush a bit.

"Where's Miss Hollis? I'm surprised she's not sitting in the back seat, reading the *Daily Mirror*." Since Conor preferred to do the driving, it gave Hollis an opportunity to catch up on war news and her sleep.

"Under the weather. Bad cold or something like that." Conor pulled the Buick out onto Horse Guards Road and headed north toward The Mall. "So, any surprise orders from your boss that I should know about?"

Emily shot him a confused look. "What in heaven's name are you talking about?"

Conor reminded her of the scene on the Vittorio Emanuel Bridge in Rome, where she had surprised Conor by revealing that she had orders from Menzies to let Wilhelm Canaris, the head of the German Abwehr, go free. It had dumbfounded Conor that Menzies didn't want Canaris bound and gagged and flown back to London. He had been even more shocked that Emily withheld the information from him until the last moments of their mission.

"I can tell you I have no such orders...this time," Emily said, turning to look out her window at the passing city landscape.

What brief conversation there was on their northward drive dried up as the barrage balloons over Regent's Park came into view. Not that they needed any reminders that there was a war on. The countless buildings they passed along the way that had been transformed into nothing but huge piles of twisted steel and rubble were the clearest reminders that England had taken more than its share of the punishment and might of the Third Reich.

With Regent's Park in the Buick's rearview mirror, Conor turned to Emily. "How are you feeling? Are you one hundred percent?"

Emily had slumped down in the seat and was resting her head against the seat back. She might have been dozing, Conor thought.

But she responded: "I'm quite fine. One hundred percent, as you say."

Conor let a minute pass before doing something foolish. "Today was the day we were supposed to get married."

Emily turned to face him. She swallowed hard, her chin trembling. She wrapped her arms around herself and squeezed.

"I'm sorry. I shouldn't have said that. Please forgive me."

Emily reached over and took his right hand. It was a moment before she spoke. When she did, her voice was choked. "Nothing important has changed. I still love you." She kissed his hand. "We'll discuss things when we get back from Italy. I promise."

Conor, his spirits still buoyed, nodded and decided he was going out of the conversation business for the rest of their drive.

CHAPTER TWENTY-FOUR

1715 Hours, Sunday, December 13, 1942
Tempsford Airfield, England

The sun had set, and the temperature was dropping. Darkness was all around them, except for the headlights of three tugs that illuminated the C-47 Dakota. He was already getting queasy at the mere sight of the plane. Conor and Emily, each hauling their own duffel bag, approached the aircraft. It was painted in a tan-and-green-camouflage scheme; the RAF roundel was prominent on the port side of the fuselage behind the cargo door. The two-man crew of a fuel truck, parked under the port side wing, were stowing hoses while playfully mocking each other.

"Emily, by any chance did you bring any of your ginger capsules along?" Emily had saved the day on their flight from Tempsford to Lisbon several weeks prior by bringing the remedy that lessened the effects of airsickness. Both Sean and Conor had availed themselves of it.

"Of course. One step ahead of you, Conor."

Standing near the cargo door of the aircraft, watching the ground crew load some crates stenciled with *P-38 J-5 Engine Parts*, was Sean Sullivan. The sight of the six-foot-tall priest in civilian clothes caught him off guard. Sean looked dapper in the dark suit. *I hope he didn't forget his old uniform*, Conor thought.

Sean turned, noticed Conor and Emily, and promptly gave Conor another back-cracking bear hug, then planted a light kiss on Emily's cheek. He seemed to Conor to be in high spirits, compared to their last encounter at the clergy house.

"Looking quite debonair in that suit, Sean," Emily said. "Maybe a little overdressed, but elegant nonetheless."

"Thank you, Emily. It's rare that I get compliments for my attire." Sean shot Conor a sharp look.

"Ah, nice suit." After seeing his comment get a quick smile, Conor continued. "Look, the trip on this Dakota won't be fun. It's not like traveling on the prime minister's converted B-24. It's going to be very noisy and cold." Both Emily and Sean nodded when he mentioned the flight on Churchill's *Commando*, which is what they'd taken to Lisbon. "Sean, you said a few days ago that you needed to speak to me about something. Maybe now is—"

"It's time. Please board the aircraft," an RAF captain said as he leaned out of the cargo door.

Conor looked at Sean ruefully and added a shoulder shrug, which Sean returned.

Emily, her duffel bag in tow, was the first up the ladder and into the C-47. Sean was right behind her. He craned his neck toward Conor before asking, "How is Emily doing?"

"Okay. She's one strong woman."

"And you?"

Conor thought for a moment. His emotions seemed to be on a never-ending roller coaster ride. He knew focusing on the mission details would give his emotions a reprieve from the cycle of highs and lows.

"Better, Sean. Thanks for asking," Conor said, patting his friend on his shoulder. "We better get on board. Some air force mechanics want their engine parts."

#

As the C-47 touched down, Conor pulled a flashlight from his waterproof duffel bag, which he had been leaning on for the full flight. He looked at his watch. It was half past midnight. His body was numb from lying on the sheet-metal floor for the past six hours. Sean and Emily moved stiffly toward the rear cargo door, followed by Conor. A member of the ground crew took the duffel bags from each before they ambled down the ladder. As soon as their feet hit the tarmac, all three stretched their cramped and traumatized muscles. Conor took in a deep breath of the warmer humid air. To Conor, it felt like sixty degrees.

"Hold on to your hats, lady and gentlemen. The show is about to begin," the grease-stained-overall-clad ground crewman said. His accent had a working-class cockney sound to it.

"Whatever are you talking about?" Emily asked.

"The drill. You got in just before the air-raid drill, miss."

The three passengers exchanged glances and then looked skyward. When nothing happened, Emily and Sean grabbed their duffel bags and headed over to an idling RAF Dodge three-quarter ton 4X4. Conor stayed and began chatting with the ground crewman. Thirty seconds later, the air-raid sirens activated. What followed was a light show unlike any Conor had witnessed before. At least a hundred streaks of light pierced the nighttime sky, like tracer rounds seeking their prey. They danced to the sound of the sirens, some reaching far out into the Strait of Gibraltar and others westward, out over the Bay of Algeciras. The entire drill didn't last long, no more than five minutes. The wailing sirens ceased first, followed by the searchlights. The crewman explained that the most important part of the drill was the time it took for searchlight and antiaircraft crews to man their positions after the radar picked up incoming threats.

Conor said thanks to the crewman and joined Emily and Sean, who were seated in the bed of the Dodge. It seemed that the two were unfazed by the drill given the lively conversation they were engaged in when he approached. Emily had just finished a series of giggles at something Sean said. Their calm and relaxed state did not surprise Conor entirely, since he knew both had been through the worst of the London Blitz in 1940.

"I'm told the drills have been frequent," Conor reported. "Between Italian bombers from Sardinia and Italian frogmen with their manned torpedoes, Gibraltar is still on high alert, even after the recent successes in North Africa. Their last attack from Sardinia was late October."

"I'm sure they don't get much sleep around here," Emily said. "Just like during the Blitz in London. Who could sleep?"

Conor piled into the Dodge's bed, which then headed toward the airfield's main building. No one talked, thanks to the roaring engine and grinding gears of the airy 4X4. Sleep deprived, hungry, and with their bodies seeking relief from the protracted and frigid flight, conversation was the least desirable activity on their minds.

CHAPTER TWENTY-FIVE

0845 Hours, Monday, December 14, 1942
Kaiser Wilhelm Institute for Physics, Berlin

Heisenberg entered Leeb's office and stopped just inside the doorway. Leeb and another man, an SS officer, stood near a window. Neither noticed Heisenberg's arrival. The officer, dressed in the fearsome black SS uniform and knee-high black leather boots, replete with a gleaming leather belt around his waist with an attached sidearm, had his back to Heisenberg. His cap was tucked under his upper arm, and he was listening to the intense-looking Leeb, nodding occasionally. Heisenberg cleared his throat to announce his arrival.

Leeb looked at Heisenberg and smiled. "Werner. We've been waiting for you."

Heisenberg strode toward the two men, finding it odd that the officer did not turn around, but instead kept facing the window. "Please excuse my tardiness, General Leeb. We were in the middle of some complicated calculations, and it was critical that we completed them."

"Yes, yes, I understand. I want you to meet Hauptsturmführer Hans Koder." As if waiting for the grand announcement, the officer spun around and clicked the heels of his glossy boots. Heisenberg noted three things immediately: the presence of a gassy, oily odor, most likely the boot polish unsparingly used that morning; the pale blue-eyed, sturdily built Koder had his right hand resting on

99

the flap of his sidearm's holster in a somewhat threatening pose; but it was the man's face that caught and wouldn't release his gaze. Several weeks prior, Heisenberg had seen a Waffen SS recruiting poster in the Alexanderplatz air-raid shelter that featured the image of a resolutely faced SS officer that was the embodiment of Aryan manhood. That image stood directly before him in the form of Hauptsturmführer Hans Koder. The fine lines of his chiseled jaw, the wavy and light-colored hair atop his head, the prominent cheekbones, the tight-lipped slash of his mouth, ears that rode tight to the sides of his close-cropped head. One distinguishing trait were the two furrows that deeply creased his forehead, that were so straight as if they were left behind by a sharp blade. He thought Koder must have recognized that he was staring at him, but Koder didn't seem bothered by his transfixion. He actually looked like he welcomed it as he fixed a steely eyed look on Heisenberg, taking the measure of him, possibly of his loyalty to the Third Reich.

"Herr Heisenberg, I am pleased to meet you. General Leeb has been most generous with praise for your contributions to the Third Reich's weapons development programs. He says you are a genius." Koder had a rapid cadence, and he ended with a slight bow. "I am in awe."

"Hauptsturmführer Koder, I am a humble man. I am only too pleased to serve the Fatherland."

"Ah, humility. A characteristic that I have little experience with, so say my comrades-in-arms." Koder smiled at his attempt at self-deprecation, which led Leeb to laugh heartily, prompting Heisenberg to reluctantly and halfheartedly join in. He thought Koder, staring at him with a fading smile, noted his lack of mirth. Koder made him uneasy.

Heisenberg cleared his throat again to move along the conversation. "General, is there something you wanted to discuss?"

"Of course, Werner. Please, both of you, take a seat," Leeb said, pointing to two high-backed wing chairs in front of his desk. After they sat, Leeb said, "It's your trip to Italy. There is a fresh development."

"Oh?" Heisenberg said, looking bewildered. The development surely involved Koder.

Leeb picked up a sterling silver Nazi letter opener replete with a shimmering swastika. He started tapping the pointed end in his palm. "Hauptsturmführer Koder will join you. And you will be lucky to have him. His Italian is impeccable. And, more importantly, I am told that Hans has earned a reputation for getting results, even in the most unusual and complicated circumstances, not unlike the one involving Ettore Majorana."

Heisenberg looked over at his new traveling companion.

"The general is too kind. I make it a goal to apply my complete set of skills in every mission for the Reich," Koder said as he brushed a few stray strands of hair from his forehead.

Now seated a mere three feet from the man, the smell of boot polish became overwhelming. "I welcome the hauptsturmführer's contributions to our mission, whatever they may be."

"I am glad to hear it," Leeb said, putting down the daggerlike opener. "Your flight to Rome leaves from Tempelhof in the morning. Before proceeding to Collepardo, you will meet with Guido Leto, head of OVRA." Leeb reached into a desk drawer and pulled out an envelope. He held it up. "Give him this letter. It states our expectations concerning their assistance."

Heisenberg leaned forward to receive the letter, but Leeb slid it across the desk's surface toward Koder. Taken aback, Heisenberg knew where he stood for the next few days. Out of the corner of his eye, he saw Koder watching him. "Leto, who I should add is a good friend of Reichsführer Himmler's, should have some additional intelligence for you. And he will assign one of his deputies to travel with you to the monastery," Leeb said, then quickly stood. "Questions?"

Koder sprang to his feet; Heisenberg rose more slowly.

"No, General. Your instructions and mission parameters are understood and will be carried out. Without fail and at whatever cost."

Koder's last words sent a shiver down Heisenberg's back.

CHAPTER TWENTY-SIX

0930 Hours, Monday, December 14, 1942
Maison Blanche Airfield, Algiers, Algeria

On Conor's last visit to the cockpit, the pilot had told him the airfield, about ten miles southeast of Algiers, was hit hard on the twenty-first of November by a flight of JU-88 bombers, which destroyed more than a dozen planes on the ground, forcing a large number of B-17s to be repositioned westward, to safer fields near Oran. Conor, perched on a crate of engine parts, surveyed the airfield as the C-47 descended through the cloudless sky, searching for signs of the carnage wreaked by the Luftwaffe. While he saw several mangled Flying Fortresses and P-38s, what he was amazed and thrilled to see was the line of P-38s surrounded by hundreds of crates like the ones they were transporting and mechanics who were buzzing around the skeletons of the fighters like a horde of angry bees, assembling what appeared to be a newly arrived aircraft along the edges of the runway. He noted the number of C-47s that were scattered all over the tarmac, unloading war matériel, and pointed out the sight to Emily as they taxied toward two battered hangars. The enormous hangar doors were missing several panels of corrugated metal, and what panels remained were twisted and fire scorched. Conor noticed numerous series of bullet holes that riddled much of the hangar's facade.

Once deplaned, all three went through the same regimen of stretches as after their first flight, while eager members of the ground crew went about unloading the crates of engine parts. There was a constant series of landings and takeoffs that made communicating a challenge. Adding to the roar from the runway and aircraft movement on the tarmac was the P-38 fighter air cover that circled the airfield. The level and type of activity was impressive.

Parked nearby among other C-47s was a Consolidated PBY-5, nicknamed the *Catalina* by the British. It was a two-engine seaplane whose upper fuselage was painted in the traditional US Navy aviation dark blue, its underbelly painted a light sky blue.

Our taxi to Italy. I hope it's a two-way fare.

Conor took in his travel companions. They had talked little on their flights, the noise level making it nearly impossible. Besides, there was time for that once they were on the ground. He had already shifted into mission mode, as had Emily. They'd all tried to get some sleep while in flight but that, too, wasn't in the cards. Conor saw the fatigue in Emily's face. The whites of her eyes were bloodshot. Her face had lost the glow Conor had seen when he'd picked her up at No. 10 what now seemed like days ago. Sean's face drooped from lack of a proper sleep. Conor, not one to throw stones, was sure he showed signs of weariness as well.

He looked around for their transportation to the Hotel St. Georges, where they were to meet up with Colonel Eddy, but saw none. He was about to head toward one of the hangars to look for a phone when his attention shifted to the blaring horn of an approaching staff car. He had expected Colonel Eddy, but it was not to be. The car screeched to a halt five yards away from the group, and the driver jumped out of the sedan in a flash.

"Conor Thorn, you sorry excuse for an OSS man, if I ever saw one." Conor hadn't heard that voice since he and Emily had left the man in the care of Emily's mother, Bertie, after their messy extraction from Sweden in early November. Bobby Heugle had taken a shot to the chest that collapsed his lung as they made their escape from the port of Lysekil. After a rudimentary surgical procedure that Emily had assisted on mitigated the danger, the trip on a British motor gun boat hadn't been the best environment in which to convalesce. But Bobby, Conor's best friend from their days at the US Naval Academy, sounded like it never happened.

"Bobby, damn good to hear your voice, even though it is annoying," Conor said, grinning.

"Well, I don't think it's annoying at all," Emily responded, which prompted Bobby to greet her first with a hug then kiss…on her lips. Emily blushed and smiled.

Bobby turned to Sean. "Hey, Padre, good to see you again. Been a while. You sure do look like you need a bed." The weary faced Sean stifled a yawn as they shook hands.

Finally, Bobby turned to Conor and slapped him on his back. The force lurched Conor forward.

"Sounds like the lung thing isn't an issue these days," Conor said, noticing Emily hiding a giggle behind her hand.

"Working like a charm. Thanks to, according to my best friend Bertie, Emily and that crazy woman Eve Lind."

"Not just crazy, Bobby. I'd throw in devious," Emily said.

"Call her what she is, a murderer," Conor added.

Bobby, looking down at the ground, nodded, then snapped his gaze back to Conor. "So, tell me all about it."

"What are you talking about?" Conor snapped. He didn't want to talk about the miscarriage in front of Emily, and that also went for his encounter on the bridge.

"The attack on Westminster Bridge. Colonel Eddy mentioned it just today. Do you know who it was?"

Damn it, Bobby.

Emily's mouth slackened. Her look of astonishment turned quickly to anger. She folded her arms across her chest and looked away. Sean, whose face registered the bombshell dropped by Bobby, picked up on Emily's reaction.

"A story for later," Conor said. "We need to get going. Colonel Eddy is waiting for us." Sean put a hand on Emily's back and escorted her to the sedan.

"Tell me you told her, Conor," Bobby said, giving him a severe look.

"Does it look like I did? Come on, let's get moving." They had taken a few steps to the sedan when Conor spotted a sailor who looked no older than seventeen trotting toward them from the direction of the Catalina. Dressed in a dungaree work uniform and a white Dixie cup service cap, he stopped in front of them and saluted, even though no officers were present.

"Seaman Eugene DiLazzaro, sirs. I'm part of the crew that's going to get you to…well, to somewhere. They don't tell me much."

Conor detected a strong New Jersey accent. He introduced himself, then asked, "Where you from, sailor?"

"That would be Newark, New Jersey, sir. Born and bred," DiLazzaro said.

"Hey, I was born there too. So were my parents. I went to Essex Catholic High School. You?" Bobby said.

"Oh, one of those rich boys." The young man grinned. "I went to East Side High. The Red Raiders."

The sailor made a dash for their duffel bags that the ground crew had offloaded and stowed near the tail of the plane. The wiry-built seaman, who had no trouble managing the three overpacked bags, stopped in front of Conor on his way to the staff car.

"We take off at sunset. That will be around 1900 hours," the now-perspiring DiLazzaro said.

"Who's our pilot, seaman?" Conor said.

"That would be Captain Jack Waddon. Top-notch, that guy…I mean officer, and a damn outstanding pilot. Been flying with him since right after Pearl," DiLazzaro replied, then sped off to load the bags in the car.

"Come on, Conor. Colonel Eddy is waiting to brief you. And you look like you could use a drink. I know I could," Bobby said.

"Bobby, it's kind of early, don't you think?"

"It's actually late," he said as he looked at his watch. "It's three in the morning in Annapolis. Our favorite bars are just closing down. Hustle up."

CHAPTER TWENTY-SEVEN

1030 Hours, Monday, December 14, 1942
Hotel St. Georges, Algiers, Algeria

The twenty-minute drive to the Hotel St. Georges was notable for one reason. Every wall, every flat surface they passed was adorned with posters of Marshal Pétain, the chief of state of Vichy France. The beady-eyed Nazi collaborator seemed to track the staff car on its journey to the hotel. Scrawled in black paint across many posters was the demand, "Death to the traitor Darlan." The threat referred to Admiral François Darlan, High Commissioner of France in Africa. He was recognized by the Allies as the commander-in-chief of all French forces in Africa. It took Darlan two long days after the initial invasion of North Africa to order French forces to cease resistance and join the Allies. He was held in low esteem by all Allies that had the misfortune to deal with him.

Bobby turned onto a main tree-lined thoroughfare and announced that they were traveling down the Rue Michelet, Algiers's Champs-Élysées. Conor saw the storefronts of high-end shops and outdoor cafés and theaters. Most, except for a café here or there, were shuttered.

"And here we are, the Hotel St. Georges," Bobby said as he pulled into a circular drive that fronted a hulking, faded yellow Moorish-style hotel. Getting out of the sedan, Conor counted five floors. The structure and the lush gardens that seemed to swallow it up could have been in Miami, given the total absence of any sign the city has been recently captured from Vichy French forces.

Conor, Emily, and Sean grabbed their duffel bags from the trunk while Bobby shooed away a couple of young boys eager to assist in exchange for a handout. Bobby made a move to help Emily, but she rebuffed him with a shake of her head.

"You can carry mine if you like," Conor offered.

"Fat chance, buster. Follow me." Bobby led them down a long passageway bound by flower beds and palm trees. A network of lattice supported a verdant canopy of vines. Passing through a crowd of US Army guards who seemed to ring the property, they entered the lobby, where there were more guards stationed at the heads of corridors that reached out in multiple directions. Hotel staff shot looks of disdain in Emily's direction. *The sight of a woman in man's clothing is too much for them to take*, Conor thought. They headed up two flights of stairs and into an expansive conference room with bone-white walls and a lavender-tinged, glazed tiled floor. The long mahogany table that sat in the center had a stack of paperwork, an ashtray overflowing with cigarette butts, a telephone, and a bottle of Old Forester along with five glasses at one end.

"I'll track down the colonel. Just wait here," Bobby said, then darted out of the room. A sizable window overlooked the harbor, the scene of Operation Terminal. It was bustling with Allied ships being offloaded by multiple cranes that seemed to dance to an unknown waltz. M4 Sherman tanks, halftracks, Jeeps, and 6X6 Jimmy trucks lined every available inch of the harbor's quays.

"Look at that," Conor said, standing between Emily and Sean.

"It is impressive. Maybe the battle for North Africa is nearer its conclusion, rather than its beginning."

"We can only pray to God that you're right, Emily," Sean said.

The three of them, transfixed by the swaying cranes, were startled when Colonel Eddy burst into the room, followed by Bobby and a diminutive aide-de-camp dressed in khaki, who took a seat by the door.

"Quite a sight, isn't it? Let's hope there isn't a similar one in Tunis's harbor," Eddy said.

Tunis was still in the hands of the Nazis and was being supplied from southern Italy and by cargo flights from Sardinia.

Eddy, a US Marine vet of World War I who lost his leg in the

Battle of Belleau Wood, approached the group, his artificial right leg emitting a slight squeak. He shook Conor's hand with the grip of a man twice his size. "Good to see you in one piece, Conor. And you must be Father Sullivan. Glad you're on board. You are the key that will, hopefully, unlock access to the monastery," Eddy said, pumping Sean's heavy mass of a hand. He turned to Emily and smiled. "Emily Bright. Heard a lot about you," he said, extending his hand.

"Conor speaks highly of you, Colonel Eddy. As does Colonel Donovan," Emily said with a smile.

"Wild Bill is quite a man himself." Eddy's eyes were locked on Emily as he held on to her hand a little longer. He seemed to be slightly taken with her. "You know," he began as he escorted Emily to a chair close to his at the end of the long table; Conor and Bobby shared a knowing glance with Bobby throwing in a wink of the eye. "Bill says that he doesn't much like that nickname. But I believe he secretly loves it. Now, if it were me, I'd want everyone to call me that, even Mrs. Eddy." Emily and Bobby chuckled.

Conor and Sean took seats on opposite sides of the table, Sean by Emily's side and Bobby beside Conor. Eddy pulled a file from the top of the stack of paperwork and placed his right hand, his fingers spread wide, on top. His expression switched from that of a gentleman who had just welcomed close friends into his home for a quiet dinner to that of a commander of clandestine forces who he was about to send out on a high-risk mission—which was exactly what he was going to do.

Conor hadn't seen the colonel since October, when he had ordered Conor to head back to London to meet with Colonel Donovan and David Bruce for reassignment. It seemed that Conor's fellow OSS agents in Tangier thought he was too brash and undisciplined—a "reckless cowboy," his partner, Chester Booth, had proclaimed to Eddy. The straw that broke the camel's—no, *Conor's*—back was nearly losing a high-level informant to some Nazi agents. It had gotten a little out of hand, Conor had to admit, but the situation had called for a little daring, an element of unexpected behavior to unsettle the Nazi agents. Tassels, the code name for the tribal leader from the mountainous Riff region of Morocco, was an important part of the OSS's underground organization of informants among the Arab and Berber tribes. And his information had aided the planning for Operation Torch.

"How's Chester doing, Colonel?" Conor asked, poking the bear.

Eddy tilted his head and leered. "That's well behind us, Conor. You've proven your point, given the outcomes of your last two missions. I think it's time to move on from the Tassels affair," Eddy said as he opened the file. "I'll get into the details about how you're getting into Italy after you tell me how you're getting inside the monastery."

"Of course, Colonel. It's pretty simple," Conor said.

It took Conor less than ten minutes to lay out his thinking on getting inside the Certosa di Trisulti. He had entertained a couple of ideas on their long trip from England and settled on one that gave them the best chance of success. As he ran through his plan, Conor kept his eyes on Sean, to see if the man's expression betrayed any concerns, but Sean remained mostly stone-faced; his head bobbed a few times, but he saw no red flags. Emily, Eddy, nor Bobby had any suggestions, comments, or complaints.

Eddy dove into the meat of the briefing. The details of their insertion near Anzio via PBY were familiar to Conor and Emily. Most of what followed was not.

"The PBY will land just north on Anzio, about a mile from the main harbor. The only nearby structure is a lighthouse. It's been inactive since Italy entered the war. Just above the beach, which isn't very wide, are the ruins of Villa Imperiale. A guy named Nero called it home. You'll need to hike up past the ruins. It's about fifty yards over rocky terrain. A bit of a challenge, but you'll do fine."

Conor worried about Sean. He wasn't used to the rough stuff.

"Once you reach level ground, your contact will meet you. There is a main road a short walk inland, about thirty yards from the edge of the ruins. Via Fanciulla d'Anzio. It's the fastest way north out of town."

"What's the story about this contact?" Emily asked.

"He's someone who came to our attention through Harold Timmons, who is a part of the US delegation at the Vatican. His name is Victor Sarandrea. He's the mayor of the small town nearest the monastery—Collepardo."

Conor and Emily exchanged bewildered looks. "Seems a

strange choice. I was thinking it would be someone who has contacts inside the monastery or does business with it," Conor said.

"Just a second, Conor," Eddy said, his voice raised a notch. "Timmons says Sarandrea has had some interaction with the administrator of the monastery. Nearly all the interaction with people outside the walls of the monastery goes through the administrator, someone named Brother Alfieri."

"Got it," Conor said, realizing he should let Eddy have the floor until he was finished.

"Sarandrea is a communist who has found a few local people sympathetic to the Allied cause. They hate the fascists more than we do. Colonel Donovan thinks the communists could be very helpful when we eventually bring the war to the Italian mainland."

One thing bothered Conor. "Colonel…" *Well, that didn't last long.* "How did Timmons contact this mayor if he wasn't allowed out of Vatican City?" Conor knew, from their last foray to the Vatican in October, that members of delegations from Allied countries were protected as long as they stayed within the Vatican's walls.

"Timmons didn't make the direct contact. A friend of his inside the Vatican, an Italian priest, contacted the pastor of the local Catholic church in Collepardo who identified the mayor as someone we could work with. Timmons sent a member of the delegation's staff, an Italian woman, to deliver a letter along with a generous amount of cash to buy some weapons. The letter stated that there would be more money if he would help some antifascist friends who would arrive soon. And the mayor agreed."

"A lot of actors on the stage, Colonel. People who we really don't know. Does that bother you?" Emily asked before Conor could get the words strung together.

"I see your point, Emily," Eddy said. His tone softened somewhat. "Thing is, we didn't have the luxury of time. This entire operation came together damn fast."

Eddy went on with one more detail: the mayor would take them to his home, which would be their base of operations.

"Do you have a photo of the mayor?" Conor asked.

"No. Not enough time to track one down. But there's this," Eddy said, handing a written description on a flimsy to Conor, who studied it, then passed it to Emily.

"Here's a list of gear we've pulled together for you," Eddy said. "We think you'll be out there for three to four days, so we packed light." Eddy passed along another flimsy, this one with a list. At the top was *Cash — 15,000 lira.* "There's a money belt and small pouch for the cash. Each of you should carry 7,500 lira in case you get split up," Eddy said. Next on the list were some items of food, such as Hershey bars, canned meat, and sardines. Next on the list was a sub-miniature Minox Riga camera, which struck Conor as an odd addition. He noted ammunition for his Colt 1911A1 and Emily's Walther PPK, as well as a spare Colt and Walther. He was glad to see they'd added some heavier firepower by including three British-built Sten semi-automatic machine guns, along with a generous supply of 9mm Parabellum box magazines. He next looked for a radio on the list. Halfway down, there it was: a Type 3 Mk II Suitcase Transceiver. Commonly known as the B2, it was the best wireless set available at that point in the war, capable of long-distance comms and effective in screening out interference. The handful of American Mk 2 grenades were a comforting bonus. He also noticed their stash included two bags of caltrops, devious but simple devices helpful in stopping virtually any untracked vehicle.

He passed the list to Emily. "Has the radio been checked out recently?" he asked, knowing it was the most important piece of equipment on the list.

"Jones did this morning. And—"

"And I did right after he did," Bobby said. "It's in good shape. Just be careful getting ashore. Those things tend to be fragile."

"Thanks, Bobby," Emily said, passing the equipment list back to Eddy. Eddy refiled it and sat back.

"This might be a good time to add something to the list of... equipment," Sean said as he reached into his suitcase and pulled out a folded white garment. Sean unfolded it, and a scapular was visible and underneath that was a cowl. He then removed a pair of lightly worn sandals from his suitcase and placed them on top of the garments. "I can't help but think that this Carthusian monk's habit might come to some use, should locating Majorana prove more challenging than you might be planning," Conor's eyes widened, and he glanced at Emily, who looked just as surprised.

"I was able to reach out to the administrator at the St. Hughes Charterhouse in West Sussex for a favor. I told them I would return it when we were done."

"Of course," Conor said. "We'll even get it cleaned beforehand."

Conor snorted at his own comment, amazed at Sean's contribution and, at the same time, wondered why no one in London or Algiers, including himself, had thought of it. "Sean, I'm impressed. You are getting too good at this espionage stuff," Conor said.

Eddy picked up from there. "When you send the message that you're ready to be extracted, include the code phrase *PAY DIRT* if you have Majorana."

Conor mouthed the phrase to Emily.

Eddy turned to look out the window as if he was searching for his next words.

"Colonel?" Conor said.

"Right. There's one more matter," he said, turning to Conor, then to Emily. "There's been a recent development. He showed up about six hours ago."

Shit. Another body in the mix?

"Joseph Feinmann. He's an American physicist who claims that he and Majorana were close several years ago, when they studied together in Rome and Leipzig, before he disappeared."

Conor slumped in his chair.

"I know…I know. Another mouth to feed. Here's the reason he's involved. He'll be able to confirm *if* this guy in the monastery is the real deal. And there are some back in the States who feel that Feinmann could help convince Majorana to sign up with us. He will also have letters from Enrico Fermi and Albert Einstein, both imploring Majorana to join the Allies in atomic research."

Conor sat up. "Has he had any training for a mission like this? The insertion and extraction ops are going to be tricky," he said, trying to tamp down the trepidation in his voice.

"He says that he's fit and capable."

Shit and shit again. This is not a day hike up the mountain and back.

Conor was sure his apprehension was obvious. He looked over at Emily, who shrugged.

"Conor, you'll be glad to hear I had to tell your friend

here"—Eddy pointed to Bobby—"five times that he couldn't go along with you."

"I think it was seven times, Colonel. In fact, I'm sure of it."

Eddy reached for the bottle of Old Forester. "I think a toast to the mission's success is in order." He lined up five glasses and added a finger of bourbon to each. He stood, struggling a bit and leaning more heavily on his left leg, and slid a glass toward each of them. Conor, Emily, Bobby, and Sean all stood, glasses in hand. "I know that Colonel Donovan didn't mince any words about how important it is to keep this genius out of Nazi hands. Do what you have to do to keep that from happening. And if you and Feinmann can convince him to come to the old U.S. of A., well, that's icing on the cake. *Sláinte!*" Eddy said as he raised his glass. The others followed. They placed their glasses on the table. Eddy refilled his glass—not the others. "Conor, one last thing from Colonel Donovan. He said—"

"Do not fuck this up," Conor said.

Bobby laughed.

"Those words have rung in my ears every hour since he last said them."

Conor, Emily, and Bobby headed for the door.

Eddy, now back in his chair, glass in hand, said, "Conor, what hand is the scar on?"

Conor turned. He was being tested. With Emily and Bobby staring at him, he said, "His right, sir."

Eddy smiled, raised his glass toward Conor in salute, then downed his bourbon.

CHAPTER TWENTY-EIGHT

1130 Hours, Monday, December 14, 1942
On Board JU-52 En Route to Rome

When Koder learned the pilot diverted to Milan to wait out a massive storm that was battering Rome, he became unglued. He pounded his fists into the armrest and berated the pilot for a lack of courage, even following him back to the cockpit to continue his tirade. The pilot, a Luftwaffe officer, refused to back down, which only angered Koder more.

Heisenberg, who sat next to Koder on the flight, could only sit by and let the episode play out, hoping they would be on the ground in Milan but for a short period. The other passengers on the flight, a mix of Wehrmacht officers and foreign service officials, knew enough to not intercede in the antics of a hot-tempered SS hauptsturmführer.

While they were on the ground in Milan, Koder continued to fume, complaining to Heisenberg that their diversion was inflicting havoc on what was already a tight schedule. Heisenberg, losing patience, contrived the need to contact his laboratory back in Berlin over an important matter, which allowed him the opportunity to escape to an office adjacent to the waiting room to place a call. He called his wife, Elizabeth, and revisited the pleasant evening they had the night before. It was a quiet dinner, as he'd sent the children over to their neighbor's apartment. A session at the piano had followed the sumptuous dinner. To Elizabeth's delight, he'd performed some of her favorite classical music: Bach, Beethoven, Brahms, Mendelssohn, but no Wagner. Elizabeth would not stand for one note of Hitler's favorite composer.

Back in the air after a two-hour layover, Heisenberg found that Koder had calmed down. It was after Koder announced to Heisenberg that he was going to report the pilot as soon as he contacted the German Embassy in Rome that Heisenberg sought to shift Koder's focus onto something Koder could lose himself in. That topic was Hauptsturmführer Hans Koder.

"Hauptsturmführer, I fear you know more about me than I you. Can you shed some light on your background?"

Koder's demeanor transformed in two ticks of the clock. Grinning, he turned to Heisenberg. "I am not...comfortable talking about my accomplishments, but since you insist." Koder paused. "Herr Heisenberg, let me say that I am a man whose good luck has never seemed to run out. Yes, I admit that sounds boastful, but we Germans should never shy away from telling the truth. Don't you agree?" Heisenberg, with a slight tilt of his head, gave Koder a quick nod as if to say, *Of course. Completely.* "You've heard of the SS-Sonderkommandos, Herr Heisenberg?

"I'm afraid not. Were you once a member?"

Those were the last words uttered by Heisenberg for the next ten minutes. Koder regaled Heisenberg of his involvement in an operation headed by a Sturmbannführer Schellenberg that led to the capture of two British Secret Intelligence Service agents on the outskirts of the Dutch town of Venlo, close to the Dutch-German border. The operation, one in which, according to the beaming Koder, he played a major role, was a key development in the lead-up to the German invasion of the Netherlands. "A more recent operation, one in which I commanded, took place behind Russian lines and involved a successful series of sabotage of key Soviet installations. That operation earned me this," Koder said as he stroked the Iron Cross that rested against his chest. "I was featured in an article in *Das Schwarze Korps.* I am sure you have heard of the publication."

Heisenberg had seen many SS officers reading the official newspaper of the Schutzstaffel, simply known as the SS, in the cafés in and around Berlin. "Yes, of course. Quite an honor, Hauptsturmführer."

By this point, Koder's earlier foul mood was a distant memory. He twisted in his seat to face Heisenberg. "Herr Heisenberg, I am so honored to be involved in this mission. From what General Leeb has told me, what you are working on will guarantee our control of the continent and all of Russia!" Koder leaned toward Heisenberg, his hot breath washing over Heisenberg's face as he continued. "I am not a deeply religious man, but I believe God is on the side of the führer. He is on the side of Germany. Don't you feel that? Just think of what life for Germans will be like when you are successful. With my help in securing the great Ettore Majorana, no one will stop Germany from taking its rightful place in the world."

All Heisenberg could do was nod. But then he thought that was not enough to placate the man and said, "Yes, Hauptsturmführer Koder, I, too, firmly believe what you say. Quite firmly."

CHAPTER TWENTY-NINE

1130 Hours, Monday, December 14, 1942
Hotel St. Georges, Algiers, Algeria

Conor, Emily, and Sean trudged down a long hallway on an upper floor. Bobby, after telling them where their rooms were and that their duffel bags had been delivered there, headed in the opposite direction. Just as Conor placed his hand on their room's doorknob, Sean cleared his throat noisily.

"Conor, would now be a good time to have that discussion?" Conor looked at an exhausted Emily, who barely managed a nod.

When Conor entered the room, Sean asked him to take a seat in a club chair next to the bed. Conor, his body racked with fatigue, melted into the chair while Sean took his seat on the bed.

Sean's right leg bounced, and he didn't make eye contact with Conor.

"What's wrong, Sean?" Conor wondered what had overcome Sean, who exhibited no signs of angst during the briefing.

Sean turned to him. "I hope by telling you this that I am doing the right thing. I have prayed for an answer to that, but none has materialized. So, I am taking a bit of a risk by revealing this to you."

Get on with it, Sean. I really need some shut-eye.

"When I returned from our...escapade in Rome in October, I was not myself for several days. I asked Cardinal Massy if I could travel to Dublin and visit with my family. I hadn't seen them since before the war began." Sean went on to explain that when he arrived, he found his sister, Constance, in poor health. Her doctor was unsure what was wrong and told Sean to prepare for the worst. Constance, given the uncertainty, felt compelled to share something she had told no one since their mother, Finola, had revealed it to her, right before she died in 1938.

"Constance told me that, while Mother was working as your family's cook and housekeeper, during your father's posting as vice-consul, she…" Sean's voice faltered. He looked away at nothing in particular, his leg bouncing faster.

"She said what, Sean?" Conor asked, completely flummoxed as to what Sean was driving at.

Without turning to look at Conor, he answered, "She was unfaithful to our father. She betrayed him by sleeping with…"

Jack.

"Jack, your father."

Conor's mouth fell open. He stopped breathing. He stopped processing. He saw Sean's mouth moving, but the sounds were stifled, like his head was under water. Sean finally turned to face him, and Conor's head rose to the surface.

"I'm sorry to reveal this news. At least, I think I am. You see, I convinced myself that it is something that both our families need to know, out of fairness to Constance." Sean's eyes filled with tears. "Constance, born on the last day of 1916, is your half sister."

Questions rattled around his head. Did his mother know? If she did, had she forgiven his father? Did his father love Sean's mother?

Jack never remarried after Conor's mother, Bridgett, drowned while saving Conor from a riptide when he was ten years old, just a couple of years after returning from Dublin. His father was handsome in a Cary Grant way and, therefore, had no trouble finding companionship. There was always some new woman making themselves comfortable at their home in Spring Lake. Jack didn't go out of his way to show that he preferred to be single. The way he carried himself made it clear that he relished being chased by single, divorced, and widowed women in and around Spring Lake and New York City, where the offices of the Republic Broadcasting System were located. Back in Dublin, Conor was too young to notice any hints that his father was taking advantage of his good looks, nor did he notice any changes in his mother's feelings toward his father. As he processed it all, Sean's revelation left him dazed.

Did my mother know?

"Do you have a photo of her?"

Sean nodded and reached inside his suit coat breast pocket, pulling out a photo and handing it to him. Constance was standing in front of a church in her Sunday finest. The resemblance to his father stunned Conor. Her cheekbones and almond-shaped eyes were a mirror image of Jack's. In the photo, Constance was smiling, lips stretched wide, but no teeth showing. Just like Jack.

Sean bent over, arms resting on his powerful thighs. "It pains me to say that my older sister, Mary, and I would tease Constance unmercifully"—he took a deep breath—"because she didn't look like the rest of us siblings."

"Why didn't your mother tell my father?" Conor asked, staring out the window. No sooner had his words been spoken than he thought maybe Jack did know he had a daughter.

"God only knows. God only knows."

Conor rose from his chair, his legs weak. "Were you ever aware that my father sent your mother any money?"

"Not that I knew of. I guess it's possible. But we never did seem to have enough money while I was growing up." Sean paused. "Conor, I—"

"Can I keep this?" Conor asked.

Sean lowered his head, then nodded. Before Conor left the room, he squeezed his distraught friend's shoulder. He really wanted to give his friend a back-cracking bear hug.

#

Outside Sean's door, he slipped the photo into his breast pocket, took a deep breath, and let it out slowly. He entered the room he was to share with Emily. She wasn't there; the door to what he guessed was the bathroom was closed. He knocked lightly and heard a soft, "Yes?"

"It's Conor, Em. You okay?"

When there was no answer, he said, "Can I come in?"

"Yes."

He opened the door and a wisp of steam washed over his face. He saw Emily standing next to a tub. The water in it was pinkish. Emily held a long towel wrapped around her and gripped tightly to her chest. Her hair, no longer pulled back, was dripping wet.

"I'm having some cramps. Nothing too serious, I'm sure. Just a little uncomfortable. I'll be fine."

Conor stepped toward her. "What can I do?"

For a long moment, Emily didn't respond. He looked at her standing there. Her beauty was heart-stopping.

"Could you stay with Sean? I need some deep sleep, and that will be too difficult with you and the cramps."

Conor winced, then nodded slowly. He had to respect that she was still reeling physically and emotionally from the miscarriage. "Let me know if you need anything. Okay?"

"Yes, I will." Emily looked away. "Let's just get through this mission. Tomorrow you can tell me about the attack that must have slipped your mind somehow. Now, please go."

CHAPTER THIRTY

1700 Hours, Monday, December 14, 1942
OVRA Headquarters, Forte Braschi, Rome

"When we meet Leto, no needless conversation, Herr Heisenberg. We must be on our way to Collepardo as soon as possible." It was the second reminder from Koder regarding their travel schedule on their twenty-minute trip from Littorio Airport to the OVRA's Headquarters in Rome. It was the first time Heisenberg detected any type of disquiet. It wasn't the type of anxiousness displayed by someone who was nervous or fearful, but of someone who was eager to meet and take the measure of an adversary.

The Mercedes from the German Embassy, its fender-mounted Nazi flags snapping in the chilly December air, pulled through the cream-colored brick front entrance to a massive installation called Forte Braschi. As they approached the entrance, their driver, a brutish-looking oberscharführer named Hermann, mentioned the fort was one of fifteen built in and around Rome. This one housed OVRA along with the Servizio Informazioni Militari, or SIM. When Hermann mentioned the fort was the location of the execution of Michele Schirru, an American anarchist convicted of planning an assassination attempt on Mussolini, Koder's eyes lit up and he leaned forward to ask how the man was executed. When the driver said he was shot, Heisenberg heard Koder mutter, *"Wunderbar."*

They were shown into Guido Leto's office straightaway upon

arriving. The air in the spacious office was tainted with the robust scent of cigars. The sharply tailored, gray-suited man standing behind an outsized leather desk chair—Heisenberg assumed this man was Leto—was looking fatigued and jowly. Another man, this one younger by ten or so years and overweight, holding a file folder, and dressed in a wrinkled, dark blue suit that was terribly ill-fitting, stood one step behind and to the left of Leto. The desk was bereft of any paperwork or accessories, except for a single black phone with an oversized handset as if fitted for someone with a large head, like Leto. The top of the desk gleamed as if it were spit shined. Heisenberg took minor note of the items that adorned the walls of the office. It was like many government offices he had been in: flags in the corners, a portrait of the country's leadership, in this case Il Duce—hands on hips and chin tilted imperiously to the heavens, a glorious warrior pose that was almost comical. It was directly behind Leto's desk. The only other item that drew Heisenberg's attention was a large, framed photo on a table behind the desk of Il Duce and Hitler standing side by side, staring intently to their left, while steel-helmeted soldiers stood ramrod straight in the background. Heisenberg wondered if it was a photo that had only recently seen the light of day in Leto's office.

"Hauptsturmführer Koder, Herr Heisenberg, welcome to Rome," Leto announced, as if he were about to grant them the keys to the Eternal City. "Please sit. May I offer you both some refreshments to help you recover from your long trip?"

As they all took their seats, except for the blue-suited man, Koder spoke. "We are in no need of recovery. In fact, I wish to be on our way to Collepardo as soon as you get on with your briefing. Time, you must understand, is of the essence," Koder said as he shoved the letter that Leeb had given him across the desk. It took Leto a moment to read it; he then nodded as he slid it back to Koder.

Initially, Leto didn't betray any reaction, possibly because he knew he was dealing with an officer of the feared Nazi SS. Then Leto nodded curtly and said, "As you wish." He reached out with his left hand, waiting to receive the file held by the man behind him.

Leto read from the file. There was nothing Heisenberg heard

that was new, and Koder must have agreed with that assessment, given the long, noisy sigh at the end of Leto's report.

"That's it? That's all the intelligence you have for us?"

Leto closed the file and reached back without looking to hand it to his assistant. "That is correct, Hauptsturmführer. The commander of the Collepardo carabinieri, Capitano Pietro Nuti, could not gain access to any officials at the monastery, though he has tried multiple times."

"Doesn't sound like an effective commander to me."

"Yes, I agree. But it is what it is. I can do nothing from here to address the situation. Except…"

"Except what?" Koder said.

"I offer the services of my most qualified deputy," Leto said, twisting to his left with an outstretched arm. "Anteo Tardino will accompany you both to Collepardo. He will…address any obstacles you may encounter in your mission."

Koder directed his attention to Tardino. His gaze ran up and down the six-foot, heavyset man. "Are you prepared to follow my orders?"

Tardino hesitated and shot a look at Leto, who was staring at Koder. Receiving no signal from his superior, Tardino cleared his throat. "Of course, Hauptsturmführer Koder, without question," Tardino said, punctuating his reply with a minor bow. "I wish nothing more than to see Ettore Majorana in the capable hands of Werner Heisenberg, Germany's most esteemed scientist." Leto, Koder, and Tardino all directed their attention to Heisenberg, who felt his face flush. If such success was achieved, it would put immense pressure on Heisenberg to get results. And in short order.

CHAPTER THIRTY-ONE

1800 Hours, Monday, December 14, 1942
Office of Commissar Vyacheslav Molotov, People's Commissariat for
Foreign Affairs, Moscow

Georgy Flyorov hadn't flown in the Yakovlev Yak-6 since earlier that year, as an officer in the Soviet Air Force. But this time the two-engine transport was flown by a woman who couldn't have been much older than twenty, and he was the sole passenger.

He was in his office at the Laboratory of Nuclear Reactions in the midst of a phone call with his friend and colleague Konstantin Petrzhak, with whom he had discovered spontaneous fission of uranium two years before, when his assistant barged in to tell him that Flyorov had been summoned to Moscow to meet with Commissar Molotov regarding a matter of utmost importance.

Before he terminated the call with Petrzhak, he whispered into the phone, "Konstantin, what do you think this summons could be about? Could it be news of increased funding for our research?"

His friend made no attempt to stifle his reaction. "Ha ha, you, my friend, are too naive. I have always said that about you. You of all people know that whatever funds there are have been earmarked for the radar and marine mine detection programs. The uranium bomb project is the ugly stepsister."

The words stung him. Maybe he was naive. But he had conviction that his project was the one project that could play a decisive role in securing the Soviet Union's future among the world's powers.

The young pilot's touchdown at Khodynskoe Field was smooth. After commending the pilot, he exited the aircraft and boarded an awaiting gray KIM-10 sedan. On the drive to the Kremlin, he recalled details of his last encounter with Commissar Molotov. It had taken place two months prior, when Flyorov was asked to organize a presentation for Molotov and several other officials from the People's Commissariat for Foreign Affairs at Flyorov's laboratory in Dubna.

He'd found Molotov unfocused and unashamedly disinterested in the overview of the lab's work. He asked no questions. He had no comments, suggestions, or observations. He seemed quite eager to return to Moscow, given the number of times he looked at his watch. The encounter was deeply disappointing for Flyorov and his team of nuclear physicists and researchers. It took Flyorov weeks to raise the lab's morale.

Upon arriving at the commissar's outer office, he was quickly announced through a desktop intercom and then told to take a seat. That had been twenty minutes ago. It became clear to Flyorov that his definition of urgent was quite different from Molotov's. Another five minutes passed. He laid his hat on a table beside his chair and opened his satchel to look for some reading material when the intercom buzzed. The dark-haired, pudgy-faced woman, with a sweeping wave of her arm, told him he was now wanted.

Molotov, hands clasped behind his back, was standing behind his cluttered desk when Flyorov entered the office. He was gazing out the window that looked over Red Square. The window was sectioned off with tape to protect the occupant from splintered glass projectiles. Flyorov was surprised, given that the threat of Nazi air raids had diminished since Soviet forces had beaten back the German Wehrmacht attempt to capture the capital early that year. Molotov didn't turn around and greet him for several seconds. When he did, Flyorov couldn't help but notice that there was an oval-shaped, coffee-colored stain on his white shirt, an inch to one side of his striped tie.

"Comrade Flyorov, welcome. I am pleased that you could come so quickly," Molotov said, pointing his chin toward a chair set in front of his desk. Molotov lowered himself into his own chair, emitting a drawn-out groan that announced the act wasn't easy on his body.

"I apologize for keeping you waiting, but I wanted to review your letters before we sat down." Molotov picked up a sheet of paper, adjusted his pince-nez on the bridge of his nose, and studied it.

The letters. That brought a smile to Flyorov's face, which quickly disappeared.

Flyorov was exceptionally proud of the fact that it had been his actions that had convinced Premier Stalin the Soviet Union must embark on its own atomic weapons program. He recalled the most impactful words in his first letter to the premier, sent in April of that year, regarding the consequences of the development of atomic weapons: *The results will be so overriding that it won't be necessary to determine who is to blame for the fact that this work has been neglected in our country.* Not seeing any results from the first letter, he, along with his friend Konstantin, had sent a second. Those words were stronger.

Molotov began to read. "'It is essential, for the sake of the Soviet Union's survival, to manufacture a uranium bomb without delay.'" Molotov looked up. "Such strong words to be directed at our leader, Comrade." All Flyorov could think to do was nod. "Do you still believe your words?"

The question was a test. He could not envision going back on those words. "Of course. The program is vital to our future. All who work on it in Dubna and in other laboratories will testify to that."

Molotov reached for a delicate bone china cup but realized that it was empty. After requesting another cup of coffee through the intercom, he reached for a pack of cigarettes. Flyorov didn't recognize the brand—Chesterfields. It sounded like an American or English brand. Maybe they were one of the items on the list of goods and war material sent by their allies. Molotov lit the cigarette with his lighter and sat back. He held the smoke between his thumb and index finger, his hand upturned. In between his first several puffs, Molotov stroked his graying mustache with the thumb and index finger of his free hand.

When his assistant brought in another cup, he sat up. "Comrade, you are to be commended for the strength of your statements. As you know, your words convinced our leader to remove our best scientists from their military obligations and return them to their scientific work, notably the uranium bomb project."

And the radar project and the marine mine project, Flyorov wanted to add, but his common sense took hold of him.

"Thank you, Commissar Molotov. Words come easily to me when it concerns the future of our country."

It was Molotov's turn to nod. "As to the reason that I have called you here." He paused. "Of course, talk of this outside this office will only end your illustrious career." He paused again to let his statement sink in. "Comrade Beria, chief of the NKVD, has made me aware that they have learned from a...source in England that an Italian theoretical scientist thought dead by the name of Ettore Majorana may have been found alive. Are you—"

Flyorov gasped. Loudly. It startled Molotov enough to make him involuntarily shake a cigarette ash in his lap, which he quickly swept off with a swipe of his hand. His look of annoyance drove Flyorov deeper into his seat.

"I take it you know the name," Molotov said. A look of astonishment spread across Flyorov's face. Of course, he knew the famous Italian scientist. He was an enigma in the field of nuclear physicists. But he had vanished. This couldn't be.

"Found?"

"Yes. Found, I said." Molotov studied Flyorov through a haze of cigarette smoke. "Have you ever met the man?"

"No."

"I'm curious. Explain your reaction. You seemed quite startled at the mention of his name."

Flyorov, stunned and thrilled by the news of Majorana's discovery, thought it might be wise to downplay Majorana's reputation and instead extol that of Soviet scientists. He knew that Stalin felt that the Soviet scientific community was second to none in the breakthroughs they had achieved under his leadership. "Many of my fellow physicists were, simply put, impressed with Majorana's ability to see solutions so clearly and easily. We, luckily, have many like him, Comrade Molotov." His first response was an understatement. His second was a lie.

Molotov beamed and nodded, then crushed out his cigarette.

Flyorov sat up and moved to the edge of his seat. "There was a rumor in the nuclear scientific community that Majorana was the one who first promoted a theory of nuclear stability bound by something he called 'force of exchange.' It was a critical development in nuclear physics. I am not sure the rumor is to be believed." Yet Flyorov did believe it.

Molotov lit another cigarette and sipped his coffee.

Flyorov waited for Molotov to return his attention to him. "He didn't publish often, but when he did, the papers were groundbreaking. He was twenty-six years old when he published his paper on the relativistic theory of particles with arbitrary spin. In it, he established wave equations for particles having arbitrary intrinsic momentum."

Molotov blew out a stream of smoke that hit Flyorov squarely in the face. Undeterred, Flyorov continued, careful to bridle his tone. "There is his 1937 paper on the symmetric theory of electrons and positrons, and in the same year, he hypothesized about the existence of the Majorana fermion, which was named after him—"

"Enough, enough, Comrade. You have convinced me that this Italian is impressive. But not as distinguished as you and your colleagues. Possibly one that could help our program though, would you say?" Molotov said, snuffing out his cigarette in the coffee cup saucer.

"Without question. But how is that possible?"

Molotov sat back and swiveled his chair slightly toward the window. He removed his pince-nez and wiped them off with a napkin. He remained quiet while Flyorov sat thinking how honored he would be to work alongside Majorana.

Finally, Molotov spun back toward Flyorov and perched his glasses on his nose. "Premier Stalin has expressed his dissatisfaction with the lack of progress in the development of atomic weapons." Flyorov had heard complaints from the heads of other labs that Molotov, overseer of all logistics of the project, was a weak administrator who didn't truly understand the program's potential in wartime and peacetime. "Given the premier's frustrations, and I completely agree with him, coupled with your appraisal of this Majorana, I believe we should move straightaway to…recruit him."

"But what if he refuses? What if he has turned to God?"

"Ha, that would be his mistake. There is no God, Comrade."

Flyorov kept his tongue.

Molotov picked up the handset to the intercom and asked to be connected with NKVD chief Beria. He hung up and steepled his hands in front of his face. "Comrade Beria will see to it that Majorana will be brought to us. He has people everywhere. He tells me that his most effective agent is stationed in Rome. Rest assured, Comrade, our program is about to take giant steps."

CHAPTER THIRTY-TWO

1830 Hours, Monday, December 14, 1942
Maison Blanche Airfield, Algiers, Algeria

Daylight was quickly fading when they drove up to the PBY. The air traffic had subsided some, at least compared to the level of activity when they'd landed earlier in the morning. Conor spied an officer wearing a short leather flight jacket and combination cap inspecting the seaplane. His flashlight beam darted around the surface of the craft, the landing gear struts and wheels, then along the edge of the wing above him. He then trained the beam on a pair of 500-pound bombs that hung below the wings. Next, the beam traveled down the swooping contour of the seaplane's hull, where it met the upper side of the fuselage. When the officer noticed Conor and his team unloading their gear, he turned off the light and sauntered over to the group.

"I'm Captain Waddon. Now, who among you is Thorn?" he asked, placing his hands on his hips. Waddon, who stood a bit north of six feet, had a slim build, a friendly face, and, from what Conor could make out, a high and tight haircut. He surveyed the group, and his eyes landed on Conor.

"That would be me, Captain. Conor Thorn." Conor extended his hand, which Waddon shook. Conor introduced Emily, then Sean, and as he was about to introduce Bobby, Waddon stopped him.

"Mr. Heugle and I are very familiar with one another. Let's

just say that I owe him a few bucks over a friendly game of poker." Waddon shook his head in mock disgust. "He bet the flop and cashed in with a royal flush. Some players never see a hand like that in their lifetime. And I do want a rematch, Bobby. You promised."

"It will be my pleasure, Captain Waddon," Bobby replied with an exaggerated salute.

"How's the ship look?" Conor asked.

Waddon turned and looked at his plane. "Done with the exterior inspection. She checks out." He turned back to face Conor. "Say, you wouldn't be the Thorn who made a late interception against Notre Dame and helped Navy beat them with a last-second field goal…would you?"

"That would be me again, Captain," Conor said.

"Aww, come on, Jack. Don't give this guy a bigger head than he already has."

"Just curious, Bobby. I won a few bets that day. Gotta bunch of friends that went to Notre Dame. So thanks, Conor. I owe you."

"My pleasure, Captain."

"So, I'm confused. You still Navy?"

"Really? Now?"

"Long story. Maybe later. We need to get loaded if we're still taking off at nineteen hundred," Conor said, looking to avoid talking about the end of his time in the Navy.

"Right. Later." Waddon turned back to the PBY but stopped when a jeep with a single passenger pulled up. The driver didn't move. Neither did the passenger, a lieutenant. It didn't take a doctor to conclude that he was half in the bag. Waddon took in the arrival and shook his head. "'Bout time, Donnie." Waddon waited for a response. When none seemed to be coming his way, he said, "You okay?"

Donnie didn't answer, except by exiting the jeep with some difficulty and giving Waddon a shoddy salute as he headed for the PBY.

"Who's that, Captain?" Conor said.

Waddon hesitated as he tracked the lieutenant to the PBY. "He's my copilot." As if he expected concerns from his passengers, he looked at his questioner. "He'll be fine. Best right seat I've ever flown with."

Waddon turned his head toward the PBY and yelled, "Eugene, on the double." He turned back and put his hands on his hips again. "Okay, here's how this is gonna go, so listen carefully."

As Waddon went through some details, Seaman DiLazzaro sprinted over and began moving duffel bags and gear over to the PBY.

Conor held up his hand to stop DiLazzaro. "Hey, Newark, careful with the suitcase. It's our ticket home."

Waddon scoffed. "And I thought we were. Okay, like I was saying, once we put down off the coast of Anzio, we'll drop two inflatables from the port side blister. DiLazzaro drops first with equipment following. Then Emily and Feinmann join DiLazzaro."

"If Feinmann ever gets here," Bobby says.

Waddon glanced at his watch. "Well, if he's not here by nineteen hundred, we leave without him."

Conor looked at Emily, who only offered a shrug.

"After Emily and Feinmann are over the side, then Conor and Father Sullivan drop into the other inflatable. Once you're ashore, DiLazzaro will bring both inflatables back and we're off." Waddon paused and looked at each of them. "But here's the key. It has to all go down fast. We don't really know what to expect, except for some rough seas."

Rough seas and inflatables. Not a comforting combination.

Waddon looked at his watch again. "I've gotta finish my pre-flight. See you on board," Waddon said, then turned on his heel and hightailed it back to his ship.

"I think I'll get on board and help get our bags stowed," Sean said.

"I'll help," Bobby said, following Sean and Seaman DiLazzaro, who were hauling their last two bags of gear. "Sailor, let me have one of those bags," Bobby said.

Conor wondered how much pushback Waddon would give if Conor asked to delay the takeoff while they waited for the overdue Feinmann.

"Well, what happened?" Emily asked, taking advantage of them being alone for a moment. "No, the better question is: Why didn't you mention anything about it?" There was heat in her tone, which was not uncalled for. He should have told her.

"After I left you at the hospital the day before they released you, I decided to walk back to the hotel. I needed to do some thinking..." Conor kept the details of the encounter a little light, including the knife play. "I will say his escape was pretty dramatic though," he said, wrapping up.

"Dramatic?"

"He went over the side of the bridge and landed on a garbage scow passing underneath. It's funny now that I think about it."

"Who was he? Did he try to rob you?" Emily asked, her attention riveted on Conor.

"No, he wasn't looking for money. Remember that guy I chased at Paddington Station the day Eleanor Roosevelt came into town?"

Emily nodded.

"It was him."

"Were you wounded?" Emily's brow was wrinkled in worry.

"Just some scratches."

Emily folded her arms across her chest like the night before, but her hard look softened. "You should have told me."

"Looking back on it now, yes, I should have. But then, I knew you were sad over losing the baby, and I thought it could wait. You had enough to deal with."

She dropped her arms, took a step toward him, and gave him a hug.

Before he could ask how she was feeling, a jeep drove up and screeched to a halt just feet from them. A dark-haired man in his middle to late thirties hopped out. The driver also exited the jeep and grabbed a brown cowhide leather suitcase from the back seat. The dark-haired man approached Conor and Emily.

"I'm Joseph Feinmann. That's Feinmann with two *n*'s. I'll be joining you on this absolutely crazy mission." Feinmann turned and eyed the PBY. "You ever flown in one of these contraptions?"

#

The port side plexiglass blister had just been secured. Waddon hadn't yet turned over the Catalina's Pratt & Whitney engines. Conor, Emily, Sean, and Feinmann had taken up positions in the

PBY's cramped living compartment, which was in the plane's midsection aft of the flight engineer's compartment and forward of the waist gunner's compartment. The air inside the PBY was a pungent blend of oil, fuel, grease, and sweat—a jumble of odors that all fighting machines shared.

Emily and Sean laid out on two canvas bunks on the starboard side. Conor and Feinmann sat side by side on the lone port side bunk. Seaman DiLazzaro, one of the two waist gunners, stood just inside the door that led to the waist gunner's compartment. There wasn't much room in there for both gunners because of the space the two inflated MK IV rubber rafts took up.

As the crew made ready for takeoff, Conor wanted to learn a little more about Feinmann with two *n*'s. "Why don't you give us a brief rundown on your background and how you landed this assignment?"

Feinmann was wearing olive green fatigues sans any identification and heavy boots. His small suitcase nestled between his feet. Conor made a mental note to store it in one of the waterproof duffel bags at some point. Feinmann's field jacket looked to be too small, the sleeves ending two inches above his wrists. Conor noticed that there was no wedding ring.

"Not much to tell. I have my head buried pretty deep into research projects these days, like many people."

"Where you from?" Emily asked.

"From all over. My father was in the foreign service, so we moved around quite a bit—Germany, Russia, Turkey. Some out-of-the-way places too, like Bolivia."

"Family?" Conor asked.

"No. Parents have passed, no siblings," Feinmann said, then paused and looked at his boots. "Wife left me after I discovered she was having an affair with one of my colleagues."

Hence no ring. Let's move on.

Conor asked Feinmann what he had been told of the mission.

"I knew Ettore Majorana well, but I haven't seen him in nine years. We spent a good deal of time together in Rome and Leipzig during the winter of thirty-two/thirty-three."

"Do you speak Italian?" Emily asked.

"Then...no. A little since. We communicated like many

scientists do: with numbers. We would exchange formulas, equations. For a while, we were inseparable."

"So, you're telling me you'll be able to determine whether this guy is an impostor of the real Majorana?"

"Yes. Quite frankly, I think that part should be easy."

"Do you think you can convince him to join the Allies in weapons research?" Emily asked.

"To join the good guys?" Conor added.

"Ha, that's what Lieutenant Colonel Groves said when we met. Almost used those same words," Feinmann said. "You two think alike."

"You didn't answer the question."

"This is what I told Groves." Feinmann glanced at Emily, then Conor. "It's a long shot for sure. All I can do is try."

Thirty minutes later, Conor, Emily, Sean, and Feinmann, now wearing headsets with throat mics so they could communicate over the roar of the Pratt & Whitneys, had taken a break from getting to know Feinmann. DiLazzaro had brought a thermos of joe in from the flight engineer's compartment, passed around tin cups, then retreated into the compartment. Conor slipped out the picture of Constance Sullivan from his breast pocket.

"Who's that?" Emily asked.

Conor looked up at Emily, lying on her side with her head propped up on a crooked arm.

"Just a new member of the Thorn family. Right, Sean?" Conor hoped he sounded skeptically humorous.

"I guess you could say that," Sean said.

"Conor?" Emily prodded.

"Later, Emily," Conor said, which was met with an icy stare from Emily. He turned to Feinmann. "So, tell me, what's Majorana like?"

Feinmann took a sip from his cup, then wrapped both hands around it, trying to soak up some fading warmth. "Quiet. An introvert. Didn't like to be a part of groups. And he certainly was never one to seek out fame. He could be stubborn. He fought off many calls for him to publish his theories, and he refused nearly all of them." Feinmann hesitated for a moment, then took another sip. "A shame, really. Science was such a big part of who he was."

"Are you surprised that he showed up in a monastery?" Emily said.

"No. Not at all. There's a possibility that he saw well beyond the vision of other theoretical physicists and found something petrifying and unspeakable, something that the world would regret—something he was powerless to stop. I sensed he was a troubled man. I think anyone who was exposed to him would have seen that. Troubled by what, I can't exactly say. He was an... unquiet genius." Feinmann nodded. "Yes, that's an apt description for my friend Ettore."

"If your description of Majorana is even slightly close to being on the mark, it doesn't sound like someone who would help us or the Nazis," Conor said.

"Maybe you're right, Conor," Sean said. "But the Nazis have done some horrendous things, even with no super weapons. They must be stopped. I am sure Majorana can grasp that."

DiLazzaro leaned into the living quarters. "Can you all swim?"

Conor was startled by the question—though now that he thought about it, he was more surprised he hadn't thought to ask it himself. Conor, Emily, and Sean either voiced an affirmation or nodded.

"What about you?" DiLazzaro asked, looking at Feinmann.

He nodded slowly.

"Good. Don't be shocked if you get a little wet on our jaunt to the beach. Maybe a lot wet."

CHAPTER THIRTY-THREE

2000 Hours, Monday, December 14, 1942
Apartment of Monsignor Puchini, Via di Porta Fabbrica, Rome

That night, the mood of the patrons seated in Puchini's favorite restaurant was somber. Il Giubileo, long used as a place to meet his various embassy contacts, was lacking its usual jovial banter, toasting, and laughter. The clinking of silverware on plates and the occasional quietly announced request from a diner was all he heard that night. The sobering news that Naples was bombed coupled with a report released by Mussolini that 40,000 Italians had been killed in action and over 230,000 taken prisoner since the war began was too much for Romans to ignore. As was the severe heartburn that his meal of saltimbocca ignited beneath his breastbone. The taste of stomach acid crawling up into his throat made him regret telling the waiter to marinate the saltimbocca in wine rather than his usual choice of olive oil.

The walk down Via di Porta Cavalleggeri toward his apartment and the cool air helped relieve his condition somewhat. As he neared his apartment, he quickened his pace when he noticed that he was being followed by a clutter of feral cats that had gotten the scent of the chopped chicken giblets he carried in a paper bag for his beloved Zitto. Rome's feral cat population seemed to grow more fearless as the war news became bleaker.

Upon entering the apartment, before he turned on any lights, he called out to his Zitto. The cat, who usually came scampering from his preferred resting spot on the living room couch at the first sound of the key rattling the door's lock, did not greet him.

He switched on a light in the foyer and called out again, "Zitto, I have your favorite dish…chicken giblets. Zitto!"

Puchini walked down the hallway that led to the darkened living area and flipped the light switch. He flinched; the bag of giblets fell to the floor. He ceased breathing for a spell, and his heart quickened. He never allowed visitors to his apartment. Not even family.

"Hello, Monsignor Puchini. Welcome home." He recognized the man who sat on his couch holding Zitto in is lap. He knew him as Dante, Silvio Dante, one of Commander Adolfo Soleti's deputies in the Vatican Gendarmerie. Zitto stared at the bag of giblets on the floor and struggled to free itself from the man's fleshy, tobacco-stained hands. Dante was in his midthirties, though the early loss of hair and a premature graying of what remained would have most people assuming he was much older. His mustache, a mix of black and gray, was neatly trimmed. Dante's pudgy face was framed by long, thick sideburns that had been fashionable in the twenties. His face showed signs of late-day stubble. His bulbous nose was a light pink, making one think that he had a cold and was constantly blowing it. But Puchini knew it was from drink. That rumor had been widely circulated around Vatican City for some time. Dante was also known for an oddity. He carried with him a small camera and would often be seen taking pictures like a tourist as he moved within the walls of the Vatican.

"What are you doing here, Dante? And how did you get in?"

Dante stroked the spotted tabby with one hand while the other held the cat firmly in his lap. "The second question is unimportant. As for the first…" His words trailed off. He answered by pointing to a large brown envelope on a side table at the end of the couch.

"What is that?" Puchini asked as stomach acid crept up the back of his throat.

"Well, there are two ways to find out. One is for me to describe the envelope's contents, and the other is for you to open it and see for yourself. I like the second way. The contents speak so clearly for themselves." Zitto fidgeted under Dante's grasp, which he then tightened instantly, producing a deep guttural hiss.

"Let the cat go."

"In due time, monsignor." He stopped stroking the cat. "Now open the envelope," Dante said in a tone that made it clear it was an order and that he was growing impatient.

Puchini kept his gaze locked on Dante and took small, tentative steps to the table. He donned a pair of wire-framed glasses from his coat pocket. The envelope was not sealed and was thick to his touch. He reached in and pulled out a stack of photos. The photo on top was a picture taken of Puchini from a distance of fifty feet or so. He remembered the occasion. He had just concluded a meeting with a midlevel member of the German Embassy at a trattoria near the embassy. He shot a look at Dante, who smiled broadly. He quickly thumbed through the rest of the photos. The context of them all was similar—Puchini with various members of embassies outside the walls of Vatican City. Some showed interactions between him and members of the American and British embassies, before they vacated their embassies and were housed inside the Vatican for their safety after war was declared between them and the Axis. At least half the photos showed Puchini receiving an envelope from his companion.

"Why are you spying on me? What have I done to warrant such treatment?"

Dante chuckled. "You very well know the answer."

Puchini dropped the photos on the table and removed his glasses. He knew where this encounter was leading. That realization felt like a heavy weight sitting on his chest, making it difficult to breathe.

"You have been selling information, sensitive information, to anyone who will buy it. Allied or Axis, communist or nationalist. Neutral or belligerent. Your services were open to anyone. We have been investigating you for some time."

"The gendarmerie or you?"

"What do you think?"

Puchini pocketed his glasses. "I have never sold anything to anyone. Yes, it is true that in my role as head of the Vatican News Agency, I have relationships with many people who hold diplomatic roles here in Rome. And some of these people are kind enough to help with my living expenses. And I humbly accept their gifts. Just like—"

"Stop talking." Dante's face was taking on the same color as his swollen nose. "Do you take me for a fool? Every one of those whom you have met have been questioned by me. Not one said they weren't paying for information."

Puchini, his knees weak, dropped onto the end of the couch. He swallowed hard to tamp down the stomach acid. A bead of perspiration rolled off his forehead into his eye.

"His Holiness and the secretary of state would be stunned to hear of your activities. I am sure they will think that your offenses rise to the level of defrocking."

"What do you plan to do?" Puchini said, staring at his tightly balled fists.

"Ah, yes. This is the most important part. It's not what *I* plan to do but...you."

Puchini fastened his gaze on Dante. "Me?"

"Yes. You have until this time Thursday to gather funds in the amount of one hundred thousand lira. You do that, and all evidence of your treachery will be destroyed, and I shall move on to other business that concerns His Holiness. You fail, and a set of those photos and my report will be sent to Commander Soleti."

"That's impossible. I have no such means to accomplish that."

"That, monsignor, is not my concern." Dante shoved the cat off his lap and smoothed out his pants. Zitto pounced on the bag of spilled giblets. Dante stood and looked down on Puchini. "You are lucky." Puchini craned his neck and eyed the man. "While I sat here before you arrived, I gave a thought to snapping your cat's neck to impress upon you that I am serious. But I don't think I would have been able to forgive myself." Dante walked toward the hallway. Without looking back, he said one word: "Thursday."

CHAPTER THIRTY-FOUR

2200 Hours, Monday, December 14, 1942
Apartment on the Via delle Fornaci, Rome

When Falco—his code name, which he always detested—arrived at the back door to the apartment building, he turned to survey the narrow lane out of habit, even though in the last four years since his posting in Rome, there had never been anyone he found suspicious. Occasionally, he spotted a familiar person dropping trash into a bin in the building's rear. Tonight, the lane was devoid of any activity.

He had been the one who picked out the apartment for his mistress. It was perfectly located to obscure his comings and goings, which were on odd-numbered days. It was only steps away from the back door of the building and allowed him to make a quick exit, should that be necessary. He limited his time with her to odd-numbered days for one reason: out of respect for his wife. He was sure she knew of his mistress's existence. A majority of powerful men in Rome had one, some more than one. When he thought of it, it made him shake his head in amazement. What his wife did not know, he was sure, was that his mistress was also the main radio operator for the Rome-based NKVD spy network.

It had been his idea to place the transmitter just two blocks away from Vatican Radio's transmitter. Transmitting on a frequency near the normal wavelength it used allowed his transmissions to hide behind those of his ecclesiastical neighbor. So far, his location had not been detected by the Servizio Informazioni Militare. When not in use, he had instructed Maria to hide the transmitter behind a massive ornate radiator.

He inserted his key and quietly entered the apartment. He stood by the closed door, pressed an ear to the surface, and listened for any footsteps in the hallway. Hearing none, he entered the sitting room. They set the radio up on a four-foot square chrome-and-Formica table that normally displayed two photos, one of Maria's mother and father, and another of her five siblings. The statue of the Virgin Mary, her head bowed and her hands clasped in prayer, was normally positioned between the two photos. It was now lying, along with the photos, on the nearby sofa. Maria was not in the room. Falco looked at his watch; their transmission window was set to open in ten minutes. He slipped off his trench coat and threw it on the couch, covering up the photos and the praying Virgin Mary.

"Ciao, Maria," he said, announcing his arrival. She walked through a doorway screened by a beaded curtain, a glass of red wine in her hand. As she handed it to him, she rose on her toes and kissed him on the cheek. "How much have you had?"

"Please, it was just a glass with my supper."

He put down the glass of wine next to the radio, then looked at her face and didn't speak. Silence always unnerved her.

She turned away. "And another half glass, but I stopped two hours ago."

"Are you clearheaded enough for tonight?"

"Of course. It is always first on my mind. It's just that…" Maria trailed off.

"Just what?"

"I get lonely. There's no one to speak to. And I've become afraid to go outside."

Falco shook his head. She was becoming more needy as their time together passed. "We'll talk of this later. Let's get ready."

The transmission from Moscow that night began with the same words as it always does: *We are from the north.* It was Falco and Maria's turn to transmit information requested during their last window. Tonight, that included information regarding Italian troop movements to the Eastern Front, specifically Stalingrad.

Falco passed a sheet of paper to Maria that included an enciphered message concerning the decision of Mussolini to reinforce the Alpini divisions: 2nd Division, the 3rd Division Julia, and the 4th Division Cuneense. As she was transmitting, Falco thought again how expensive the information was to come by. He made a mental note to ask for added funds in their next window. Moscow's response followed quickly. Maria transcribed it, and then they signed off. She handed the transcription to him and started to break down the transmitter. Falco saw her hands were shaking. He had no time to inquire what was wrong as he was eager to read what Moscow wanted from him.

It took him slightly longer to decipher Moscow's response because of its length and the unusual nature of their request—unusual enough that he deciphered it twice. The process was laborious. It was a mixed alphabet substitution cipher, where the ciphertext alphabet starts with a keyword and removes the repeated letters from a plaintext alphabet, then follows the keyword with the remaining letters in the alphabet in the leftover order. The keyword for that night's mixed alphabet keyword was *marmont*.

The message laid out details of a mission to extract an Italian physicist who was living in a monastery east of Rome. He was to apprehend him and make his way to Switzerland with him via the Switzerland–Italy rail line. The man's name, Ettore Majorana, was vaguely familiar to him. He remembered seeing photos of Majorana in the newspapers when he'd first arrived in Rome from Florence. He was a frail-looking man, diminutive in stature.

Maria came from the kitchen with another glass of wine. She stood at his back and read over his shoulder. "Why is this scientist so important?"

He shrugged, turned around, and wrapped his arms around her waist. He rested his head on her breasts and she returned the gesture by wrapping her free right arm around his neck.

He turned his head a little so she could hear him. "Maybe we don't have enough scientists. Perhaps they are all on the Eastern Front, fighting the Nazis." He rose from his chair and went into the bathroom, where he burned the decrypt and flushed it down the toilet.

Falco was too tired for sex. He had been up early, meeting with various members of his network, reaping the rewards of their spy craft. His wife would be surprised to see him that night. As he put on his trench coat, he could see Maria was taken aback.

"Where are you going? Are you not staying?" she asked, the fingers of her hand, now shaking, covering her mouth almost in fear of what he was about to say.

"My son is ill. I need to see him." He turned away but turned back again when he heard her whimper. "What is wrong with you? You've been acting strange tonight."

She moved to the door to the hallway and blocked it. The aggressive move surprised him. "I am worried. I have seen trucks in the neighborhood for the past few days. Detection trucks."

The muscles in Falco's face loosened, and his jaw dropped. "Why didn't you mention this before?"

"I don't know. I…" She hesitated. "I didn't want to anger you. I was worried that you would break off our relationship if I angered you."

Falco let a string of swear words fly and began pacing, his hands in his pockets. It was clear the location was close to being burned. He stopped pacing and softened his demeanor and slowly slipped off his coat, which caused Maria's face to brighten. He approached her. "It's fine. I'm not worried. There is a plan for this type of development. You should not worry." He wrapped his arms around her and hugged her. The glass of wine, nearly finished, was still clutched in her hand. She pushed away, turned, and took a step toward the kitchen. He smashed the leaden cudgel he surreptitiously pulled from his coat pocket into the side of her head. Her eyes closed immediately, even before the sound of the wineglass smashing to the floor filled the room.

He bent and checked for a pulse. It was weak. He dragged her to the bedroom, where he found an empty wine bottle on the nightstand. He brushed a movie magazine off the bed and dumped her body on the covers. Before it stopped bouncing on the mattress, he was on top of her, wrapping his hands around her throat. He waited for thirty seconds before he checked her pulse, finding none. He then raised her eyelids, where he saw burst blood vessels in the whites of her eyes.

Ten minutes later, after packing up the transmitter and wiping down all the surfaces, he looked around. He didn't need to worry about any personal items—he'd never brought any there. No change of clothes, no personal items, nothing.

Out in the lane behind the building, he tossed the apartment key in a trash bin and headed home, wondering exactly how he was going to kidnap an Italian scientist who seemed to have found God.

CHAPTER THIRTY-FIVE

2230 Hours, Monday, December 14, 1942
Off the Coast of Anzio, Italy

The luminous dial on Conor's watch said 22:30 hours when he first noticed that Jack Waddon had throttled back the engines and they'd begun their descent toward the Tyrrhenian Sea off the coast of Anzio. The PBY hit the water's surface with a jarring slam that made the narrow, corrugated panels that comprised the catwalk in their compartment clang loudly. The second jolt was half as jarring, a sign that Waddon knew how to handle his PBY. But as the plane settled onto the sea, it wasn't hard to notice they had landed in rough waters, given the pitching they were experiencing.

Wearing life jackets under their combat packs, they shuffled into the already crammed waist gunner's compartment and watched DiLazzaro slide open the port side plexiglass blister. The rush of clean, cold sea air filled the compartment in a flash. DiLazzaro and the other waist gunner wrestled the inflatables through the tight opening and dropped them into the sea, DiLazzaro handed over the leads to each raft to his partner. He sat on the bottom edge of the blister's opening and turned around.

"It's pretty rough, Captain. Just like you said," DiLazzaro shouted.

Conor's head swiveled toward the bow, and he saw Waddon leaning into the compartment. "Good luck. Stay dry. And get moving," Waddon said, his voice getting louder with each word.

Conor gave a thumbs-up and turned back to see the second waist gunner passing DiLazzaro their duffel bags and the packs with their equipment. The last thing to be passed down was a waterproof duffel containing the brown leather Type 3 MK 2 Transceiver suitcase radio, followed by Emily and Feinmann, into DiLazzaro's raft. Conor was next to climb out. As he dragged his left leg over the bottom edge of the blister, he caught his first glance of a star-filled sky. He splashed into the inflatable, which was already awash with seawater, then reached up to help Sean down into the rear of the raft and handed him a paddle. DiLazzaro's inflatable was already headed toward the beach, which Conor estimated was a mile away.

Conor and Sean dug deep into the churning sea with their paddles. Wind was whipping at the sea's surface, creating whitecaps, which threw off salty spray that stung Conor's eyes. Up ahead, Conor saw Emily and DiLazzaro paddling furiously, pulling at the surface with their paddles. Feinmann was gripping a rope that ran along the top edge of the inflatable with two hands.

Get to the beach. Get. To. The. Beach.

Both inflatables made progress, but Emily and DiLazzaro were pulling away, increasing the distance between the two inflatables. Conor had been worried that Sean, not used to a physically demanding operation, would lose some steam on the way in, just as was happening. A powerful wave lifted Conor and Sean at least five feet, then dropped them into a watery trough. Then another wave lifted them again, giving Conor the opportunity to pick out Emily and DiLazzaro up ahead. Then Emily and DiLazzaro's raft disappeared behind another wave. A second later, he heard Emily's first shout: "Feinmann!"

"Emily," Conor yelled, breathing rapidly.

"It's Feinmann...He went over."

He can swim, and he has a life jacket. Keep your cool. This is not a repeat of the Chesapeake Bay fiasco. This is not a repeat...

"Come on, Sean. Paddle harder...faster, and don't stop. Just head for the sound of the waves crashing on the beach. I've got a floater to find."

The only response from Sean was a series of grunts as he ramped up his efforts. Conor slipped over the side and swam toward where he'd last spotted Emily and DiLazzaro's raft. The combat pack and his life jacket restricted his arm movement, slowing his progress. He headed for what he could make out was someone thrashing about. Feinmann came into view—or at least, his arms flailing in the air did. A wave propelled him toward Feinmann, and he threw his arm around his neck before the same wave pushed the man farther away.

"Joseph…I got you. Calm down," Conor said, his mouth within an inch of Feinmann's ear. "We're going to head for the beach, so don't fight me. Just let me do this."

Conor's thoughts darted from the Chesapeake training incident to the present. It was in that moment that he first heard the crashing of waves on a beach. When his mind folded back into a moment from the Chesapeake, he felt a tug on his legs. Something was pulling him away from the beach. It was something from his dark dreams. It had to be. He could hear waves pounding the beach. Then he realized he wasn't just reliving a dark moment from the Chesapeake tragedy—it was happening now.

He let out a fierce yell and kicked his legs with all the force he could gather, then kept on kicking until a wave lifted them high in the air and drove them toward the beach.

Another wave forced them down, this time onto the beach, where both men lay on the sand, waves breaking over them. Feinmann was puking up seawater. Conor got his legs under him and rose as Emily and DiLazzaro ran up to them. Emily started to shove her hands under Conor's armpits, but he waved her off. DiLazzaro, his hands gripping Feinmann's life vest, dragged him out of the surf and deposited the physically spent scientist on the hard, packed sand at the water's edge, then knelt beside the gasping man.

"I thought you said you could swim," DiLazzaro said, seawater running down his face.

Feinmann leaned over and vomited again. "I lied."

Sean appeared, struggling to drag the inflatable loaded with their gear. When he reached the group, he collapsed in an exhausted heap.

"Why would you do that? We would have been better prepared," DiLazzaro said. "Maybe added a third raft."

"And maybe left you behind," Conor said, rising to his feet.

"I shoulda known when you didn't answer me right away," DiLazzaro said.

Feinmann struggled to his feet. "I didn't want to be the only one who said he couldn't swim." He shook his head. "It was vain of me. I'm sorry."

Conor didn't have time to deal with vanity at that moment. He, Emily, and DiLazzaro scrambled to unload their gear from the inflatables and move it all up the beach. Once unloaded, they tossed their life vests into the rafts. DiLazzaro grabbed the leads to the two rafts, lashed them together, and headed out into the surf, back to the PBY.

Brave man, that Newark guy.

He turned back. "Good luck to you all." Then a wave hit him.

#

After watching DiLazzaro paddle out into the surf, Conor led Emily, Sean, and Feinmann up the beach, each carrying a duffel bag. Conor had the duffel loaded with weapons and other toys while Emily handled the Type 3 Transceiver. Feinmann, carrying a smaller duffel, looked drained and still shaky from his battle with the angry sea. He stayed close to Sean. Once they arrived at the base of the rocky gradient, Conor looked up. The trail from the beach rose rapidly and disappeared in darkness about ten yards up. He pulled a flashlight from his duffel and directed the beam up the trail.

"What did Eddy say? 'Shouldn't be too much of a challenge'?" Conor said. It might be just fifty yards, but to Conor, it looked much steeper than Eddy let on.

"We need to get moving. We're behind schedule. Don't want to miss our ride," Emily said.

"Okay, I'll lead. Then Sean. Then Feinmann. Emily, you pull up the rear." Conor pulled his Colt 1911A1 from his shoulder holster and drew back the slide to chamber a round. Emily, her semi-automatic already in her hand, ejected the magazine of her Walther PPK, inspected it, and reseated it back into the grip. Conor looked at Sean. "You all right, so far?"

"So far," Sean answered as he ran his hand through his sea-soaked hair.

Conor nodded. "Let's get moving."

His waterlogged clothing combined with the nighttime air chilled Conor. But the hike, more arduous than expected, served to keep much of the cold at bay, as long as they kept moving.

Ten minutes later, at the top of the trail, he dropped his gear alongside a crumbling porous limestone wall of the Villa Imperiale. The road Eddy mentioned should have been due east of their position, about thirty yards distant. It wasn't visible from his position though, and neither was their contact. Two minutes later, Sean appeared, his breathing labored, and let his duffel bag fall to the ground before slumping against the wall to catch his breath. Feinmann followed suit. Emily, however, looked none the worse for wear as she dropped her gear next to Conor's.

"Pretty quiet," Emily said.

"That could be good and bad," Conor said. "Let's leave Sean and Feinmann here so they can recover some, and you and I search for the mayor." Sean gave them a feeble wave as they set off.

The growth along the side of the path was about knee-high and danced in the nighttime breeze. Conor thought about leaving the path to eliminate the sound of his boots crunching on the gravel when he heard someone up ahead. A pinpoint light appeared, a match burning white-hot, then flickering out.

"*Sei in ritardo*," a male voice said.

Conor aimed his flashlight where the match had appeared and turned it on. Whoever it was, they were blinded by the light and raised an arm to shield their eyes.

"He says we're late," Emily said.

"I got that," Conor said. Their contact lowered his arm when Conor used the flashlight to scan the man, from his head to his feet, then back to his face.

"Where's the mayor? Where's our contact?"

"What do you mean?" Emily asked.

"This guy is a foot taller than our contact and younger. Just ask him, Em."

Emily asked, which elicited a stream of protestations from whoever was standing before them. Emily leaned toward Conor, who kept his Colt and flashlight pointed at the mystery man. "He says the mayor is no longer in the picture. His name is Dominic Canali. He mentioned something about the mayor—"

"Has...disappeared. It is just as well," Canali said in passable English. "As he lost his enthusiasm for the people's cause. He was lacking as the leader of our small, fiercely committed group."

"Do you mean he's dead?" Conor asked.

"Ahh, all I know is that he is no longer in Collepardo."

Conor shot a look at Emily. "What do you think?"

"We don't have any options. We can't stay here."

"I suggest we leave this place. My truck is this way," Canali said, pointing in the road's direction. "Was there not to be a third?" No sooner had he asked than Conor heard gravel-crunching footsteps stopping just behind him. "Aah, yes. The man of God. But he brings a friend. A fourth. We were not told of a fourth person."

"Plans change. Sorry we couldn't get you on the phone to tell you," Conor said.

"Who are you?" Canali said.

"Joseph—"

"Quiet!" Conor said. Emily turned to Feinmann, her index finger pressed against her lips.

After they loaded their gear into the back of an aged and di-lapidated Fiat delivery truck, its driver-side door painted in now faded and flaking lettering announcing that it was owned by the *Café Vecchio*, they boarded. Emily sat in the middle of the front seat, Conor in the front passenger seat. Sean and Feinmann had to suffer, sitting on wood boxes that contained tomatoes according to the colorful labels. They were on the road for only two minutes when Conor started the questioning.

"Do mayors usually just disappear around here?"

"I would not know...ah, I did not catch your name, signore."

"I didn't throw it, Canali." Conor hoped the man detected the tone of distrust in his response.

"No, you did not. As for your question, I would not know. I have only lived in Collepardo and have known just two mayors in my lifetime. The first died of a stroke while making love to his mistress. Quite the...scandal. Is that the right word, signora?"

"That works, Mr. Canali. Tell me, what have you been told of why we are here?" Emily asked.

"The mayor, Signore Sarandrea, briefed me, as I was his second, with what he said was all that he knew: that there were people who needed to find someone hiding at the Certosa di Trisulti and that, in exchange for a generous gift of support, our small but determined group of antifascists were to assist in whatever way we were asked."

Conor scoffed. Canali had recited the answer, as if it were written for him—an actor who didn't flub one word, Conor thought.

He pulled his flashlight from his field jacket pocket and twisted in his seat toward the rear of the truck. He trained its beam where Sean and Feinmann were seated. Sean's head was canted against the truck's side wall, Feinmann leaning up against Sean, his head nestled on Sean's shoulder, fast asleep. The man was drooling. Conor turned back around.

"We know nothing about you. Fill us in," he said.

"I manage the Café Vecchio. It is owned by the mayor and his wife. The mayor and I are…were close. His wife and I…ehh, not so much."

"Your English is very good. Why is that?"

"Thank you. I take pride in it. I have a brother in America. In Boston. Little Italy. He owns a restaurant there. It is small but profitable. I have worked there in the summers for the last few years, when the tourists come to visit. I love America. I—"

"Do you know anyone inside the monastery?" Conor asked, quickly growing weary of Canali's faint adulation of America.

"Yes. My wife, Claretta…she is sometimes sickly, which necessitates visits to the monastery's pharmacy. It specializes in herbal remedies. The brothers…they are quite industrious and skilled in making medicines from the plants that grow around the Certosa. Brother Alfieri, the monastery's administrator, knows me well. He is very strict about outsiders entering the monastery."

That's not what I wanted to hear. He hadn't thought they opened the place up on the weekends to let the townspeople gawk at the monks, but them being strict about no visitors was not good.

"And I know of a plumber from Collepardo who has been working at the monastery for several days."

"Name?" Emily asked, before Conor could form the word.

"Bruno Fabrizio."

Conor snorted. He had a chemistry teacher back in high school named Fabrizio.

"Fabrizio and me, we are not on speaking terms. He does poor work that I, as manager of the café, will not pay for." Canali turned his head toward Emily and Conor. "He hates me."

CHAPTER THIRTY-SIX

0300 Hours, Tuesday, December 15, 1942
Apartment of Dominic Canali, Collepardo, Italy

Immediately after they arrived at Canali's apartment, located above Café Vecchio, Conor and Emily stashed their gear in the attic, since the apartment was anything but spacious. On their drive from Anzio, Canali had said there were only two bedrooms, so the sleeping arrangements were going to be catch-as-catch-can. The apartment was well-kept but sparsely furnished. Next to the compact kitchen was the sitting room with a simple wood table and four battered chairs, a couch along the wall, and two stuffed armchairs, angled facing the couch, that looked like they were secondhand. There was a rickety set of double doors which led to a narrow balcony that only had room for several flowerpots that still contained offerings, now dead. The aroma of a recently cooked meal still hung in the air, reminding all of them they had eaten little since they'd left the Hotel St. Georges.

Conor, Emily, and Sean took seats at the table along with Canali. Feinmann sat on the couch. Conor wasn't long into the discussion of their next moves when he noticed Feinmann drift off. He was about to say something when Emily touched his arm.

"Let him sleep. I'll pull him aside later and fill him in with what he needs to know," she said.

"All right. I'll be brief. We all need some rack time," Conor said. "Canali, do you know where this plumber lives?"

"Yes. He owns a small farmhouse north of town. About a half-mile off the main road. Why do you ask?"

"Because he's our first stop this morning, before we head to the monastery."

"Purpose?" Emily asked.

"I think we should at least try to color in some more information about the monastery. I feel we don't know enough."

Emily nodded her agreement and turned to Canali. "Let's start with you. You said that you've been there several times for medicines. What else can you tell us?"

"As I said, I've only been to the pharmacy. They don't let people access any other area except for Christmas and Easter. They are very protective of their monks and their property."

"Maybe you should go over the plan one more time," Sean said. "I don't want to make any mistakes."

Conor had realized that a guns-blazing approach would fall short and only set alarm bells ringing. "Like I said back in Algiers, we use the soft approach by deploying our secret weapon."

Emily turned to Sean and winked, anointing Father Sean Sullivan the secret weapon.

"You and Canali will go knock on their door. Canali will say that he is only helping his new Irish friend. Someone who stopped at the Café Vecchio asking for directions to the Certosa di Trisulti. Sean will explain that he is experiencing a crisis of faith and is seeking permission to enter the monastery for a brief spell and could he please meet with the prior. Assuming that they will either balk or just say no to someone who shows up on their doorstep, Sean will ask if they received the letter from Cardinal Massy, his superior. They will say no because we sent no letter, but Sean will present his copy of it."

Sean leaned forward. "What if—"

"They don't grant you a meeting with the prior? Which is who, Canali?"

"That would be Father Misasi. He's been there since 1937. He's…"

Conor held up his hand to stop him. "If they say come back another time, you ask for a tour of the place before you leave. If they say come in and meet with Father Misasi, you plead your case for a room, so you can come to terms with your crisis, and while you're there, do some recon and locate our man. Canali will be our go-between, since we can't really show our faces on the premises. He'll show up looking for more medicine and ask to see his new friend." There wasn't any reaction from anyone at the table. All he heard was Feinmann's snort and a gulp of air.

After a slight hesitation, Sean sat back in his chair, which creaked loudly, and then he cracked a smile. "I haven't done any acting since I was a wee one, when I played Scrooge in *A Christmas Carol.*"

"I'm sure you were a hit. Okay, let's get some sleep. Tomorrow could be a big day."

Less than ten minutes later, Conor, Emily, and Sean had settled in, Canali leaving one light in the kitchen on while he retired. Conor and Emily were in the two worn stuffed armchairs, and Sean shared Feinmann's couch. Canali had doled out some blankets that barely kept them warm. Sean closed his eyes and bowed his head for thirty seconds, which was followed by the sign of the cross.

"Include us in that prayer, Sean?" Conor whispered.

"Of course…I have for days." He was asleep less than a minute later.

"Are you going to tell me about that picture you had on the flight?" Emily said.

Conor had been expecting the question, and as much as he wanted to catch some z's, he told her. Her gasp was loud enough to stir both Sean and Feinmann.

After a long pause, Emily said, "Many families have secrets. And they are often better kept secret given the hurt they can cause if revealed."

Conor nodded. "And what secrets does the Bright family have?"

Emily was silent for a while before telling him that someone who had once been part of her life, a RAF pilot she was told had been shot down in Northern France and was presumed dead, had visited her in the Underground War Rooms. The Luftwaffe shot him down in May 1940, over the beaches of Grande-Synthe, just due west of Dunkirk. He was severely wounded, and a French family took him in. Once he was well, he joined the French resistance for a time and eventually, with their help, made it to Spain. They couldn't talk at length that day, as she had important work to do, so they agreed to meet the next day. The day before her miscarriage.

"I can tell you this because I know you'll understand. I once loved him."

Conor hoped Emily did not hear the quick intake of air. Was this back-from-the-dead man the reason she put off their wedding? Did she still love him?

Emily, as if she were tracking his inner pangs of doubt and disappointment, went on: "Or I thought I did…until I met you. Then I truly knew what love was."

CHAPTER THIRTY-SEVEN

0600 Hours, Tuesday, December 15, 1942
Apartment of Dominic Canali, Collepardo, Italy

Conor and Emily were leaning against the door to a small garage off an alley behind the café. The early morning air was brisk. Puffs of breath rose and quickly disappeared in the darkness that the sunrise would soon overtake. They were waiting for Canali, Sean, and Feinmann, the last of whom had woken up feeling queasy.

"Did you manage to sleep?" Conor asked as he shoved his hands in his pockets.

"No. Not really. Never could sitting up in a chair."

Conor nodded. "Tell me his name. The RAF pilot."

Emily levered herself off the door, took a few steps into the alley, then turned to Conor. "His name is William Richardson. He grew up not far from Southend-on-Sea. In Chelmsford. A fine gentleman. I told him I was so relieved that he was alive. But…"

"But?" *I hate buts.*

"I also told him I had moved on and so should he."

"How did he take that news?"

Emily tilted her head to the side and looked as if she was recalling the scene. "He looked hurt. For just a moment. He took it like the gentleman he is."

Conor nodded and pried himself off the wall and pulled his hands from his pockets. "Is he the reason you wanted to call off the wedding? Maybe seeing him caused you to have some doubts?"

Before Emily could respond, Canali, Sean, and Feinmann appeared on the back stairway leading from the apartment to the alley.

CHAPTER THIRTY-EIGHT

0700 Hours, Tuesday, December 15, 1942
Vatican City, Palace of the Governorate, Rome

Cardinal Secretary of State Maglione sat at his desk mentally preparing for his meeting with Colonel Adolfo Soleti, the commander of the Vatican's Pontifical Gendarmerie Corps, the Vatican's own police force. The pope's soldiers were tasked with the protection and security of Vatican City and its extraterritorial properties in Rome as well as locations outside of the city. Their responsibilities also included guarding against political threats and espionage emanating from the Allied and Axis powers that would threaten the neutrality of the Vatican. Maglione's preparation was necessary because of the mounting level of distrust he held for Soleti. But it didn't alarm Maglione that he didn't trust Soleti. He didn't trust a majority of the cardinals, bishops, and archbishops of the Roman Curia, the central body who conducted the affairs of the Catholic Church. The level of dishonesty, self-dealing, and backstabbing bordered on treachery in Maglione's mind.

With Soleti, it was a less-complicated issue of trust. He was too often not deferential—not to Maglione, but to the institutions that comprised the sum total of the Roman Catholic Church. Soleti would often only reluctantly agree with priorities and initiatives that Maglione championed. He would regularly cite that some of the initiatives Maglione wanted the Gendarmerie Corps to oversee did not come under their official purview. Soleti complained about staffing concerns and the lack of resources for training. He had to remind Soleti that he, the cardinal secretary of state, decided what was within the corps' purview, which, on most occasions, elicited a movement of Soleti's head that Maglione sometimes took as both a yes and a no. A half nod and half shake. A movement that Soleti must have practiced often while working in elevated roles inside OVRA, his previous employer, since it came off so naturally. Appointed the prior year, Soleti was still adjusting to life inside the walls of Vatican City. The length of the adjustment period also annoyed Maglione.

Soleti was escorted into Maglione's office by a member of his staff, and after some casual conversation about the overall status of the corps, Maglione shifted the conversation.

"No doubt you've heard Mussolini's recent announcement?"

"Which one are you referring to, Your Eminence?"

"The loss of life. He reports that forty thousand Italians have been killed in action since war broke out. And nearly a quarter of a million are prisoners of war."

Soleti winced. "Those are depressing numbers." His face affected a look of sadness that Maglione didn't buy. "No one can argue that."

"Heartless and maniacal politicians waging war against humanity, against their own people. They may someday pray to the Lord for forgiveness. It is my hope that the Lord will ignore their pleas."

"Something tells me, Your Eminence, that the people you are speaking of do not believe in God. Therefore, prayer is an act not in their repertoire."

"Yes, Colonel, I may give them too much credit." Maglione shifted in his chair, readying himself for another change in subject. "Your source in OVRA, have they mentioned the name Ettore Majorana?"

It was Soleti's turn to fidget in his seat. "Yes. More than one source has mentioned the rumor of his miraculous reappearance."

Maglione had held out hope that news had not reached any government entity, especially the OVRA. It was foolish of him to believe that news of Majorana would have not been leaked beyond His Holiness, himself, and Father Misasi. Pope Pius XII, in 1938 when Majorana disappeared, was the cardinal secretary of state for Pope Pius XI. He approved, along with Pope Pius XI, of Father Misasi's petition to take in the suffering and broken scientist. They were concerned by near maniacal ramblings of Majorana's to Father Misasi when he'd first arrived at the Trisulti Charterhouse about washing his hands of those who sought to develop weapons capable of massive carnage. Majorana had made clear his intention to have nothing to do with any phase of their development. The Holy Father was extremely fond of the Carthusian order and thought it was the perfect place to hide Majorana, at least until the looming war was over.

"Would it be correct to assume that Signore Leto has shared this information with his German counterpart?" Maglione asked, hoping against hope that such news didn't travel that fast.

The question prompted Soleti to squirm and stammer a touch. Maglione thought the man may be doing it to give himself time to think before replying. "Your Eminence, there does seem…to be interest on the part of the Germans in Majorana. It should not be surprising to you."

"At what level is this interest?"

"I am told that it exists at top levels." Soleti paused, seeming to mull over how much to divulge. "They are sending a contingent to the monastery to establish contact with the subject."

His biggest fear realized, Maglione asked, "When did you learn of this?"

This time, the pause was more prolonged. "It must have been a day ago, I believe."

"When were you going to notify me of this?" a peeved Maglione shot back, despite knowing the answer didn't really matter. When Soleti opened his mouth to reply, Maglione flicked his wrist, killing Soleti's response. He sat silent for a moment, his thoughts on what he knew could not happen: Majorana in the hands of a ruthless regime intent on continuing their oppression of the Roman Catholic Church.

Soleti's throat clearing snapped Maglione out of his reverie. He reached into a desk drawer, pulled out a letter, and shoved it across the desk. "Go to Certosa di Trisulti and meet with Father Misasi. Give him this letter. It orders him to turn Majorana over to you.

Bring him immediately to this office. He will be safe here. And, Commander, I forbid you to share any of this with your OVRA sources. Am I understood?"

Soleti took the letter and slipped it into his breast pocket. A familiar smile crossed Soleti's face, one that Maglione always felt betrayed condescension.

CHAPTER THIRTY-NINE

0715 Hours, Tuesday, December 15, 1942
Sanctuary of Our Lady of the Cese

Bruno Fabrizio had tucked a copy of *Il Messaggero* snuggly under his arm, protecting it from the steady rain that was falling as he strode down the path from the Certosa to the sanctuary. When he entered the sanctuary house, he found the main room empty. There was a weak fire hissing and spitting in the fireplace. He called out Brother Bini's name. Seconds later, he heard footsteps coming from the rear of the house. When Brother Bini entered the room and glanced in Bruno's direction, his expression turned from a pinched look of worry to the wide-eyed look of a boy who had just seen the red-suited Babbo Natale on Christmas Eve.

"Bruno!" Majorana yelped. "I was hoping it was you. Did you bring it? The newspaper?"

Bruno nodded once, sharply. Of course, he had already scanned the pages that contained personal messages and ads concerning employment opportunities. He had thought about leaving the newspaper on the table and taking his leave, but he decided otherwise. And now, he felt sorry for Majorana, a feeling that caught him off guard.

Majorana hurried over to him and took the newspaper, spreading out the broadsheet on the wooden table and, his slight frame partially bowed over the table, frantically searched for the appropriate page. Finding it, he ran his index finger down each column.

After the first pass, he shot a split-second glance at Bruno, who briefly looked away. Majorana made another pass, dragging the tip of his finger down each column, this time more deliberately. He stopped and stood erect for several silent moments, staring out into the open space of the room.

"You did mail the letter, yes?" Majorana murmured without turning to look at Bruno.

"I did what you told me to do, Brother Bini." He watched as Majorana's erect posture melted to a point that Bruno thought he was about to faint.

"Please leave, Bruno. Find work in the monastery today. Not here."

#

Majorana scanned the newspaper one more time with the same crushing results, then rolled it up and laid it on top of the sputtering fire. A plume of smoke rose from the newspaper as if in protest at being placed there. Then it burst into flame, followed by pops in quick succession. His hopes of a reunification rose in the chimney along with the last vestiges of the newspaper.

He began walking in a tight circle around the room, his hands seeking warmth inside the wide sleeves of his robe. He began to chant softly in Latin, the Salve Regina, seeking some guidance from the holy Queen, Mother of Mercy. The monophonic, single-pitch melody always soothed his mind, which was constantly racing. This went on for less than a minute, and then he began mixing in questions among his chants.

"Was this a simple mistake?" *Eia, ergo, advocata nostra, illos tuos.* "Did I check the publication date of the newspaper?" *Misericordes oculos ad nos converte.* "Could it have been the wrong edition?" *Et Jesum, benedictum fructum ventris tui.* "Did Bruno lie to me?" *Nobis post hoc exsilium ostende.* The next questions put an end to his chanting and walking. "Does my family wish that I stay away and not return? What would be the reason for that decision? Did I hurt them so deeply they cannot find forgiveness in their hearts?" Majorana spun around and headed for the door. He yanked it open, letting it slam against the wall, then raised his cowl, hanging his head as he trudged up the path to the monastery.

Father Misasi must be told.

#

The prior sat hunched over at his desk, his nose just inches away from the document he was scanning, his glasses nestled on the tip of his nose. He looked up when Majorana slipped through the partially opened door and advanced toward the desk.

The sunlight streamed in from a large, curved bay window behind him. The translucently thin curtains on either side of the window were cinched halfway down their length to allow a generous amount of sunlight to fill the office. In the corner of the room, there was a single kneeler that faced a sizable crucifix. The kneeler's pad displayed two indentations where it had welcomed, many times over, the bony knees of the elderly prior.

"Aah, Brother Bini, I am surprised to see you." The prior stole a glance at a pocket watch that sat beside the document he was reading. "Shouldn't you be immersed in the Lectio Divina?"

Majorana hung his head. The Lectio Divina is a meditative reading of the Bible. It was a part of the structured day of Carthusian monks. But today, he was too disturbed and disconcerted to sit reciting psalms. "Prior, I have come to unburden myself," he said, his voice low and gravelly.

Misasi took off his glasses and sat back. "Do you mean you have sins to confess, Brother?"

Majorana lifted his head. "No, Prior. I have not sinned. But I have done something that you will be…displeased with."

Misasi inclined his head toward a chair set alongside the desk. Once he was settled, Misasi, elbows on his desk, pressed his hands together as if in prayer. "Go on, Brother Bini. What have you done that you think I will not approve of?"

Majorana had convinced himself that the only reason for his family's lack of response was that they never received the letter. He was unwilling to accept that the letter was lost by the mail service. No, not in Mussolini's Italy. It had to be that it was never sent. His family loved him. Which, Majorana realized years ago, was the engine that drove his shame and disgust with himself. How could he leave his family in such a deep emotional limbo?

Majorana looked down at his hands, which were lying in his lap. He saw them tremble. He placed his left hand on top of the scarred right hand and gripped it tightly to quell the tremble. "Prior, I have attempted to contact my family, seeking their forgiveness." He blurted the words rapidly.

Misasi dropped his hands and laid them, palms down, on his desk. "You...you... How did you do that?"

Majorana raised his head and looked directly at the prior, whose face betrayed the look of someone deceived. Majorana divulged his dealings with Bruno Fabrizio: the letter he sent to his family in Rome, the lack of a response in the newspaper, his feeling of utter shame for having gone behind the back of the prior, ending with a description of the hollow feeling left by the nonresponse. When done, he returned his gaze to his hands.

"Brother Bini, I am almost shocked beyond words. Are you happy here?"

"Of that I am certain, Prior. But I have been dealing with a growing feeling over the past year that I did something so horrible to my family, and I wanted...I *needed* their forgiveness." He paused and looked at Misasi. "I am ashamed to say that God's forgiveness has become insufficient."

Misasi gasped.

"Prior, I owe you so much. You have worked hard to protect me since I arrived. I am indebted to you and the Vicar of Christ for... saving my life. Had His Holiness not approved my request to be taken in, I would have—"

"Why do you want to leave now? It makes no sense to me." Misasi said. "The war has come to the mainland. I know news of the bombings of Genoa, Milan, and Taranto have been circulating around the Certosa, according to Brother Alfieri. And Rome will soon be next, no matter how much His Holiness protests."

Majorana, ensconced within the walls of the Certosa, did not fear the violence that had come to the shores of his country. But his family in Rome faced those fears every day.

Father Misasi was about to speak again, but Majorana raised his hand and bowed his head.

"Two weeks ago, while sitting in the sanctuary, the Virgin Mary appeared to me. Just as she appeared to the hermit who came to the sanctuary seeking the life of penance in the sixth century. She told me that God the Father commanded me to go to my family and seek forgiveness for my selfishness. That…" Majorana gasped for air. "That they have suffered long enough."

Majorana sought some sense that Father Misasi truly understood the gravity of what he had just confessed. He only saw a glimmer, but then the glimmer faded. "Why not tell them that you are alive and happy but not tell them where you are?"

"Father, that would only relieve some of their suffering. Besides, the Virgin Mary said I must go to them. There was no doubt what she told me." His head dropped into his hands, and he sobbed. "Now you understand the pain and grief I have been dealing with."

Father Misasi rose and took a step toward Majorana. He placed his hand on his head and prayed.

CHAPTER FORTY

Feinmann, who was still dealing with a bout of nausea, delayed their departure for the Fabrizio's farmhouse. Canali's wife served up some potato leek soup, which seemed to quell his roiling stomach, or at least, so said Feinmann. His words did not match the wan look on his face. But their trip to Fabrizio's was a waste of time. Canali was told by his wife—who, according to Canali, wasn't thrilled to see him—that he had already left for the monastery. She asked if he was there to pay him for past services. Canali's answer displeased her so much that she heaved a saucepan in his direction.

The hard-riding Fiat truck jostled the five of them as they made their way along an undulating, pitted, two-lane road whose standout feature was a series of eight hairpin turns that Canali seemed to have no respect for, given the speed at which he took them. It had snowed overnight, but the early morning sun that beat down from a cloudless sky was transforming the layer of snowfall into a slushy mix. The roadside brush strained under the weight of the heavy, wet snow. Emily, who again sat in the middle between Canali and Conor, tucked her pants into her calf-high, well-worn boots. She looked like she was ready for anything. Sean and Feinmann were in the rear, perched on their tomato crates.

"Tell me about the local police," Conor said.

169

Canali leaned forward, nearly lying across the steering wheel. He turned to look at Conor. "It is a small force." He paused as if thinking about something, still staring at Conor. "Five men, including its commander, Capitano Nuti." The hair on the back of Conor's neck stood up because Canali still hadn't turned back to look at the road. "He has led Collepardo's carabinieri for five or so years." Conor lunged forward, his right arm pointing at the road, which prompted Canali to return his attention to it.

"Do you get along with him?" Emily asked.

"I must admit, no. He thinks I had something to do with the disappearance of Mayor Sarandrea," Canali said, his wide eyes affecting a look of incredulity.

"Did you?" Conor asked.

"Of course not. He was my comrade. But the capitano does not believe me." Canali drilled his left index finger into his ear and jiggled it back and forth furiously. He ceased and let out a sigh, perhaps a signal he had achieved his purpose. "One more thing: there is a garrison of newly conscripted troops, very young men, training nearby in the mountains. Nuti has established a relationship with their commander. In fact, he has entertained the commander at my café."

Which could mean, Conor thought, he couldn't completely eliminate the commander and his troops from his list of possible adversaries.

Conor marveled at the size of the monastery as they approached. The road out of Collepardo passed close by the monastery, hugging the north wall. Canali pulled the Fiat to the side of the road, opposite a single-story building built into the wall. He explained it was the gatehouse to the monastery. Across the road from the monastery was a ten-foot stone wall, much of it crumbling, losing the battle against time and the elements. Above and beyond the wall was a forest thick with pine trees and low mostly leafless brush.

Conor craned his neck toward the rear of the truck and trained his gaze on Sean. "Ready for the Father Sean Sullivan show?"

Sean smirked, signaling he didn't appreciate Conor's attempt at relieving the tension, but he nodded.

"Okay then. Canali, you and Father Sullivan are on. Good luck."

\#

Sean crept past Feinmann, who whispered good luck, and crawled out of the back of the truck. He smoothed out his cassock, stretched briefly, taking in the scent of the pine forest that seemed to surround the monastery, then grabbed his small, tattered travel case. Canali, wearing a greatcoat that was in a similar condition to Sean's case, straightened his faded necktie.

"Shall we, Father?"

"Lead the way, Dominic."

The block wall of the single-story gatehouse was a sun-faded yellow, its paint flaking. There was evidence of this all along the wall; paint chips from it had left a yellowish stain on the granite stones inlaid in the road in front of the structure. In the middle of the wall was a doorless arched entryway that led into a darkened foyer. Inside the foyer, there was a single light bulb hanging from the ceiling, doing its best to shed some light but failing miserably. The air inside the foyer was fusty. Sean heard water dripping but couldn't make out where from.

Canali poked a button on the side of a wide wooden door that looked like it had been varnished a hundred times over. Sean couldn't hear any results from the action, but Canali didn't seem to be worried. A minute later, the door opened into the foyer, and Sean stepped back.

A monk stood before them. His cowl sat on his shoulders. His face carried an annoyed expression, as if they had interrupted a crucial function or task. Canali greeted Brother Alfieri and introduced him to Sean. The short-statured brother inclined his head and looked into Sean's eyes. The gaze was piercing as Alfieri extended his hand and Sean took it. Sean's grip swallowed up the bony hand, its skin roughhewn and dry to the touch.

"Sullivan. You are Irish?" Alfieri asked in passable English while still holding Sean's hand.

"I am, Brother Alfieri. Born in Dublin."

The brother looked Sean down, then up, his eyes lingering on Sean's travel case. "Aah," he murmured, taking his hand back and turning to Canali. "And what brings you here today, Dominic? More medicines for Claretta, possibly?"

"Actually yes, Brother. But I am also doing my new friend a favor by driving him here. Otherwise, he would have had to walk all this way. This weather…it is not so good."

Alfieri fastened his eyes back on Sean but said nothing for a second lengthy pause. "Dominic, go straight to the pharmacy. Brother Lazio will be happy to help you."

Canali took his leave, but not before he shot a quick wink at Sean.

"Why are you here, Father?"

"Brother Alfieri, I come here today to ask to see the monastery's prior, Father Misasi. I seek permission to enter Certosa di Trisulti."

Alfieri, his arms now tucked inside the sleeves of his robe, stood silently, head still inclined, looking up at Sean.

"I have found myself immersed in a deep crisis of faith. I need the time and space to sort things out."

"Things, Father? What would those 'things' be?"

"I…don't know where I could begin," Sean stammered. Despite the chilled dampness in the foyer, sweat rolled down Sean's spine. "I have a copy of a letter from my superior. Cardinal Massy, the head of the Catholic Church in England," he said, shocked he'd almost forgotten to mention it. "Has the prior received it?" He reached into his travel case and pulled out the letter he had affixed Father Misasi's name to that morning.

Without providing a response, Alfieri quickly snatched the letter from him, reminding Sean of a frog snatching a bug out of the air. Sean was sure that if it hadn't been addressed directly to Misasi, the letter would have been opened on the spot by the suspicious monk.

"Wait here, Father Sullivan. I will present your circumstances and letter to the prior." In a flash, Alfieri about-faced and shut the door with a slam.

Sean's entire upper body sagged as the tension seeped from his muscles.

#

When Sean was finally escorted into the office of the prior, he found the man holding a paper up to his face. The sight looked to Sean like he was trying to detect a scent on the document. As he got closer, Sean saw it was the letter he had given to Brother Alfieri.

Father Misasi rose from his chair. Sean expected an extended hand to shake but none was offered. The prior nodded to the chair beside his desk.

"Cardinal Massy's letter was quite convincing, Father Sullivan. He is very concerned about your present state of mind, religiously speaking, of course."

"Yes, Prior. He is as concerned as I am. Maybe more so. We have grown close over the years."

"How long have you been engaged in your struggle?"

"Doubts would come and go, and I brushed them off as something that all souls who have devoted their lives to Christ have at one time or another."

The prior nodded behind steepled hands.

"But the doubts continued to come, and they would linger. I decided I needed to address them head-on. But I couldn't do that while still performing my duties in service to Cardinal Massy."

Father Misasi lowered his hands and leaned forward. "Your request is something we do not take lightly. But it is imperative that we cannot let it be known that we have become a spa for those who have fallen prey to doubts. It is something I need to think through thoroughly and pray over…obviously. Give me a day to do that, Father."

"I completely understand, Prior."

Misasi, his brow furrowed, folded the letter, and replaced it in the envelope, then set it on his desk. He seemed lost in thought for a moment. Finally, he said, "Father Sullivan, why have you come to Italy in search for answers? Especially with a war on, it seems rather dangerous. There are monasteries and retreats in England, I am sure."

Sean squirmed and cleared his throat. This was a question that had not come up in the planning sessions with Conor. How stupid of him not to have thought about it. "Prior, I have spent many years in Rome working with Cardinal Massy while he was assigned to the Vatican. The cardinal sent me to return to the Vatican on official business. The cardinal suggested that, once that business concluded, I stay in Italy and seek resolution to my situation. He also felt that being from a neutral country, that I would be safe."

Misasi's slow nodding indicated he was satisfied with Sean's quick thinking.

"Prior, before I leave, may I ask for a tour of the charterhouse? I have read a great deal about the Certosa di Trisulti and the history of the Carthusian order. It would be a great honor in case you decide against my request to be taken in."

"I think I can arrange that, Father Sullivan. The Certosa is a sacred place I am most proud of."

#

The tour, such as it was, took less than ten minutes. It was five minutes longer than Brother Alfieri wanted it to be, Sean thought, given the brisk pace and sparse annotation he offered as they went about a small section of the monastery. Sean guessed that he saw no more than a tenth of the vast Carthusian monastery.

The pace and lack of commentary didn't keep Sean from being impressed with the pharmacy, which was opulent in its design, the cabinets and shelves chock-full of oval-shaped containers of hundreds of herbs. Its domed ceiling was painted in deep-hued oranges and shades of teal. Harp-playing centaurs mingled with cherubs and flights of angels on the mural. The floor of the pharmacy depicted an intricate mosaic that must have taken artisans months to complete. But most impressive was the air, which was thick with a mix of perfumed smells and pungent odors. The assault on his olfactory senses was almost murderous.

They sped down hallways and stairways, through gardens that featured oddly sculpted boxwood shrubs monks must have been toiling over for decades. There were no flowers in bloom that time of year, which did not detract from the impressive, stately gardens. But there was no sign of Majorana. It appeared the population of monks must have been in hiding, as he saw none on his tour. When he questioned Brother Alfieri, he greeted Sean with a puzzled look.

"They are doing what monks do this time of day. They are praying. But soon, they will be about the monastery, performing their assigned tasks."

After a brisk walk through the Church of St. Bartolomeo, they crossed a large courtyard. The granite flagstones were inlaid in circular patterns. The gaps between the stones hosted shoots of now-dormant grass. A small nonflowing fountain was dwarfed by the expansiveness of the courtyard. They walked along a cloister and into a building that looked from the outside to be much older than many of the other buildings. It had few windows, and time had stained the stone facade with blackish streaks of soot. They entered through a narrow doorway with a low clearance, forcing Sean to crouch to enter.

"We are quite proud of our library. It hosts over thirty-six thousand volumes," Brother Alfieri said, spreading his arms wide for emphasis. The room featured a mezzanine with spiral staircases at each end. Along the four walls, shelves of books sat, all with ancient-looking spines. Tables were scattered about and placed on each was a single kerosene lamp and nothing else.

Brother Alfieri let silence rule the moment, which made it easy to hear the heated words being spoken on the other side of the library wall nearest the door to the courtyard.

Sean heard two voices; one voice seemed more impassioned than the other. Sean was curious as to Alfieri's reaction. The monk appeared to know who the verbal combatants were and instead of looking shocked, he shook his head slowly, not shying away from showing his frustration.

"Father Sullivan, this way. I will take you back to the gatehouse," Brother Alfieri said, heading to the door in a near-sprint.

Apparently, the tour was over, but the argument which had prompted the tour's hasty conclusion seemed to be in full swing.

CHAPTER FORTY-ONE

0800 Hours, Tuesday, December 15, 1942
Certosa di Trisulti Charterhouse, Outside of Collepardo

Head bowed, hands stuffed in his sleeves, Majorana's determined stride took him toward the kitchen. Bruno hadn't shown up at the sanctuary that morning so he, knowing there were other plumbing issues near the monastery's kitchen, headed there. He needed to confront Bruno and...and what? He wasn't clear what he would do. He was broken. He didn't pray looking for guidance, fearing God would tell him to forgive the man, regardless of the reason he didn't mail the letter. Majorana felt shame overcome him for not being more forgiving.

He reached a short flight of stairs that descended into a narrow cloister running along the wall of the kitchen. He stopped and watched as Bruno, about twenty feet away, on his knees and facing Majorana, shoved a wire down into a drain. A cloud of cigarette smoke hung over his head. Majorana glided down the steps into the cloister and removed his hands from inside his sleeves. Head up, he took long strides toward the unaware plumber.

Majorana bent down and jerked Bruno's right arm up. The plumber's cigarette fell from his lips and into the drain as Bruno pulled his arm free. "What are you doing? What do you want?" Bruno struggled to his feet, almost losing his balance.

Majorana shoved him against the wall and leaned in. Bruno was at least a foot taller than Majorana, but it did not deter Majorana as he shouted, "You never mailed the letter, did you? You lied to me when you said that you did what I asked you to." Majorana felt a rage that shocked him. It was foreign to him, a feeling that he hadn't experienced since he was a young child playing football with his brother, Luciano, in the hallway in their home in Rome. His brother was always better than him and he never let a moment go by during their games without telling Majorana so.

"What I said was true, Brother."

"No, no, no. You are lying to me. But I can't determine why. I won't believe that my family would not respond. That's unfathomable to me."

"You have destroyed your relationship with them. If you are a genius, why can't you understand that?"

Majorana's rage peaked, and he began shouting at Bruno, spittle filling the air between them. Bruno shoved Majorana, who stumbled backward and slammed into a stone column, banging his head. His vision flashed with sparkling lights. "Leave me be, Brother. I want nothing to do with this letter. Or with you."

When his vision stabilized, Majorana pushed off the column, about to reengage with Bruno, but he sensed the presence of someone at the top of the stairs he had come down. He turned to look and found Brother Alfieri staring at the two men.

Before Brother Alfieri could make a move toward them, Majorana bolted down the cloister. He heard Brother Alfieri's sandals rapidly slapping the tile floor behind him. Majorana pulled open a door at the end of the cloister and slammed it shut behind him. The loud, crisp snap of a deadbolt accompanied Majorana's heavy breaths.

CHAPTER FORTY-TWO

0800 Hours, Tuesday, December 15, 1942
Kaiser Wilhelm Institute for Physics, Berlin

"You look..." Leeb hesitated. He needed to be careful with his choice of words. "Drained, my friend. You seem to have the entire weight of the Fatherland's armaments industry on your shoulders." He stopped breathing—it was a poor choice of words, given the fact that the entire responsibility for the Reich's ability to make war against the Allies was, in fact, on his guest's shoulders. Without his wry smile to indicate he was being ironic, it would have sounded stupid. Nonetheless, he attempted to more fully gloss over his silly comment before the startled Albert Speer could respond. "What I mean to say is that you need to delegate. Delegate. Delegate. You cannot do your job without a qualified and loyal staff. I stress the term *loyal*."

Speer, Minister of Armaments and War Production and close ally of Adolf Hitler, was as unnerved as Leeb had ever seen him. The sight of the troubled man unsettled Leeb.

"It isn't the job, Emil. While it is a massive undertaking, it is one that I can handle."

"Then why do you look so morose?"

The thirty-seven-year-old Speer, pacing in front of Leeb's desk, was smoking a cigarette—his fourth in as many minutes. He stopped and faced Leeb, giving him a hard look.

"Did you know that the Luftwaffe, just two days ago, flew in one hundred tons of supplies to Paulus's Sixth Army…the trapped Sixth Army?"

"I did not."

"Well, then you probably don't know that one hundred tons is not enough." Speer, his double-breasted gray suit coat unbuttoned, his tie loosened and askew, jabbed his cigarette in an ashtray firmly enough to have ash and butts spill out on the desk. He quickly lit another and resumed his pacing, but at a faster rate.

"They won't make it out of Stalingrad. Hoth's Fourth Panzer Army can't break through Russian defenses."

"Hoth is a skilled and cunning leader. He will succeed. I am sure of it."

Speer seemed to ignore Leeb's attempt to lift Speer's despondency.

"Todt was right, you know." Speer stopped pacing and took a seat. Fritz Todt, the previous Reich Minister for Armaments and Ammunition, had died in a mysterious aircraft crash in February of that year. A flight that Speer, at the last minute, had decided to forgo. "He complained to the führer that, without better equipment and more supplies for the Wehrmacht, it would be better to end the war on the Eastern Front." Speer waited for a reaction from Leeb, who sat stone-faced. "He complained to the führer. Do you believe that, Emil?"

"Certainly not the action of a wise man."

"No. No, it wasn't. But the sad thing is, he was right." Speer sat silently, lost in his thoughts; he seemed less agitated. Then he shot forward in his chair. "Emil, tell me of your program's recent successes. What has Heisenberg been working on?"

It was Leeb's turn to pace. He explained that progress on the pile was positive, but the speed was slow. "I have put a great deal of pressure on Heisenberg. He seems to be responding as I had hoped."

"Hardly the type of news I was expecting." Leeb ceased pacing and stood behind his chair. He grabbed the top of the chair back and squeezed with both hands. He heard his knuckles cracking. "Emil, your program is quickly falling out of favor with the führer. He is pushing me to allocate more funding to the V-weapon program. It is nearly impossible to say no."

"I understand, Albert."

Speer jumped out of his chair, startling Leeb, and resumed his pacing. "I don't think you do. There is a test of the V-1 weapon scheduled for eight days from today at the Peenemünde facility. If it is successful, I expect a call from the führer. A call that could cause funds from your project to be diverted to the V-weapons program," Speer said, his voice raised.

Leeb had had one success after the other ever since he entered the Wehrmacht in 1901, from Flanders to Poland, up through the ranks, from adjutant to general. Not one misstep. Not one failure. Yet his Uranprojekt might prove to be his undoing. "I do have a development to report that could have a significant impact on our progress." Speer stopped pacing and turned to look at Leeb.

"Go on."

Leeb circled around his desk and approached the red-faced Speer. It took Leeb three minutes to reveal the story of Ettore Majorana being discovered in the monastery in Italy.

"Do you believe Heisenberg when he says this man could be the difference between success and failure?"

"I do. So much so that I have sent him and an SS officer by the name of Koder to Italy to bring the Italian to Berlin. Heisenberg states that his brilliance cannot be overstated."

Speer turned and stared out the window, nodding slowly. Leeb retook his seat. After several seconds, Speer returned to his chair and reached down for his leather briefcase. He pulled out a thin file and opened it. "I have been copied on a speech that Goebbels is scheduled to give on New Year's Eve." Joseph Goebbels, Reich Minister of Propaganda, was the most fanatical Nazi in Hitler's inner circle. "One line of the speech stood out for me. 'Wherever we look, we see mountains of problems... Everywhere the path ascends at a steep and dangerous angle and nowhere is there a shady spot to stay and rest.'" Speer looked up and stared at Leeb.

"It sounds rather defeatist. Don't you agree?" Leeb said.

Speer shrugged, which stunned Leeb. For such a prominent member of Hitler's inner circle to give voice to defeatist thoughts was breathtaking.

"What I do know is that we are in great need of a 'shady spot,'" Speer said. Leeb, his face pinched, tilted his head in confusion.

"What I am saying is that we need a major success, and soon. The war is not going well for us. We need the V-weapons program to be successful." Leeb slumped in his seat. "And we need your program to be just as fruitful. I wish you... No, I wish *us* luck with enlisting this Majorana in our fight. A fight for the life of the Third Reich."

CHAPTER FORTY-THREE

0805 Hours, Tuesday, December 15, 1942
En Route to Certosa di Trisulti Charterhouse

"How much farther?" Koder asked the burly driver, Hermann. The answer, that they were now only ten minutes away from the monastery, did not help Koder's anticipation. He was sitting forward on the edge of the rear seat, constantly craning his neck to see out the windshield.

Heisenberg, Tardino, and Koder were in the Mercedes, following a carabinieri sedan driven by Capitano Nuti. One of Nuti's officers sat in the passenger seat. They were racing along the rolling, constricted roadway, making excellent progress when Nuti's sedan slowed to a stop. Koder rolled down his widow and stuck his head out.

"It's an old man with his damn donkey," Koder said more to himself than to anyone. "Blow your horn, dammit," he shouted to the lead car. Several horn blasts from the carabinieri sedan did nothing but elicit high-pitched brays from the stubborn animal. "You, Hermann," Koder snapped at the driver. "Get out and push that jackass off to the side of the road. And Tardino, you help him. We're wasting time."

Hermann, Tardino, Nuti, and his man all attempted to coax the donkey off to the side. Two men tugged at the reins and two men pushed from behind, which Heisenberg thought was a bit too risky. The old man, no taller than five feet, watched as the men struggled, spinning his cloth cap in his hands and blabbering away at the group. Koder cursed and bolted from the car, Heisenberg close behind. He admitted to himself that he was rather enjoying seeing Koder get rattled…by an obstinate donkey, no less.

Koder hustled over to the braying donkey. It was loaded with bundles of firewood lashed together with string. The old man was mumbling something Heisenberg couldn't understand at first. Then he realized he was praying. Koder screamed at the men: "Push. Push."

The hefty Tardino was the first to back off. He mopped his forehead with a handkerchief. "It's no use. This donkey doesn't want to go anywhere."

Koder swore and snatched his Walther PP from its holster. Tardino and Heisenberg were the first to see the gun, but the old man wasted no time transitioning from praying to shouting. Heisenberg hoped Koder was only going to fire in the air, to frighten the animal into moving. Koder had other ideas. He shot the donkey in the head. Heisenberg, standing next to Koder, gasped as his knees weakened at the sight of the brutal act.

"Why the hell did you do that?"

"Shut up, Tardino," Koder hissed.

The weeping old man collapsed on top of his donkey, wrapping his arms around its neck as blood seeped from the wound, drenching the sleeves of his tattered coat.

Tardino took a step toward Koder. "This man depends on that donkey for his livelihood. You could have—"

"I could have what? Stood here all day staring at him and his donkey? We have an urgent mission that must be completed without delay. And you—"

With shocking dexterity, the old man sprung to his feet, and a high-pitched stream of Italian filled the air. His right hand in his coat pocket, he charged the gaping Koder, who after a slight delay raised his Walther and shot the man in the face, dropping him to the ground in a heap of human detritus. The others, standing next to the donkey, were splattered with blood and brain matter. The shot blew out the back of his skull. No one moved or spoke until the sound of the Walther echoing off the surrounding hills ceased.

"The fool was reaching for a weapon. I had no choice but to

defend myself," Koder said in full voice. "Herr Heisenberg, check his pocket." Heisenberg didn't respond. "Check the fool's pocket… now."

Heisenberg crept toward the fallen man and reached in his pocket. He didn't find a weapon. He removed from the old man's grasp a rosary, its beads made of a dark polished wood.

Koder holstered his Walther, unmoved by Heisenberg's discovery. "Push the donkey to the side of the road. Nuti, when we have finished at the monastery, take care of the body." He holstered his weapon and headed back to the Mercedes. "Move, all of you," he shouted over his shoulder. "We're running behind schedule."

CHAPTER FORTY-FOUR

0810 Hours, Tuesday, December 15, 1942
Mayor Sarandrea's Office, Collepardo

The sign above the entrance of the three-story building was simple: *Sindaco Ufficio.* The mayor's office was on the street level of the apartment building, across from a prominent fountain in the middle of the town's piazza. From the outside, Falco was prepared to be unimpressed.

The door to the office had warped with time. The bottom of the door scraped along the floor as he opened it. It would only open halfway. Falco slid through the constricted opening sideways and with some effort shut the door.

"I told the mayor every day the door needed to be replaced, but all he would say is *'domani, domani.'* But tomorrow never came."

The woman who greeted him sat at a cluttered desk on one side of the cramped space. On the other side of the room was another desk free of anything but a picture frame with a photo of a middle-aged man sitting on the edge of the fountain in the piazza, his legs crossed at his ankles. He was smiling at the picture-taker. There was a black ribbon draped diagonally across the high-backed wooden desk chair. It appeared to Falco that his contact was no more.

"What happened to the mayor, *senora?*"

The woman, fiftyish and blotchy faced, dabbed at the corners of her puffy eyes with her handkerchief. "No one knows. Here one day, gone the next. No one knows." She took a deep breath and hacked into the handkerchief. A refined gesture it was not.

"You must miss him," Falco said. "I mean, you seem upset that he is gone."

"Upset!" The woman's retort made him flinch. "Of course, I am. Now all the work falls on my shoulders until the next election. And that is months away. They do not pay me enough to do the work of two." She paused. Her agitated demeanor shifted to one of curiosity as she fastened her gaze on him. "Who are you? Are you from the national police? Are you here to look into what has happened? You dress like you are from Roma."

Falco held up both hands to stop the steady stream of questions. "Yes, I am from Roma. But I am only a childhood friend. I was hoping to reconnect with Victor."

"You should go talk to his wife. I don't talk to her; she is a witch. I told him that many times."

"Where might I find her?"

"The café…across the piazza. They own it," she said, and then she paused. "Now, maybe she is the sole owner. Someone should ask her some questions."

Falco offered the grieving woman a hint of a bow and left.

#

The tables in front of the Café Vecchio were gathered in a corner of the patio, one stacked on top of another. The chairs were nested in two groups. The tattered and frayed awning used to cover the patio had been rolled back to the café's facade. He stepped inside and was hit with the robust smell of espresso mixed with the sweet smell of baking bread. There was a handful of people seated at three tables, heads close together, talking indistinctly. Some were drinking wine, others had small cups set before them. A raven-haired woman, middle-aged and slender, was snapping a towel across a table, clearing it of crumbs, and then she wiped it down.

Falco took a table with several cups and plates left by previous customers waiting for the woman to clear it. He watched her move about the floor briskly, eventually making her way to his table.

Without greeting him, she collected the cups and plates, making the most noise possible.

"The owner won't be pleased if you break something," Falco said.

She recoiled suddenly. "I *am* the owner, I'll have you know. And I'll break anything I like."

"Where is your husband?"

She took a step back and tossed the towel over her shoulder. "Who's asking?"

"I am from the Ministry of Industry and Commerce. I have some business with him."

She snorted. "I have business with him too, but you and I need to get used to being disappointed." She rambled on about her workload now that her husband had disappeared, adding that the manager he had hired—someone named Canali—was just as worthless. "He comes and goes like *he* is the owner. Another communist bastard, just like my husband. Both lazy excuses for men."

A fellow comrade named Canali sounded like someone he needed to chat with. "Maybe you should run for the office of mayor, *senora*."

She grunted. "Do I look stupid?"

CHAPTER FORTY-FIVE

0815 Hours, Tuesday, December 15, 1942
Certosa di Trisulti Charterhouse, Outside of Collepardo

Conor, Emily, and Feinmann, grouped between the truck and the wall across from the gatehouse, surrounded Sean. "I tried very hard not to lie. I believe I succeeded. I am having a crisis of faith, and if Father—"

"Sean, what happened?" Conor said.

"Yes, well...Father Misasi said he needs time to think about and pray on my request, which didn't surprise me. After I met with Father Misasi—who seems to be a reasonable sort, by the way—as planned, I requested and was granted a tour of the monastery. It was a hasty one, given by the monastery's administrator, the man who greeted Dominic and I at the gatehouse. He was very disagreeable. I don't know why but—"

"Sean" was all Conor had to say to get him back on point.

"Yes, so at the end of the tour, we were in the monastery's library and—"

"You saw Majorana?" Emily blurted.

"No." Conor and Emily hung their heads.

"Of course, it wasn't going to be that easy," Emily said.

"Brother Alfieri said that the monks were sequestered in prayer. But maybe not all the monks were in prayer, because we heard two men arguing. I didn't get a look at who they were, because Brother Alfieri led me to the gatehouse like I was a Protestant looking for a handout."

All of them were so focused on Sean, they didn't notice Canali approaching the truck. "Father Sullivan has returned," Canali said. "Have you found Majorana, Father?"

Conor shut Canali down with a wave of the hand. "Sean, get the habit out. I'm going

inside," Conor said, which sent Sean to the rear door of the truck with Conor following. Sean started to explain how to get inside through the gatehouse. "Well, I'm not getting inside through the gatehouse, that's for sure." Conor looked at Emily, who had joined them. "I'm going over the wall. I need you to stay here," he said to her as he took the folded monk's habit from Sean and began slipping it over his head. Emily protested, but he cut her off.

"I don't want these guys to fend for themselves if anyone comes asking questions."

"All right. I'll give you ten minutes," Emily said, looking at her watch. "Not a minute more. Then I'm going over right behind you."

"Em, this monastery is huge. I'll need much longer than that to do a decent search."

Emily gave him a stony stare. He did his best to ignore her as he slipped out of his boots and into the pair of leather sandals. She started to speak, but Conor held up both hands to stop her.

"I'll find him and then we'll beat it out of there. Just be ready to leave when we come out."

Conor yanked out one of the duffel bags. He pulled out a coil of rope with an attached grappling hook.

"Do you have your map?" she asked.

He patted his breast pocket. "Yeah, right here."

She rushed him and gave him a quick hug. "Watch your back," she purred in his ear.

"Come on, Em, they're monks. Men of God."

CHAPTER FORTY-SIX

0820 Hours, Tuesday, December 15, 1942
Certosa di Trisulti Charterhouse, Outside of Collepardo

Conor, the map of the monastery in his hand, wasn't sure where he should go after landing inside the wall. He started adjacent to the gatehouse and moved clockwise, opening any door that wasn't locked, which was the large majority of the doors. He ran into several groups of monks who didn't recognize him and asked questions. He only gave them short responses in his best Italian when they asked who he was. He knew his best wasn't good enough, but he made sure that his response included the name *Prior Misasi* before hastily moving on. The look on their faces communicated clearly that they weren't buying it. When he would take his leave after each confrontation, he heard the monks chattering among themselves.

He knew he had little time left before the packs of monks organized a more aggressive reaction to his roaming around their home. As he approached the end of a hallway, he heard raised voices, then found a set of stairs he stood at the top of. A short distance down the cloister, two people were facing off. One was a stout man dressed in soiled clothes. A drain cover plate lay next to a wire snake. He'd found the plumber. The other, a monk, was looking at Conor. He was short and fraily built; his face was flushed and his long nose that drooped at its tip to his upper lip couldn't be missed. He still had one hand planted on the plumber's chest. Conor wanted to ask the plumber some questions, but the monk ahead of him didn't look like the cooperating type. As Conor approached slowly, the long-nosed monk didn't take his eyes off him.

"Who are you?" the monk asked in Italian. The plumber, the guy Canali called Fabrizio, backed away from the monk. A look of relief crossed his face as Conor's approach stole the monk's attention.

"Brother…Brother Bonvini," Conor said, using the name of a pizza joint in his hometown.

"I don't know any Brother Bonvini. What are you doing here, and how did you get in?"

Conor was about to jump in with the story Sean concocted about being sent by the prior of the Pisa Charterhouse to request some special herbs from the pharmacy when, from the direction that he had come, about a dozen monks appeared. They were carrying shovels, metal garden rakes, and large pruning shears. Even though not one monk looked younger than sixty, Conor wasn't about to pull his Colt from his waistband and make a bloody stand in the cloister.

"Do you have any identification?" the brother standing next to Fabrizio asked.

Conor's negative answer prompted a search by one of the rake-wielding monks. When he pulled the 1911A1 Colt from Conor's waistband, the group of monks let out a gasp in unison. Two minutes later, minus his Colt, Fabrizio and Conor were both standing on the granite stones outside the gatehouse. The throng of monks who had escorted them out of the monastery stood just inside the gatehouse foyer, staring at Conor and the plumber.

Conor didn't have to clean his habit before he returned it to the charterhouse in England—the monks of the Certosa di Trisulti were now in possession of it.

CHAPTER FORTY-SEVEN

Conor shoved Fabrizio into the front seat of the truck and followed right behind. He fielded rapid-fire questions from Sean and Emily, but none of his brief answers did much for their moods as they headed south, away from the monastery.

"That black Fiat sedan parked at the monastery. Who was in it?" Conor asked.

"We don't know," Emily said. "It just arrived a minute ago. Canali didn't recognize him or the car. He looked like he was in a rush though."

Conor took in Emily's answer with some concern but decided to focus on Bruno Fabrizio for the moment. He leaned forward to see past the rattled-looking Fabrizio seated next to him and told Canali to drive back to Fabrizio's farmhouse.

For the next minute, Conor sat silently, questioning what he could have done different inside the monastery. He noticed Canali had picked up speed. The road back to Fabrizio's farmhouse wasn't the best maintained road he'd ever been on. Conor twisted around and saw Emily, Sean, and Feinmann being jostled around in the rear. He was about to tell Canali to ease off the gas when Fabrizio started screaming in Canali's ear. It took Sean, with a few firm admonishments, to calm both Canali and Fabrizio down.

"What were they talking about?" Conor asked, turning to Sean. "I didn't catch most of it."

"Shoddy work. No payment. Fabrizio called him a 'bloody communist.'" A pause. "He actually used a nastier word."

"Oh, and each said something about the other's wife. Need more?" Emily said, seated across from Sean and Feinmann on her own crate.

Conor turned and glanced at her, and she greeted the look with a smirk.

He snorted. "Ask him where Majorana"—Conor felt Fabrizio flinch at the name—"would have run off to."

It was a brief question, and she gave an even briefer response. "He has no idea," Emily reported.

Fabrizio turned his head and looked at Emily. He rattled off something to her that Conor only partially understood. He was trying to figure it out when Canali took a hard right turn onto the single-track dirt road that let up to Fabrizio's farmhouse. Sean, Feinmann, and Emily were almost knocked off their crates in the windowless rear of the truck. He thought he heard Feinmann dry heave.

#

Heisenberg, still mulling over the horrific scene they'd left on the road earlier, sat looking out the rear passenger window. He noticed up ahead a panel van pull off the road after a severe turn and head up a narrow dirt road. The truck quickly disappeared in a thick cloud of dust. It seemed no one else took notice except maybe the driver.

Koder, tightly clutching a pair of black leather gloves, gave Heisenberg a sideways glance. Heisenberg sat back and let out a long breath. He wished he had some water to sip to rid his mouth of the sour taste left by the incident with the old man and his donkey.

Koder then looked directly at him, but Heisenberg did not want to engage. "Tell me, Professor, why have you been so quiet and…sullen? I would have expected some level of excitement from you."

"Hauptsturmführer, I am readying myself. I am concentrating

on managing my expectations regarding the meeting with Majorana."

"Ah, by 'managing' do you mean stifling your expectations?"

"No. I know Majorana. He can be…stubborn. I'm not quite sure what to expect, really."

Koder nodded, but Heisenberg knew it wasn't because he'd agreed with him. "You see, Herr Heisenberg, that is where we are different. I hold high expectations for our mission. Stubborn or not. We have ways to bend the will of people into acceptable levels of cooperation." Koder slapped the leather gloves into the palm of his hand. The crack made Heisenberg flinch. "I have no doubt that your friend will be traveling back with us tomorrow."

"I hope you're right, Hauptsturmführer. I truly do." He meant the proffered agreeable response to shut Koder down. It didn't work.

"You know that *Weihnachten* is only ten days away. Think of it this way, Professor: we are bringing back to the German people a wonderful holiday gift!" Koder's tone was inauthentic, if not outright condescending. "Wouldn't you agree?"

Tardino, in the front passenger seat, shot Heisenberg a fleeting glance, which Koder noticed. "Do you agree with my outlook, Tardino?" Koder said.

Tardino responded with an imperceptible nod.

The cabin of the Mercedes fell quiet for long minute except for the steady growl of the sedan's engine. "Tardino, was there any problem getting Capitano Nuti to make arrangements for the army conscripts to meet us at the monastery?"

"No," he said flatly. He stole a look at his watch. "The truck with fifteen men should be at the monastery in fifteen minutes."

"Excellent. Hopefully, they will not need to search the monastery for our brilliant scientist," Koder said, punctuating his statement with another sharp slap of his gloves into his hand.

This time, Heisenberg didn't flinch.

CHAPTER FORTY-EIGHT

0910 Hours, Tuesday, December 15, 1942
Certosa di Trisulti Charterhouse, Outside of Collepardo

The old priest was nervous—just the way Soleti wanted him. Obviously, commanders of the Holy Father's Gendarmerie Corps hadn't been frequent visitors. And if Misasi had a tendency to be territorial in any way, the letter from the Cardinal Secretary of State Maglione that he was now reading would certainly stymie them.

The letter in Father Misasi's hand trembled as he pushed it across his desk toward Soleti. There was perspiration collecting on his upper lip.

"Do you have questions, Father?"

Misasi dabbed at his face with a handkerchief. "No. No questions." His voice was softer than when he'd first greeted Soleti.

"Then I have one. Where is he?"

"Actually, I don't know. I know where he should be, but Brother Bini hasn't adhered to today's daily schedule as we require him to. His confused and emotional state of mind is, undoubtedly, the cause."

"Why don't you explain what has transpired here for the past two days, so I have a better understanding of the nature of the dilemma we have on our hands?" While Misasi recalled the events of the past two days, Soleti palmed a pack of Nazionali cigarettes and extracted one, causing the priest to pause his recollection.

Soleti motioned for Misasi to continue once he finished lighting his smoke. Another five minutes passed, and Misasi finished his report about a letter, a plumber, and a confused and unstable monk who was roaming about the monastery untethered to its reality.

"You said that…Brother Bini had a confrontation with this Fabrizio. Before we search for the brother, I want to talk to him."

"As you wish," Misasi said, pushing a small button on the edge of his desk. In the two minutes it took someone to appear, Soleti flicked his ash twice on the parquet floor, spurring a scowl from Misasi each time.

When Misasi asked a brother called Alfieri to see the plumber, Fabrizio, he said, "I have sent him away for arguing with a brother. That can't be tolerated. I am sorry, Father."

Soleti stood, dropped his cigarette to the floor, and crushed it with the sole of his shoe. "Was it Brother Bini?" Soleti asked.

For such a simple question, the monk standing before him took his time answering, convincing Soleti to disbelieve whatever came out of his mouth.

"No, it was me."

Soleti's raised a single eyebrow. "Oh, I see. What did you two argue about?"

This time the answer came quickly. "He is taking too much time on the repairs that we hired him to do."

Soleti nodded slowly. "Send someone for him."

CHAPTER FORTY-NINE

0950 Hours, Tuesday, December 15, 1942
Sanctuary of Our Lady of the Cese

Majorana lit a lamp and surveyed the sanctuary's main room. Below the wall where the plumber had been working was a mound of debris. Some pieces of lath and horsehair plaster were snapped off toward the bottom of the wall to allow access to the pipe that had burst. It was an untidy, muddled mess—the same state Majorana's mind was in.

He rubbed the back of his neck, felt the perspiration that was running down his back. He began walking in circles, frequently stopping to ask himself a question. His gaze snapped from one object to another, and he did more neck rubbing, a hand to his chin while he stopped again to think.

"Father Misasi has protected me for so long. How could I have done this to him? He is too old for this...this stress. His efforts have now been completely undone." His pace quickened and the circles became more constricted. "Undone by me and the faithless plumber." His eyes welled up as he realized he couldn't remain in the hands of Father Misasi for much longer.

"But where will I go?" Majorana asked, his voice thick with fear as he came to a stop. "Could Father Misasi find another monastery for me?" He had too many answerless questions. "What about fleeing to the Vatican with Father Misasi's help?" No, no, no. He recalled what Father Misasi said about the Vatican. Too many spies and men who would do anything to solidify and enhance their power, not to mention the lure of selling information to the fascist government, OVRA, and military intelligence. "Think, Ettore. Think. They say you are a brilliant man!" But he couldn't think. Anxiety was choking the life out of any cogent thought. He craved a cigarette, but he had none. He should have taken the pack the devious Bruno offered.

"No, I need to pray."

He seized the lamp from the table and headed toward the rear of the sanctuary, to the chapel.

It was exceptional for its limited space—there were no pews, only kneelers for four people. At the altar, there was room only for one celebrant. The room, meant for solitude and prayer, was unadorned except for a lone crucifix.

"It will come to me. A plan will come to me, with the help of God, my savior."

CHAPTER FIFTY

1015 Hours, Tuesday, December 15, 1942
Farmhouse of Bruno Fabrizio, Collepardo

They settled in a cramped sitting room. Two walls exhibited water stains that were expansive where the wall abutted the ceiling and then slimmed down like icicles as they traveled to the floor. The sitting room was decorated with a slight nod to the coming Christmas holiday. A puny pine tree only three feet tall stood in the corner of the room. There were wax candles the color of dark cherries that sat on a mantel above a dormant fireplace. There were two stuffed armchairs that faced and flanked the fireplace. Conor had spun one around and pushed Fabrizio into it. He'd grunted when he hit the seat cushion. Conor sat in the other armchair with Emily, Sean, and Feinmann standing behind him like they were posing for a family picture with the patriarch seated in front.

The four of them drilled holes into the slack-faced Fabrizio. Canali hung back, hugging the wall of the sitting room, having been scowled at by Fabrizio's wife, who was now hiding in the kitchen, which was situated just off the sitting room.

Fabrizio's eyes darted from one inquisitor to the other. He started to rise, but Conor shoved him back into the chair. Fabrizio didn't like that; the look on his face turned stony.

"I'm curious, Bruno, why was Majorana arguing with you?" Conor asked.

Fabrizio opened his mouth to speak, then...nothing. He watched his wife emerge from the kitchen.

Conor pulled his Colt semi-automatic from the small of his back and placed it on his lap.

Emily rattled off something in Italian that Conor couldn't fully comprehend. "What, Em?"

"I told him to tell us what we want to know, and we will leave his house peacefully," Emily said.

Conor picked up his Colt, which triggered a panicked outburst from Fabrizio's wife.

Sean, arms folded across his chest like a barroom bouncer, said, "Listen to your wife, Bruno. She wants us out of her house pronto. Or you will not be welcome in her bed."

Fabrizio threw a look at his wife, who returned it defiantly. The threat worked—Bruno started blabbing: "He accused me of not mailing a letter for him to his family."

"Did you?" Emily asked.

Fabrizio looked at his wife, then lowered his head. "No. I gave the letter to her brother," he said, pointing at his wife. "He is a deputy with OVRA."

"When?" Emily asked.

"A week ago." Conor realized it couldn't have been long after that when the Nazis first learned of the reemergence of Majorana. Plenty of time to put their own operation in motion.

"Why?" Conor said.

"Money. I wanted the reward money…for us." The man raised his gaze and leaned forward. "The war—it is coming to our doorstep soon. I wanted the money to buy false papers to get us to Switzerland. For me, my wife, and my daughter."

"How do you know there's a reward?" Conor said.

"Tardino. My brother-in-law. He found out the family never revoked it. I was counting on the family to—"

"Pay up," Conor said, as he looked around the sitting room. The furniture and rug had seen better days; Fabrizio's clothes were tattered and faded. The knees of his pants, which were held up by a length of rope, were patched. Fabrizio could have used the money. "If you tell us where Majorana is hiding, and we find him, I'll see to it that you get three thousand lira." Fabrizio gave Conor a puzzled look. Conor silently cursed his ragged Italian. "Em, tell him."

When Emily finished, they could all hear Fabrizio's wife gasp. Fabrizio's slackened face grew taut. "What will you do to him? You won't..." His voice trailed off as his eyes lowered to take in Conor's Colt.

"Suddenly, he has a conscience," Conor said. "No, we will not kill him, just keep him out of German hands. Now, where did he go, Bruno? My patience is gone."

Fabrizio rubbed his hands back and forth on his thighs. "The sanctuary." He gave quick directions on how to get there, and Conor rose and slipped the Colt back in its resting place. Fabrizio's shoulders loosened as he slumped low.

"Canali, I need your truck to get back to the monastery. That work for you?"

Canali nodded.

"Feinmann, you stay with Canali. If all goes well, you'll be chatting with your friend soon."

As they headed to the door of the house, Fabrizio's wife, teary and red-faced, stepped toward her husband and slapped him upside his head, then bent down and pressed his head to her bosom.

CHAPTER FIFTY-ONE

1015 Hours, Tuesday, December 15, 1942
Certosa di Trisulti Charterhouse, Outside of Collepardo

Soleti had just told Father Misasi to gather several brothers and had given instructions to search for Majorana, first in his quarters, then elsewhere and, once found, to bring him to his office. He wanted to be back in Vatican City before dark. Soleti cut short Misasi's attempt to protest by slamming his hand down on his desk.

"You did read the letter, did you not?" Soleti asked.

A silence stretched for several beats. The meek expression on Misasi's face signaled his compliance. The father had reached for his buzzer to summon the monastery's administrator when the office door slammed open, and Brother Alfieri was shoved into the office by a gun-toting, carabinieri officer with heavy black stubble that made him look like he was wearing a mask. Behind the stubbled man was an imposingly sized German SS officer, his cap tucked under his arm, his blond hair cropped close on the sides of his head. The shockingly blue, piercing eyes that didn't blink drew Soleti's gaze in. Behind the officer was a smallish man whose features were blotted out by the SS officer's physique. Pulling up the rear were two other men. The heavyset Tardino, he recognized. The other man, shorter in stature, he did not. Soleti damned himself for moving too deliberately to find Majorana.

"Apologies, Father, these men were insistent that they see you," Alfieri blurted before he turned to beat a hasty exit.

The stubbled man grabbed a handful of Alfieri's tunic and steered him over to a bench along a far wall and loomed over him, his pistol in his firm grasp.

"I am Hauptsturmführer Koder." He introduced the others.

Heisenberg, another German, looked sickly with his blanched complexion. Soleti was sure he detected a slightly upturned corner of Tardino's mouth as he dipped his head, acknowledging the reacquaintance.

Koder marched behind the desk, his bootheels hammering the wooden floor, and took Misasi's seat. He flung his cap onto the desk and began to remove his black leather gloves with painful slowness. Misasi's face registered shock at the maneuver, then irritation. Soleti laid a hand on Misasi's arm and guided him to the chair in front of the desk. Acquiescing, Misasi looked up at Soleti for guidance, and Soleti responded with a faint nod.

"I am here to collect Ettore Majorana. Where is he?"

"There is no one here by that name," Soleti said.

Koder finished removing his gloves and, with a final flourish, flicked them on top of his cap. "And who are you?"

Soleti remained silent, calculating his response. Koder's glassy stare signaled his annoyance at Soleti's hesitation. "Commander Soleti from the Vatican Gendarmerie Corps."

"Ah, the pope's errand boy. Sent to bring back their possession. Am I correct?"

Soleti chose not to answer.

His silence elicited a sneer from Koder. "Bring Majorana to me," Koder said.

"I am sorry about your hearing loss, but I said that we do not know this man," Soleti said, his voice raised.

Heisenberg stepped forward and handed Soleti a photo of Heisenberg and Majorana seated at a table, both dressed in white shirts, ties loosened at the neck, open bottles of beer on the table along with a chess set.

He handed the picture back to him. "As I said, we do not know this man."

Koder had had enough. He sprang from the chair and unholstered his Walther. Anger turned his complexion a light red. Tardino followed suit but more slowly and less threateningly.

Heisenberg retreated to the bench and sat alongside Brother Alfieri.

Koder glanced at his watch. "Tardino, go to the gatehouse and let in the troops. Make sure each one has a photo of Majorana. Tell them to search every room. Bring me Majorana!" Koder turned to Soleti. "I hoped this would have unfolded in a more cooperative manner. But backup plans are often the best way to go. Wouldn't you agree, Commander?"

"Go ahead and search. His Holiness will make his feelings known to the German ambassador."

Koder snorted. "And the German ambassador, being a loyal Nazi, will promptly

disregard the pope's feelings." Koder, seemingly satisfied with the proceedings, retook his seat, laying his Walther on the desktop. "We shall all await the arrival of the great Ettore Majorana." He swiveled in his chair as Soleti lit up a cigarette and paced. Soleti gave Misasi a sideways glance and saw the man's ashen face—the old priest had had an extremely unusual day for a prior of a quiet mountainside monastery.

Soleti walked over to a window behind the desk. Koder, his hand resting on his Walther, tracked him with squinted eyes. Soleti could feel the Beretta tucked inside his shoulder holster. This SS officer was sloppy for not having him searched. Soleti gazed down and saw a handful of soldiers, all seemed to be in their late teens, dressed in ill-fitting, dull, olive green uniforms scurrying through the courtyard and the gardens that lay beyond. They held photos that flapped in the breeze as they hustled about. *What are the chances that they find him?* Soleti wondered. *The Certosa was massive with, undoubtedly, countless dark corners and nooks to hide,* he concluded. Fifteen minutes later, news arrived.

Tardino, winded, barged into the office. "He is nowhere to be found. They have searched everywhere."

Koder stood suddenly, the backs of his knees toppling the chair. The tenseness in Soleti's body dissipated more quickly than it had built up.

Koder spread his hands on the desk and leaned toward Misasi. "The plumber. The one Majorana used to send the letter. Where is he?" Koder asked, spittle falling to the surface of the desk.

Misasi sputtered a few unintelligible words.

"We know of no such letter. But the monastery's plumber is not inside the monastery today, so I've been told," Soleti said. Before he could press him further, Soleti continued. "This mystery man, why are you so interested in finding him?"

Heisenberg stood and started to say something, but Koder held up his arm in something akin to a Nazi salute to shut him down.

"Find him. We will return to collect him. Failure in turning him over will only lead to the sacrifice of the—"

Soleti cut him off. "Your business is done here. Now leave."

#

The two heavy trucks transporting the Italian conscripts headed back to their camp, leaving a low-hanging cloud of exhaust that stubbornly clung to the ground. Koder sat in the Mercedes, leaning forward, watching Nuti have an animated conversation with the monk who took them to the prior's office.

"Tardino, go get—" Before he could finish his order, Nuti turned and trotted toward the Mercedes. Koder rolled down his window. "What have you learned?"

"I asked the brother if there were any other visitors to the monastery in the last day or so. After some prodding, he said that Dominic Canali, a manager of a local café, visited and brought along a priest, an Irishman, to see the prior. But he looked like he wasn't telling me everything, so I shoved my gun in his gut. He then told me that there was an American inside the monastery under false pretenses earlier today."

Koder recoiled. Heisenberg muttered something under his breath.

"He threw him and the plumber out before we arrived."

Koder stewed. He was surprised the Americans moved so quickly. He sat back to consider his next move. Nuti leaned against the Mercedes, and Koder picked up foul scents off the man's stained black carabinieri uniform. Splotches of the old man's blood and brains had dried a dark red color on the red stripes that ran down the outside of Nuti's pant legs. He started to crank up his window, then stopped. "Where does this plumber live?"

"In a farmhouse down off the road back to Collepardo. About two miles or so from here. There is a narrow dirt road that leads up to the house."

Koder rolled up his window. "You heard him. Head to the farmhouse." Hermann turned over the Mercedes's engine.

Tardino rolled down his window and communicated their destination to Nuti, who loped back toward his car, but before he could get there, a dark Fiat nearly clipped the carabinieri capitano.

Recognizing the driver, Koder sat back and looked at Heisenberg. "Now, where might the commander of the Vatican's gendarmerie be headed?" Koder snapped his fingers twice, and the Mercedes lurched forward. "Hopefully back to Rome."

CHAPTER FIFTY-TWO

1130 Hours, Tuesday, December 15, 1942
Farmhouse of Bruno Fabrizio, Collepardo

Koder sat in a well-worn armchair that reeked of something he couldn't place. The specifics didn't really matter; it was just unpleasant. They needed to get what he'd come for and leave as quickly as possible. Heisenberg sat across from him in an identical armchair. He noted Heisenberg hadn't been very talkative since the incident on the road to the monastery. Typical for someone who hid in a laboratory while others fought for the Fatherland. He looked at his watch, frowned, then shot a look at Tardino, who was sitting at the table with his sister while they all waited for Nuti to search the house for her husband. She was whispering something to him. "What did she say?" Koder said.

Tardino hesitated. "She says that she doesn't like the German with the black uniform in her home. She wants to know why I brought you here."

Koder stifled a laugh. He would not waste his time explaining that Germans in black uniforms would win the war for Germany. Just as Koder was about to order Tardino to search for the searcher, Nuti came down a narrow stairway with an unshaven, unkempt man in his forties, one arm twisted behind his back.

"He was hiding in a closet, under a blanket," Nuti said. Koder saw his wife cover her mouth briefly, then whisper something to Tardino, her brother.

Koder motioned to Heisenberg to give up his seat, and Nuti shoved the plumber into it, almost colliding with the slow-moving Heisenberg. Koder took in the sight of the rattled plumber, whose red-rimmed eyes flicked from Koder, to his wife, to Tardino, and when they settled back on Koder, he asked, "Where is he?"

Fabrizio lowered his eyes and hunkered deeper into the chair, as if the soft, odorous fabric could protect him from his inquisitor. Koder signaled Tardino with a finger snap, who responded with a single nod.

"Bruno," Tardino said. "One last time. Where is Majorana?"

Bruno's grip on the chair's armrest tightened. He directed his attention to Tardino. "You were never going to get us the reward like you said. You lied to me."

Koder wanted nothing to do with their family drama. He needed to move this along. "Tardino, shoot her in the knee."

Tardino drew in a short but loud breath, and Heisenberg murmured something. Nuti lowered the arm that held his pistol, his mouth agape.

"Do it," Koder said. The sister's expression turned from anxious to terrified, her rapid breathing evident to all. Her eyes darted from Koder to her brother then back to Koder. She repeatedly made the sign of the cross.

"Shoot her," Koder said. "In…the…knee." A pause. "Do it now."

Tardino looked at Fabrizio, whose eyes were directed down into his lap. Koder heard the plumber murmur. "What did you say?" he asked.

The man cleared his throat and said: "He may be in the sanctuary…near the monastery. If he's not there, I don't know where he could be."

Koder stood, glad to be free of the stinking chair. He leaned over toward the plumber and, with a gloved hand, lifted the broken man's chin up. He looked into his eyes. "Are you telling me the truth?"

The plumber hesitated. That was all he needed. "Tardino, shoot her in the knee."

Tardino bolted from his chair and made for the door. Koder cursed the man, stepped forward, and did the deed himself.

Fabrizio clawed out of the armchair, rushed to his screaming wife's side, and knelt. Koder grabbed the collar of his shirt and pulled it toward him. "Herr Fabrizio, friend of Ettore Majorana, tell me everything you know."

CHAPTER FIFTY-THREE

1210 Hours, Tuesday, December 15, 1942
Sanctuary of Our Lady of the Cese

The three interlopers rushed down the gravel path from the monastery to the sanctuary. Conor had seen nothing like it before. It wasn't the building itself, but its location. It sat inside the mouth of a cave. The roof of the cave hung over the structure like an awning. While it was partly sunny, the building was shrouded in a shadow. The few windows there were emitted no light.

The door was unlocked. They slipped inside and found themselves in an open, faintly lit room. They turned on their flashlights. It was frigid and sparsely furnished—a table with a single oil lamp, an open Bible, four chairs, a cold fireplace with a stack of twigs in a copper tub, a kitchen with a single counter along the far wall, a sink, and some dishes, but no stove. Conor lit the oil lamp, which flickered and threw their cautiously moving shadows on the walls. There were crucifixes on each wall along with paintings of the Virgin Mary. The lower section of one wall had been excavated, exposing ancient-looking plumbing. A rusted-out section of pipe lay on the floor. Conor signaled Emily and Sean to stop and pointed to his ear. He listened and heard nothing but what he thought was water dripping on the sanctuary's tiled roof. Moisture seeping through the cave's roof, he assumed.

He moved toward the back of the building. As he passed Sean, he held out an arm to stop him, leaned down, and with his mouth an inch from Conor's ear, said, "Monasteries, churches, and sanctuaries, especially ones this old, often had secret rooms where valuables and even people could hide from thieves."

Conor nodded.

A narrow and low-ceilinged hallway led from the front room to the back of the sanctuary, where a door stood at the hallway's end. About ten feet from the door, off to the left, was a chapel that was half the space of his pint-sized basement room at Claridge's. There were two kneelers placed in front of the altar; an oil lamp sat on top of one. Conor placed his hand on the glass of the lamp. It was warm. He got Emily's attention and pointed to it.

Conor motioned for Sean and Emily to huddle. "Look for hiding places. Look to see if there are any trapdoors, and check for marks on the floor to see if furniture has been moved around."

He left the two of them in the chapel and headed down to the end of the hallway. The door was slightly ajar. He nudged it open, listened, and only heard water dripping in the darkness of the cave. The air was heavy, cold, and damp. He pointed his flashlight straight ahead, revealing an enormous cavern that began to taper at the far end of the flashlight's beam.

"Emily," Conor said in a hoarse whisper.

Emily and Sean stuck their heads out of the chapel doorway.

"We need to check this out."

CHAPTER FIFTY-FOUR

1215 Hours, Tuesday, December 15, 1942
Café Vecchio, Collepardo

Falco, seated in a corner of the café, had an unobstructed view of its bustling main room. The patrons, numbering close to twenty, chatted away while they ate, drank, and smoked. The waiter was a young man in his late teens with a ruddy complexion and a severe case of halitosis. There was an elderly woman behind the bar operating an espresso machine like a concert pianist, her hands moving so swiftly they nearly blurred.

The mayor's wife, and now possibly the sole owner of the café, appeared to be in a much less riled mood than during their first encounter. She was even pleasant when he approached her upon arriving and reintroduced himself. But when he asked if Canali, the communist bastard, had returned to work, her mood shifted dramatically, though only momentarily. It seemed she wasn't letting her missing manager ruin her mood. When she told him that he would know when Canali arrived because she was going to rip his head from his shoulders, he couldn't help but grin.

He ordered a cappuccino and smoked while he waited for the recalcitrant manager to show up. With his contact, the mayor, missing, he needed to enlist his comrade's help in tracking down the elusive Majorana. He looked at his watch. The two men he ordered to join him from Rome should be arriving at the café in two hours, so he had time.

Which he didn't need, given the good fortune that fell on his shoulders when a man in his twenties, nearing six feet, entered the café and immediately became a target for the mayor's wife. The heat she brought down on the man was intense. So much so that several patrons decided it was time to move on.

Falco approached the two, who were standing in the middle of the café. Canali, who still had his head on his shoulders, tried to skirt around the woman, but she was not having it. Falco let her run out of steam a bit more before he took Canali by the elbow and whispered in his ear. He reacted the way Falco had predicted—by jerking his head, his mouth gaping. Mentioning Moscow to a communist often prompted such a reaction.

Falco led him toward the front door with the irate woman steps behind. He pulled a lira note and passed it to her. The gift served its purpose as she stopped her pursuit and fell silent. Outside on the patio, Falco grabbed two chairs from the stack in the corner and told Canali to sit. He pulled a pack of cigarettes from his suit coat pocket and offered one to Canali, who looked at Falco warily, then accepted. Falco noticed Canali's shaky hand, and when Canali saw he noticed, the man gave the cigarette back to Falco, who shrugged and lit up.

"My first question is the most important. Where is the mayor? I had business with him."

Canali surveyed the piazza and the entrance to the café over his shoulder, then asked, "What is your name?"

"I'll ask the questions. You answer them."

"How do I know you aren't some OVRA agent sent to wipe out my group?"

"If I were, we wouldn't be sitting on a patio having a smoke. You'd be sitting in the back of my car in handcuffs on the way to Rome." Falco paused for effect. "Unless I decided to shoot you first."

Canali digested his response. "I'll take that cigarette now."

Falco smiled and passed his pack to him. Canali fumbled with the pack before accepting a light. "Well?"

"He lost his zeal for the party. He no longer held the fascists responsible for what they have done to the people." Canali leaned in and in a lowered voice said, "He had to go." Canali drew heavily on the cigarette smoking it down a quarter of an inch. "I am in charge now." Backing up his claim, Canali released a lungful of smoke through his nostrils ending with a sly grin.

It was Falco's turn to digest information. "In charge of what, exactly?"

"I have four men. We are recruiting. I plan to have triple that in the next few months," Canali said, beaming. He tapped ash from his cigarette toward the ground, but a wind gust blew it in his lap.

"What did you do with the mayor? Just so I have the full story."

"We took him up into the mountains. Far from here." Canali took another deep drag and flicked the butt to the ground. "He cried like a child."

Falco crossed his legs and took in the piazza. Low clouds blunted the heat from the sun. The few people that traversed the piazza hurried along, heads bent, hands in pockets.

Four men. He was hoping for a stronger presence. "You know of an Ettore Majorana?"

Canali was stone-faced but replied, "Of course. You are looking for him?"

"Yes."

"There are others looking for him as well. Or am I telling you something that you already know?"

The twinge of disappointment at the news came and went. "I'm not surprised. Who are they?"

"Two Americans and an Englishwoman. They have a priest with them. To get inside the monastery."

"Do they have Majorana?"

"No. No one knows where he is."

"Where are they now?"

Canali scanned the piazza again. "Searching the sanctuary where Majorana apparently stays. It shouldn't take them long. They were to meet me here."

Falco nodded and glanced at his watch, thinking now would be a good time for his two men to arrive.

"There's more."

Falco looked up.

"Someone visited the monastery this morning. A man. He was alone. I didn't get a look at him."

Falco didn't react.

"The monastery doesn't get visitors from out of town often."

Falco thought about telling Canali not to worry about the visitor. But he reconsidered. "We shall wait and see if your friends return with their quarry," Falco said.

Canali's head bobbed in agreement.

"Oh, one more thing. I expect full cooperation from you and your men. Should you decide to play the various sides against the other, I will kill you like you killed the mayor. We'll see if you cry like a baby."

CHAPTER FIFTY-FIVE

1220 Hours, Tuesday, December 15, 1942
Sanctuary of Our Lady of the Cese

The temperature in the cave was bone-chilling. They found nothing, save some graffiti on the walls that neither Sean nor Emily was willing to translate for Conor. On the way back into the sanctuary, Sean bumped his head on the top of the door casing, causing him to mumble hotly under his breath. Conor was about to suggest they take another pass through the few rooms in the sanctuary when he heard muffled voices outside. The layout of the sanctuary didn't offer many places to hide based on their initial search for Majorana.

Think of something before it's too late.

"Come on, back into the cave, it's the best—"

"No, let me handle it," Sean said.

Conor started to protest, but Emily touched his arm. "Don't worry. He's a priest dealing with a crisis of faith. And a sanctuary is a good place to deal with that."

#

Sean raced to the table and sat. He could feel a trickle of blood creep down his scalp toward his forehead. He ran his hand across the crown of his head. As he wiped his hand on the cassock draped over his thigh, the door flew open. He feigned surprise by leaping from the chair as if he was prodded by a hot branding iron. A man in a dark uniform stood in the doorway holding what was most likely a gun. The sun backlighting him made deciphering his features difficult. He was over six feet with broad shoulders, and Sean could make out the forms of at least three other people behind him. The lead man was the first to speak.

"Who are you?" he asked, his head swiveling from one side of the room to the other. He took several steps deeper into the room, which made it easier to see the uniform of the SS officer. Sean was expecting someone from the monastery, not a Nazi. "And what are you doing here?" There was a snarl in his tone, as if Sean had invaded the man's own home. Three men followed him inside, one a dark-haired short man, the other two shy of six feet, one heavier than the other, who was sporting a couple days' growth of a beard. The SS officer's scowl betrayed his level of anger.

"I could ask you the same question."

The officer turned his head but kept his eyes on Sean. "Herr Heisenberg…all of you, search the building," he barked over his shoulder. He circled the table as the short man rushed past, followed by the unshaven man, pistol in hand. The other, the heavyset man, lingered. "Move," the SS officer shouted.

The fat man glared at the Nazi, then sauntered past the table, the officer tracking him with a piercing look.

He turned his attention back to Sean. "What I'm doing here does not concern you."

Sean shrugged and turned his attention to the pistol the Nazi held hip high, then to the open Bible on the table. He heard heavy footsteps toward the back of the sanctuary.

"Do you know Ettore Majorana?"

"No," Sean said, not looking up from the Bible. He noted the passage: Proverbs 19:5: *A false witness will not go unpunished, nor will a liar escape.*

"Do you know *of* him?"

Sean shot a look at the Nazi. "Of course, anyone who lived in Italy in 1938 knows of the scientist who…was guilty of committing the mortal sin of suicide." Sean paused.

The officer seemed like he was about to speak when the small man and the bearded one emerged from the rear of the sanctuary. "There is no sign of him in the sanctuary. Tardino is searching in the cave, behind the building," the bearded man said. No sooner had he finished his report than the one called Tardino entered the room.

The SS man didn't look pleased. "Did you do a thorough search?"

"Yes, of course. Just some empty bottles of wine…and rats. Plenty of rats. Nothing more."

The peeved officer swore and jammed his pistol in its holster. "Get back in the car. We're leaving," he said, his tone radiating disgust.

"Why is a German officer looking for a dead man?" Sean asked.

The officer placed his hands flat on the table and loomed over Sean. The taut skin surface flushed when he leaned over. "How can you be so sure that he's dead? Was a body recovered?" Not waiting for a response, the Nazi turned on his heel and headed for the door. "Your head is bleeding."

#

Conor worried that the echoing noise of he and Emily scurrying about for cover could be heard by the man who entered the cave, sweeping the confines briefly with his flashlight. But he disappeared quickly after taking a piss.

The door to the sanctuary creaked open, and Conor, from his place tucked away in a crevice, could see the shadow of Sean filling the narrow doorway. He pried himself free and whispered for Emily.

They made for the door, sloshing through puddles of fetid water, disturbing several rats in the process. Conor stopped at the doorway. Sean looked anxious to say something. He opened his mouth, but Conor put his index finger to his lips, silencing him. "Tell me later," he whispered. They entered the sanctuary and took seats at the table, and then he doused the oil lamp. The three sat wordlessly in the darkened space for ten minutes. Then fifteen. Water from the cave's roof sounded like a metronome when it hit the sanctuary's roof. Emily tapped the back of Conor's hand. He barely made out her likeness but knew she was getting impatient. He was too. Conor was about to give up on his ruse to flush out Majorana when they heard footsteps on the wooden hallway floor coming from the direction of the chapel.

When the footsteps stopped, he turned on his flashlight. Emily followed suit.

"Hello, Ettore. Tell us, where is the secret room?" Conor asked in Italian.

Ettore Majorana, dressed in the white tunic, scapula, and cowl of a Carthusian monk, stood with an arm shielding his eyes. Conor and Emily redirected the flashlight's beams, and Majorana lowered his arm. His answer came back in sotto voce Italian.

"He said it is behind the altar," Sean said. "But, Conor, there's something you need to know."

CHAPTER FIFTY-SIX

1300 Hours, Tuesday, December 15, 1942
Carabinieri Capitano Pietro Nuti's Office, Collepardo

The passive expressions on Heisenberg's and Nuti's faces only inflamed Koder's rage more, as did Tardino's glum stare.

"Capitano, why don't you have someone inside the monastery that you can depend on for information? Any effective police force would have someone indebted to you inside such a large operation."

Nuti exchanged looks with Tardino. "Sir, as you said, it's a monastery. It's filled with people that talk to God and keep to themselves. We've had no reason before today to even think we needed an informant inside."

Koder knew he was grasping for anything to explain their lack of success. He paced for a long moment; hands clasped behind his back. He stopped and turned to the silent group. "Am I the only one to come up with ideas? Heisenberg, where is your brilliance? I see no sign of it. And, Tardino, what of the power and expertise of the mighty OVRA? This is your homeland. Yet you just sit there sucking the oxygen out of the room. What a damn waste!"

Nuti cleared his throat loudly. Koder snapped his head around to face him. "What?"

"Dominic Canali is, somehow and for some reason, in the middle of this."

"Yes. Go on."

"Maybe a conversation with his wife will yield some information about what her husband has been up to. Something to help her…"

"Her what?" Koder shot back.

"Her lover."

"Your mistress…" Koder said, his words trailing off. "Can you trust her not to mislead you?"

"I believe so. We planned on meeting tonight. If her husband is mixed up with something involving your Majorana, she will know."

CHAPTER FIFTY-SEVEN

1310 Hours, Tuesday, December 15, 1942
Vacant House Next to Café Vecchio, Collepardo

Canali had planned for them to keep Majorana, if they found him, under wraps at a vacant house next to Café Vecchio, while they regrouped and packed up their gear for the trip back to Anzio. Sean's news flash concerning the arrival of the SS lit a fire under his desire to get out of Collepardo as quickly as possible. Conor pulled the van up to the rear of the café and backed it into the single bay garage across the alley. They hustled Majorana through the rear entrance of the two-story house. Once inside, the air was thick with the scent of death. A rat? Mice? They walked down a short hall into a large room and found Feinmann, head resting on his arms, seated at a large oak table fast asleep. His briefcase was unlatched and the flap open. When they situated Majorana at the table, Feinmann awoke and raised his head, leaving behind a pool of drool.

"Ettore. Do you...do you remember me?"

Majorana took in his face and swallowed hard, only managing a faint nod and a weak attempt at a smile.

Two candles in the middle of the table flickered. A ribbon of smoke from each weaved its way up toward the ceiling. Conor opened a window that fronted the piazza for relief from the foul air. Majorana's flinty expression barely changed since they left the sanctuary, except for the abbreviated reaction to seeing someone from his past.

"Sean, go over to the café, tell Canali that we're back and need him to do a few things. First, we need one of his men to guard the house, then I need him to load up our gear in the back of his truck. Don't tell him about our guest," Conor said.

"All right. I'll try to get some food. Ettore looks a bit drained."

Majorana looked suspiciously at Sean, as if he were trying to make sense of why a priest was helping an American and a Brit spring him from his home of the past four plus years.

#

A thick cloud of cigarette smoke billowed above the heads of the patrons at the bustling café. Falco kept his eyes on Canali as he moved about the front room. He seemed to be on his own, as there wasn't a sign of the mayor's wife. Canali would occasionally disappear into the kitchen but always returned within a minute, loaded down with a tray of food or an armful of wine bottles. There were instances where Falco caught Canali staring at him, forcing Canali to break off his gaze like he was caught staring at a woman's bosom.

When a broad-shouldered priest entered the café, the buzzing subsided as nearly all the patrons turned to size up the priest, signaling that he was not a regular of the café or of Collepardo. The black-haired man of God stopped just inside the café's entrance and scanned the room. Canali, behind the counter talking to the older woman who was operating the espresso machine, didn't notice the priest's arrival. Falco tracked the priest's path to the counter. Halfway there, he noticed the priest signaled Canali with an inclined head to follow him into the kitchen.

Canali shot Falco a brief glance before following the priest.

Falco stubbed out his cigarette in the ashtray, gathered his overcoat, and trailed Canali into the kitchen. The priest's back was to Falco. He was speaking to an attentive Canali in Italian, his Irish accent quite clear.

"So, Dominic"—the priest whipped around so quickly he nearly lost his balance—"this is the friend you mentioned." When the priest took in the sight of the Beretta Falco gripped in his right hand, Falco was sure he saw his red-tinged cheeks lose their color. Men with guns did that to people. Even men of God.

#

Conor, worried why Sean hadn't yet returned, was about to jump into a line of questioning when Feinmann reached inside his briefcase and dragged out a book about twelve inches wide. It was the 1939 edition of *Jane's Fighting Ships*. It prominently featured a heavy cruiser at anchor on the cover. He slid the book over to Majorana, which drew a smile from the wide-eyed monk.

"Thank you, Joseph. You remembered."

Conor, confused, raised both hands, palms up, and shot Feinmann a quizzical look.

"I recalled that years ago, I saw Ettore was carrying around some books about famous naval battles and fleets of various nations," Feinmann said as he watched Majorana flip through pages of the book. "And assuming that the monastery wouldn't have such books in their possession, I thought he might like to indulge his interest."

Conor allowed a bit of indulging, but then remembered what his file said about Majorana's language skills. "Where did you learn English?"

Majorana closed the book with a thud and pressed the heels of his hands into his red, sunken eyes.

Conor waited.

"I had a teacher, another monk. He was an American. Brother Larsen. He was from Salt Lake City. He left the Mormon Church and came here to the Certosa in 1939. You've heard of Mormons?"

"I've heard of them. Served with some on convoy duty. Good people."

Majorana cocked an eyebrow. "You are in the navy, the American Navy?"

"Was."

"What type of ship?"

"A destroyer."

"What class?"

The question startled Conor. "Clemson-class."

"Ah, four stack, two steam turbines, top speed thirty-five knots, twelve twenty-one-inch torpedo tubes, four four-inch guns."

Feinmann laughed. "See! What did I tell you?"

"Well, well, that's impressive," Emily said.

"What was your ship called?" Majorana asked. There were two subjects that deeply pained Conor to think about, much less talk about: the deaths of his wife, Grace, and their son, and the sinking of the USS *Reuben James*, the first US ship sunk during the war, even though it was before the Japanese attack on Pearl Harbor. Of the crew of 144, only 44 survived. Numbers he would never forget.

"It's not important. We have more—" Conor heard heavy footsteps. More than one set, coming from the rear of the house. Sean and Canali's man, he assured himself. But his assurances went up in smoke when he saw Sean enter the room followed by a lanky guy with a gun pointed at Sean's back.

Conor and Emily, stony-eyed, sprung to their feet, each with their gun of choice in hand.

What happened next caught Conor completely off guard. The man stowed his Beretta inside the pocket of his overcoat and smiled broadly.

"I am Adolfo Soleti, Commander of the Pontifical Gendarmerie Corps of the Vatican City State," he said, capping his introduction with a partial bow. "And this must be Ettore Majorana, or should I say Brother Bini?"

The reactions in the room were mixed. Sean, Canali, and Majorana registered expressions of disbelief, while he and Emily were more subdued, as if they'd expected to run into someone from the Vatican at some point. As far as Feinmann's reaction was concerned, his blank face told Conor nothing.

Emily leaned toward Conor. "He's the one who arrived at the monastery while you were inside."

Conor nodded. "Welcome to the party, Adolfo. But it breaks my heart to say that it is already time for you to leave."

"Not before I make my case to you and thank you for finding the slippery Brother Bini." Soleti turned to Majorana. "Father Misasi is very distraught over your absence. He wishes you to come with me back to the monastery."

"That will not happen. Trust me." Both Majorana and Soleti reacted to Conor's pronouncement with different expressions—Majorana's of dread, Soleti's of mock surprise.

"I understand why you are here. Why you have…taken Ettore against his will. You fear that the Germans have the same ideas as you do: to tap the brilliance of this poor man to further your weapons programs."

Majorana squirmed in his chair and looked at Feinmann with eyes that stabbed at his old acquaintance. Behind Soleti, Canali was shuffling backward to the rear of the house.

"Canali, where do you think you're going?" Emily said.

Soleti turned around and said, more to Canali than to the others, "Nowhere. He and his people are badly needed if we are to keep Ettore out of German hands."

"There is no *we*, Soleti. You don't seem to understand that." Conor pulled the slide back on his Colt to help convince Soleti that he meant what he said.

Soleti held up his hands in front of his chest. "All right. I will go. But can I offer you any assistance in your efforts to take him away? This is a foreign country to you. I can be of great help. Maybe I can offer the safety of Vatican City to you all until the war is over."

Emily gripped her Walther with both hands and pointed it at Soleti's chest. Soleti smiled and nodded.

"Yes. I understand. You refuse my assistance." He turned to leave, then stopped just before the hallway that led to the rear of the house. "Should I wish you luck?"

"You don't need to. But you need to stay out of our way," Conor said.

CHAPTER FIFTY-EIGHT

1400 Hours, Tuesday, December 15, 1942
Vacant House Next to Café Vecchio, Collepardo

"Soleti. He's not going away just because I asked him. You don't get the job of running the Vatican police by taking 'get lost' from…"

"Some American smart aleck?" Sean said.

"Maybe you should have told him you're Catholic," Emily added, smiling slyly.

"I get it. A little levity to lighten the mood. But I'm serious. That guy's not out of our hair just yet."

Canali excused himself to make arrangements for the guard and to load their gear. Sean offered to help and followed Canali out of the room. When they left, Conor, Emily, and Feinmann joined Majorana at the table.

"Feinmann, give Ettore the letters," Conor said.

Feinmann responded with the look of a man who had just been asked to show a bad report card to his parents.

"Hand over the letters from Fermi and Einstein," Conor said. "You have them, right?"

"Enrico? He…he…" Majorana stammered.

"He what?" Emily asked.

"He knows I'm alive? And Albert?"

"Yes, they do. And they are quite happy that you are," Emily said.

Conor turned to Feinmann. "What gives?"

Feinmann closed the flap of his briefcase and snapped the clasp in place. "I lost them. Somewhere, I just don't know where."

Conor's face flushed. He should have checked that Feinmann was ready to pour on the pressure once they found Majorana.

"Surely you're joking," Emily said.

"I wish I were. There was such a rush to get ready to leave that I must have left them behind."

Emily's jaw clenched. "Did you read them? Can you at least tell Majorana what they said?"

"No, I didn't read them," Feinmann said. He slipped his briefcase off the table and wrapped his arms around it, pulling it close to his chest like a shield.

"What the hell are you here for?" Conor asked, realizing that snapping at the man wouldn't produce the letters.

"I'm here to convince Ettore to spurn any German entreaties…"

"And?" Conor asked.

"And…" Feinmann said, shifting his gaze to Majorana, "to join the Allies…if that can be done without compromising his beliefs."

Majorana leaned forward, his arms nesting in his sleeves. His calmness, given the day's events, surprised Conor.

He opened his mouth to speak, then didn't.

"What, Ettore?" Emily said.

He cleared his throat. "What my friend asks of me, I cannot agree to."

"Why is that?" Emily asked.

Majorana tilted his head forward and closed his eyes.

It's not a time for prayer, Conor thought. It was time for some answers. "Why do you want to leave the monastery?"

Majorana opened his eyes, his head still bowed. "I am deeply religious, but I feel I am a prisoner there. And my family. I have been told by the Virgin Mary to return to my family." He raised his head and continued. "Do not misunderstand. I am indebted to Father Misasi. He has been like a father to me."

"What was your plan if you reunited with your family?" Emily asked.

"To ask their forgiveness and seek their help in leaving the country."

"Where would you go?" Feinmann asked.

"South America…possibly Argentina." Majorana's head bobbed from one questioner to another.

"Have you been in contact with your friend Werner Heisenberg?" Conor asked.

When Majorana turned to Conor, he immediately lowered his eyes. The corners of his mouth curled upward faintly, as if he was recalling a pleasant memory. "No. I wrote several letters to him but never sent them."

"Why did you leave the field of physics? You were among its leaders, or so I'm told," Conor said.

Majorana sunk down into his robe, pulling the cowl over his head. The image was of someone hiding, withdrawing—like he'd hidden from the world of theoretical physics. "I have known as early as 1934 of the enormous source of energy that the atomic nuclei could produce. Fermi's group didn't realize that they actually produced nuclear fission in 1934. They only recognized it in 1938. I want nothing to do with it. Physics has been on the wrong track since the early thirties. I saw no way to correct that. So I left that world."

"Are you saying that you would never work with the Germans or the Americans on their nuclear projects?" Emily said.

"No. Never. I would ask my friend Werner to shoot me. I would ask my friend here, Joseph, to do the same. As you know, it seems that I am incapable of taking my own life."

Conor eyed his watch, wondering why Canali and Sean hadn't returned, then turned to Majorana. "What if the Nazis threatened your family if you didn't join their program?" Conor said.

Majorana flinched deeper into the cowl, his expression slackened. "What did you say?"

"What if the Nazis—"

"They would do such a thing? Werner would let them do that?"

Emily chuckled. "You've been inside too long, Ettore. The Nazis have done much worse," she said, and let that percolate in the physicist's brain for a moment. "And your friend Heisenberg could do nothing to stop them."

Majorana sat up and lowered his cowl. "But if I am dead, threats against my family would be pointless. Yes?"

Conor glanced at Emily, whose raised eyebrows said it all.

Majorana was a couple of moves ahead of them. "You've got a good point there, Ettore," Conor said.

"Conor, why not let Joseph and Ettore move upstairs? Canali says there is a bed and a couple of chairs. Ettore looks as if he could use some rest before we head back," Emily said.

Conor shook his head. "I don't know, Em. We need to get out of here. Soon. It's just a matter of time before the Nazi Sean ran into gets the local police to start knocking on doors looking for Majorana." He paused a beat. "Just for a few minutes...until we get loaded."

Emily nodded her agreement.

Loud sounds from the rear of the house startled all of them. A breathless and ashen-faced Sean appeared with a frazzled look on his face that told him one thing...they were in deep shit.

CHAPTER FIFTY-NINE

1420 Hours, Tuesday, December 15, 1942
Alley Behind the Café Vecchio, Collepardo

When Sean announced that Canali couldn't get the truck to start, Conor wanted to throw something at the wall but thought better of it when he told himself that there weren't many engine problems that he couldn't figure out and fix. Except if the block was cracked, or the starter was fried, or there was a blown piston. Then he wanted to throw something again.

He left Emily to keep watch over Majorana and headed out with Sean to see what he could do. They approached the ramshackle garage across the alley, the swinging doors open wide, revealing the van's side engine cover raised and resting on top of the hood; Canali was bent over the spare tire that was nestled in the front left fender, talking to himself.

"Back off, Canali. Let me have a look," Conor snapped. Canali backed off. "What did it sound like when you turned it over?"

Canali shook his head and ran a finger across his neck.

Conor got the message. Not a sound out of the engine. That in itself was a clue. He bent down and surveyed the small block engine. He quickly spied a bracket just below the fuel tank that had been loosened on one side. Whatever it had once held in place was missing. He didn't have any experience with Fiats, but he did with British cars. He stretched forward to take an inventory on the far side of the engine. By process of elimination, he determined what was missing. He turned his head to Canali and Sean. "Someone took the ignition coil. Who did that?" Conor asked, rising to face Canali.

Canali slapped his forehead with the palm of his hand and let loose a string of Italian that contained a few choice words that Conor recognized. They weren't complimentary.

"The witch. The owner of the café. She is the one. I am sure of it," Canali said.

"Go get her. We're running out of time," Conor said.

"We don't have to," Sean said, his gaze directed into the alley. "I believe she just arrived."

Conor turned and took in the sight of a woman with glossy, dark chocolate-colored hair and a trim figure holding what looked like the ignition coil in her hand. The smirk on her face communicated her satisfaction at possessing it. There was a smudge of grease on her forehead and right cheekbone. She rattled off something in Italian through bared, clenched teeth.

Sean did the honors. "She says now that bastard Canali can't use my van like it's his own. It's hers." The woman stepped toward Conor, reached for the engine cover, and started to put it back in place, but Conor put his hand out and slid the cover back on top of the compartment.

"I'll need that back, lady," Conor said, trying to snatch the part from her hand but whiffing.

More rapid-fire Italian. Sean said, "She wants to know who we are."

Sean responded quickly. "We are friends of Dominic Canali," Sean said in Italian. "We're just borrowing his…the truck, just for an hour or so."

"Canali has no friends," she said and turned to leave, then stopped. "And he has no job. No job with me."

Conor got the message and blocked her, thinking he might have to clobber her and stuff her in the back of the garage so they could be on their way.

"Might I suggest a deal?" Sean said, intervening.

"There's an idea," Conor said.

"*Senora*, we would like to rent your truck for a fair price," Sean said. "What would you say to four thousand lire?"

The woman's eyes bulged, but she blurted out, "*Cinque.*"

Sean nodded.

Conor ran his hands through his hair. "Sean, slow down," Conor said. "That doesn't leave me with much in case we need to bribe some people to get back to Anzio. I don't think—"

"Excuse me for interrupting, but we don't have a lot of time. The longer we're here, the chances that we get picked up rise… meaning not in our favor."

Conor grimaced. The Irishman was right.

"So how do you Yanks say it? Fork it over," Sean said.

Conor shook his head, unbuckled his belt, and pulled it free. He unzipped the zipper that ran the inside length of the belt and extracted several banknotes. He peeled off five one-thousand notes and before he fully extended his hand, she snatched it from him and replaced the bills with the coil.

"Nice doing business with you, *senora*," Conor said, silently cursing the delay in their departure for Anzio.

Just as the witch took her leave, Emily joined them, telling them that the guard had arrived. Conor let Canali and Sean take care of replacing the ignition coil and he and Emily returned to the Canali apartment. He explained to Emily once they arrived that his thoughts had drifted to Feinmann's earlier admission that he misplaced the letters from Fermi and Einstein. Not that the letters, assuming they would have complimented and implored Majorana to join the Allied atomic weapons program, would have done much good considering Majorana's steadfast stance against any participation in the programs of either side.

"What if he was lying and he has the letters?" Conor asked.

"But why lie? That makes no sense. He's just forgetful," Emily said.

But the idea that there was more to his forgetfulness troubled him. He looked over at the duffel bags, the suitcase radio, and small valises belonging to Sean and Feinmann that were stacked next to the door, ready for their departure. Conor pulled Feinmann's valise from the pile and laid it on the table in the sitting room.

"Really? You think you need to do that just because he forgot some letters?" Emily asked.

"They weren't some *having a great time…how are you* letters.

They were important. They could have convinced Majorana to join the Allies."

He freed the straps from the brass buckles and opened it. At first glance, nothing unusual. There were two layers of folded shirts, underneath those was a pair of brown corduroy pants. A closer look at the pants unearthed a bulge under them. Conor slipped his hand under and pulled out a thick wad of US currency. All one-thousand-dollar bills. The wad was as thick as the book Feinmann presented to Majorana the previous day. Conor handed the cash to Emily and continued rummaging through the valise. "I know what you're going to say. That we got cash too before we left. But that's at least $25,000." Before Emily could answer, he felt another bulge. It was a High Standard HD .22 small-caliber pistol wrapped in an oil-stained rag.

"What the hell?" Conor said.

He dropped the pistol on top of the pants, jostling them enough to reveal something red beneath. He pushed the pants aside—another book. *The Communist Manifesto* by Karl Marx and Friedrich Engels. The red-bordered cover featured a large hammer and sickle above the author's names.

"What is this guy up to?" Conor asked.

"Wait a second," Emily said, then went into the kitchen and brought back a small knife. She dumped all the valise's contents on the table and sliced through the soft cloth lining of the lid. Finding nothing, Conor suggested she do the same to the bottom's lining. The initial slice revealed a manila envelope an inch thick. Conor took a deep breath, untied the thin string from the round clasp, and poured the contents onto the table—a series of documents and blueprints, several with the heading *RADAR–Radio Detection and Ranging.*

Conor and Emily exchanged looks. He was fairly certain he knew what Feinmann was, but one thing he was fully certain of was that he didn't want him alone with Majorana. "Go back to the garage and get Canali and Sean to hurry up and load the gear. Then meet me next door. We need some answers from Feinmann."

Emily headed for the back stairs of the apartment as he started to repack the valise. Before he closed it, he took a closer look at the Karl Marx book. He fanned through the pages to see if anything fell out. He noted that some pages had notes scribbled in the margins. The handwriting was difficult to decipher.

He was trying to read one of them when two muffled gunshots sounded. He wasn't certain whether they came from the café or the vacant house. He pocketed the HD .22 pistol and headed down the stairs to the piazza. It was nearly empty except for two elderly couples on the far side of it, seemingly oblivious to the gunplay. Two patrons from the café stood on the patio, glancing nervously about the piazza and speaking indistinctly. Conor moved cautiously toward the house, which was set back further on the piazza than the café, and spied a black, four-door sedan parked on the side of the house, no driver or passengers. As he reached the front entrance of the vacant house, he saw the door was kicked in; splinters from the doorjamb littered the floor inside.

He stood at the landing of the stairs leading to the second floor. With his Colt gripped in both hands, he took the first few steps; his neck craned up the stairs. Ten steps ahead, the stairs took a hard right turn, and then another three steps put him on the second floor. He heard murmured voices. He stopped inching up the stairs to listen. He heard what sounded like something being dragged along a wooden floor. He resumed his creep. A loud squeak pierced the air with his second step. He froze and looked down at the offending stair. Then he heard a grunt. He looked up. All he saw was a dark-clad, hulking body falling from the second floor two feet from his face. The falling body flattened Conor. The side of his head smashed into the nose of a step. Before he blacked out, he felt warm blood roll down his cheek.

#

The rear door to the first floor of the house flew open; the door-knob pounded a hole in the plaster wall. At the first sight of the smashed in front door, Emily winced. "Bloody hell." Her Walther PPK drawn, she shuffled across the floor of the sitting room, past the table they sat at earlier with Majorana, toward the landing. There were droplets of blood on the floor leading outside. She turned and saw the body of a middle-aged man, short, stout; he was one of Canali's men. He was lying in the middle of the staircase on his back, facing up, his head toward the landing. A round had gone through his right eye. She stepped over the dead man and slowly made her way up the stairs. Taking each step softly, on the balls of her feet, she hugged the exterior wall of the stairway, her right shoulder dragging along the wall as she did. She could hear the raspy sound of her rapid breathing. Emily stopped and looked down the stairs. Sean was staring up at her. He moved to the side of the dead guard and took his pulse. Emily resumed her advance. At the top of the stairs, she stopped, turned, and signaled Sean stay put. She cocked her head and listened. Her mouth went dry. There was the faint burbling sound of someone breathing through a throat thick with mucus. She glanced at Sean, who stared at her.

There were two doors, one on either side of the landing. One was closed; the other, on the left, slightly ajar, was where the gurgling sound was drifting from. Emily inched closer to the open door. Stopped, listened. A gulp of air, and she burst into the room, kicking the door all the way open. Feinmann was prone on a blanket on the floor next to the bed. Majorana was gone. "Damn it." She lowered her PPK. "Sean," she shouted.

Sean rushed past her and knelt beside Feinmann, rolling him over on his back. Blood soaked his white shirt, the contrast of the red on the white vivid. Feinmann's eyes were shut, his mouth was moving, but the words couldn't be heard.

Sean opened his shirt. "Chest wound. Not good."

Emily knelt beside the scientist. "Who are you?"

Feinmann turned his head toward her voice and opened his eyes, but they fluttered, then closed again.

"Those documents…and all that money. What were you going to do with them?" Emily asked.

Sean held the man's head in his lap and began praying, his hands making the sign of the cross.

"To Russia," Feinmann said. A rivulet of blood and mucus coursed out of each side of his mouth. He coughed for several seconds; his eyes still closed.

Sean stopped praying.

"I was going to take my friend to Russia." His voice was giving up.

"Why?" Sean asked. But Emily thought she knew why.

"It's wrong…not to share our research… We're allies."

"How were you—" But one final cough, louder than the others, interrupted her. The blood and mucus that followed this time were darker, denser. Emily's half-asked question were the last words Feinmann heard.

The heavy smells of blood and spent rounds fought each other for dominance in the small room.

"Where's Conor?" Sean said as he laid Feinmann's head on the blanket.

That was the question she had been asking herself ever since she heard the gunshots. Emily rose to her feet and looked at the bed. The indentation on the mattress was about the same size as the small-framed Majorana. "If we find Majorana, we find Conor."

CHAPTER SIXTY

1435 Hours, Tuesday, December 15, 1942
Apartment of Dominic Canali, Collepardo

Emily left Sean to pray over the lifeless body of Canali's partisan. Conor's disappearance hounded her. He was either giving chase, or he had been taken as well. But by now, they could have dumped him in an alley like some unnecessary baggage.

She returned to the Canali apartment and found him in the kitchen, consoling his distraught wife, Claretta. She buried her head in her husband's chest, muffling her sobs. Canali's arms wrapped around her as he whispered in her ear.

"What's wrong?" Emily asked, then realized that it wasn't her business. Or maybe it was.

"I don't know. She has asked for my forgiveness, but she won't tell me why she needs it," Canali said. "What has happened?"

"Majorana and Conor are gone. Feinmann is dead. So is your guard."

Still holding Claretta, Canali, eyes blinking rapidly, said, "Franco...*morto*? Nooo."

Then Claretta's weeping hit a high pitch. Emily thought the news of Franco's murder explained the ramping up of her hysterics, but what initially made Claretta break down was what interested her more. She stepped closer to the couple. "Claretta, why are you so upset? Tell me," Emily said.

Claretta lifted her head and began jabbering.

Emily struggled to understand what she was saying between sobs. Canali, who seemed to understand, jerked his head back and pushed her away, keeping her at arm's length. She fought to get closer, but he wouldn't allow it.

Sean entered the room, his hands painted with Feinmann's blood.

Emily looked at him, then back at Canali. "What, Dominic?" she asked.

Canali buried his face in his hands and shook his head.

Emily placed a hand on the man's shoulder, which put a stop to the head shaking, and she spoke. "Claretta said something about Nuti, the carabinieri chief, and a meeting last night. What else did she say?"

Canali walked over to the table and dropped into a chair, his chin resting on his chest. "She just told me of her affair with the bastard Nuti. But…that's not the worst of it." Canali raised his head and looked at Emily as Claretta stood, her chin quivering. His gaze slid from Emily to his wife. "She says she told him she wanted to break it off, but he threatened to tell me if she didn't tell him about my involvement with you and why you were here. She told him you were hiding Majorana next door. And now Franco is dead." He pointed at his wife. "All because of her."

Claretta moaned.

Emily took three long strides toward Claretta and grabbed her upper arms and squeezed. "Where did they take him, Claretta?" Emily said. Getting nothing but her whimpers, she shook the woman. "Where?"

"Emily, don't—"

She turned. "Quiet, Sean," Emily barked, then looked at Claretta. "Tell me where."

Claretta's softly enunciated answer was tinged with regret but lacked the panicked sorrow of her confession: she did not know where they went. When she mentioned the German officer in a black uniform and someone from OVRA, Emily's own level of panic reached a boiling point. Claretta had betrayed them all. She shoved the woman away.

Claretta sprinted from the kitchen. Seconds later, a door slammed.

Emily looked at Canali. It was time to move. "Dominic, find someone you can trust to bury the bodies. Can you take care of that?"

He sat rubbing his eyes with the heels of his hands.

"Dominic?" she prompted him.

He nodded.

"What about Conor?" Sean asked. The front of his cassock, stiff with caked dried blood, caught her eye.

"I have to think that, if he's still alive"—Emily shivered at her words—"they took him with Majorana. My first guess is the carabinieri station. If they're not there, they're most likely already on their way to Rome." She cocked her head in Canali's direction. "We need your men, Dominic. As many as you can get here."

"Why?" Canali asked weakly.

"We're going to bust into your local police station. Can't be too hard." Emily pulled her Walther from her jacket pocket and ejected the magazine. She could almost feel the piercing stares from Canali and Sean. Before she could return their looks, there was a knock at the door. All three exchanged rattled glances, as there was another knock.

Emily motioned to Canali to answer it.

Canali stood but before opening the door said, "*Sì?*"

"I'm looking for Conor Thorn," someone replied in Italian.

Canali shot a look at Emily. She motioned with the Walther to open the door, then concealed her gun behind her back. Canali opened the door enough for Emily to glimpse a short man with a sinewy, short frame. He saw Emily and his eyes bugged out. "It's me, Eugene DiLazzaro. You remember me...from the PBY."

Emily, mouth gaping, was sure her face betrayed her astonishment.

"Yeah, I know. I get that look a lot." DiLazzaro strode into the room with a wide grin. "Hey, Father. Nice to see you again...still in one piece, I see."

"You have thirty seconds to tell me how the hell you got here," Emily snapped.

"Yeah...great story. When I went back in the direction of the PBY, I couldn't find it. It probably drifted down the beach because of the tide. I gave up when I heard its engines start up. If I didn't get back in a specific time frame, the plan was for them to take off and I was supposed to hide until the pickup day."

Emily looked at her watch, so DiLazzaro picked up the pace like he was making the call at the Ascot Racecourse.

"Being Italian American, they thought my chances were good. I knew you guys were headed to Collepardo, so I gave some guy I met near Anzio some money for clothes and came here too. I heard you mention something about Café Vecchio in Collepardo, so I stopped in and asked some questions. Some woman there told me the manager had been hanging around with some people she didn't know, and here I am," DiLazzaro said, taking in a lungful of air. "I thought you could use some help." He smiled and looked at Emily, then Sean.

Emily almost expected him to take a bow. The performance was authentic, and as incredible as the story was, she believed him.

"I speak fluent Italian. And I'm pretty damn good with a gun." DiLazzaro looked around and asked, "Hey, where's Conor?"

"You're just in time to help us find him."

CHAPTER SIXTY-ONE

1440 Hours, Tuesday, December 15, 1942
Carabinieri Stazione, Collepardo

"You." That was all his old friend uttered when Heisenberg first showed his face outside the puny cell that held a solitary prisoner: Ettore Majorana. The blood spatter on his white robe told Heisenberg what Nuti and his two men wouldn't—there had been a human cost to taking Majorana from the American. It was a long minute before Majorana spoke again, and when he did, he spared no rage. "Two men shot, one dead. Another close to death." A vein in his forehead pulsated, his words forced through pursed lips. His eyes welled up with tears. "One was our...our friend." Majorana shouted the last two words. The knuckles on both hands were white as they gripped the iron bars of the cell door.

"Who...who are you talking about?" Heisenberg said. "I wasn't told anything. I—"

"It was Joseph. My friend Joseph Feinmann. And yours too! They shot him in the chest."

"Oh God...I didn't know," Heisenberg's words softly trailed off.

Majorana drew a quick breath. "All of this bloodshed is because of me." He dropped his head, tears falling to the floor, leaving dark marks on the gray slate.

"I did not know that Joseph was involved. I had no idea." Acid churned in Heisenberg's stomach. He grabbed for a bar on the cell door to steady himself and pressed his fingertips against his large sloping forehead as if to rid his mind of the devastating news. Feinmann had been a favorite of his. He was always willing to join in the spirited discussions at the seminars Heisenberg organized.

Majorana raised his head, the whites of his eyes streaked with red. "And to see that they involve you sickens me."

Majorana's reproachful words stung him. "I didn't know they would go so far as to kill anyone. You must believe me, Ettore," Heisenberg said.

"Why, Werner? Why have you done this?"

"I am under tremendous pressure from those who oversee my program. They threaten me. That is fine. But they have threatened my family if I fail at developing a useful atomic weapon. I am desperate."

"What you and the Allies are chasing must never be caught."

"Ettore, listen to me," Heisenberg said, his words a harsh whisper. "You will be back in Italy soon. This I will promise." He drew closer to the cell door and in a soft voice said, "I hope to deliver a weapon that has a very limited impact. But I need help with some...theoretical issues. When I was told that you were alive, I knew you and only you could help me solve them. And you will be responsible for saving many lives, not just my family, by bringing this horrible war to an end. Trust me, Ettore. I will not let them harm you."

"And what of my family? If they can threaten you and your family, they can do the same to mine. I have washed my hands of the direction that people like you and Fermi and Bohr have taken the field of physics. You are being manipulated by bloodthirsty politicians and maniacal despots. If you proceed, there will be so much bloodshed that God could never forgive." Majorana turned away from Heisenberg and nearly fell onto a wobbly cot on the far wall of the cell. With his back to his former friend, Majorana began to weep.

#

"Thank you for allowing me some personal time with him," Heisenberg said, hoping his words would mollify the ill-tempered hauptsturmführer.

Koder, seated behind Nuti's desk, his black-booted feet propped up, waved a dismissing hand in his direction. "And what came of your reconciliation?"

"Quite little, I'm afraid. Honestly, Hauptsturmführer, I think it a waste of your and my time to take him to Berlin. As far as assisting me and my team, he is dead set against it." Heisenberg grimaced at his use of the word *dead*.

Koder stared blankly at Heisenberg. He let his boots slide off the desk, hitting the floor with a thud. "It is not your decision to make, Herr Heisenberg. My mission was to bring him back to Berlin, and I plan to fulfill this mission like all the others assigned to me."

Heisenberg had expected just such a response, but he felt obligated to put words to his remorse regarding the whole affair.

"But your report has convinced me we will also take some of his family back to Berlin with us. I believe you stated that his mother is still alive, along with some siblings?"

Heisenberg's jaw muscles tightened, and his chin jutted out toward Koder.

"I'll take that as a yes."

The mention of family jolted Heisenberg. He needed time. For exactly what, he did not know. He cleared his throat. "May I make a suggestion, Hauptsturmführer?"

"Go on," Koder said, rising from the chair and stretching his back.

"I suggest you send someone back to the sanctuary to collect any books and papers he may have stored or hidden there. They may be useful to me and my associates."

"Ahh, an excellent idea. I will have Capitano Nuti do just that."

Nuti cracked open the office door and poked his head in as if answering the mention of his name.

"There is someone here from the German Embassy. It concerns him," Nuti said, inclining his head toward Heisenberg.

Koder nodded slowly, acknowledging the news, then looked suspiciously at Heisenberg.

"Show him in," Koder said, adding instructions to send two men out to the sanctuary to collect Majorana's books and papers. He paused, then stepped toward Nuti and said something indistinct. Nuti smiled and nodded as if he were just invited to a dinner with Mussolini. Koder turned back to Heisenberg, looking pleased with himself. "Herr Heisenberg, what have you done to warrant a visit from the embassy?"

"I assure you nothing that will embarrass you or me," Heisenberg said, hoping Koder did not detect the tinge of doubt in his voice.

Koder pulled his tunic down by the hem and sat. The gentleman from the embassy was middle-aged, with a scrawny build. There was a trivial number of lonely strands of hair that laid on the top of his head in a swirl. His hands nervously rotated his felt hat by the brim. After he entered, he made a sputtering introduction, which annoyed Koder. Heisenberg thought embassy staff in Rome probably didn't see many SS officers.

"Hauptsturmführer, Ambassador von Bergen received word that Herr Heisenberg is needed back in Berlin immediately."

Koder gave Heisenberg a sideways glance.

"It seems that Herr Speer is demanding an in-person report as to the progress of his work. Decisions as to funding must be made. That is all the ambassador was told, Hauptsturmführer." As soon as he finished, he ceased toying with his hat.

"You are here to transport him, I take it?"

"That is correct." The news displeased Koder given his scowl, but a shrug of his shoulders communicated his displeasure was short-lived.

"Herr Heisenberg, because of me you have good news to report to Herr Speer and General Leeb, do you not? Majorana will soon be joining you!"

"Another suggestion, Hauptsturmführer? Might I take Majorana with me? The sooner he is—"

"Stop," Koder said, his arm held up in opposition. "Of course not. For the simple reason that I do not trust you." The man's icy stare chilled Heisenberg. "Majorana will be in Berlin soon enough. I will make sure of that." He slammed both hands down on the desk, the handset of the desk phone bouncing in its cradle. "Now, it is time to see what this American spy can tell me—something I have been looking forward to all morning."

CHAPTER SIXTY-TWO

1505 Hours, Tuesday, December 15, 1942
Carabinieri Stazione, Collepardo

It had been at least thirty minutes since two uniformed men had dragged him into the room and sat him in a chair in the center. The space, approximately twenty-foot square, seemed like it was little used given the stale, exhausted air. The chair faced the front of the building, and he could tell they were on the second floor—through two windows that overlooked the street, Conor saw the peak of the roof that covered the building's entrance that he was hustled through earlier.

After one man bound his hands and then his feet, he left, leaving the second man, who was clearly keeping himself busy by chain-smoking cigarettes, to stand guard somewhere behind him. The room, its wood plank floor covered in a thick layer of dust, looked out to the east. The afternoon sun streamed into the room, catching thousands of particles of dust in its beams.

Conor's head pounded from crashing into the edge of the step back at the vacant house. When his hands were being tied, he'd looked down at his left thigh. He didn't feel or see the lump in his front pocket where the case with his cyanide pill was stored, not that he could have easily retrieved it with his hands tied.

While he waited for the inevitable interrogation, he eyeballed two propaganda posters pinned to the wall in front of him. One depicted a pith-helmeted worker carving the letters *S.P.Q.R.,*

Roman Senate and Peoples into a wood sign calling for fascist agriculture workers to come to Ethiopia, land that Mussolini had invaded in the mid-1930s. The other featured a man with angular features—an angry, brow-furrowed Gary Cooper look-alike—gripping a semi-automatic rifle calling for volunteers to join the Black Brigade. His black shirtsleeves were rolled up to his elbows, exposing vein-popping, bulging forearm muscles that made Conor think of Popeye the Sailor Man cartoons.

He had recalled his training when he was being tied up. His hands were the key to his escape. He'd kept his palms together and elbows far apart, the separation in his wrists hopefully producing the needed slack to allow him to shimmy one of his hands free... later. He noticed that the guard took little time with the knot, which was helpful. That and the thickness of the rope, about an inch in diameter, should render the process less arduous. To keep him from using his bound hands as a club, they'd added a length of rope that extended from the loop around his hands to the loop that bound his feet together at his ankles.

The sunlight and dust caused him to sneeze five times in close succession, which made his head pound more fiercely. He heard the guard laugh behind him. "What? No God bless you?" Conor said.

"*Che cosa?*"

"I said—"

The door banged open, and he heard the heavy footfalls of several men on the plank flooring. There was some muttering going on behind him, first in German then in Italian, that Conor couldn't make out. Then a SS officer, his black uniform impeccably tailored, walked from behind him to stand three feet away, directly in front. The good news was, based on Sean's description of the Nazi who searched the sanctuary, this was the same guy and not another SS sociopath.

"A chair!" the Nazi shouted.

This was the first time he'd gotten a look at the blue-eyed, blond-haired SS menace. Square jawed with well-defined features, he smiled revealing near perfect teeth except for two lower teeth, incisors maybe, that were honed to a sharper point than others.

A flurry of movement produced the requested chair which was

placed inches away from Conor. The Nazi took a seat, their knees nearly touching, and tossed Conor's cyanide pill case on his lap.

"I assume the pill has gone missing?" Conor said.

"You won't need it. Spies are shot. I'm sure you know that."

"Fine. You keep the pill. You may need it someday when the Allies are rolling through the Brandenburg Gate."

"So, is that what you and your British lackeys dream about?"

"Not a dream, but it is your nightmare. One closer to coming true every day."

Two other men stepped forward and flanked the Nazi, neither of whom looked German. One of little height and many pounds, dressed in a dark, heavily wrinkled suit, seemed sullen as if he was the one in Conor's chair. The other, in a carabinieri uniform, appeared as if he was looking forward to watching his favorite movie.

"So, tell me, what organization dropped you behind enemy lines? Was it that organization run by a group of cowboys...what is it called? The OSS. Or do you work for the British? The SOE perhaps?"

"Does it really matter? But maybe you need to know so you can write it in your diary. *On this day I met a handsome American.* Something like that, right?"

The slap across the face wasn't telegraphed. The second back-handed slap, with the other hand, surprised him more. Conor's ears rung with greater intensity, which was a condition he hoped he wouldn't have to get used to. They'd been ringing since his head was introduced to the stair in the vacant house.

"How were you going to get Majorana out of the country?" the blue-eyed Nazi asked as he rubbed his hands together.

"We already have our tickets on the next liner headed to Lisbon. A luxury suite complements of the OSS...no, the SOE... No, maybe it's the FBI...oh shit, I forget."

That made the blood rush to the man's face. "Nuti, go get Hermann. Now." The one who looked like Conor's predicament was his favorite movie took off. Thirty seconds or so later—Conor wasn't much for counting when his head was pounding like a jackhammer—a circus-strongman-sized creature, also decked out in a drab gray SS service uniform, showed up.

Blue eyes started asking questions in short bursts, like he was using a German MP40 submachine gun, not waiting for an answer. Conor thought it was because he'd ceased speaking at all. After each burst of questions went unanswered, Hermann did his thing. The first blow to the side of his head drove Conor off his chair, sprawling him to the floor. Hermann picked him up by the waist of his trousers and roughly reseated him. When Conor whispered "*Danke, Hermann*," the goon's nostrils flared.

When Conor again failed to answer a series of questions about the status of the Allied weapons development program, Hermann squinted at his boss. Or at least Conor thought so, but he couldn't be sure since he was seeing two Hermanns and two black-clad SS bosses by that time. The two bosses pointed at Conor's gut. A second later, a pile driver of a punch landed—Conor would later think this was the one that might have cracked a rib. Luckily for him, it made him vomit, sprinkling specks of bile all over the gleaming surface of Hermann's and his boss's black leather boots.

"Hauptsturmführer Koder, shall I continue?"

So, the boss is Koder.

Koder, his lips curled in a nasty snarl, stopped wiping the puke off his boots and glanced at his watch. "No, leave him." He continued in hurried German: "I will take him and our new friend with us to Rome, then to Berlin. There, we have people properly trained in getting answers from spies." Koder looked at his watch again. "We leave when we have Majorana's books and papers in our possession."

Conor heard Koder say something about wanting an escort before he traveled out of range of Conor's ringing ears. It was a minute later that Conor realized he was alone.

Thank God for sloppy Nazis.

CHAPTER SIXTY-THREE

1520 Hours, Tuesday, December 15, 1942
Carabinieri Stazione, Collepardo

Soleti, accompanied by his newly arrived men from Rome, was told to wait for Capitano Nuti, who was busy questioning an American spy. The admission from the glib officer manning the front desk surprised Soleti.

When he was taken back to Nuti's office ten minutes later, he registered only a moderate amount of surprise when he saw Koder was in attendance.

"Anteo," Soleti said as he gave Tardino a slight nod.

Koder noted the interaction. "You two know each other, I take it."

"We find ways to use each other," Soleti said, "without crossing lines that would have us both…out of work…or worse."

"What are you doing here?" Koder said.

"I have information you will be interested in," Soleti said, but Koder surprised him by offering a blank face. "In exchange for this information, I would like to take Majorana back to the Vatican. There he will be safely out of Allied reach."

Koder scoffed and stared at Soleti.

"What information?" Tardino said.

"I am aware of the location of two Allied spies, one American and one British, and…Ettore Majorana. You take the spies and I'll take Majorana. I am sure the spies, given the effective methods of the SS, will divulge much in the way of valuable information about each organization they spy for."

"You're wasting our time," Koder said. "While you were sleeping, we took the initiative and have already taken the American *and* Majorana. As far as the British spy, that would be a distraction I don't have time for. Now, go. Return to that nest of spies you call the Vatican."

Soleti struggled to mask his surprise. "Ah, it seems I have underestimated the effectiveness of the SS, not to mention the OVRA," he said, offering a slight nod in Tardino's direction. "My mistake. But at least you can permit me to see Majorana. Just so I can report to the cardinal secretary of state that I found him alive and being treated with respect."

"Why would I allow that?" Koder asked.

"It is a harmless request that would allow me to speak to the secretary of state and His Holiness regarding the wise and magnanimous behavior of Hauptsturmführer Koder."

Soleti was sure he saw Koder's chest swell. "Go see your monk. You have ten minutes with him," Koder said, then wheeled around to Nuti. "Go with him. And watch them both closely."

CHAPTER SIXTY-FOUR

1540 Hours, Tuesday, December 15, 1942
Carabinieri Stazione, Collepardo

Conor's vision still hadn't fully realigned itself to producing just one of everything, the ringing in one ear rose and fell like it was tuning in a signal on a shortwave radio, and his split lips remained swollen. The taste of blood in his mouth had receded, but the amount of blood he'd swallowed was causing some stomach upset. Other than that, he was still breathing, although not without some pain radiating from an angry rib.

The wind rattled the windows as he shimmied his hands together, creating some heat. Slowly, the hand movement caused the rope from his wrist to slip down the back of his hands, toward his knuckles. When he heard muffled voices coming from outside the room, he stopped to see if he could decipher anything. When the voices lowered, he continued with the shimmy dance. It took longer than he expected to inch the rope over both sets of knuckles, but a measure of patience later, he hit the jackpot. It took much less time to untie the slipshod knot that secured his feet and even less to pry the slim blade from his right shoe's insole. It wasn't much of a weapon, but it was all he had.

His best way out was through one of the windows and a short drop onto the roof over the station's entrance. What that route lacked was covertness. A saying about beggars and choosers popped into his pounding head. He dragged his aching body over to one window; it was nailed shut, the square heads of the two nails on each side of the window frame were set at least a quarter of an inch below the surface. They'd also nailed the other window shut, but as far as he could tell, it was with only one nail, and its head was much closer to the surface. The handle end of the knife was thin, so getting a firm grip was difficult. The good news was the steel blade and tip were sharp. He dug at the wood around the nail head and in little time could grab it and wriggle it out. He pocketed it—*Hell, it could come in handy*—gripped the bottom of the window and lifted. It rose with accompanying screeches…but only six measly inches. He put more muscle behind his effort and succeeded in raising it another four or so. His head still ringing, pounding, and throwing a fit, he wondered if ten or so inches would be enough to slide his frame through.

It was. But as his chest slid through, the bottom of the window scraped the length of his left rib cage, igniting a bolt of pain that traveled up through his neck, into his brain, adding to the pandemonium. When he dropped near the peak of the sloping slate roof over the entrance, he crouched and took a series of long, slow breaths to calm himself.

He counted five people in two groups walking on the street within fifty yards on either approach to the station. No one seemed to notice the man with the bloodied and bloated face squatting on top of the small roof, but it was time to move.

He slipped down the slope and looked below. It was an eight-foot drop. He seized the edge of the last row of slate tiles and lowered his legs over the side, slowly…slowly, then fast…fast. The slate tile proved too slick, and he lost his grip, then crumpled to the ground in a heap, almost blacking out from the jolt of pain from the left side of his rib cage. But he recovered—he had to. He clambered to his feet and peered around the corner of the entrance. An old man, bundled up in a dark gray coat, was staring at him. When he smiled, Conor saw he was missing multiple teeth. His nose hairs mingled with the hair of his gray mustache like they were old friends. The man laughed. Something told Conor the old man had escaped from the same room at one time in his youth. He gave the man a snappy salute and beat a path out of there.

Every step told him he wasn't in good shape—but maybe good

enough to rain down some shit on Koder's planned escape from Collepardo.

CHAPTER SIXTY-FIVE

1545 Hours, Tuesday, December 15, 1942
Carabinieri Stazione, Collepardo

Majorana was on his side, balled up with knees to his chest, when Soleti approached the cell.

"Wake up, Ettore," Nuti said. "You have another visitor." Nuti leaned against the block wall opposite the cell and lit a cigarette.

Majorana stirred and rolled over on his back. He had his cowl pulled up, covering half his face. He eyed Nuti and asked him for a smoke. Nuti shook his head, but Soleti pulled a pack of Macedonia Extras from his breast pocket and offered the open pack to Majorana, who sat up, then stood. He took a cigarette in his slim, lean fingers, and Soleti extended his lighter through the iron bars. Majorana closed his eyes and drew on the cigarette deeply. He held the tar-laced smoke in his lungs for three seconds, then released it through his nostrils.

"I have been sent by Cardinal Maglione, do you know who that is?" Soleti asked, expecting some reaction but getting none other than another deep draw on the Macedonia. "What is your name?"

Majorana opened his eyes. "Brother Bini." Tendrils of smoke rose to the ceiling as the brother gave Soleti a cold, hard stare.

Soleti gave Nuti a sideways glance. "He's lying. And you have five minutes left," Nuti said.

"Are you here to take me to the Vatican?" Majorana asked.

"I hoped to do just that, with the blessings of Father Misasi. But—"

"Is the prior safe?" Majorana asked.

"He is. Do not worry about him."

"But I do. He has been so kind to me. Like a father," Majorana said, dropping the cigarette on the floor and stubbing it out with a sandaled foot.

Soleti heard Nuti snort and shot him a glance. Nuti had smoked his cigarette down, the red tip nearly burning his lips.

"I was about to say that it seems that I do not have the power to take you to the Vatican. The Germans, with the help of local authorities and the OVRA, have the upper hand. I wish that were not so."

Majorana turned and sat on the thin, stained mattress. The sleeves of his robe swallowed up his hands. He bowed his head. Soleti didn't know if he was praying.

"They have not harmed you?" he asked quietly.

A long pause. "Not yet."

"That's it. Time's up." Nuti grabbed Soleti by the elbow and led him out of the cell area.

Before the door closed behind them, Soleti heard Majorana praying.

CHAPTER SIXTY-SIX

1555 Hours, Tuesday, December 15, 1942
Carabinieri Stazione, Collepardo

Soleti shook free from Nuti's hold on his elbow as he walked him past Nuti's office to the front entrance. Through a wide window that looked out on the hallway, they witnessed Koder screaming at Tardino and a burly man dressed in an gray service uniform. Both he and Nuti stopped and took in the dressing down. The space between Koder and the two other men was spittle filled. Both Tardino and the other man leaned back out of range of Koder's damp outrage.

"What now?" muttered Nuti.

"Maybe you should go in there and see," Soleti said.

Nuti looked at him as if he'd asked him to sample a taste of dog shit.

Soleti saw Tardino's face harden, and then Tardino pointed at Koder. "Why didn't *you* order Hermann to stay with the American? His escape isn't our fault alone. He's—"

Nuti and Soleti heard nothing more from Tardino because Koder cut him off with a backhanded blow that snapped the man's head back. Nuti winced as the blow landed and a trickle of blood made its way from a nostril, down his lip, into the corner of his mouth.

"*Mio dio*," Nuti said under his breath.

"*Mio dio*, how could you let the American spy get away, Nuti?

257

You people are very…careless," Soleti goaded. Nuti chose to ignore the question.

But Koder wasn't quite done. "Your insolence and carelessness will be reported to your superiors. Now get ready to depart for Rome as soon as the men return from the monastery." Koder turned and caught sight of Nuti and Soleti standing in the hall. "Nuti, get in here at once. And you, Soleti, get out before I have you arrested."

CHAPTER SIXTY-SEVEN

1615 Hours, Tuesday, December 15, 1942
Apartment of Dominic Canali, Collepardo

On the way to Canali's apartment, Soleti concluded that his best, and likely only, option was to throw in with the American and British agents, now that the American had found a way to get free from his captors.

A woman opened the door to the apartment halfway and greeted Soleti with a hard stare. Soleti, followed by his two men, bull-rushed their way past her and in response, the woman slammed the door shut and retreated into the kitchen. The British agent was the first person he recognized. One other, a thin man somewhere in his twenties, was a new face. The British agent and the new man had been conversing when the woman opened the door. The British agent broke off and approached him, unzipping her olive green jacket to purposely reveal a semi-automatic pistol stuck in the waist of her wool pants. In the afternoon sunlight, he noticed for the first time that she was quite beautiful, despite the masculine outfit and bulky boots. Her light brown hair hung to her shoulders, and her almond-shaped green eyes seized on the three visitors with a hot intensity.

"Soleti, what are you doing here? We were clear: we need nothing from you."

"Aah, but I have news. Your American friend has escaped. Where he is now, I do not know, but he is free from the hands of the SS and OVRA." He glimpsed relief quickly replaced by suspicion. "I thought it important that you were aware of this, Miss…?"

The woman eyed him closely. "And you know this how?"

"I have just come from the carabinieri stazione, where I met with Ettore Majorana. And of course, Hauptsturmführer Koder, who was not pleased to see me."

Before she could reply or react, Canali and the priest from the café barged into the apartment. Soleti's men, startled, moved for their holstered guns, but Soleti waved them off. Both Canali and the priest looked surprised. The Irishman moved toward the woman.

"Emily, everything all right here?" Sean asked.

"Yes, Emily, is everything all right between us?"

She eyed Soleti. "Like Koder, I'm not pleased to see you either. But I appreciate the news you bring."

"Will he return to this location?" Soleti said.

"There's a chance of that," she said.

"I want to clarify that we share an objective: that Majorana not fall into the hands of the Germans. You, at this point, have failed in achieving that objective. I offer my services and that of these two very capable men in reversing the situation."

She turned and conferred with the priest. Soleti saw it as an opportunity and turned his back to them, then grabbed Canali's upper arm in a viselike grip. "How much did the Americans and British pay you to help them?"

"Nothing. They just promised to supply arms and possibly some training."

"Of course they paid you. It's what they do. Where is the money?" Soleti tightened the vise. His two men stood to either side of Canali, who was now perspiring.

"It's in a safe place."

"It's here, in this apartment, isn't it?" Canali didn't respond. "You killed the mayor for the money, didn't you?" Canali tried to free his arm, but Soleti persisted. "I am sure that Capitano Nuti would be interested to hear that you are responsible for the mayor's *disappearance*."

Canali stiffened.

"Maybe just as interested as the American would be to learn

that you are working for the Russians. Deceiving them along with the Holy Father."

Canali yanked his arm free and stepped toward the woman in the kitchen.

Everyone froze when the front door banged open, this time to reveal the worked over American agent. "Can anyone join this party? Sorry, I forgot to bring the beer."

#

"DiLazzaro, what the hell?" Conor shut the door. "Remind me to ask you what the hell you're doing here. But first, I need to hear what Soleti is doing here." Conor turned to Soleti. "We laid it out for you, didn't we?" he said, trying to keep a slight limp from being noticed as he slid past the Vatican cop.

"Your escape seems to have deeply angered Hauptsturmführer Koder," Soleti said.

"Well, I won't lose sleep over that," Conor said. "Now, I'll ask you to leave so I can get reacquainted with my friends."

"Conor, a word?" Sean said. Soleti retreated with his two men to a corner of the room.

Seeking some relief, Conor took a seat at the table, and Sean did the same. Emily stood near them, as did DiLazzaro. "I believe Soleti when he says he wants nothing to do with Koder or the OVRA. He wants what we want: to keep Majorana out of their hands," Sean said leaning in. "We could use him and his two men if—and I am sure that it's your plan—we're going to take Majorana back."

"We don't need help. I have it figured out."

"Conor, I trust this man," Sean said.

Sean's point about Soleti and his men made some sense. Conor looked up at Emily. "Where's Feinmann?"

"Dead," she replied. "Took a round to his chest when they took Majorana. I had Canali and one of his men bury him." She leaned over. "Conor, you look like—"

"A DeCamp bus to Newark just rolled over you and left you for dead," DiLazzaro said.

"A bus named Hermann." He looked up at Emily again. "I'll be fine, Em."

"You better be. We've got work to do."

He nodded. "What do you think about Soleti and his boys? Think Sean's right?"

"Time's running out. I think we have one more chance at getting our man. So yes, I do."

Conor processed for a bit, peering over at the Vatican men huddled together in the corner. The two new men looked like twins, each stretching out to over six foot and both sporting broad shoulders and sizable upper arms. Soleti darted a look over his shoulder at Conor. "Okay. But we need to keep eyes on all of them. Sean, go give Soleti the news."

Conor stood. He was sure Emily didn't miss the contorted look on his face as he did. She certainly didn't miss his bruised face and swollen lips. He turned to Canali, who was standing next to Claretta. "We're not safe here. Or next door. Is there somewhere else we can stay until we hit the road?"

Canali said something to Claretta that Conor couldn't make out. She replied, and then Canali spoke up. "The only place is the garage. There is a back room. We keep empty crates and broken chairs and tables from the café there."

"Okay. That will do. Do you have a map of the area?"

Canali nodded and left the room. Emily took his face in her hands. "Your nose, is it broken?"

He felt her warmth on his damaged face and realized he could have fallen asleep in her hands then and there. "I don't know. I'm too numb to figure that out."

Canali returned with a map in hand.

"Let's go. Eugene, Em, Sean, grab our bags. Leave Feinmann's bag and clothes here, but take the cash and the documents. Leave the copy of *The Communist Manifesto* for Canali and his friends."

Conor noted a twitch on Soleti's face at the mention of the book. He knew the Vatican had it in for the communists. Up and down the ranks.

CHAPTER SIXTY-EIGHT

1630 Hours, Tuesday, December 15, 1942
Garage Behind the Café Vecchio, Collepardo

They squeezed past the café's Fiat into the back room. Eugene, after he gave Conor the Reader's Digest version of how he got to Collepardo, made himself useful by clearing the center of the room and propping up a damaged table with the back of a chair. The air was thick with dust kicked up by Eugene's efforts. The light from a lone light bulb illuminated the particles, giving the impression it was snowing.

Conor opened the map and laid it across the table, kicking up more dust. He located the road that led from Collepardo to Rome, which was southwest. He cleared his throat, but a banging at the door to the garage stopped him. He looked at Canali and inclined his head toward the door. Emily handed Conor his spare Colt, and everyone but Sean and Eugene pulled their weapons.

A conversation in heated Italian seeped through the door to the storage room; voices were raised. An elongated moment passed, followed by Canali entering the room with three men in tow, no one more surprised to see Bruno Fabrizio than Conor.

"Canali, what the hell is going on?" Conor asked, jabbing a finger in Bruno's direction.

"He says he wants to help. He wants revenge."

"For what?" Emily asked.

"He said the Nazi officer shot his wife in the knee."

Bruno, as if on cue, dove into his story. His face flushed, and a vein in his neck bulged. Sean gave a running translation for Conor. Conor surveyed the reactions of the crowd, and all seemed repulsed by the recounting of Koder's barbaric act—except Soleti. *What barbaric act did Soleti engage in?* Conor wondered.

Bruno cried as he finished his story, his last words squeezing out of a thick throat.

"He said he blames himself for not telling them right away where Majorana was hiding. He wants revenge but also to redeem himself in his wife's eyes," Emily said.

"No," Conor said firmly. "He'll just get in the way. Tell him to go home and take care of his wife. I will take care of the German. I have some revenge to take out myself."

"You're in charge, Conor, but…being Italian myself, I can say that he has a right to avenge what he says the Nazi pig did to his wife," Eugene said.

"Like you said, I'm in charge," Conor replied, "and I say we don't have time to babysit. It's still a no. Em, tell him."

Emily spoke to Bruno for a long minute, patting him on the shoulder as his head hung low. She unbuttoned the top button of her shirt, reached under it to pull out a small fabric purse, unzipped it, and removed three one-thousand lira banknotes and handed them to Bruno.

"The deal was three thousand lira *when* we had Majorana," Conor said.

"Well, we did have him at one point," Emily said. She patted Bruno on the shoulder and thanked him. A stunned Bruno wheeled around and left the room.

"That was a kind gesture, Emily," Sean said.

Conor winked at her, then said, "Can we get back to business?"

Conor looked over at the other two men who came in with Bruno, one clearly quite young, maybe even eighteen, the other at least fifty. Both had rifles that looked like they were used in WWI and had stiletto-style daggers at their belts. Conor didn't recognize the rifles, but he saw they were bolt action and magazine fed. The younger one also had a revolver tucked into his waistband. Their eyes were wide-open and looked plenty eager. Maybe too much so. Like he was on the training mission on the Chesapeake.

Eagerness fueled by a growing sense that nothing could kill him, or those around him. He survived a near drowning as a youngster. He survived, in an indirect way, the sinking of the *Reuben James*. His last two missions with Emily also saw him come out the other end unscathed. His audacity, his unbridled ego, got someone killed on the bay that stormy night. An operation with too much risk with absolutely nothing to gain. A tragic miscalculation. He owned it. His second thoughts about the plan he had devised for the retaking of Majorana were quelled one minute only to bubble up to the surface the next minute. But this time, there was too much at stake. His plan was audacious but that's what their current situation called for.

"Eyes and ears on me," Conor said as he pulled the nail he dug out of the window frame from his pocket and turned his attention to the map on the table. He held up three fingers. "There will be three teams," he said, looking around the room, all eyes drilling holes in him. As he spoke, Canali translated for his men. "Team one: Canali, one of Soleti's men, and DiLazzaro. Team two: me, Sean, Soleti, and one of his men." He needed to keep Soleti where Conor could put him down if he had to. It was something in his gut that made him distrust the man. "Team three: Emily and both of Canali's partisans." With the nail, he stabbed the map at a section of the Via Trisulti, the road that led out of town, where there were a series of hairpin turns, and scratched a circled around one specific bend in the road.

"The café's van and Soleti's car need to be pulled along the side of the road after this turn. Koder and his people won't see them, meaning they won't get that far." He took a quick look around the table. Everyone was looking at the map, except Soleti, who was looking at Conor. When their eyes met, Soleti's gaze slid to the map.

"Team one will take a position coming out of the turn. When you get there, toss out the caltrops." A murmur rippled through the group. Conor reached into one of the bags and pulled out a handful of the devices.

"It's an anti-vehicle weapon. It will take out their tires." That got Soleti's men and the two partisans laughing and slapping backs. "I heard Koder say he wanted an escort, so I think there will be two cars. Koder and Majorana should be in the second vehicle. That's the way I'd do it. Take the lead vehicle out. Team two will take a position at the sharpest point in the turn and hit the second vehicle, who will have to stop when the first car stops." Heads nodded all around.

"Team three will take up a position leading into the turn, here," Conor said, scoring the map with an X. "Emily will have a set of binoculars and will signal me when she sees the two vehicles approaching.

"Team three will toss some caltrops on the road *after* the two vehicles pass, to keep the second vehicle with Majorana from reversing and escaping after they see the first vehicle get in trouble." Conor hauled three haversacks from the duffel bag and explained each team would have, on top of their personal weapons, a Sten Machine Carbine with seven magazines and four Mk 2 hand grenades. Conor, Emily, and Eugene would carry the Sten guns. Conor looked at his watch.

He stowed the nail in his pocket. "Listen, we need to get in position as soon as possible because we don't know when they'll be leaving the police station. So we may be playing a waiting game once we get in position. Just be patient. Remember, the key objective of this mission is to take Majorana, and to do that it's critical that we stop the lead vehicle. We're counting on the element of surprise. Any questions?"

"What do you plan to do with Majorana after he's taken?" Soleti asked.

"Not up to me to do anything except get him out of Italy. Alive."

Soleti stepped away to talk to one of his men.

Conor turned to Sean. "I don't expect you to get involved if there's gunplay, but you can help get Majorana secured."

Sean nodded.

"But take this." Conor handed Sean a small pistol. "It's a Baby Browning. Low caliber. Hard to kill someone with it."

Sean shook his head in protest. "Don't ask me to—"

"Just take it for self-defense. Slow down someone with a shot to the shoulder, leg, or arm. You carried one similar to it on our mission to find the missing document from Ike's diary."

"To protect the Vatican's diplomatic pouch."

"Well, now you'll use it to protect yourself, which is more important than a diplomatic pouch." Sean gave in and slipped the Browning inside his cassock.

Conor turned to everyone. "All right, teams, mount up."

CHAPTER SIXTY-NINE

1700 Hours, Tuesday, December 15, 1942
Via Trisulti, Southwest of Collepardo

Conor, at the wheel of the Fiat, struggled to see out the windshield because of the heavy snowfall. The single wiper screeched along the surface, barely clearing a patch of glass slightly bigger than a cocktail napkin. Despite the visibility challenge, he thought the falling snow would help hide the caltrops.

Conor counted the hairpin turns as they drove. Soleti was close behind with his two men. Conor drove past the fifth hairpin and pulled the Fiat to the side of the road, careful not to get too close to the edge of the gully. Both vehicles emptied, and without being prompted, the teams formed up and raced to their positions.

Conor motioned to Sean, Soleti, and Soleti's man to drop into the shallow ditch, and then he walked into the middle of the road. Dry, any speed above twenty miles per hour would be not only dangerous but stupid; snow-covered, Conor pegged a safe speed around ten miles an hour. He raised his binoculars and zeroed in on Emily's team. He saw Emily doing the same thing, standing in the middle of the road with her binoculars trained on the section of road approaching the hairpin. That section of road sloped downward, which allowed Emily a good look at any vehicles headed their way. From where Conor was, the heavy snowfall made it nearly impossible to see that section of road clearly.

"Oh, shit," Conor said through clenched teeth.

"What? What is it?" Sean said.

"It's Emily, she's running down the road toward us. Stay here." Conor took off, his haversack bouncing on his back. He met Emily thirty yards from his position.

"They just reached the top of the rise and are on the downslope," Emily said, panting. "There are three vehicles. Three, not two. In the lead is a truck, an army truck. I can see soldiers in the back, hanging over the sides with rifles."

"Not the escort I was counting on."

"There's a black sedan next, a Mercedes I think, in the middle. A smaller vehicle is behind it."

"Fucking Koder. Okay, we'll stick to the plan. No other choice. Get back in position and make sure to spread the caltrops after the third vehicle," Conor said, already turning to head back to his location.

\#

Eugene DiLazzaro didn't think the guy from the Vatican police looked so happy to be lying on the side of a ditch in three inches of the white stuff. He got it. He'd never liked snow either. In Newark, when it snowed, it looked pretty for all of thirty seconds; after that, you could have it.

While he spread the two dozen caltrops across a section of road, he saw Canali and the Vatican guy in what looked like an argument. The snow had a muffling effect on their voices. As Eugene kicked snow with his boots to cover as many of the caltrops as possible, he saw the Vatican guy slap Canali. Eugene swore under his breath. As he turned to head back to the ditch, he watched as the Vatican cop pulled out his gun and shot Canali.

Eugene slid into the ditch like DiMaggio into home plate. "What the hell have you done?" Eugene looked down at Canali's twitching body.

"He was going to run. I couldn't let that happen."

Eugene felt for a pulse on the side of Canali's neck. It was slow and weak. The Vatican guy got in Eugene's face. He hated when guys did that.

"There is no time. I hear a vehicle. It sounds like a truck…in low gear. Leave him."

#

Conor lowered himself to his haunches and took another look down the road beyond Emily's position while he briefed the others. He pulled the Sten gun from his haversack. At the crack of a pistol, Conor snapped his head around. It had come from down past the hairpin, where the first team was positioned.

"What trigger-happy fool was that?"

"I'd bet that other American… He looked nervous to me," Soleti said.

"That's funny, so did your guy," Conor shot back, drawing a hard look from Soleti.

CHAPTER SEVENTY

1710 Hours, Tuesday, December 15, 1942
Via Trisulti, Southwest of Collepardo

Koder was peeved. He had admonished Hermann to slow down just a minute before, and given the excessive fishtailing the sedan was doing, he needed to do it again.

"Hermann, what did I tell you? Slow down! We can't afford to find ourselves in a ditch buried in snow."

Koder turned his head and looked past the sulking Majorana at the passenger next to him. Majorana had reacted maniacally when he first saw the prior, Father Misasi, his hands bound behind his back and mouth gagged, being dragged into the carabinieri station along with all of Majorana's papers and books. At first, Koder wasn't sure what rankled the monk more: seeing the prior or his precious books. In the end, it didn't matter to Koder.

"Enjoying the ride, Father? I'm sure you and the other monks don't get out much." Koder couldn't understand Misasi's panicked reply, which also didn't matter to him. What did matter to him was what taking Misasi signaled to Majorana: that he would stop at nothing in completing his mission.

Koder reached forward and tapped Tardino on the shoulder. "Do you know where Majorana's family lives?" A sideway glance saw Majorana stiffen—just the reaction he wanted.

"Yes, but just the mother and one brother and sister. The others, no. Why do you ask?"

Koder sneered. Tardino was a simple man. "I have decided to take them with us back to Berlin. As added motivation for Ettore. People will do anything to save the lives of their family. It's human na—"

The gunshot killed his thought. "Stop. Stop the car." The Mercedes slid to a halt, and Hermann flashed his headlamps to signal to the truck up ahead. "That gunshot. You heard that, didn't you?"

"Yes. It was probably someone hunting for dinner. The people, they are hungry," Tardino said, his words dripping with rebuke.

Koder gave a dismissive wave of his hand. "Is there another route we could take?"

"No. One road in and out of the mountains," Tardino said.

"Hermann, get out and make sure the driver of the truck heard the gunshot and to not stop for anything. They must be on high alert."

#

Conor lifted his binoculars and looked down the road. The truck and the other two vehicles were stopped fifty yards from Emily's position. The driver of the Mercedes, Hermann, jumped out of the car and trotted, slipping and sliding, up to the driver's side of the truck. It was a quick conversation, as the truck began moving again almost immediately. By the time Hermann reached the Mercedes, the distance between the truck and sedan was stretching beyond thirty yards and closing in on Emily's position.

The snowfall had picked up its intensity, the flakes bigger and wetter. He dropped his binoculars into the haversack as he watched the truck pass Emily's position. It took another moment for the truck to pass Conor and his team, who had melted into the thick roadside underbrush. Conor counted six soldiers, three on either side of the bed, wearing heavy greatcoats, rifles resting on top of the bed's wooden side slats. As they passed, Conor shifted his gaze down the road. The Mercedes had passed Emily's team and was closing the distance to Conor.

#

"Holy shit! Conor said something about the element of surprise, but he meant the other way around," Eugene said. "How many do you count?"

"Three, but probably more. I don't have a full view of the truck bed. The driver is the only one in the cab," Soleti's man said.

"You're in charge of these," Eugene said, handing over the haversack with the grenades. "Make sure you let the truck roll over the caltrops before tossing them."

Coming out of the hairpin, the truck picked up speed. When the front tires hit the field of caltrops, the sound of the punctures was softened by the snow-covered road, as was the hissing sound of escaping air.

"Now!" Eugene drilled a short burst from the Sten into the truck's cab, taking out the driver, who slumped over the wheel. The first grenade rolled under the truck's rear, and when it triggered, it sent the bed two feet off the ground. The force of the explosion pushed the truck toward the ditch on the opposite side of the road. The grenade explosion and the truck's movement kept the soldiers off balance, making it difficult to get off shots anywhere close to their targets.

Eugene let loose two, then three short bursts from his Sten, raking the back of the truck. Another grenade landed a foot from the rear tire and sent a plume of dirt, snow, and slivers of wood from the truck bed's wooden side skyward when it detonated.

Three soldiers leaped from the truck, landing upright but quickly losing their footing in the wet snow. Two collapsed to the ground. Two more bursts from the Sten riddled their prone bodies. Eugene redirected his attention to the truck. One soldier, rifle-less, bounded over the far side of the truck and started for the woods. Soleti's man tossed another grenade, this time under the truck's chassis. Eugene buried his face in the snow as a blistering hot wave of air rushed over him. Eugene scrambled to his feet and headed for the front of the burning truck, searching the woods for the runner. Ten yards away, the body of the soldier was lying at the base of a boulder, the side of his head split open, dark blood melting the snow beneath his head.

He turned back, expecting to see his partner, but he was alone.

#

"Speed up. Don't stop," Koder shouted. He counted three explosions and several bursts of automatic gunfire. Hermann downshifted and sped forward.

"The truck up ahead, it's blocking the road," Hermann said, hitting the brakes. The Mercedes skidded and ended up sitting sideways in the middle of the road.

"We can't sit here, you fool. Go around them."

Hermann spun around in his seat. "There is no room," he shot back.

CHAPTER SEVENTY-ONE

1715 Hours, Tuesday, December 15, 1942
Via Trisulti, Southwest of Collepardo

"Reverse at once, get us out of here," Koder yelled. He sat forward and grabbed the back of the front passenger seat, pulling his Walther from his holster with his other hand. Hermann shifted into reverse, realigned the direction of the sedan, then stomped on the accelerator. The sudden motion pushed Koder up against the back of Tardino's seat. Their heads nearly collided. Koder eyed Majorana holding the hands of the priest, whose cheeks were tearstained. "They will not take you alive. I will make sure of that."

The Mercedes traveled erratically, swerving from side to side. "Nuti's car—it's in the way."

"Ram it…push it off the road. Just get us out of here."

#

The Mercedes, positioned between Emily's team and Conor's, reversed and was closing on a small two-door Fiat that had stopped in the middle of the road. Conor, Soleti, and his man stood on the lip of the roadside ditch; Sean remained hidden in the thicket. Conor spied the two partisans and Emily scampering back into the brush after depositing the caltrops behind the Fiat.

The Fiat reacted to the Mercedes speeding toward it by also

reversing. Conor couldn't hear, but he watched the rear tires of the Fiat fall flat, followed by its front tires, then continue to reverse, swerving side to side. The Fiat slid to a rest with its right driver's side facing the reversing Mercedes, whose own tires had fallen prey to the field of caltrops, though it hadn't slowed the heavier Mercedes's momentum. It smashed into the side of the stalled Fiat. The driver's head cracked the side window before he slumped over to his left into the lap of the passenger.

Conor and Soleti closed the distance between themselves and the Mercedes, which was still bulldozing the smaller Fiat as it continued to plow up the road. The Fiat, its radiator spewing steaming water, was turned sideways, perpendicular to the road, its left side digging into the roadbed, tilling up snow and gravel. Eventually both vehicles came to a stop.

The entire scene played out in seconds. Emily and the two partisans emerged from the brush, guns drawn, Emily yelling at the Fiat's occupants to get out of the vehicle.

Conor saw the driver of the Mercedes and a passenger in the front seat, but the back seat was lost in shadow.

The Fiat's passenger Conor recognized from his interrogation—the carabinieri capitano who licked his chops while Conor took a beating as if he was a heavy bag—emerged partially from the Fiat, using the door as a shield. He fired one shot, downing one of Canali's partisans. Emily let loose a two-second burst from the Sten carbine, shattering the door's window. The outgunned cop fired one more shot—his last—and Conor saw Emily go down on one knee as she let loose one more two-second burst. Her target dropped to the ground. Conor stopped breathing…but Emily got up. The driver, if he was alive, wasn't moving. The other partisan emerged with his rifle trained on the battered Fiat, yelling at the driver to get out. Still no movement, the partisan approached the open left side door and stepped over the lifeless body of the carabinieri officer and fired three shots into the Fiat's interior.

Conor, Soleti behind him, moved closer to the Mercedes, where there was still no one moving. Conor advanced toward the front of the car. He was close enough now to make out Koder and Majorana and a third man he didn't recognize in the rear seat. Emily moved toward the rear of the Mercedes. Stopping ten feet away, she took a knee, her Sten's stock nestled in her shoulder. Conor noted the blood dripping onto the snow around her left foot.

Sean was just behind Conor, Soleti, and one of Soleti's men. "Conor…the back seat," Sean said. "It's Father Misasi…the prior. Please be careful. He's an innocent."

"As long as he stays where he is, he should be safe," Conor said as he kept his eyes locked on Koder. "Get out of the car, Koder. And do it slowly."

Inside the Mercedes, there was no movement.

#

At the sound of a burst from a machine gun, Koder turned and looked out the rear window. Through the wisps of steam coming from the damaged Fiat, he watched Nuti grab his chest and fall to the ground. The American was standing twenty feet away; the Vatican commander and another man were standing behind the American along with the priest from the sanctuary. He assumed the men in the lead truck were no longer to be depended on.

Koder grabbed Majorana's arm and dragged him from the vehicle, keeping the Mercedes between himself and his assailants. The Mercedes provided some protection but not enough. Koder handled the slender Majorana like a rag doll. The nose of his Walther was pressed against the side of Majorana's head. Being so frailly built, Koder knew that Majorana was not much of a shield. As he inched toward the front of the Mercedes, past the passenger door, Tardino slipped out of the sedan with his hands raised.

Koder eyed a man in a dark suit running toward his adversaries who then stopped and whispered to Soleti. The American took note.

"I count seven against three. Tough odds, I'd say," the American said. Sweat dripped down Koder's spine. "Hermann, get out of the car," the American said.

"No, stay where you are," Koder said. He was running out of options: give up his prey, or kill him so no one wins. He stopped level with the front right wheel and glanced at Tardino, who stood two feet to his left, his arms still raised in defeat. "Do something, you worthless piece of shit," Koder said. The Nazi flags on the Mercedes's fenders snapped in a rogue gust of wind.

The American and the woman slowly closed in on him, he toward the front of the Mercedes, she toward the rear. Soleti and two men were just behind the American. The priest and another man held back.

"Where are your vehicles? I shall need them. You surely didn't walk all this way."

The American laughed. "You're going nowhere, Koder. But I'll make you a deal. Let Ettore go, and we'll leave you and what's left of your party here to make snow angels. How's that?"

"I'll make *you* a deal. I won't put a bullet in the genius's head as long as you step back and tell me where your vehicles are."

#

"No deal," Conor said. The next thing he was going to say depended on his assumption that the arrogant Nazi thought he was going to get out of this intact. "Go ahead. Shoot him. Our mission was to make sure you didn't take him back to Germany alive."

Koder had the expression of someone who'd just watched his opponent go all in when he held only a pair of twos.

Just then, the Mercedes's driver's side rear door popped open, and Misasi's plump body rolled out onto the ground, landing with a grunt. Sean had taken two steps toward the fallen priest when the driver, Hermann, decided it was time to screw things up. The door opened a crack, the nose of a Mauser semi-automatic peeked between the windshield pillar and the door's edge. Before Hermann could site a target, Conor tapped out two-second burst, shattering the door's window and the windshield. Emily added two rounds. The Mauser fell to the ground.

Tardino moved suddenly, taking Conor's attention from Hermann. Conor watched Tardino rip Majorana from Koder's grasp and haul him backward, toward the crippled Fiat. Hermann bent down and reached for the Mauser with a bloodied hand; two bursts from Emily's Sten felled Hermann, whose lower body was still in his seat, but his upper body slumped to the ground, the crown of his head resting in an inch of snow. His dead eyes stared at Conor. Koder extended his Walther at the retreating Tardino and got off two rounds before Conor released a short burst across the roof of the Mercedes, sending Koder's Walther flying into the ditch.

Sean sprinted over to Misasi and, shoving his large hands under his armpits, began to drag the priest toward the ditch behind Conor and the others.

Koder, his right hand bleeding, took two steps backward, creeping closer to the undergrowth that bounded the thick woods along the road. Conor launched himself across the hood of the Mercedes, sliding feet first, and planted both boots into Koder's chest. The men hit the ground.

Conor's right elbow hit the road's surface hard, his Sten gun jarred out of his hand. Koder struggled to his feet and swayed. Conor, his rib injury reminding him it had gone nowhere, scrambled to his feet and advanced on the dazed Koder, kicking just below Koder's knee and scraping the man's shin downward, bringing Conor's full weight to bear on the man's foot.

A guttural yelp was followed by the snapping of the small bones in Koder's foot. Koder stumbled backward, which freed his damaged foot from under Conor's boot. Conor jabbed the base of his palm into Koder's chin, snapping his head back, then drove his fingers into the man's eyes. He followed the move by hooking his left leg around Koder's legs and shoving him backward to the ground. As Koder fell, Conor landed on top of him, squeezing all the air from Koder's lungs. Fighting back his rib pain, Conor rolled off and stood. Before Koder could move, he raised his right foot and stomped, using his full body weight, on Koder's neck, crushing his windpipe. His pale blue eyes bulged briefly then settled but didn't close. They remained focused on the cloudy winter sky, as if still searching for a way out.

Conor clutched his aching rib cage and, panting heavily, looked at Majorana and Tardino, both standing several feet away at the rear of the Mercedes. Neither of Koder's two rounds had found their mark, as far as Conor could tell.

"Conor, look," Sean, across the road from the Mercedes, said, pointing in the direction of the burning truck. "Eugene and Canali." Eugene held up Canali whose left arm was wrapped around Eugene's neck, his right hand pressed into his own gut. Canali's coat was blood-soaked. Their progress was slow. Canali's right foot dragged, leaving a trail in the snow. Eugene laid Canali down on the roadside near Sean, who was tending to Father Misasi.

Soleti took several steps toward Conor, his expression stricken, but pursed lips and flared nostrils betrayed his anger. Soleti said something to one of his men that Conor couldn't understand, but his gut told him Soleti was working with a different playbook.

"You took out the truck, Eugene. Good man. A bit of a surprise, huh?" Conor asked.

"You're telling me. And that wasn't the only surprise."

Emily moved toward Canali and took a knee to watch Sean pull his bloody coat from his wound. "He's in bad shape but alert," Sean said.

"Conor, I have to tell you something," Canali said in a weak voice.

Before Conor could respond, Tardino moved to pick up Koder's Walther.

Emily shouted, "Conor!"

But Tardino shook his head. "No, no, no. No worry." He snatched the Walther from the edge of the ditch and pumped two rounds into Koder's knees, then muttered something in Italian.

"What did he say?" Conor asked.

"He said it was for his sister," Emily said.

So, Bruno does get his revenge, Conor thought.

Tardino's knee-drilling drama had everyone's attention, which was why no one noticed Majorana was on his feet, making a run for it. He headed straight into the thick woods beyond the ditch. Sean, one of Soleti's men, and Eugene, his Sten gun over his shoulder, tore off in pursuit, Eugene in the lead. If Conor had to chase anyone, they wouldn't have any trouble getting away, so he waited—for all of one minute—until the four men emerged from the woods.

Eugene and Soleti's man each held on to one of Majorana's arms and led him toward Conor, Emily, and Soleti. An out-of-breath Sean followed behind. Soleti's second man made a snap move and joined his partner, then yanked Eugene away and slammed him to the ground before he pulled his own gun and nudged Sean and Majorana toward Soleti.

Soleti's men flanked their two captives and stood behind Soleti, facing Conor and Emily. Soleti motioned with his Beretta at Tardino.

"Move over here, Tardino, with the others," Soleti said.

Tardino obliged slowly.

"Toss all your weapons into the ditch," Soleti said, pointing his thumb toward Koder's last stand. "All of you, toss guns, satchels… everything into the ditch."

"What the hell are you doing, Soleti?" Conor asked.

But Canali answered instead: "Meet Agent Falco. He's doing the bidding of the NKVD. And he plans to take your genius friend back to Moscow."

"Double-dealing communist," Tardino said, spitting on the ground.

Conor swore under his breath.

Shit. Always trust your gut, Wild Bill said.

Soleti again ordered them to toss their weapons. "And if you don't, you'll have to say goodbye to Father Sullivan," he said, his eyes hard. The lone partisan was the first to toss his rifle.

"Em, Eugene, do it. We can't lose Sean…or Majorana," Conor said.

The three of them tossed their Sten guns and satchels toward the ditch, the Sten guns landed just at the ditch's lip. Before Conor returned his attention to Soleti, a shot rang out followed by another. Soleti collapsed to the ground, reaching for his lower left leg. Soleti's man next to Sean also dropped to the ground and clutched his upper thigh. Sean stood perfectly still, the Baby Browning in his hand, a look of shock on his face. Emily and Eugene leaped toward the ditch and pounced on their Sten guns; Conor had his Colt already drawn from his shoulder holster and fired off a round into Soleti's other man, who went down in a heap.

Majorana collapsed to the ground, pulled his knees to his chest, and started weeping. Sean, no longer being held at gunpoint, dove on top of Majorana to protect him. Soleti, recovered from the shock of being shot, raised his Beretta and aimed at Conor, but his action was met with a burst from Emily's Sten gun, putting him down for good. The wounded man next to Sean started to drag himself away. Eugene, Sten gun back in his hand, advanced toward him. Before he got too close, Conor put a round in the man.

Conor did a quick survey and spotted Tardino with Koder's Walther PP, this time pointed at Conor.

"I was just going to give this to you," the smiling Tardino said as he lowered the gun and tossed it toward Conor.

"Good decision, Tardino," Conor said.

CHAPTER SEVENTY-TWO

1720 Hours, Tuesday, December 15, 1942
En Route to Collepardo

Puchini's grip on the leather strap attached to the inside of the Lancia's passenger door was viselike. Luciano Majorana was driving like a man possessed. He had told him so several times. When they found themselves in the midst of a snow squall, Puchini closed his eyes and prayed.

"Have you told me everything you know about the monastery and how this became known to you?" Luciano said, his words clipped and clear.

Eyes still closed, Puchini shook his head. The question had now been asked of him three times. His answer was always the same. "Luciano, as God is my witness, there is nothing I have not told you."

"And you swear you have not shared this news of my brother with anyone in or known to my family?"

This was a new question. Puchini opened his eyes and was greeted with the sight of the windscreen of the Lancia framed in a ring of ice, the wipers caked with a sleeve of snow. When he was slow to answer, Luciano reduced speed and cut his glance sideways. "I have done what you asked...I did not share any information with any other member of the Majorana family or their friends." He turned to Luciano, who resumed his study of the road ahead.

Luciano was tall and lanky. When they started their journey

to the Certosa di Trisulti earlier that morning, he had been seated upright, his dark hair brushing the roof. Now, nearly two hours later, he was slumped forward toward the steering wheel, the eyes behind his round, tortoise shell glasses focused forward.

"I thank you for that, Monsignor. I do not want any more sadness brought upon my family or friends should this Carthusian monk not be who he claims to be. They have been through enough."

"I understand completely. But as I said when we met to make our arrangements," he glanced furtively at Luciano, "the information I was provided with seems incontrovertible."

"So you say, Monsignor. So you say."

Several minutes passed. The snowfall lessened, and with it the Lancia picked up speed. Luciano sat back. "Tell me what you know of this plumber. What was his name?"

"Bruno Fabrizio." Puchini spent the next five minutes reciting all that Tardino had reported about his brother-in-law. He made certain to sound angry when he recounted the fact that Fabrizio refused to mail the letter.

Luciano eyed Puchini. "What he did by not mailing the letter was wrong. There is no doubt in my mind about that. But if he had done nothing, you…I would not know of Ettore and the monastery." Luciano opened his mouth again as if to say something but shook his head slowly.

"What is it, Luciano?"

"The monastery…the Certosa. Salvatore and I searched dozens of monasteries, but they were all not far from Naples. It sickens me that we did not press on to regions farther flung. That is a grave error that I will have to live with the rest of my life, Monsignor."

Puchini left Luciano alone with his thoughts for a number of minutes, wondering if he should be concerned that Luciano did not react when he mentioned making arrangements earlier. The reward, though it fell short of Dante's demand, would go a long way to satisfying him until he could raise the balance.

"Luciano, your family's reward. You have it with you?" When his question went unanswered, Puchini turned to the man. "I only ask because the orphanage is in such dire need. The children are not getting enough to eat. Their stores of food were supposed to last for the winter, but the situation has become critical."

"No. It would be foolish to travel with that amount of money," he said, clearly irritated. "If this man is our Ettore and he returns with me to Rome, you will receive the money."

"Of course, I understand—"

Luciano shot forward and swiped at some condensation on the inside of the windscreen. "*Mio dio,* what has happened here?"

CHAPTER SEVENTY-THREE

1730 Hours, Tuesday, December 15, 1942
Via Trisulti, Southwest of Collepardo

"We have company, Conor."

Conor looked at Eugene, who was zeroed in on something beyond Conor. He wheeled around and saw a silver sedan rolling to a stop thirty yards from their position. He couldn't get a clear look at whomever was inside. "Son of a bitch. Just what we need," Conor said. Tardino had already left for Collepardo with Canali and the prior in Soleti's car, and they were just about finished getting Majorana and their gear in the Fiat panel truck, ready to head out to Anzio, all the while fearful that the smoke from the burning Italian troop carrier would attract some activity. They had spent way too much time on the road and needed to make short work of this onlooker.

The driver emerged. He was over six feet tall with dark, wavy hair and round glasses. His overcoat collar was turned up. He walked toward them but pulled up when he noticed their weapons.

"What has happened here?" the driver said. He lost some color as he took in the sight of the burning truck and the bodies that were laid out near it. "Who are you people? You don't look like you are with the Royal Army."

Conor turned to Emily and Sean, who was wrapping a flesh wound on Emily's lower leg. "Finish loading up, we're leaving."

The driver approached Conor. By then, a passenger exited the sedan. A priest.

"Conor," Sean said. "I know that priest. He's—"

"You are an American? Are you responsible for this horror?" the driver said in a raised voice.

Conor raised his Sten gun.

"Luciano! Luciano!" The shouts came from inside the truck and were quickly followed by an emerging Majorana, who hustled past Emily, Eugene, and Sean before they could stop him.

Conor cut him off with an outstretched arm to his chest. "Stop." *No. You're kidding me. Not his brother.*

The driver stood motionless, arms at his side. His face lost its color. He took a knee and Conor could see that he was breathing rapidly. He placed his right hand on his heart and looked down at the ground briefly, then back up at Majorana. He took off his glasses and squeezed tears from his eyes with his free hand.

Conor knew Ettore had two brothers. The briefing file reported that they both searched for Ettore for months after his disappearance.

Conor's gaze darted between the kneeling man and his passenger, who was approaching the group tentatively.

"Luciano...my brother," a breathless Majorana said.

His hand still on his chest, Luciano began to mouth words, but no sound came until Majorana slapped Conor's arm away and stepped closer to Luciano.

Luciano held up his hand, stopping Majorana. "Ettore...why? What you did to your family...it was wrong. Why?" Luciano struggled back to his feet. Majorana lowered his head and said nothing. Luciano turned to Conor. "I am here to take Ettore back to his family."

"And I am here to make sure that doesn't happen. Is that clear?" Conor said. Luciano started to protest. "Your brother is alive. That's going to have to be enough for now." Conor turned to Majorana. "Get back in the truck." Conor nodded to Eugene, who snapped to and grabbed Majorana by the arms. Majorana struggled, but Eugene had too good of a grip on the man's lean frame.

"Wait." The shout from Luciano caused Majorana to cease struggling. "May I examine him?"

Conor tilted his head quizzically. "Examine? What the hell for?"

"To ensure that you have the right man and not an impostor. You may have been taken in by this man. Yes, he looks like my brother but…"

"Conor, we need to get moving," Emily said.

"Yeah, I know, we're almost done here," Conor said over his shoulder. "Go ahead. Have at it. You have fifteen seconds. But I'm telling you, he's going with us."

Luciano took steps toward Majorana. Eugene freed his arms. Luciano reached for Majorana's right hand and betrayed no reaction when he saw the scar on the back of his hand.

"Okay. That does it. The scar on the right hand," Conor said, motioning to Eugene to grab Majorana. Before he could, Luciano grabbed Majorana's face with both hands and tilted his head back.

"Open your mouth," Luciano said, with the cold detachment of an overeager dentist.

Majorana paused briefly, then opened his mouth. While Luciano played dentist, the other priest drew closer.

Luciano nodded at his findings, then released Majorana's face. "This is not my brother. You have an impostor on your hands." Majorana jerked his head back and started at Luciano, who turned and walked up to Conor. "My brother had his wisdom teeth pulled when he was ten years old. Look for yourself. This man still has his teeth. And the scar, that was a well-known descriptive fact at the time of his disappearance. It could have easily been duplicated."

Conor smiled. The teeth play impressed him. "You are an American," Luciano continued. "It is dangerous for you to be here. Leave this man here and take your leave. Your presence here will not be divulged by me to anyone."

"No deal, Luciano. I have to call your bluff for the simple reason that you can't prove what you're saying is true."

Luciano's eyes bored into Conor's. "But I do have proof. I have his dental records."

Conor retuned Luciano's steely gaze, not expecting that response. "Cough the records up."

Luciano reached into his breast pocket and handed Conor a document folded in thirds. He opened it. The paper was faded; its edges jagged and the ink on the lower third was partially smudged. The name at the top of the record in faded type was *Ettore Majorana*.

There was a list of procedures that started in 1909. The entry for a visit in 1916 stated that he had oral surgery to remove his wisdom teeth. Conor handed the document to Emily who glanced at the document briefly, then at Conor.

"Take a look, Em," Conor said. "Let's see if Luciano is stupid enough to lie to us."

Majorana complied quickly, opening his mouth and tilting his head back. After Emily took a brief look, she turned to Conor. "Not a wisdom tooth in sight," Emily said. "Now let's get out of here."

"Well, Luciano, time to back off," Conor said.

"Luciano, go," Majorana said. Luciano turned to Majorana. "You tried. But this is for the best. If I stay in Italy, at the Certosa or in Rome with you, there is a risk that the Germans will force me to work with Heisenberg. They have tried already. Many people died because of their plan. They will threaten our family to make me cooperate with them. So I must leave. But after the war I shall contact you and we will be together again."

Luciano, after a long pause, turned and looked at Conor.

"It's the only way to guarantee his safety," Conor said. "The Nazis won't stop until they have forced him to do their bidding."

Luciano nodded and turned back to his brother. "As you wish, Ettore." Luciano stepped toward Majorana, and they embraced. Majorana broke it off and looked up at his taller brother. "Please forgive me. I was troubled and did not know what to do."

"You, what is your name?" The priest, Luciano's passenger, spoke for the first time. He was staring at Sean, who seemed to note the imperious tone, as did Conor.

"Father Sullivan. We've met, Monsignor Puchini. Several years ago."

"Why are you, a priest, involved in this…this…kidnapping? It is shameful," Puchini said, his arms gesturing wildly. "Ettore belongs with his family. He will be safe there with the help of His Holiness and the Vatican's gendarmerie," Puchini said, becoming red-faced.

Conor snorted. "You have no idea what you're talking about. We're wasting time here."

"Luciano, you can't let them take Ettore. You will never see him again. He must return with us…with you to Rome. After all these years, you must return him to his mother. I insist."

"Ettore is right. He would be too valuable an asset for the Germans. He must leave the country. It is enough for me, for now, to know that he is alive."

Conor turned to Emily and made a head movement toward the truck. She took Ettore by the arm and led him away. Conor looked at Luciano. "We need time to get out of the area. Keep your unhappy friend from talking to anyone about this. For your brother's sake." Conor waited for an answer. Luciano stood stone-faced.

"Luciano, you must not conspire with these scoundrels. The authorities must be informed." Puchini wheeled around and headed to Luciano's car. Conor thought about placing a round in the man's calf, but Sean had another idea.

Sean sprinted past Conor, grabbed Puchini by the shoulder, and spun him around. The right cross he landed on the priest jaw did the trick. Gravity won the day and the unconscious man hit the ground as if all his bones had turned to jelly.

Conor strode toward Luciano. "We have a deal?"

Luciano took a deep breath and let it out slowly. "Yes. I will keep the monsignor from creating any trouble for you. But you must promise that nothing or no one will harm my brother."

"Nothing or no one, Luciano. That's the plan."

CHAPTER SEVENTY-FOUR

1830 Hours, Tuesday, December 15, 1942
En Route to Anzio

Eugene drove while Sean, seated next to him, was half turned in his seat, his arm draped over the seat back. Conor and Emily sat on wooden crates in the back, opposite Majorana. For the first thirty minutes, no one spoke. Most likely, everyone was too busy processing the circus they were putting behind them at forty miles an hour.

Majorana looked glum. He nestled his head inside his cowl, shielding half his face, closed his eyes, and rested his head against the side of the truck. Conor took the time to check the bandage wrapped around Emily's calf wound.

Eugene was the first to start the conversation, though it was more like a monologue. He didn't leave out much detail in describing how he and Soleti's man made quick work of the truck of soldiers.

"He told me that Canali was going to run, that we couldn't depend on him. I almost peed my pants when he shot him. Sorry, miss," Eugene said, glancing over his shoulder. "I checked his pulse, and it was still ticking, and I started to tell the guy, but that's when the truck showed up. I almost peed my pants again." Another quick glance. "Sorry, miss."

"Eugene, you're going to have a great story to tell your grand-kids," Sean said, giving Eugene's shoulder a light slap.

"I could say the same for you, Sean," Conor said.

"Except for the grandkids part," Emily quipped.

Conor snorted. "Never thought you'd actually have to use the Baby Browning."

"Like you said: I used it to slow someone down. Left the rest to you and Emily," Sean said.

For the next five minutes, the only sounds were the racket and rattles the Fiat gave up as it sped toward the Anzio coastline. The sixth minute belonged to Majorana.

"I will not help you. I cannot help you with any project that would lead to the development of a massively destructive weapon." That declaration emanated from inside his cowl. The firmness and conviction intoned in it was of no surprise to Conor.

"Why, Ettore?" Emily asked. "We've told you that the Nazis are merciless and must be stopped. You saw firsthand the ruthlessness of Koder. There are thousands upon thousands who are more pitiless and cold-blooded than him."

Majorana's face emerged from his cowl, and he leaned forward. While he spoke, he made little eye contact. "Over time, in the science that I immersed myself in, I saw something terrifying and inhumane. I began to believe that physics, and those who studied it, were on the wrong path. The discovery of atomic energy and the massive power that it holds is not something that God wants. I knew that before my time at the Certosa. My time there only reaffirmed my thinking." Majorana gazed at Sean, who nodded sympathetically. He lowered his gaze once more as he continued speaking.

"Contributions to the study of theoretical physics would thrust upon me a share of the deaths that will come from the development of these weapons, and that share of deaths drove me to leave the field of study and retreat...disappear. I believed then, as I do now, that I possess a clear insight into what is to come regarding the power of a handful of atoms, and I chose to not be a part of it. That decision is my right." He paused.

Conor leaned in, but before he could speak, the man continued.

"I am not done." Another pause. "I foresaw, as far back as 1934, after a series of experiments, the enormous energy that would come from atomic nuclei. The target nucleus of uranium, in dividing itself into two nearly equal parts—that is, into nuclei of elements with an atomic number of about half that of uranium—releases an enormous amount of energy. This energy is a hundred times greater than that which is released in common nuclear processes and a million times greater than what is released in typical chemical processes, such as combustion." Majorana looked at Conor, then Emily, as if he were searching for some sign they understood. "Any scientist, whether he is a God-fearing man or not, should not endeavor to devise such weapons. I am convinced that man is not capable of using the enormous amount of energy responsibly." Majorana sat back and retreated into his cowl. His hands did the same, disappearing into his sleeves once again.

Conor swallowed hard. Majorana had laid out his position again in clear, no uncertain terms. There had been no equivocation in his voice. But then again, he'd had over four years sitting in the Certosa to pull his thoughts together—maybe more time than that, as it sounded like the thoughts he'd expressed were what had originally driven him there.

The Fiat bounced along at a steady rate, though if Eugene was trying to avoid the ruts and potholes along the way, he was doing a piss-poor job. "How much longer, Eugene?" Conor asked.

"Hmm, maybe another hour, less if I can get more juice out of this clunker."

"No, no, an hour is okay."

"Ettore, will you come to the United States with the understanding that you will not be required to work on any program that you have moral objections to?"

Without moving, Majorana said in a calm and slightly admonishing tone, "How can you, Conor Thorn, guarantee that your superiors will not force me to do exactly that? Just as the Germans, they want to win the war at all costs, do they not?"

Conor gave Emily a side-eyed glance, then looked at Sean. In their expressions, he saw they had also heard something in Majorana's words to agree with.

"Why didn't you give us that speech earlier, at the house?" Conor asked.

Majorana leaned forward again. "Because I didn't think you were going to succeed in getting me in the back of a truck, on my way out of Italy with you."

"You underestimated us," Emily said.

"Possibly. Are you sure Father Misasi was going to be taken back to the monastery?" Majorana asked, genuine concern in his voice.

"I have to trust Tardino will do as we asked," Conor said, not fully believing his own words.

"I don't. You may have miscalculated."

"Like you did about our chances of success, Ettore?" Emily said.

Majorana's fiery eyes bored into Emily. "If I hear of any misfortune that comes to Father Misasi, I shall blame you."

CHAPTER SEVENTY-FIVE

1830 Hours, Tuesday, December 15, 1942
Capitano Nuti's Office, Carabinieri Stazione, Collepardo

A young, acne-scarred carabiniere opened the office door and leaned in. "The bodies…what do you want us to do with them?" he asked, his face pallid. Tardino eyed a wet stain on the officer's uniform shirt. The stench of vomit seeped into the office. He sat at Nuti's desk, leaning on his elbows. He held a handset to his ear, twirling its cord around the index finger of his free hand, waiting to be connected to Guido Leto.

Tardino gave the question a brief thought. "I only care about the German. Wrap the body in something…a tarp or a blanket, and put him in the back of the car I arrived in." The pale-faced man turned to exit. "And don't steal any of his belongings. Especially the Iron Cross medal. You understand?"

The officer nodded and left, leaving Tardino to consider his call. He assumed there would be repercussions felt within OVRA and inside the Mussolini government over the deaths of Koder and Soleti. The Vatican would have to do some inventive explaining why the commander of their gendarmerie was assisting American and British agents in kidnapping a member of the Carthusian order. He had already composed much of his story about how Hauptsturmführer Koder completely mishandled his mission, due in large part to his ignoring Tardino's counsel.

But Tardino's chat with Canali may have provided a shield from any criticism as far as OVRA was concerned. He could only look at Canali's face for brief moments. He'd tied Canali to the back of the chair in front of the desk; the man was slumped to one side, blood draining now from his nose, mouth, and ears. The blood that soaked his coat from the ambush was now dried. As Tardino was beating information from him earlier, some dried flakes of blood had fallen to the floor.

Tardino's hand that played with the handset's cord had bloodied knuckles. As he nestled the handset between his shoulder and ear, he pulled a handkerchief from his pocket, spit into it, and wiped clean the bloodstains just as the other end of the line clicked.

"Yes, I am here. Have you found him?" Tardino asked, his tone clearly registering his impatience.

"Yes, please hold for a moment," said Leto's assistant.

There was a rattling as the handset was passed from one hand to another. "Tardino, I haven't heard a report from you since you left. I am fighting off requests for information right and left."

Tardino took a deep breath and began recounting his story from the notes in front of him, interjecting some facts from memory. "Koder, a brave man, but he refused to listen. That is what ultimately led to the escape of the monk."

"This is distressing news. It will not be received well by any party. Are you sure you did everything to ensure success? Do not lie to me."

"Everything in my power." There was a stretch of silence. Now was the time to polish his image. "But I have news that should lead to the recapture of Majorana and the agents responsible for his kidnapping."

"Go on."

Tardino proceeded to explain that his interrogation of the leader of the local communist partisan group had uncovered information that the agents and Majorana were headed to a rendezvous point on the shores of Anzio, to be picked up by a seaplane. "I suggest that the Regia Marina dispatch patrol boats as soon—"

"Yes, yes. I will take it from here, Tardino. Put that partisan under arrest. Then get back here. I want a full written report on my desk first thing in the morning."

"Yes, of course. But, sir, the partisan succumbed to his wounds, suffered in their attack."

The only response from Leto was the handset crashing into the cradle. He had no doubt Canali would have been a problem if he had lived. But that's what Tardino tried to always do: solve problems.

CHAPTER SEVENTY-SIX

1950 Hours, Tuesday, December 15, 1942
Beach Fronting Villa Imperiale

"It ain't much, but it was home for a spell while I figured out what to do after my flight back to Algiers disappeared," Eugene said.

"It ain't much is right," Conor replied, taking in the unstable beach cabana. Someone had thought it was a good idea to build a row of closets with a narrow door leading out to a deck the size of an unfolded copy of *The Stars and Stripes*. But the more he thought about it, it was something that could come in handy to swap out of a wet suit filled with sand. There wasn't a cabana in the row that looked like it had been reunited with a paintbrush in quite some time. The same could be said for the interior. There was a bench seat along one wall that measured about five feet. Majorana took one side of the bench, and Sean offered the other to Emily, which she declined, so he took it. A layer of sand, blown into the cabana from under a two-inch-high gap under the door, coated the floor. There was no power, which made sense. The salty fishy scent in the stale air was assaulting. With the five of them gathered inside the confined space, Conor felt like he was riding the A train during evening rush hour—except there was no room for Ella Fitzgerald or Duke Ellington.

"I raided the other cabanas and found some old beach towels that didn't do too much to keep the chill from reaching my bones," Eugene said as Emily picked up a towel and actually thought it would be a good idea to take a whiff.

She gagged. "If you try to sleep with this within arm's length of your nose, it will do nothing but bring nightmares."

"Well, it did, come to think of it. Of Italian POW camps." Emily and Sean chuckled, which prompted a smile from Eugene.

"We won't be here long. And no one will be sleeping." Conor paused. "By the way, what did you do with the rafts when you didn't make it back to the PBY?"

"I knifed them, then buried them. Took me about an hour."

"Good thinking." Conor asked Eugene to run the aerial out along the roofline of the cabanas so he could contact Colonel Eddy in Algiers.

Conor and Emily slid down the wall of the cabana and sat, pulling their knees up to their chests. He reached into his haversack and pulled out two Hershey bars. He handed one to Emily and one to Sean, who broke his in half and handed the other half to Majorana. The physicist hadn't uttered a word for quite some time. A sign of resignation or silent resistance, Conor wasn't sure. Majorana, eyes shut, held the chocolate bar up to his nose and drew in its sweet smell.

"Here's what I don't get, Ettore," Conor said.

When Majorana's eyes opened, they were staring at Conor. The Hershey bar remained under his nose.

"Why not walk out of the monastery, go to your family, and just ask for forgiveness?"

His gaze slid away before he responded. "It would have been too cruel to just reappear after all this time." He lowered the Hershey bar to his lap. "What I did to them initially was more than cruel. I had to give them a choice."

"Choice?" Sean asked.

"Yes. They could forgive and receive me, they could forgive and not, or they could just say nothing."

Forgiveness was an act Conor had given some thought to since Sean had delivered his bombshell about Jack's infidelity. He needed to know if his mother knew, and he was going to find the answer to that before giving any thought to forgiving his dad.

Majorana's eyes welled with tears. Emily and Conor took note.

"What troubles you, Ettore?" Emily asked, touching his knee lightly, making him flinch.

He wiped his eyes with the back of his scarred hand. "It was selfish of me to have sent the letter in the first place. I was a fool to think I could return to a normal life after opening up old wounds. It is good that the letter was not sent." His voice was husky. "If I had never written that letter and went on with my life at the Certosa so many people would still be alive—including my friend Joseph." At that, Majorana's chin dropped to his chest and his shoulders heaved.

A heavy silence followed, but Conor couldn't think of one life lost on the mission that he would lose sleep over. Maybe the partisans that didn't want to live under the thumb of the fascists.

"Ettore, we are taking you back behind Allied lines," Conor said. "We've accomplished the most important part of our mission. But understand this: your role as an asset to the Allied weapons development program would shorten this damn war. And that would save lives. Thousands of lives."

"Not just in Italy, not just in Germany, Ettore," Emily added. "In every country dragged into this horrible war, including thousands of people in the Pacific theater." She paused. "How could God condemn a man who did something that saved more people from dying than would have died otherwise?" She leaned across to Majorana, her face inches from his. "He couldn't."

Majorana jerked his head up, his dark pupils floating in a sea of red. "But you're not listening to me," he bawled. His fist closed on the Hershey bar. "I cannot do that." Conor closed his eyes and tilted his head back. "Have any of you or your people thought that I might actually harm the progress of your weapons program?"

That got Conor's attention. "Sabotage. That's what you're talking about?" Conor realized that it didn't have to be an overt act of sabotage. It could come down to an equation or two where one numerical or symbolic component wrongly cited could waste weeks of work.

Majorana didn't answer. He didn't have to. Nobody moved or spoke for a long minute.

"I will not help any warring power to create a weapon capable of such mass destruction." Majorana paused and took in his audience one-by-one. "I would die first." Another long minute passed. The Tyrrhenian Sea's surf crashing on the Anzio shore the only sounds.

"Sean," Emily cried out.

Conor opened his eyes to Sean holding Soleti's Beretta pointed at him.

CHAPTER SEVENTY-SEVEN

2010 Hours, Tuesday, December 15, 1942
Beach Fronting Villa Imperiale

"Sean, what in hell are you doing?" Conor asked, a sour taste springing to life in his mouth.

"You can't force a man to do something he finds morally reprehensible."

Sean's words hung in the rank air. *Actually you can force a man to do just that.* Didn't make it right though. But that was for the higher-ups to figure out. He just needed to get Majorana out of Italy and have another crack at convincing him to help the Allies.

"It seems that Sean's religious fervor has been relit," Emily said. "Isn't that right, Sean?"

Sean looked at Emily and nodded. Then he reverted his attention back to Conor. "Don't force him to go to the US."

"Why? He won't be forced to do anything he doesn't want to."

"You can't guarantee that. You give those tasked with winning the war too much credit."

"You are overstepping your role in this operation, Sean. We're friends, but you're making a mistake," Conor said.

"No. I'm just doing what God called on me to do a long time ago: to help and care for those who can't do it themselves." He paused and looked down at the Beretta he gripped in his right hand. "Here's Soleti's gun. I meant to give it to you sooner."

Conor took the gun and let out a breath that he had held for a long minute. He leveraged his body off the wall and stood, staring at Sean all the while.

Emily rose along with him, but he wheeled around and stomped out of the confined, overcrowded space, brushing past Eugene. He stopped on the edge of the tiny deck, breathing out short, shallow breaths. He was angry. Not so much at Sean for the stunt with the gun, but because he knew enlisting Majorana to assist the Allies was not in the cards. Once he delivered him to Colonel Eddy, what they did with Majorana was out of his hands. He swung back around and barged into the cabana. His abrupt reentrance made everyone but Majorana jump.

"If we let you go, what would you do?" The question triggered another jolt, one more pronounced from Emily than Sean or Eugene. Majorana fastened his gaze on Conor, his lips stretched into a slight smile, and he cocked his head to one side, seeming to mull the question over. He had a dreamy look, as if he was thinking of an answer to what he would do with a million dollars.

"Conor, you can't be—" Emily said.

"I'm not talking about letting him go here. If we did that, there's no guarantee that he wouldn't fall into the hands of the Nazis."

Majorana leaned forward and rested his elbows on his knees.

"I'm talking about later." Conor turned to Majorana. "Well?"

"As I said to you earlier, I would make my way to somewhere in South America. Maybe Argentina or Venezuela."

Sean's eyes widened. "If we get him to a port, he could book passage to a neutral country," he said in words that sizzled with his excitement.

Conor shook his head slowly, second thoughts creeping into his head. "How do we know that the Nazis won't track him down somehow? The Abwehr has spies in more countries than I can count."

"If that were to happen, he can take this." Emily pulled her cyanide pill from her jacket's breast pocket. "A suicide pill. He must do what he couldn't in 1938."

"Why would a man who has been in a monastery for over four years dedicating his life to God commit a mortal sin by killing himself?" Conor said.

"To keep from being—"

Majorana held up his hand, shutting Sean down. "To keep from being forced to help create a weapon that would kill thousands upon thousands of innocent people, as I have stated before. Yes, I will take that pill if I am forced to." Majorana rose. "Before, on the boat to Palermo, I was nothing but a child emotionally. My life was not *my* life. I am a very different person now. Besides, I cannot trust that you will not take it out on my family if you were to find out that I did not fulfill my side of our bargain."

A brief moment of silence was shattered when Eugene burst in with news that he had finished stringing the aerial. No one offered a response. "Hey, is this a wake? Did someone die?"

Conor gave Eugene a sideways glance. "Not yet." He looked at Emily, who was leaning against the wall, staring him down. Sean was doing the same thing. Both were waiting patiently for a response. Conor looked away from them and focused his gaze on Majorana. "Okay. I have a plan." He turned to face Eugene and placed his hand on his shoulder. "Eugene, when you started out on your trip from here to Collepardo, did you see any homes nearby with chicken coops?"

CHAPTER SEVENTY-EIGHT

2130 Hours, Tuesday, December 15, 1942
Hotel St. Georges, Algiers, Algeria

Colonel Eddy was not a patient man. Especially when it came to dealing with academics, even though he considered himself one, his focus being literature. When he found himself dealing with that sort as the president of Hobart College and then William Smith College in the years leading up to World War II, he often had to remind his loquacious professors and department heads to be more concise in their reports and presentations.

His late-night debriefing of Chester Booth, a former an-thropologist and archaeologist from Yale and one of his agents attached to his intelligence operations in North Africa, took him back to those days. Booth had just arrived back at the hotel from a meeting in Oran with some Berber tribal leaders. It took him more time than was necessary to get to the list of Berber demands in exchange for their assistance connected to Operation Torch.

"Chester, you finished?" Eddy asked, slouching back in his chair, his hands steepled.

"Yes. But while I have you, I wanted to know the status of the operation in Sicily. The one where Thorn was to be assigned. Is it still on the table? And is he—"

"It depends, Chester." Eddy was aware of the shaky relationship Thorn and Booth shared. Booth didn't miss many opportunities to throw out an icy comment about his former partner, mainly focused on Thorn's recklessness. What it came down to for Eddy was that Thorn just outright scared the forty-year-old former professor out of his wits.

"Depends?"

"If he comes out of this current mission alive," Eddy said. He was about to change the subject when Heugle entered his office, a flimsy flapping in the breeze as he approached.

"Colonel, it's from Conor," Heugle said, handing the message over. Eddy couldn't miss the half smile.

"Am I going to be happy or angry?"

"Just depends on your expectations. He's alive."

Eddy sat up and scanned the message. "God damn it!" He tossed the flimsy on the desk, but it floated, landing softly. "Send a message right away: 'Do you have our man?'"

"Already did, Colonel. No response. He's off the air."

Eddy shook his head. "Can't be good news if he doesn't mention that he has him."

He sat back and raised his artificial leg, then let it fall on the corner of his desk with a thud. He turned some assumptions around in his head. A mention that "they" were ready for an immediate pickup without a mention as to their numbers or the use of the agreed-upon code phrase for a successful mission—PAY DIRT—left him with two assumptions. One, Majorana was in the hands of the Nazis or dead. The second was that Thorn or Bright didn't send the message because they were compromised. Neither did anything to quell the acids churning in his stomach.

"I've told you before, Colonel, you can't depend on someone like Thorn with his cowboy mentality. He can't—"

"Chester, shut up. You don't know what the hell you're talking about."

"Easy, Bobby," Eddy said. "Send a message every ten minutes stating, 'PAY DIRT... with a question mark.' Keep me posted." Eddy turned to Booth. "We're done here, Chester."

CHAPTER SEVENTY-NINE

2200 Hours, Tuesday, December 15, 1942
Beach Fronting Villa Imperiale

Rays of moonlight laid down a vivid path across the Tyrrhenian Sea to the beach. On their southern flank, there was no evidence the city of Anzio was inhabited, given the absence of houselights or streetlights. While the setting was quiet and settled, Conor didn't forget that they were in enemy territory. He set a two-man watch schedule. Each watch would have two Sten guns and two hand grenades. He and Emily split up, so there was some experience on each shift, and there were always two people with Majorana at all times, just in case he had second thoughts about the plan.

Conor and Sean sat on the deck outside the cabana, doing their best to keep the icy wind coming off the onrushing waves from giving them hypothermia. Sean squeezed into Emily's waist-length field jacket, which, thankfully for Sean, was a couple sizes too large for her.

"You put a scare into me, Father Sullivan. You know that, don't you?"

"Not my intention, Conor Thorn. I don't even remember having the gun in my hand. It was as if someone had taken over my body. I felt something that I can't explain."

"Well, don't worry about it. I decided not to include anything about it in my final report."

Before Sean could reply, Conor cocked his head and shot a finger up toward the sky. "Hear that?"

"What?" Sean said, craning his neck to search above them. "I don't see anything."

Tiny dark blotches in a tight formation blanketed the sky above. "Up there, around twenty thousand feet. Probably Liberators, heading north," Conor said.

"God bless the poor souls wherever they're headed," Sean said, his words trailing off into a quiet request for God's blessing.

"Sean, you weren't going to shoot me, were you?" He knew the answer to the question that he asked half in jest.

"Oh, come now, Conor. We have history. Our families are linked. I am at peace with our family's…shared history. And as for you and Emily, I care for you both. I would lay my own life down to see that you both survive this war."

Conor placed his hand on Sean's shoulder. "You are a good man, Sean. I mean that." He peeked at his watch and was about to announce that their shift was over when he heard the low rumble of powerful engines. It reminded him of the throaty roar of the four Packard engines on Motor Gun Boat 622, the Dog Boat, that had ferried just six weeks prior Emily, Bobby, and him out of Sweden with the Luftwaffe and a Nazi E-boat nipping at their heels.

Emily appeared at Conor's side.

He glanced at her. "You heard it too?"

"Who could forget that sound?" Emily asked.

Conor scanned the horizon with his binoculars. Caught in the moonbeams was the silhouette of the engine roar's source. "We have visitors. An Italian MS patrol boat about a mile off the coast, headed south. They pack a decent amount of antiaircraft power."

"It could be a routine patrol," Emily said.

"I hope you're right, but something tells me you're not," he said. He lowered the binoculars. "I should have listened to my gut."

"What do you mean?" Sean asked.

"I left Canali and Tardino alive. That was stupid of me."

"Conor, we couldn't take Canali with us. He needed medical attention that Tardino promised he would get. It was the right thing to do," Emily said.

"She's right, Conor," Sean added.

"All I know is if that patrol boat doesn't keep heading south,

Tardino did more than get Canali medical attention—he reached out to his boss in Rome."

CHAPTER EIGHTY

2215 Hours, Tuesday, December 15, 1942
Beach Fronting Villa Imperiale

"Shit." Conor lowered his binoculars and shook his head. He took another quick look.

"What, Conor?" Emily asked.

"The MS boat reversed course…it's now headed back north." Conor handed his binoculars to Emily. "Em, stay out here with Sean, and keep watch offshore while Eugene and I set up the radio again. We've got to get word to the PBY that they should expect company on their approach. Let me know when that boat returns," Conor said before disappearing inside the cabana.

"He blames himself for a lot, doesn't he?" Sean said.

"He does," Emily replied, the binoculars to her eyes as she scanned out to sea. She lowered the field glasses and pressed a finger to her lips, waiting until she was sure there was no sound of the boat's engines. "That's what makes Conor, Conor," she said.

Sean stayed quiet for a long moment. Emily knew what was coming. Men, even priests, had trouble addressing such matters. "Have you come to terms with…" Sean trailed off.

"Losing the baby?"

"Yes," he said, Emily noting the relief in his tone.

"Not completely. I wish I had a different answer."

"I understand. It's so devastating. If I could offer this as some comfort. Matthew, chapter nineteen, verse fourteen, 'Let the little children come to me and do not hinder them, for to such belongs the kingdom of heaven.'"

Emily smiled and squeezed her friend's arm. "Thank you, Sean. That helps," she said, her voice a near whisper. She wished she believed her own words.

"How are you two getting along?"

Emily had expected that question too at some point, and she had come up with at least three different replies, none of which would shed much light on the state of their relationship. "We've had little time to talk about anything, really. So I don't know how to answer that. I told him we needed to finish this mission, then we'd try to figure out what we should do next."

Sean nodded.

"Speaking of relationships, I'm glad yours with God is on surer footing."

This time, he sucked in a lungful of air and looked toward the heavens. "Thank you. When I was first ordained, I felt I wasn't going to save people...just comfort them. That's all I was focused on. My adventure with you and Conor in Rome weeks ago left me feeling...confused. I found myself in situations I was unprepared for and didn't understand. I found them exciting—the type of excitement I felt when I was a young, wet-behind-the-ears boy brawling in Dublin pubs for money. I'm a little more clearheaded now...I think."

"So no more collaborating with MI6 or the OSS for Father Sullivan?"

Sean shrugged. "Well, I didn't say that exactly. After all, we can't let the Nazis win this bloody war, now can we?"

CHAPTER EIGHTY-ONE

0130 Hours, Wednesday, December 16, 1942
On Board PBY-5 Flight to Anzio Coast

Ten minutes into the flight out of Maison Blanche Airfield, Bobby had commented to the pilot, Jack Waddon, that he was impressed with how loose the crew was. But in the minutes after they received the radio message from Algiers about Italian naval patrols the coast off Anzio, the crew was all business. The joking and ribbing on the intercom ceased when Waddon ordered the test rounds from the Browning.50 caliber waist guns and the.30 caliber bow and tail guns. The PBY-5's vibrations traveled up Bobby's legs like a dull electrical shock.

"Approaching the coast, gentleman, so eyes wide-open," the coolheaded Waddon said into his throat mic.

Bobby wore a spare headset and stood inside the navigator/radio compartment, leaning in the open doorway to the pilot's compartment, humming "Silent Night."

"You know we can all hear you, right?" Waddon asked.

"Sorry. Just passing the time," Bobby said.

Waddon took over the controls from his copilot, Donnie Doyle, and gave Bobby a sideways glance. "How long have you known this guy, Thorn?"

"Too long. I've tried to cut him loose a few times, but he's a bit clingy. He—"

A series of tracer rounds sliced through the air by the sliding hatch to the left of Waddon.

"Whoa, that was too close. Someone down below doesn't want any visitors tonight," Waddon said. "Buckle up, boys. The Italians have come knockin'."

Doyle, his hands wrapped around a pair of binocs trained off the starboard side of the PBY, muttered something Bobby couldn't make out. "What do you see, Doyle? How many boats in the reception committee?"

"Lucky us. I can only see one. He's about a mile off the shoreline heading north."

Waddon started a turn to port. "O'Hara, starboard side gets first crack. Get that fifty zeroed in on that bastard and don't let up until the next turn. Then I'll circle around and let port side have at it. Shorty, if that doesn't get the job done, you're up, so get your five-hundred-pounders ready."

#

Conor had been tracking the PBY more by sound than sight, but he could make out a light blue, dark, cloudlike image as it traversed the nighttime sky. It was currently on a southward course, parallel to the coastline, its port side fifty-caliber emitting a steady stream of rounds that riddled the MS boat's deck. But the pounding delivery of high-caliber machine guns, followed by the screaming white-hot tracers, confirmed the Italians had also located their ride home. He redirected his binoculars back to the location of the patrol boat, tracking the tracers backward. It was traveling in a tight circle about a mile off their beach location.

The sound of the patrol boat attack brought Eugene running.

"Will they turn back because of the patrol boat?" Conor asked, still tracking the boat.

"If it's Captain Waddon, no way. He's probably smiling ear to ear that someone is trying to kill him."

CHAPTER EIGHTY-TWO

0135 Hours, Wednesday, December 16, 1942
On Board PBY-5 Off the Anzio Coast

Waddon put the PBY into a tight banking turn to starboard.

"Jack, the Eyeties are circling off the beach just north of Anzio. They must have found our passengers," Doyle said.

"Shorty, hear that? Couldn't get any easier. So get set. Get those bombs on target. Uncle Sam paid a lot for'em," Waddon said.

"How good is your bombardier?" Bobby asked.

"Not now, Bobby," Waddon yelled as he leveled out the PBY and headed for the circling patrol boat. Tracers streamed past port and starboard sides of the fuselage. Several rounds found their target, ripping through the thin skin of the fuselage just to the left of Waddon. Holes the size of large fists allowed a rush of air into the cockpit that quickly dispersed smoke from electrical gear that was beginning to cook.

It was nearly impossible for Bobby to see their target. But he could hear the bombardier muttering something. Seconds later, Shorty's highly charged announcement that the five-hundred-pounders were on their way was met with Waddon putting the PBY in a steep banking turn to port. He pulled back on the yoke with only his right arm. That was when Bobby saw the blood.

"Doyle, pull it back," Waddon said through gritted teeth.

"I got it, Jack," Doyle said. No sooner were Doyle's words out when two loud explosions could be heard over the roar of the Pratt & Whitneys.

"Bull's-eye, Shorty," someone said. "The damn deckhouse and foredeck are on fire and..." A pause. "Yep, it's dead in the water and on fire, at least what's left of it."

"Skipper, this is port side waist. O'Hara's hit. He's bleeding bad."

"I'll take over," Bobby said.

"No, the navigator is next in line. But go check on O'Hara. See what you can do. But stay out of the way as much as you can," Waddon said.

Bobby dropped his headset and raced through three compartments, ducking low as he slipped through the doorways in each bulkhead. He snatched the canvas first-aid kit off the last bulkhead before reaching the waist gunners. Despite the open blisters in the compartment, the smell of cordite was robust. He found O'Hara and tended to his shoulder and upper arm wounds.

He dropped packets of sulfa on the two wounds and started to wrap his mangled shoulder. After finishing the hasty bandaging, he administered a syrette of morphine to comfort the sailor. The replacement waist gunner turned to the port side waist gunner and slapped his back. They looked gleeful, but only for a short moment. The sight of O'Hara's put an end to their backslapping.

He took O'Hara's headset and put it on. "I've done what I can do for O'Hara, Jack. We need to get him home."

"Right. But we need to do what we came here for. When we land, jump to it, and move fast, boys."

#

Three minutes after the patrol boat exploded, Conor heard the PBY splash down, followed almost instantly by engine shutdown. The group of five passengers were wading in knee-high swells. Conor's Sten gun was slung over his shoulder, and he held one duffel bag. Emily held the other, while Eugene carried the suitcase radio. Sean was standing right behind him, holding on to Majorana, who was having trouble remaining on his feet in the rushing surf. The phosphorescence of the water was the only source of brightness, except for the moon's slivery light.

Conor heard paddling. Then a hoarse voice asked, "Conor, that you?"

Why am I not surprised?

"Is that—"

"Yes, Sean. It's Bobby Heugle," Conor said. Bobby, ten feet away, slid out of the inflatable and waded toward Conor, towing the raft behind. A second raft followed Bobby. "Don't tell Colonel Eddy that I bought my way onto this mission. In fact, don't tell him anything at all," he said, slapping Conor on the shoulder.

"What did it cost you?" Conor asked as he hoisted his duffel bag into the inflatable. Seeing Bobby was a relief, signaling that they were close to the end of their mission.

"A bottle of Old Forester. Just one."

"Let me guess: from Eddy's stash?"

"That would be correct, my friend. Now let's get out of here."

#

The wind gusts carried the acrid smell of burning fuel from what remained of the patrol boat. The two inflatables struggled to make their way through the surf churned up by the same gusts that blew smoke from the fiery hulk. As they closed the distance to the PBY, Conor saw that the starboard side blister was open, and two crewmen had deployed the short three-rung ladder. Two crewmen stood inside the blister, bent over the bottom edge of the opening, arms outstretched.

The first inflatable to pull alongside carried Sean, Eugene, and their gear. Conor counted at least five whoops and *holy shits* when the two sailors first glimpsed Seaman Eugene DiLazzaro.

"We thought you was dead, Eugene," one sailor said.

"Nope," Eugene said as he helped Sean up the ladder and through the blister opening. "It takes a lot to knock off this guy."

Conor was the last one onto the plane; Sean, Eugene, and Majorana had already moved forward into the living quarters below the mechanic's compartment. Waiting for him inside along with his team was Jack Waddon, leaning against the bulkhead, and a crewman who was wrapping Waddon's left arm, from his elbow to his hand, with a roll of gauze. Just above his bicep, a rubber tourniquet was tied off.

"Turn 'em over, Doyle. Time to go," Waddon said in a full voice. "Welcome back, Mr. Thorn. And thanks for bringing our friend Eugene back with you. We kinda missed the guy."

"The least I could do, seeing as he was so helpful, Captain," Conor said. He gave a nod to the bandaged arm. "Who said flying big, slow planes in enemy territory was a piece of cake?"

"No one I know…absolutely no one I know." Waddon turned and started to tuck his tall form through the bulkhead doorframe when Conor said, "Captain?"

Waddon stopped and twisted his torso back toward Conor.

"Do you have a minute? There's been a slight change in plans I need to run by you."

"A minute, Mr. Thorn. Like you said…enemy territory." The two Pratt & Whitneys coughed to life as the blister behind him closed.

CHAPTER EIGHTY-THREE

0430 Hours, Wednesday, December 16, 1942
El Kettani Beach, Algiers

When Conor told Waddon what he needed to do, at first, Waddon wasn't having it. He was worried about being questioned by someone higher and grew angry with Conor for even thinking about putting him and his crew in that position. In an earlier, testy exchange with Emily, she expressed some of the same concerns as Waddon. She cited her growing unease that if any one of the crew mentioned a stop at El Kettani Beach, difficult questions would certainly arise. Emily's doubtful expression after he asked her to trust him shook his own trust in himself.

"What do I tell higher-ups when they come knocking?" Waddon asked for the second time.

"Don't lie," Conor said. "Tell them you were following my orders. I'm in charge of this mission, and I told you that there was a change in plans, but I didn't tell you why plans had changed. That's it. End of story." Conor paused for a series of heartbeats. He needed Waddon's buy-in. "Plus, no one on your crew even knows what the mission orders were. Eugene even mentioned that no one tells the crew anything. Isn't that right?"

Waddon considered Conor's answer. "Okay," Waddon said, his voice wavered. "But it sounds like you could make yourself a messy bed to sleep in, Conor."

"Maybe, Jack. I'm...we're counting on your crew following

your orders that no one discusses the mission with anyone. And if anyone does come snooping around asking questions, tell them the mission details were decided well above your pay grade, and they need to find me." For the first hour of the flight, they removed their headsets and all rested. No one actually slept except Bobby, who sat on a section of catwalk and leaned up against the bulkhead. Emily and Conor, seated on the port side canvas bunk, propped against each other. Sean and Majorana shared the lower bunk on the starboard side. Eugene had stayed in the waist gunner's compartment, regaling his crewmates with stories of his time behind enemy lines. O'Hara, the wounded waist gunner, occupied the top bunk on the starboard side.

An hour into the flight, O'Hara stirred. Sean and Majorana went to him. Majorana held the young man's hand while Sean prayed, ending with making the sign of the cross with his right hand over O'Hara's bloodless face.

Conor and Emily watched the two men of God comfort the young man. Emily leaned in and cupped her hand around his ear. "Does this really have a chance of working?"

Conor didn't answer at first. He had his doubts for sure. It was going to come down to his relationship with Colonel Eddy, which was a bit of a mystery to him. That Eddy was the one who sent him back to London to be reassigned after Conor screwed up in Tangier, almost getting a high-level informant killed, didn't fill him with confidence. The shrug he responded with was his only answer.

The PBY's splashdown was rough, but as the plane settled into the surf, their movement toward the El Kettani Beach, about two miles along the coast west of the Port of Algiers, was smooth. The engines were cut, and the port side blister was rolled up. One raft was being fed through the blister opening when Conor popped through the bulkhead.

Emily, Sean, Majorana, and Bobby, joined Conor and the two waist gunners.

"Sean," Conor said, tugging on the sleeve of his cassock. "Any questions?"

Sean smiled wryly. "No, it's pretty simple: get ashore with my friend Ettore, find some transport, and head to Casablanca. I'll contact some friends there posted to the Sacred Heart Cathedral to assist with securing transit visas, fake ones if necessary. Ettore's being Catholic will help smooth out the process, I'm sure. And Feinmann's cash will definitely open doors. Then book passage on a neutral ship headed west."

Conor, knowing that it wasn't going to be the breeze Sean thought it would be but not having time to explain why, confirmed with a pat on Sean's shoulder. "That's about it. Then make your way back to England. You'll have to figure that out on your own. Maybe your friends can help with that too. Conserve the cash in case you need some to get back to England."

Conor turned his attention to Majorana. "We delivered on our deal, my friend," Conor said. The timber in his voice had a finality to it. "You deliver on yours."

Majorana looked at Conor, then Emily. "Ettore Majorana has passed away. God bless his soul. I have already picked out a new name. It is—"

"Don't tell me," Conor said. The less they knew, the better. "And don't tell Sean."

CHAPTER EIGHTY-FOUR

0800 Hours, Wednesday, December 16, 1942
Hotel St. Georges, Algiers, Algeria

Conor, Emily, and Bobby hadn't made it past the threshold of Eddy's office when Eddy stood and leaned on his desk with his hands and snapped, "Heugle, I'll deal with you later." Eddy turned to Conor with an icy stare and opened his mouth, but the portly lieutenant colonel standing rigidly next to Eddy's desk held up his hand to cut him off.

"Where's Majorana?"

Conor looked at Eddy.

"Lieutenant Colonel Groves," Eddy said. "This here is Conor Thorn and Emily Bright. The other guy you don't want to know."

"Well, I'll ask again: Where is Majorana?" Grove's tone made his anxiousness and annoyance clear. Conor didn't blame him.

"He didn't make it. He's dead. Along with Feinmann."

Groves's rigid posture surrendered to the news as he plopped down in a chair in front of Eddy's desk.

Conor and Emily approached the desk, Bobby hanging back. Eddy left them standing.

Emily jumped in first with how Feinmann died. As she delivered the news that he had classified documents pertaining to the development of radar, Conor pulled the documents from his haversack and dropped them on Eddy's desk. The news stunned Groves enough to make him stop biting his lip over the Majorana news.

"How did Majorana die?" Groves asked.

Conor's turn. It took him ten minutes to relate how they had found and taken him before he was then subsequently kidnapped by local police. "We set up an ambush when the SS and OVRA were on their way to Rome," Conor said. "In the firefight, the SS officer felt the need to use Majorana as a shield. When Majorana struggled to free himself, a trigger-happy partisan let a round go, and Majorana took it in his upper back. There was no saving him. He bled out."

"You have proof of this, I assume," Groves said.

"Yes, sir," Conor said, nodding to Emily, who pulled their compact camera from her haversack and handed it to Eddy. "There are several pictures of him on that roll," Conor said.

"We did the best we could, sir," Emily put in.

"Which…in the end, was not good enough," Groves said. He rose, took his combination

hat off Eddy's desk, and walked, not so quietly, out of the room.

Eddy dropped into his chair. "Groves…he had high hopes."

"So did we, Colonel. I know it's little consolation, but the Nazis don't have him either.

Like Emily said, that was the best we could do." Conor glanced at Emily, who nodded solemnly.

CHAPTER EIGHTY-FIVE

1200 Hours, Wednesday, December 16, 1942
Hotel St. Georges, Algiers, Algeria

Conor waited until the clock behind the bar chimed for the twelfth time before he raised his glass. "To the famous theoretical physicist Ettore Majorana. May he rest in peace."

"If Sean were here, he'd say, 'May the good Lord forgive us our duplicity,'" Emily replied, her glass of bourbon raised. They both had taken a hot bath after their meeting with Eddy and grabbed some food with Bobby. He almost felt human again.

Conor smiled, and they clinked glasses. He drained his, Emily taking a healthy swallow before lowering her glass.

"But it was the right thing to do, right?" Conor said.

Emily, wearing an emerald colored dress that she borrowed from an accommodating WAAC officer that set off her green eyes magnificently, nodded and sat back. Conor thought she had never looked more beautiful. "Speaking of Sean, I had a nice conversation with him while you were on watch."

"And?" Conor asked, raising his empty glass, signaling the bartender with two fingers for another round.

"He gave me some details about…your sister Constance."

"Oh, you don't say?" Conor said, his tone playful, something he hadn't felt like in quite a while.

"I do. She sounds like a lovely woman. He said Constance was much loved by him and his two other siblings and their parents.

He said she was particularly fond of their brother Timothy. He's different mentally than the others but liked to go salmon fishing as often as he could, liked to fish with a four-foot-long piece of aged oak."

Conor laughed at the image. *Sounds like my type of fishing buddy.*

"Apparently Constance was his loyal fishing companion."

"I have vague recollections of Timothy and Mary, but not much of Constance," Conor said. The next round arrived, and he took a sip.

"Maybe it was because, as Sean explained it, Constance was never far from her mother's apron strings. When she wasn't with Timothy fishing, she was right by her mother's side." Emily paused and then sat forward, studying Conor in silence with her shimmering green eyes. Being alone with her, time slowed for Conor. He hoped it was the same for Emily. "Are you going to confront Jack about Constance?"

Conor drew in a deep breath. "How can I not? He needs to know he has a daughter he didn't know about. He needs to make sure she knows she can always reach out to him…to us, for anything that she needs." It was his turn to lock his gaze on her. "Isn't that the right thing to do?"

"I don't know. Neither did Sean. We both agreed that it could make for a better life for Constance, or it could have just the opposite effect."

Two young army lieutenants, neither one looking older than twenty-one, entered the sparsely populated pub in a raucous fashion and took seats near the bar, their entrance spoiling the calm.

"Are *we* going to make it through this war?" Conor asked.

Emily sat quietly, seemingly comfortable with her nonanswer and the uneasiness that she must have known her silence caused him.

"That was a question, Em."

"Yes, I know." She looked over at the two boisterous lieutenants who were exchanging nasty jokes about Arab women.

"Hey, cut that crap out, you two. There's a woman present," Conor shouted.

"Thank you," Emily said, patting the back of his hand. "But I've heard worse." More silence.

Conor sipped his bourbon and waited impatiently.

"I never told you I asked the prime minister to be taken off this mission."

Conor cocked an eyebrow at her admission. "I told Colonel Donovan that you shouldn't have been assigned to it in the first place. I told him you had been through too much and needed time. What was *your* reason?" he asked.

Emily sat forward and brought folded hands up to her chin. "It's true, losing our baby deeply affected me. I wasn't in the right place, emotionally or mentally. I feared that, being so distracted, I would muck up something and possibly get someone hurt. I couldn't bear it if that happened."

"Okay, I get that. That was part of why I told the colonel that you needed time. But why call off the wedding?"

"Really, much the same answer. Don't you think things between us happened…swiftly? I wasn't just dealing with the loss of our child, but also with being pregnant." Emily unfolded her arms and leaned over the table. "Need I remind you we only met on October fifth. That's…what? Ten weeks ago?"

Conor grinned. "You remember the date? I'm flattered. Must have made an impression."

Emily shook her head in mock surrender. "If *I* can continue." She lowered her eyes to her untouched glass of bourbon. "At that point, being married before the baby was born no longer was the most important thing."

Conor reached over and grabbed her hand. It was warm and soft. She raised her eyes.

"I told you at the Equus Bar…on December fifth, by the way, I didn't propose because of the baby. I did it because I love you. Need I remind you, I told my dad that I was going to do it *before* you delivered your news." Conor released her hand and pulled back to let her consider his words. A sip of bourbon later he said, "I should have proposed as soon as we got back to England from Sweden… before I left for the States. I knew then it was going to happen."

"Why didn't you?"

"It was the whole Seaker thing. It was still too fresh."

Emily was there when Seaker confessed. She had the full picture.

"But that is behind you…us now. The Seaker thing. Not Grace." Emily patted the back of his hand. They sat there like that for a while. Conor, having gone over the words in his head, was about to propose once again when he picked up a squeaking noise coming from behind him—a noise he recognized. It was the persistent squeak from Colonel Eddy's wooden leg. The two rowdy army lieutenants beat a path to the bar's exit.

Eddy approached their table and tossed a black-and-white photo on the table. Conor and Emily both stared at it. It was of Ettore Majorana lying on his stomach, his head turned to the right, revealing his profile. There was blood pooled below his mouth, a ripped open, blood-soaked shirt showed an entry wound in his upper back. His right arm was extended at a ninety-degree angle, which placed the hand close to his face. The back of the hand displayed a scar several inches long. "Not the result we were looking for. You could say not a home run…but maybe a double."

Conor, careful to modulate his relief, said, "I would agree, Colonel," even though he thought it was closer to a triple.

Eddy asked for some additional information about Feinmann for his report. When he and Emily spilled more details, Eddy sat back and folded his hands across his stomach, seemingly lost in thought.

"Do you think Majorana would have made much of a difference for the Allies if he'd made it out alive?"

Conor offered up a short answer. "Frankly, he wasn't the same man that Fermi and Heisenberg knew—the brilliant physicist, whose mind far outstripped his colleagues."

"Colonel, over four years in that monastery changed him," Emily said. "That would change any man."

"Groves is furious. Gave me an earful. I'm sure Colonel Donovan will get one too." Without another word, Eddy snatched the photo off the table, pushed off the armrests of the chair, and made his way out of the bar.

Conor, eyes wide and eyebrows raised, looked at Emily and swiped his fingertips across his brow, flicking faux sweat from his hand.

"Didn't know you were an expert photographer," Emily said.

Despite the fatigue and the alcohol, her eyes were sparkling. She smiled softly. "You know what I'm thinking?"

"Of course, I do."

CHAPTER EIGHTY-SIX

2200 Hours, Wednesday, December 16, 1942
Hotel St. Georges, Algiers, Algeria

"I told you that I was buyin'. And don't tell me that you're tired and need to get some sleep. You're just grumpy that I cleaned you out."

"Again." Jack Waddon was a man of few words, whereas Bobby was a man of many, which was a polite way of saying he talked too much. That night, Jack's word count dwindled with each losing hand during the three-hour session of Texas Hold 'Em that just concluded.

The hotel's bar that Bobby was dragging Jack into with a firm grip on his elbow was teeming with officers, male and female, from, what Bobby could see through the haze of cigarette smoke, various services and several countries. Bobby was quick to notice that the linen topped tables that were scattered about the bar with members of the Woman's Army Auxiliary Corps in attendance was where you would find the higher-ranking officers seated, with the lower ranking officer's looking on from the bar with sad, droopy faces as if they discovered that there was nothing under the Christmas tree for them.

Bobby steered Jack to a couple of bar stools toward the end of the bar that stretched along the long wall of the rectangular room. There was a small dance floor on the far side of the room and a four-piece band, all in neatly pressed khakis, had set up adjacent to it. They were doing their best with "You Can't Say No To A

Soldier", but all it did for Bobby was wish that Joan Merrill was there to sing it. There were several couples dancing, the men all major in rank and above. Bobby ordered a round of Old Forester, one finger for him, two for the brooding Jack.

Bobby scanned down the long bar and saw that a couple of lucky navy lieutenants were paired off with women, one of which was dressed in civilian clothes—a pleasant surprise. He hadn't seen a woman in a dress since his time with Conor and Emily at the United States Legation in Stockholm several weeks prior. Halfway down the bar, one of the lieutenants with his back to Bobby and Jack knocked over his glass of beer and created a commotion by loudly blaming the army captain next to him, who responded by turning to face his accuser and then stood up. The lieutenant turned to face the captain, who was the size of a New York Giants lineman fresh off the Polo Grounds field. The lieutenant got the message and backed down, then noisily ordered another drink, this time a whiskey.

"Jack, isn't that your right seat down there making a scene? What's his name, Doyle?"

Jack eyed the line of guests down the bar and nodded. "Yep. That's Donnie Doyle. Engaged in his second and third favorite things. Drinkin' and chasing a skirt."

The quartet took a break, which made it slightly easier to pick up on nearby conversations. The one conversation, at least one side of it, that immediately rose above the rest was the one that Doyle was engaged in with a blue-eyed brunette officer smartly dress in her WAAC uniform.

Doyle's back was again turned toward Bobby and Jack, but they could hear clearly what the WAAC officer was saying, and it captured the attention of Bobby and Jack right quick.

"And why would you want to drag me to this beach of yours? What did you call it? El Kettani Beach?"

"We had to make an unscheduled stop there just yesterday," Doyle said.

"And just what do you have in mind, Donnie?" the brunette asked as she shook a Pall Mall from a packet.

Doyle responded with an exaggerated shoulder shrug and picked up his whiskey.

"Did you hear that, Jack? He—"

Jack slid off his stool, finished off his shot of Old Forester, and headed toward the best right seat he had ever flown with. Bobby was startled by how quick Jack moved. Before Doyle's empty whiskey glass hit the bar, he had Doyle by the upper arm and half off his stool.

"Sorry, ma'am. Let's go, Donnie. We've got an early morning."

"Jack, what the hell…"

"I said, let's go."

Jack whisked Doyle toward the exit like Doyle was on fire. Bobby was about to slide a cheek on the vacant stool but was beaten to it by the lineman fresh off the Polo Grounds. He started to protest when a khaki-clad man with no identifying patches, a full head shorter and twenty pounds lighter than Bobby, slipped off his stool two spots down from the newly engaged brunette. The man's slight stature helped render him difficult to see among the other bar patrons. It was Stevens, Colonel Eddy's aide. Things had never been on track between the two since Stevens heard Bobby call him a twerp under his breath a few days after Bobby arrived in Algiers.

"What was Doyle talking about?" Stevens asked. Bobby caught the whiff of wine on his breath.

"Stevens, didn't spot you sitting at the bar. If I did, I would have bought you a round. Do you—"

"Cut the crap, Heugle. What was he talking about…the beach, about an unscheduled stop?"

"Come on, Stevens. He's in the bag. You can see that, can't you? It's an issue he's dealing with. Probably why he's not in the left seat."

"What about the beach? He mentioned—"

"A beach, probably some beach back in the States. I think he's from California."

"El Kettani Beach isn't in the States, Heugle. Do you think I'm stupid?"

Bobby wanted to tell Stevens he didn't think so, he knew so, when he brushed past him and headed for the exit.

#

Emily sat alone at a table in the expansive *La Salle des fêtes*, the main banquet hall for the hotel. The room's ceiling extended thirty feet above and was supported by thick burnished wood beams that traversed the main part of the banquet room, which was ringed by a series of columns topped by wide, horseshoe-shaped archways the color of alabaster. Her rattan chair squeaked and cracked with each minor movement. While she waited for Conor to show up, she watched the small number of staff clear tables after a joint American, British, and French dinner that, rumor had it, was attended by General Eisenhower, British Admiral Cunningham, and the troublesome French Admiral Darlan.

Emily had asked one of the staff for a glass of water, which hadn't arrived yet when Bobby shouted her name from the banquet room's entrance. She twisted in her chair in the direction of her name and glimpsed Bobby rushing toward her, snaking through the maze of empty tables and chairs.

"Jeez, I've been looking all over for you guys. Where's Conor?" Bobby asked as he plopped down into a chair across from Emily.

"He's trying to get a message through to his brother, Johnny. He said he might have some luck using a radio in Colonel Eddy's Communications Room. He wanted—"

"We've got a problem. And it could be one that sinks all of us. I hope to God he doesn't run into Eddy. It won't be pretty."

"What in God's name..." Emily's voice trailed off. When Bobby wrapped up his account of his and Jack Waddon's meeting with the copilot Doyle and his drunken pronouncements about their beach diversion, her mouth went dry. She swallowed hard and leaned forward. She folded her hands and rested her chin on her thumbs. "How much did Doyle say exactly?"

"Not too much, thanks to Jack Waddon's quick moves. The WAAC Doyle was trying to impress lost interest right away. But, like I said, Stevens is our problem. And by now, probably Eddy also."

Their attention shifted to the footsteps coming toward them. Conor sat and scanned their faces intently. "Who died?"

Another rapid recounting of the scene at the hotel bar left Conor as ashen as his tablemates. Emily made a case for being on the offensive, coming clean. Both Bobby and Conor greeted her argument with vigorous headshaking.

"No. I don't think that's the right move. The colonel has a lot on his plate. Our mission is done. He's moved on."

"You hope," Emily said, rubbing her forehead with the fingertips of both hands. Emily worried Conor wasn't thinking it through. Running with the first idea to pop into his head. "And what if he hasn't moved on? What then? What's the explanation, Conor?"

Conor waited before he replied. As he waited, he surveyed the room. A staff member approached and placed a glass of water on the table. He picked it up and drained it. Emily swallowed hard again but said nothing. She was still waiting for an answer.

"We wait and see what Colonel Eddy does. There's a chance he'll do nothing." It was the most unsure and scared she had ever seen him.

The three of them sat there for several minutes; the only sound was the squeaking and cracking of their rattan chairs.

CHAPTER EIGHTY-SEVEN

0730 Hours, Thursday, December 17, 1942
Maison Blanche Airfield, Algiers, Algeria

Conor's face felt heavy from lack of sleep. It was as if the force of gravity around his head was double the norm. Emily's face appeared equally troubled. They didn't talk much that night. Conor tried a few different topics, but Emily wouldn't bite. He hoped she wouldn't bring up the problem with Doyle's sloppy bar chat, but it wasn't going to be.

She asked the question. "We have to have a response. What is it?"

Conor told her that he was still working it out.

"You're joking, right?"

He didn't think she really wanted an answer, so he didn't give one.

"Run it by me, Conor. You owe me that." Conor wanted to say that it was she and Sean that first felt that letting Majorana go was the best idea. And they sold him on it. But he realized that was a response below him, serving no useful purpose. So they slept, or tried to.

The C-47 Skytrain that was to take them and several other passengers to Gibraltar and then onto London was parked on the tarmac very near where Jack Waddon's PBY-5 had been parked just a half hour before. They watched the PBY load up and taxi out to the runway. Jack Waddon waved at them as he went about his preflight. Conor thought no contact was the right move. Better the three of them weren't seen together.

Emily looked at Conor. "No Eddy. And we board in ten minutes," Conor said, biting the inside of his cheek.

"What were you going to tell him? Or are you still working on it?"

"Em, I'm just going to tell him that Majorana wasn't going to work on anyone's weapons project. And—"

"That, if forced, he would have done what he could to destroy whatever they had already accomplished."

"Right."

"But the beach. What about the beach?"

"Emily, Eddy never asked about Sean. Where he was. Did you pick up on that?"

Emily didn't have time to answer. The jeep that carried Colonel Eddy and his aide, Stevens, who was at the wheel, sped toward them like they didn't see them in their path. At fifteen feet from them, Stevens swerved sharply to the right and stopped, locking the jeep's front and rear wheels.

"I'm glad we caught you," Eddy said. His choice of words made Conor's stomach flip like he was on the steep downslope of a roller coaster. He moved closer to Emily ready to grab her if she need someone to break her fall. Conor looked at Stevens, his face the picture of smugness. "I'm just about finished with my report to Colonel Donovan and wanted to double check a couple of things."

Conor resumed breathing again. He took in a deep breath, as if he'd just surfaced from a deep dive. "Sure, Colonel. Ask away."

"Tell me again what Majorana said about being enlisted to help the Allies. I'm looking for exact words."

"Well, maybe not exact words, but he made it very clear he would die before he would be forced to assist with either weapons program," Conor said.

"Pretty strong words. He was aware of what the Nazis are doing, right? The camps. The persecutions?"

"We made sure he did, Colonel."

"He also said he if he had the chance to throw a wrench in either program's machinery, he wouldn't hesitate. He would have been a disaster." Emily added quickly before Conor could follow up. He waited, expecting Eddy to say that they should have let the Nazis have him.

Eddy nodded slowly and let a long moment pass. He swept the tarmac taking in the building activity of unloading cargo and refueling. A look of puzzlement crossed Stevens's face. "Tell me something, I forgot to ask this in all the hubbub after your arrival...where's Father Sullivan?" Eddy said. A look of puzzlement crossed Stevens's face.

Conor didn't get that far in his earlier discussion with Emily so he grabbed her arm before she could offer her explanation. "He asked me if we could make a quick detour to a beach west of Algiers. He had some important church business, for Cardinal Massy, to tend to. He said the detour would save him some travel time. So we helped him out. He, after all, came through for us. And I know Colonel Donovan has been bending his ear about joining us on a full-time basis. He said he'd make his way back to England when he was finished.

"He said something to me about the Lord's work never being done, Colonel," Emily said, shaking loose from Conor's grasp.

Eddy gave Stevens a quick side glance, complete with a disapproving smirk. "Have a safe flight. I'll send Colonel Donovan a message that you're on your way back to London. Tell him for me that we're behind schedule for our pre-invasion ops for Sicily."

CHAPTER EIGHTY-EIGHT

1030 Hours, Thursday, December 17, 1942
Kaiser Wilhelm Institute for Physics, Berlin

Heisenberg's nausea was persistent, refusing to bow to any of the remedies that his wife suggested. It had plagued him ever since his return from Rome. At first, he attributed it to a horrendously turbulent flight. But that was two days prior. Seated at his cluttered desk in his office, he struggled to maintain focus on a report from Carl von Weizsäcker on the lab's progress during his absence. What he had thus far taken from the report was disheartening, adding to the funk that washed over him after his confrontation with Ettore in the Collepardo jail cell. The sight of his longtime friend and collaborator behind bars had left him cold and fueled the rapid change in his outlook for his Uranprojekt.

A spike in his nausea made him reach for his wastebasket. He placed it between his legs, closed his eyes and took deep breaths to quell the resurgent waves of queasiness.

"Are you well, Werner?" He opened his eyes and took in the sight of General Leeb, whose ghostly complexion alarmed Heisenberg. The skin under his reddened eyes sagged.

"I…I am fine, General. An upset stomach is all it is." Leeb studied him. "Oh, excuse me, General. Please, take a seat," Heisenberg said as he scrambled to his feet to clear some papers and books from the chair adjacent to his desk.

"No, no. Don't bother. I shall not be long," Leeb said as he looked about the office. He zeroed in on a photo on the wall above his desk taken in Copenhagen in 1933. It featured Niels Bohr, Heisenberg, and Ettore Majorana. Bottles of Carlsberg beer littered the table; an ashtray overflowed with spent cigarettes. His gaze on the photo lingered. "I have just come to tell you that your friend Majorana has fallen through the grasp of Capitan Koder. He was taken by American and British agents."

Heisenberg reached for the wastebasket and vomited. Leeb turned to Heisenberg, then took a step backward. Heisenberg wiped his mouth with a handkerchief and slid the basket under the desk. He had prepared himself for the failure in his mission to enlist his old friend in his cause ever since their discussion in the Collepardo jail. The Ettore he had seen that day was different. More convicted. He would have been no help to him. "Please excuse me, General."

Leeb stared at him. "Koder is dead."

Not fully surprised that Koder's luck had run its course, Heisenberg nodded slowly. He wondered if Tardino or the plumber had killed him. The thought hit him that the owner of the donkey was resting more peacefully.

"So if you have any promising news to report, now would be a good time. I expect a call from Minister Speer anytime now."

Heisenberg stammered. He looked at von Weizsäcker's report. "General, I am still reviewing reports as to recent work done in my absence. I shall have something for you shortly." Before Leeb could respond, his assistant knocked on the doorjamb to announce that Speer had called and was on hold.

Leeb's deadpan look betrayed his disappointment. "He will ask if Majorana will now work for the Allies." He paused. "Will he?" His eyes seemed to plead for a reassuring answer.

"I believe strongly that he will not, General. He convinced me of that when we last spoke. Minister Speer can rest easy."

Leeb nodded. "Well, that's something. Bittersweet as it is."

Heisenberg stood and watched Leeb take his leave.

He looked at the photo above his desk, at the man who was Ettore Majorana before he turned his life over to God.

EPILOGUE

1200 Hours, Thursday, December 31, 1942
Westminster Cathedral, London

String pulling, for some, is an art form. In wartime, it is as valuable a skill as there is. In fact, virtually little—significant or not—gets done without employing some pressure, some compliment, or some words that could be considered threatening. Who you were and who you knew were effective substitutes for money, although having a fair amount of money to spread around didn't hurt matters any. It usually meant things came together faster.

Colonel Donovan had pulled some strings with his favorite tailor on Savile Row, which yielded a new, expertly tailored dark blue suit. Emily had pulled some strings at No. 10 Downing Street—actually she pulled some strings with Prime Minister Churchill—and had Sean's siblings flown into London from Dublin.

Not to be outdone, Conor had had Colonel Donovan call in some long overdue IOUs with some army brass and had his brother, Johnny, pried away from Patton's Second Armored Division and flown out of Morocco. That was some serious string pulling, Conor had said to Colonel Donovan, who had just responded with a "friends in high places" quip.

Conor stood, his back ramrod-straight, and took in the sight from his elevated position in front of the altar, beneath the baldacchino—that's what Cardinal Massy, seated directly across from

Conor on the edge of the nave, called it on the tour of the cathedral he had given Emily and him the day before. The impressive structure formed a gilded canopy over the altar. Eight columns of yellow marble supported the baldacchino, and a massive Byzantine-style crucifix hung above it, dominating the altar.

Maggie, his sister, who was Emily's maid of honor, joined Conor. She was wearing a bright yellow dress that set off her blazingly red hair brilliantly. Standing behind him and to the side was Bobby Heugle, who wouldn't, or couldn't, stop staring at Maggie, his former girlfriend. Getting Bobby sprung from the clutches of Colonel Eddy, especially after the colonel found out about Bobby bribing his way onto the PBY flight to Anzio, was no simple feat. But somehow, as far as Conor was told, David Bruce, head of the OSS London office, had something on Colonel Eddy. Enough to make Eddy change his mind about approving Bobby's travel request.

Father Sean Sullivan stood front and center with the resplendent altar to his back. His eye-searingly white vestment was topped with a red-trimmed white stole that hung around his neck and crossed his puffed-out chest. Sean had only arrived back from his sojourn to Casablanca two days prior. Given the commotion during the days leading up to the ceremony, Conor had had little chance to corner his friend for details about his time with Majorana, or whatever he was calling himself now. All Sean had said, which put Conor and Emily at ease, was that Majorana's gratitude was endlessly expressed, and that Sean saw him safely board a Panamanian-flagged freighter bound for Colón, Panama, which was due to arrive two weeks later. That was enough information for now, Conor thought.

Looking out at the gathered guests, he spied his father, Jack, and Johnny, who appeared to be telling jokes to his date, who battled to contain her laughter, no matter how many dirty looks Jack shot their way. Conor marveled at how quickly Johnny had found someone to bring to the wedding. He had only landed in England the previous afternoon. Conor had asked his father to convince his Uncle Mickey, an NYPD detective and Conor's favorite uncle, to come to London, which was, according to Jack, the first time Mickey had been out of the country or on an airplane. Jack had told him Mickey didn't loosen his viselike grip on the armrests until they touched down at Southampton. Mickey was now sitting next to his brother, Jack, gawping at the impressive interior of the cathedral and jotting notes in a small notebook, just like the skilled detective he was.

Conor located a few other guests seated behind his family—Colonel Donovan, David Bruce, and some London-based reporters that worked for his father's radio network, RBS.

On the other side of the wide aisle, seated in the first pew, was Bertie Bright, Emily's mother. Her prim-and-proper pose was almost completely undone by the smile that stretched across her face. Conor and she had struck up a warm relationship. She had an uncanny knack for getting whatever she wanted out of him, including Conor's middle name, Capability, which he kept from as many people as he could manage. Keeping the widow Bertie company was Elizabeth Nel, Churchill's secretary. Behind them were several other members of Churchill's staff, mainly from No. 10. And seated tightly together as if they were drawing warmth from each other were Sean's siblings: Mary and Constance sat on either side of Timothy, who was equally as big as, if not slightly bigger, than Sean. Constance and Mary were dressed in what looked like their best outfits, Mary in a lavender dress with a lace collar, while Constance wore a bright floral-patterned blouse with a blue, pleated skirt. Their matching hats were smartly perched at opposite angles. They had arrived at the cathedral just in time for the ceremony.

Sean raised his right arm so imperceptibly that Conor almost missed the signal to the person in the organ gallery at the far end of the cathedral. Conor had felt fine up to that point. It was when he first glimpsed Emily, on the arm of Ian Fleming, her closest friend, in an elegant, white, floor-length wedding dress and a wispy veil covering her face, that his stomach flipped—and then flipped again. He must have wavered some, because Bobby cleared his throat and said something indecipherable. The buzzing in Conor's head could only pick up the word *steady*.

If someone had asked Conor for details from that point forward, he'd stammer like a kid who had skipped school and was asked by his mother what he'd learned that day. He remembered the scent he detected as Emily stood beside him—lavender. Then it was her eyes—her vivid, almond-shaped green eyes scintillated, seeming to give off waves of joy wherever she looked. Conor was fairly successful at expelling memories of his and Grace's wedding ceremony at St. Patrick's Cathedral. The few that slipped through passed quickly.

It was a quick ceremony, since it didn't include a mass. Emily and Conor answered all of Sean's questions without any flubs, and after the "I dos" and the long kiss that sealed the deal, Conor and Emily paraded down the aisle, glancing at Bertie, who was drying tears that wouldn't stop. They waved at Jack and Johnny, who gave Conor a thumbs-up. When they passed Sean's siblings, even though he had seen a photo of her, Constance's facial similarity to his father shocked him. He pointed out Constance to Emily, who gave her a finger wave, prompting a blush and slight smile.

For New Year's Eve, the temperature was mild, so the bride and groom stood outside the main door to the massive cathedral. Conor draped his new suit coat over Emily's shoulders and received a peck on the cheek for his gesture. The guests filed out, and it seemed that everyone had somewhere to be. The handshakes and hugs flew by like a P-51 streaking across the sky. Only Jack, Johnny, Mickey, the wedding party, Sean's brother and sisters, and Bertie lingered. Sean's siblings grouped around their older brother, as if protecting him from an invading horde. It was clear from their reverential looks that they loved Sean.

Conor called out to get his attention and motioned him to come over.

Sean looked concerned.

He thinks I might have changed my mind.

Conor and Sean had had a quiet moment after Conor arrived at the cathedral, when they talked about how Conor wanted to handle introducing Constance to Jack. Conor wasn't sure then and now how to take Sean's reaction.

"You all right with that?" Conor had asked, looking for clarity. "Didn't you say Constance would be okay with it?"

"Yes, but she's having second thoughts."

"Doesn't she deserve to have the truth out in the open?"

Sean had stammered, which was unlike the wordy Irishman.

Conor had waited. "Maybe you and she need time to think this through more thoroughly," Sean had said. "And really, is this the right day to do it?"

"Sean, we're all going to be thrown into the wind in the next day or so."

"What does Emily say?"

Conor's plan had been taking hits. It wasn't necessarily dead from a thousand cuts, but his plan was on very feeble legs. Even at the outset, he thought it was a little shaky but he, being a bit pig-headed, had stubbornly pressed forward. He felt strongly that one should be held accountable for their actions. But was it his right to be the one who initiated that accountability, he now wondered. "She doesn't want anyone hurt—my dad, Constance, and for that matter, your brother and other sister. She says everyone will be shocked. She's not pleased with me."

"So why do you want to handle it this way?"

"Because…because…" It had been Conor's turn at the stammer game. He had taken in a deep breath and exhaled slowly. "Because I'm angry. I'm sure my mother knew. And how can that have not hurt her…deeply?"

Sean had had a quick response. "She's gone, God bless her soul. The risk of hurting so many just because you're angry isn't right. I think this is between you and Jack—take it out on him. Better yet, tell him you know, that you're saddened, and that you forgive him."

Conor had bitten his lip, something he did often when he was younger and unsure of himself. He'd nodded.

Sean had closed his eyes and let a breath go as if he had been holding it for a while.

That's where they had ended the discussion earlier that day.

Now, Sean started to make introductions, but Conor stopped him. "Let me handle the intros, Sean." Sean's rattled look wasn't diffused by Conor's reassuring nod.

"Maggie, Johnny, Dad, this is Timothy, Mary, and Constance Sullivan. They're Sean's brother and sisters. They've come all the way from Dublin to share this great day with Emily and I."

Jack couldn't take his eyes off Constance, who wouldn't make eye contact. When Jack extended his hand, she shook it with lightning speed and let it go just as fast. The Thorn kids exchanged greetings with the Sullivans. Johnny listened to one of Timothy's fishing stories. Maggie gave Mary and Constance warm hugs, while Bobby, his arms around Bertie, joked about something with Sean and Emily. Jack continued to stare at Constance. Conor wondered if Maggie and Johnny picked up on the resemblance.

"Okay, now onto the Savoy. It's time to toast this marriage, and..." Conor surveyed the group and settled his gaze on his father. The group, hanging on his last words, were staring at him, including Emily. "And we can also raise a glass...or two to Constance, whose birthday is today. I want to make sure that she feels like the very special person she is." Conor didn't take his eyes off Jack, who unlocked his gaze from Constance to take in Conor. Jack's mouth was partially open, his forehead creased with several lines arranged tightly. Jack shifted his attention back to Constance, who was now returning his look. "And I almost forgot...Dad, you're buying." After responding with cheers and birthday wishes, the group started to drift away.

Accountability could wait another day—maybe quite a few days. He was glad he'd listened to Emily—his wife.

Emily, her arm entwined in his, squeezed his arm and didn't let go. Just like he wasn't going to let her go. Ever.

DID YOU ENJOY
THE UNQUIET GENIUS?

You can keep reading by grabbing a free short story
that pits Winston Churchill against the leader of the
Soviet Union, Joseph Stalin, when you join my newsletter.
You'll also get the prologue and chapter 1 of *The Torch Betrayal*,
the first book in the Conor Thorn Series, and notice of
upcoming releases, promotions, and personal updates.

Sign up today at:

WWW.GLENNDYER.NET/SUBSCRIBE

You can help other readers (and this author!)
by leaving a review for *The Torch Betrayal*, *The Ultra Betrayal*,
and *The Unquiet Genius* on Amazon.

Don't worry—it can be short and to the point!

If you didn't get a chance to read the first two books
in the Conor Thorn Series, *The Torch Betrayal* and
The Ultra Betrayal, you'll find them at Amazon.

You can connect with Glenn Dyer at:
www.instagram.com/glennduffydyer/
www.facebook.com/GlennDyerAuthor
www.twitter.com/duffy_dyer
www.glenndyer.net

AUTHOR'S NOTE

As was the case with the first two books in the Conor Thorn Series, *The Torch Betrayal* and *The Ultra Betrayal*, the third book, *The Unquiet Genius*, is inspired by a true story. I find myself often chasing down mysteries related to the events of World War II. Missing battle plans for Operation Torch that were never recovered inspired *The Torch Betrayal*; a Polish mathematician/engineer who possessed knowledge of Britain's code-breaking efforts and vanished shortly after being flown to England as the Nazis closed in on Paris in 1940 inspired *The Ultra Betrayal*. Playing with "what if" scenarios after uncovering these mysteries provided the basis for the main plot lines for the first two books in the series. Let's jump into the process of separating fact from fiction in *The Unquiet Genius.*

While sifting through *Great Mysteries of the Past: Experts Unravel Fact and Fallacy Behind the Headlines of History,* a publication by Reader's Digest, I came across the story of Ettore Majorana, an Italian theoretical nuclear scientist and professor who boarded a ship in Naples, Italy on March 25, 1938, destined for Palermo, Sicily. Before he departed, he had written two letters. The first one, left behind in his room at the Hotel Albergo Bologna, was a surprisingly brief missive to his family that made it clear he had decided to end his life. It read: *"I've got a single wish: that you do not wear black for me. If you want to bow to custom, then bear some sign of mourning, but for no more than three days. After that remember me, if you can, in your hearts, and forgive me."* The second letter he wrote and mailed before he departed to his superior, Antonio Carrelli, the director of the Institute of Physics at the University of Naples. That letter read in part, *"I have made a decision that was by now inevitable. It doesn't contain a speck of selfishness, but I do realize the inconvenience that my unanticipated disappearance may cause to the students and yourself."* While Majorana's words are less clear as to his intentions, coupled with his letter to his family, one could easily assume the worst.

Majorana arrived in Palermo early the next morning, March 26, not having taken any final acts to end his life. He wrote a second letter to Carrelli. But, at the same time, he sent a telegram. It was concise. *"Don't be alarmed. A letter follows. Majorana."* The second letter to Carrelli was more forthcoming. *"I hope my letter and telegram have reached you together. The sea has rejected me and tomorrow I'll return to the Hotel Bologna, perhaps traveling together with this same letter. I have, however, decided to give up teaching. Don't take me for an Ibsen heroine, because the case is quite different. I'm at your disposal for further details."*

There were reported sightings of Majorana in Naples the next day, but he never met with Carrelli to provide those *"further details."* Instead, poof, he vanished. A man who resembled Majorana was reported to have sought admission to two monasteries in Italy but was rejected. Then the trail got cold. Ice cold.

In the early 1940s, both Nazi Germany and the Allies were pursuing the development of atomic weapons. The Soviet program didn't come together in any meaningful way until the latter part of 1942. The development of a deployable weapon was a daunting task for the Allies and Nazi Germany, requiring massive amounts of money, materials and, most importantly, brilliant scientific minds to propel the development of these ground-breaking weapons. In the 1930s, Nazi Germany had created an environment inside its borders that made life untenable for Jewish scientists, forcing them to seek refuge across Europe and the United States. This fact had a negative impact on the pace of Germany's atomic weapons project, the *Uranprojekt.* The theoretical approach to the program, as opposed to the experimental approach, was led by Werner Heisenberg, a dear friend of Ettore Majorana and a key character in *The Unquiet Genius.*

A mind like the one possessed by Majorana would have been

a critical, game changing asset for the Allied as well as the Nazi atomic bomb projects. The premise of *The Unquiet Genius*, once I did further research on Majorana's life, became clear. Adhering to the theory that he sought refuge in a monastery in Italy, I assumed that, had news of this found its way to the Allies and Nazi Germany, both sides would want to ensure that Majorana did not fall into the other's hands. In addition, they would make supreme efforts to convince the troubled yet brilliant physicist to join their programs. And away we go. Or, actually, away Conor Thorn and Emily Bright go!

Chapter 3 is the first mention of the Certosa di Trisulti monastery. Also referred to as the Trisulti Charterhouse, it was at first a Benedictine abbey founded in 996 by Saint Dominic Abbot. Pope Innocent III approved the construction of the current iteration starting in 1204. He, being very fond of the Carthusian order, assigned the monastery to them and the Carthusian order maintained the monastery until 1947, when the order transferred the monastery to the Cistercian Congregation of Casamari Abbey. The Carthusians, also known as the Order of Saint Bruno of Cologne, after its founder, is an enclosed religious order of the Roman Catholic Church and includes both monks and nuns. At one time the Certosa was home to approximately 100 monks and workers. Sambuca, the anise-flavored liqueur, was according to some, invented at the monastery in the early 1800s.

The Sanctuary of Our Lady of the Cese is an ordinary, aged-looking structure set in an eye-popping location. I hope my description was somewhat successful in painting an accurate image in the reader's mind. If you ever travel to the Certosa di Trisulti, you should make time for the short walk to the sanctuary. The story of its establishment as told by Brother Bini is accurate, according to my research.

I deeply regret that the COVID-19 pandemic kept me from traveling to the monastery. I have journeyed to many of the settings in the previous two books in the Conor Thorn series. For *The Unquiet Genius*, my research was chiefly done via the internet. Where would we be without Google? In addition to the internet, I was fortunate to have been referred by Eric Reguly, who is the European Bureau Chief for Canada's Globe and Mail, to Benjamin

Harnwell. He is the founder and president of Dignitatis Humanae Institute, a group that is involved in fostering human dignity as an essential element to the survival of civilization. Benjamin is also the director of the Trisulti Charterhouse. He was kind enough to interview the last prior of the monastery, Don Ignazio Rossi. His interview provided a great deal of information as to the daily operation of the monastery during World War II.

One interesting aside regarding Benjamin Harnwell is that he was a partner with Steve Bannon, Donald Trump's former chief strategist, in an effort to establish a school for far-right nationalists at the Certosa di Trisulti, named after the institute founded by Harnwell. Their nineteen-year lease that was granted in 2017 was revoked in March 2021 by Italy's Council of State, the top administrative court in Italy citing that the lease was awarded based on "declarations made at the time of the bid that were subsequently shown not to be true" (Italy's Council of State 40-page ruling).

I employ the use of historical characters quite often in the books I write. It is a device I use knowing the responsibility to portray these figures as accurately as possible. That requires a great deal of research, which I do quite willingly. I sometimes get carried away with the research at the expense of actually plopping my rear end in the chair and hitting the keyboard.

In chapter 7, the subject of Operation Freshman and Gunnerside is broached during the meeting between Winston Churchill and Frederick Lindemann, physicist and scientific advisor to Churchill. The key objective of both operations was the destruction of deuterium-producing facilities in Norway. The deuterium, used as a moderator in uranium reactors and produced in large quantities at the plant in Vemork, Norway, was a critical component in Nazi Germany's atomic weapons program. As was explained, Operation Freshman was a horrendous failure. Operation Gunnerside, however, was more fruitful. In February 1943, a team of Norwegian commandos trained by the British SOE did succeed in destroying the heavy water production facility. Supplies of the deuterium oxide that remained on hand were later shipped to Germany, but the ferry that was carrying the valuable cargo was sunk by elements of the Norwegian resistance. A fascinating overview of the Nazi atomic weapons program, including Operation Gunnerside, is depicted in

The Heavy Water War, a highly recommended video series directed by Per-Olav Sørensen and written by Petter Rosenlund. The Nazi perspective is presented through the eyes of Werner Heisenberg.

I mention briefly in chapter 9 that the reason for Conor's assignment back in the States was to work with Jack Taylor on developing an OSS infiltration training program for agents assigned to maritime units. The OSS Maritime Units were established in April 1942 at the request of Bill Donovan to train its agents in specialized amphibious operations such as inserting operatives into enemy territory. According to OSS history as quoted in Patrick K. O'Donnell's *First SEALs: The Untold Story of the Forging of America's Most Elite Unit*:

"To get from ship to shore in secrecy and in stealth is a special operation with a technique akin to no other. It belongs, strictly speaking, to neither Army or Navy, yet is needed by both. Approaching enemy shores, either for the purpose of depositing personnel or equipment or merely for reconnaissance, can ably be accomplished by submarines, fast surface craft, or disguised fishing vessels."

I chose the Consolidated PBY-5 because I love the plane and wanted to spend

some time in researching it and its role during WWII, which encompassed many types of missions. A very useful and well-researched book on the exterior and interior details of the PBY-5 was *Consolidated PBY-5A Catalina: Walk Around* by David Doyle.

The character of Jack Taylor, introduced in chapter 2, is another historical character. Taylor served as a chief instructor at the Maritimes Unit's training facility at Smith Point in Maryland, but his service as an OSS operative extended well beyond the shores of Maryland. Taylor, a dentist, yachtsman, swimmer, and pilot, not only chalked up many missions for the OSS in the Aegean Sea operating from a base he established in Bari, Italy, but in October 1944, he was captured by the Gestapo after parachuting into Austria with three other OSS operatives to spy on German supply lines. In March 1945, Taylor was transferred to the Mauthausen-Gusen concentration camp located in northern Austria. He was a part of the slave labor force, and while there, collected intelligence about atrocities that were committed in the camp. Taylor was scheduled to be executed at least four times but was saved as a result of the actions of his fellow inmates. Taylor also testified at the Nuremberg Trials. Needless to say, this man led one hell of a life. It's another example of the thousands of personal stories emanating from WWII that should never be forgotten. Patrick K. O'Donnell, a first-rate historian, has a great deal of detail about Taylor in his *First SEALs: The Untold Story of the Forging of America's Most Elite Unit.*

In the chapter where Bill Donovan mentions sending Colonel Eddy to Algiers, I took the opportunity to lay out the details of the Allied assault on the harbor facilities that took place on November 9, 1942, as a part of Operation Torch. Reading about this battle, which Rick Atkinson described so deftly in book one of his Liberation Trilogy, *An Army At Dawn,* (Henry Holt, 2002), what so moved and impressed me was the jaw-dropping bravery of all who took part. I wanted to share some of the details in *The Unquiet Genius,* in the hope that the men and their actions would not be forgotten.

In chapter 12, Werner Heisenberg, General Emil Leeb, and Kurt Diebner all make their first appearance. All three are historical figures that I hope I have portrayed realistically. Of the three, Werner Heisenberg is the most enigmatic when considering his role in the *Uranprojekt* (informally called *Uranverein*). Heisenberg, who was awarded the Nobel Prize in 1932, was not widely admired by the Nazi-led government. He was labeled, after the Nazis came to power in 1933, as a "White Jew" for adopting and teaching the theories of Jewish scientists like Albert Einstein. With SS Reichsführer Himmler leading the charge to oust him because of his perceived Jewish sympathies, Heisenberg was eventually, and surprisingly, given a reprieve and drafted into the *Uranprojekt.* His role in the project has been dissected by historians for years. Heisenberg was careful not to overpromise Nazi higher-ups about the timeline for the development of a deployable nuclear weapon. Some feel that Heisenberg, seizing on the immense power of a nuclear weapon, deliberately slowed the progress of the weapon's development, while some believe the main reason for the lack of timely development was mainly due to his ineptitude. This debate rages on.

Heisenberg survived the war and was eventually picked up,

along with Kurt Diebner and several other German scientists, in the OSS's 1945 Alsos Mission. This mission's main objective was to learn the secrets of the Nazi atomic bomb project and exploit the program's research, facilities, and, most importantly, its scientific staff. Heisenberg was eventually flown to England, along with others, including Kurt Diebner, on July 3, 1945. He and the others were interrogated extensively. When questioned about the *Uranprojekt's* failure at developing an atomic bomb, Heisenberg reportedly said, *"We wouldn't have had the moral courage to recommend to the Government in the spring of 1942 that they should employ 120,000 men just for building the thing up."* (Macrakis, Kristie, *Surviving the Swastika: Scientific Research in Nazi Germany*).

Heisenberg died February 1, 1976. In my research, I have been amazed at how many key figures in the Nazi government, armed forces, and other key sectors lived for many years beyond the end of the bloody conflict. Among them, Kurt Diebner died in 1964, and General Emil Leeb died in 1969.

The reader is introduced to Cardinal Luigi Maglione, Vatican secretary of state under Pope Pius XII, in chapter 15. Maglione, another historical character, did not survive the war. He died August 23, 1944, approximately eleven weeks after Rome fell to the Allies.

In chapter 20, we meet two more key historical figures, Enrico Fermi and Lieutenant Leslie Groves. All of the background information in this chapter was taken from my research, including but not limited to, the location of the first nuclear reactor, its components, and what operational milestones it achieved.

Fermi's relationship with Ettore Majorana went as far back as the 1930s when Majorana joined Fermi's "Via Panisperna Boys," a group of young, budding physicists who were given free reign by the University of Rome La Sapienza. Fermi was as impressed with Majorana's intellect as he was frustrated by Majorana's almost complete refusal to publish the results of his research and studies. Fermi's quotes regarding Majorana's stature in the field of nuclear physics were actually uttered by him.

Fermi won the Nobel Prize in 1938, the same year that he and his Jewish wife fled Italy for the United States to eventually work on the Manhattan Project, the code name given to the U.S. atomic bomb project. It was also the same year that his friend and former protégé disappeared.

Klaus Fuchs, the German-born theoretical physicist, makes his entrance into the drama in chapter 22. The time span of his assignment to the Tube Alloys project coincided nicely with my need to have information as to the discovery of Ettore Majorana in the Certosa di Trisulti reach the Soviets. His handler was actually the person code-named *"Sonya,"* whom I described from photos produced from my research.

The unsuspected Fuchs went on to work for the Manhattan Project in August 1944, and after the war, he returned to the United Kingdom and labored at the Atomic Energy Research Establishment as head of the Theoretical Physics Division. Fuchs admitted in 1950 that he was a spy for the Soviet Union and served nine years in prison. When released, he returned to East Germany to resume his career in physics. He died in East Berlin in 1988.

I ever so briefly touch on the issue of French forces in North Africa and their resistance during Allied landings during Operation Torch in November 1942. By the time Conor and Emily arrive in Algiers on December 14 in chapter 27 to meet with Colonel Eddy, many battles had been fought and much ground taken from the Afrika Corps. French forces in December were firmly behind the Allies after much wavering between the Allied cause and their allegiances to the Vichy government headed by Marshall Pétain. While I address this issue briefly, during the months of planning leading up to the invasion of North Africa by the Allies on November 8, the central question on the mind of every Allied leader was whether the French forces would fight the invading Allies or would they lay down their arms and welcome the Allies. Every effort was made to convince French military leaders to opt for the latter. But the central question was not answered until days after the invasion began.

During the flight from Milan to Rome in chapter 28, Heisenberg and Koder engaged in a conversation where the subject of one operation that Koder was a part of early in the war comes up. That operation, which took place two months after hostilities began with the invasion of Poland on September 3, is referred to by British Secret Intelligence Service as the Venlo Incident. It was

a Sicherheitsdienst (SD) operation that
involved secret meetings set up by a German refugee between British SIS agents and participants that were posing as German officers interested in overthrowing Hitler and then seeking peace terms with Britain. Eventually, the refugee's efforts to arrange the meeting became known to the Sicherheitsdienst. Sturmbannführer Schellenberg, who played a major role in *The Ultra Betrayal,* took part in subsequent meetings, posing as lower-level German officer. At the last meeting, Schellenberg promised to bring a general to the next meeting, but instead SS-Sonderkommandos surprised the SIS agents, named Best and Stevens, and took them as prisoners. Best and Stevens, after interrogations by the Gestapo, were sent first to the Sachsenhausen concentration camp then to the camp at Dachau. In April 1945, both agents were transported along with 140 other prisoners to a hotel near Niederhorf in South Tyrol, where they were liberated by advancing U.S. Army units on May 4, 1945. Following their initial capture in 1939, Hitler used the involvement of a Dutch agent in the meetings as proof of cooperation between the Dutch and the British, thereby justifying the German invasion of the Netherlands in May 1940.

Chapter 30 includes a brief mention of the execution of Michele Schirru for planning the assassination of Benito Mussolini. Schirru, born in Sardinia, was a veteran of World War I and politically active. After arriving in Rome on January 12, 1931, he began to study the comings and goings of Mussolini as Il Duce traveled about the city on government business. He was arrested on February 3, tried by the Special Fascist Court and executed on May 29 by 24 Sardinian soldiers who volunteered for firing squad duty. Schirru died while screaming "long live anarchy, long live freedom, down with fascism." In a bizarre twist, Mussolini, after the execution, publicly praised Schirru's service to Italy in World War I and his bravery for voicing his convictions at his darkest hour.

Chapter 31 features two more historical characters, this time representing the Soviet Union. Vyacheslav Molotov, who held the position of minister of foreign affairs, among several other positions, and Georgy Flyorov, a Soviet nuclear scientist. Molotov was considered the second most powerful leader in the Soviet Union and did occupy an oversight position of the Soviet nuclear weapon development program. He was staunchly loyal to Stalin even after Stalin's death. Molotov, given his support of Stalin and his opposition to Stalin's successor Nikita Khrushchev, was expelled from the Communist Party in 1961. He died in 1986.

Georgy Flyorov did indeed write two letters to Stalin encouraging the development of a uranium bomb and expressed fears that other world powers might have already surpassed the Soviet Union's fledgling efforts. He died in Moscow in 1990.

Albert Speer, a close ally of Hitler's, was the Minister of Armaments and War Production. In chapter 42, I depict Speer, during his meeting with General Leeb, as a man who was a bit panicked by current developments in the conflict. Speer's reputation was complicated. Speer worked hard to position himself as a loyal, "good Nazi." Not fanatical, but apolitical, and someone who regretted that he failed to discover the atrocities committed by the Nazi regime. He was arrested and found guilty of war crimes and crimes against humanity at the Nuremberg Trials, primarily for the use of slave labor in war production plants. He served his prison term and was released in 1966. While in prison, he wrote several books, which were considered efforts to reshape his reputation and called by many the "Speer Myth." He died after suffering a stroke in London in 1981.

In chapter 58, in discussions between Majorana and Conor, and Emily and Father Sullivan, Majorana mentioned that he thought he would, with his family's help after reuniting with them, escape to South America, possibly Argentina. Moving forward to chapter 83, Conor and Emily part ways with Majorana and Father Sullivan as they head to Casablanca to seek passage for Majorana to points west.

This development in the story was prompted by rumors that surfaced years after Majorana's disappearance. Rumors such as a landlady who was renting a room to a physicist in Buenos Aires came across the name Ettore Majorana in the physicist's papers. She told the scientist that her son had known a man by that name who was pursuing a career in engineering. Another story emerged in 2008, when a caller phoned in to the Italian program *Chi l'ha visto* (Who Saw Him) and related a story about a friend who claimed in 1955 to have met Majorana while living in Argentina. The caller was later introduced to the man, who was now called Mr. Bini, while visiting Valencia, Venezuela. Another friend who was present, an Argentinian, told him later that he, the caller, had just met "Mr. Majorana." He described a man that closely resembled Majorana, who was 50–55 years old. A photograph was taken and eventually made known to Italian authorities, prompting an investigation by the Rome Attorney's office. After studying the photo, the investigation concluded that there were ten specific points of similarity between old photos of Majorana and the photo taken sometime in 1955 in Argentina. But, for some unknown reason, it wasn't until February 2015 that an official statement was released by the Rome Attorney's office and reported in the Italian *Corriere della Sera* newspaper that Majorana "was alive in the period 1955–1959 and was voluntarily living in the Venezuelan city of Valencia." However, the same newspaper article went on to state some prominent people, who knew much about Ettore Majorana, doubted the conclusions of the Rome Attorney's office, citing their strong belief that Majorana had a spiritual crisis and ended up in a convent.

Based on my research, weaving a story that eventually found Ettore Majorana on his way to start a new life somewhere in South America made tremendous sense to me. As a writer, when you're knocking your head against the wall as you labor at pulling a compelling story together, you hope that you wind up with a balance between verisimilitude and surprise. I hope I arrived at something close to that target.

I hope these author notes helped to color in some additional background behind some of the story elements and characters of *The Unquiet Genius*. Share what you think with me at glenndyerauthor@gmail.com.

ACKNOWLEDGMENTS

Writing a novel is hard. Damn hard, at least for me. I am extremely lucky to have many people in my corner as I plug away at producing what I always hope is an entertaining, enlightening, and compelling story. Their feedback, suggestions, and answers to my endless questions were invaluable. Any errors in this work of fiction are mine.

First up is my family. My wife, Chris, and our children Tom, Mike, and Riley are always ready to offer advice that keeps the story from going off the rails. Tom was one of my early beta readers that offered up some very sound advice, especially in the outline phase. While we're on the subject of beta readers, my other beta readers include Bill Hobbs, Jim Grieme, and Danielle Urban. They very willingly offered up their time and thoughtful comments that went a long way in helping me avoid stepping in a plot pothole.

To my fellow authors Steve Berry, Jack Carr, James R. Benn, James Thayer, and Anthony Franze, I am humbled by your inspirational support.

I wouldn't be half the writer I am if it weren't for the steady hand and insightful guidance offered by my primary editor Gretchen Stelter. The issues, no let's call them mistakes, that she catches that completely slip by me have me whispering to myself *"Wow, she's good!"* Thanks, Gretchen.

The very late stages of the editing process were ably handled by Kimberly Hunt of Revision Division. Her professionalism and suggestions were spot on and very much appreciated.

To my brother Mike, a Navy veteran, thanks for answering the myriad questions about terminology, procedures, and all things military. It nice to have someone like you to depend on.

To very dear friends, Lou DiLazzaro Jacobs and Bruce Waddon, for giving me permission to use the names of their fathers, both veterans of World War II, for two characters in *The Unquiet Genius*. I was extremely fortunate to have known both of their fathers. Eugene DiLazzaro, who served in the U.S. Army, and Jack Waddon, who served in the U.S. Army Air Force, were truly classic examples of the Greatest Generation.

Once again, when I needed some feedback on weapons available during World War II, I turned to Chris Grall at Tactiquill. Besides his knowledge of weapons of the time, he has a great eye and ear for storytelling.

I was extremely fortunate when I started out on my author's journey to have come across Jane Dixon Smith, who has expertly handled the cover and interior designs for all three books in the Conor Thorn Series. She is unbelievably patient in answering all of my countless questions and requests concerning the process of bringing a book into this world. Many thanks, Jane.

Thanks to a very supportive colleague from my broadcasting days, Rob Stevens, the video wizard who produces the book trailers for the Conor Thorn Series. He is another artist that has the patience of a saint and the creativity of a master artist.

I must recognize the help of a family friend Tom Solomon who was kind enough to offer his services when I was scrambling for some inspiration. He never balked at lending a hand. And he was, like many people mentioned here, very patient with me, fielding my requests with enthusiasm. Many thanks, Tom. It turned out pretty good.

I often have to reach out to people looking for information and answers to questions about history and various fields of study. I would like to thank John Belz, professor of physics and astronomy at the University of Utah. As I said earlier, I own any mistakes in the manuscript related to the field of nuclear physics. Eric Reguly, European bureau chief for the Globe and Mail, Benjamin Harnwell, and Father Rossi for their help in learning about the history of the Certosa di Trisulti during World War II. A special clap on the back goes to my nephew Shane Axtell for translating the interview between Benjamin Harnwell and Father Rossi.

The Unquiet Genius is my third novel. It would be an understatement to say that I am still learning how to develop my craft. Besides working with great editors, much of that learning comes from reading accomplished authors in the thriller genre, but not limited to it. I'll start out with Steve Berry, Jack Carr, James R. Benn, Brad Thor, Don Bentley, P. T. Deutermann, David Poyer, Daniel Silva, W. E. B. Griffin, Herman Wouk, C. J. Box, Kate Quinn, Alan Furst, Jack Higgins, Robert Dugoni, Brad Taylor, Phillip Kerr, John Lawton, Steven Hartov, Anthony Franze, Thomas Kelly, Harlan Coben, and John Altman. Thanks to you all for being so inspiring.

As I did in the acknowledgments for *The Ultra Betrayal*, I wanted to mention the OSS Society, which honors the accomplishments and sacrifices made by members of the OSS during World War II. The OSS Society was established in 1947 by General William Donovan, as the veterans of the OSS. Please take a look at their website osssocity.org and think about making a donation to their efforts to establish a National Museum of Intelligence and Special Operations. So many stories that can now be told, so many stories that should never be forgotten.

PRAISE FOR THE TORCH BETRAYAL

"The disappearance in 1942 of a page from a secret document concerning Operation Torch…drives Dyer's suspenseful espionage thriller…Jack Higgins fans will find a lot to like."
—BookLife/*Publishers Weekly*

"Atmospheric and tense, with plenty of treachery and a heavy dose of history. What more could you ask for in a thriller? Take a walk on the perilous side and check this one out."
—Steve Berry, *New York Times*, *USA Today* & Internationally Bestselling Author

"Welcome to 1942. Glenn Dyer is your tour guide to the world of spies and betrayal in the lead-up to the Allied Invasion of North Africa. You're in good hands, so settle back and enjoy the fireworks."
—James R. Benn, author of *Road of Bones*, A Billy Boyle World War II Mystery

"…what sets Dyer's book apart from the others in the genre is his unfailing attention to historical detail and great writing."
—The BookLife Prize

"...a classic spy story in the vein of John Le Carré or Daniel Silva..."
—BlueInk Starred Review

"*The Torch Betrayal* is the best mix of genre standards from a fresh voice...crisp writing, plot reveals that pop like firecrackers, and cinematic excitement..."
—*Foreword*/Clarion Reviews

"A well-crafted espionage tale set during World War II."
—*Kirkus Reviews*

"In this highly entertaining tale...Dyer has hit all the notes in the thriller genre."
—IndieReader Five-Star Review

PRAISE FOR THE ULTRA BETRAYAL

"Brilliantly researched and filled with fascinating characters from the pages of history, Glenn Dyer once again brings World War II espionage to life in his latest Conor Thorn thriller. *The Ultra Betrayal* exceeds all expectations."
—Jack Carr, *New York Times* bestselling author of Savage Son

"A tantalizing premise set among the ominous atmosphere of World War II, there's sizzle and plot twists galore — more than enough to satisfy any thriller reader."
—Steve Berry, *New York Times*, *USA Today* and #1 Internationally Bestselling Author

"*The Ultra Betrayal* is blessed with a plot that zings along like a ricocheting bullet that finds its mark in the last electrifying pages. Meticulously researched and filled with fascinating characters, this one is sure to please."
—James R. Benn, Author of *Road of Bones*, A Billy Boyle World War II Mystery

"Dyer's series, which started with *The Torch Betrayal*, is one of the more underrated spy franchises set during WWII, and a perfect fit for fans of Alan Furst. And Conor Thorn is a really fantastic hero, who doesn't get the attention he deserves."
—The Real Book Spy

"Conor Thorn is back with a vengeance in Glenn Dyer's compelling new World War II thriller, *The Ultra Betrayal*. History and thriller lovers alike will stay up reading late into the night until the final breathtaking twist. Don't miss this one!"
—Anthony Franze, Author of *The Outsider*

"*The Ultra Betrayal* is a masterful historical spy thriller where morality pushes people to their breaking points . . . The cast is staggering in both its number and variety; all characters are developed in clear terms, though whom can be trusted—aside from Emily and Conor—is always in question."
—*Foreword*/Clarion Reviews

PRAISE FOR THE UNQUIET GENIUS

"Glenn Dyer does it again with *The Unquiet Genius*, his third work of World War Two historical fiction. With characters both familiar and obscure from the pages of history, Glenn weaves a fascinating story of action and espionage that has become the hallmark of his must-read Conor Thorn series!"

—Jack Carr, *New York Times* Bestselling Author of *The Devil's Hand*

"For readers who like action, this is the perfect book. If those who like the lines between good and evil as clear as a fifty-yard line, this book is for you. For those who like suspense that unravels as gracefully as a silk tie, this book is for you. And for those who appreciate accurate historical details...this book is for you."

—IndieReader

"*The Unquiet Genius* is a well-written, suspenseful and deeply researched thriller that thrusts you into the atomic arms race during the critical days of WWII...Buckle up and get ready for the ride."

—Steven Netter, Best Thriller Books

"This rip-roaring, Nazi-punching World War II thriller will keep spy fans on the edge of their seats."

—BookLife/*Publishers Weekly*

"*The Unquiet Genius* is a high-stakes spy thriller about the fight to do the right thing, no matter the cost."
—*Foreword/*Clarion Reviews

"A high-stakes World War II thriller inspired by true events and full of drama and fast-paced action."
—*Kirkus Reviews*

"Glenn Dyer's *The Unquiet Genius* has it all—action, suspense, and the endlessly fascinating World War II era and makes a worthy addition to the author's gripping espionage series."
—IndieReader